THE PUZZLE

David A. Wardle

Copyright @ 2024 David A. Wardle

All rights reserved. No part of this publication may be reproduced or transmitted by any means, electronic, mechanical, photocopying, recording, by future technology or otherwise, without prior permission of the copyright owner.

First published in Great Britain 2024.
1 Holm Court,
47-49 Westway,
Caterham CR3 5TQ

This is a work of fiction. Names, characters, businesses, organizations, places, events and incidents either are the product of the author's imagination or are used fictitiously. Any resemblance to actual persons, living or dead, events, or locales is entirely coincidental.

ACKNOWLEDGMENT

I would like to thank Stuart Gibbon for his help on police procedures and other details.

Prologue

Somewhere in the US – 1997

Someone was going to die that night. Maybe two people, if the fates were kind, but at least one.

The shadowy figure crept silently up the stairs. On the landing he turned for the master bedroom. The door was open, and he could see a sleeping woman in the four poster bed. He walked over, making no sound on the thick carpet, and gently lifted the quilt off the bed, dropping it to the floor.

The silencer of his gun travelled across her silk nightgown, tracing a line down her body. The touch was so light that it did not disturb her. She gave a slight semi-conscious moan as the gun reached the end of its journey. The second time he used more pressure, and she woke with a start. The intruder had already established where the bedside lamp was, and he clicked it on with his free hand. It was 3 am. He briefly wondered whether the glow of the lamp would filter through the bedroom curtains. He didn't think so. It was not much more than a reading lamp but there was sufficient illumination for his purpose. He saw the woman's eyes widen with fear at what she saw.

"Hello, Beverley. Long time, no see."

The figure by her bed was clad all in white. An all in one protective suit including hood. She could only see the face but did not recognise it, nor the voice, but then all her attention was on the gun.

"Come on Bev, you must remember me. The last time we met we were in this bed together."

Then she got it. "Sly," she croaked, her eyes widened further.

"Took you long enough. Obviously, I wasn't that memorable. Do you sleep with all your daughter's boyfriends?"

He remembered that day, five years ago, all too well. He had spent the night in this house with Alice in her bed, despite thinly disguised disapproval from her parents. The next day, a Sunday, Alice got up early to go riding and her father had given her a lift on his way to the golf club. Sly had turned over to go back to sleep when there was a knock at the bedroom door and then Alice's mum came into the room in her nightgown.

"Morning Sly," she greeted him, in an unusually low, husky voice. "I just wondered if I could do anything for you. Breakfast? Or maybe you're hungry for something else?" Her right hand was rubbing suggestively near her crotch.

Sly was a bit confused, not only was he still a bit sleepy but he had been sure that Alice's mother hated him. Maybe it had been an act whilst the others were around. There was no doubt about it she was a fantastic looking woman.

"You seem a bit tongue tied, Sly. What do you say now," she said pushing the straps of her nightgown off her shoulders and letting it drop to the floor. Automatically, Sly held up the bed covers for her to crawl inside. "No. I want you in my bed." She turned to leave, then at the door looked back. "Bring that with you, will you," she purred, indicating the discarded garment, then she was gone closing the door behind her.

Sly was still bemused but which nineteen year old boy wouldn't be flattered to be seduced by his girlfriend's totally attractive mother. Her slim, taut body and long, flaming red hair made him forget all about Alice. He picked up the nightgown then left for the master bedroom. On entering he could see Mrs Barrett-Smythe lying in a suggestive pose on the bed. She eyed him longingly. "I see you're up for it," she purred, provocatively, her eyes on the mound in his shorts. "Get over here."

It was fast and frenzied, far better than he had experienced with Alice, and that apparently was what her mother wanted to hear because she kept whispering to him to keep telling her that, which he did. He never noticed the slightly ajar wardrobe door.

Two hours later they were in the kitchen where Beverley was starting to make lunch. Her husband and Alice were due back in a short while.

"Sly, while I'm peeling these vegetables can you lay the table for me."

Not used to helping around the house, Sly was too far under her spell other than to agree. She turned from the sink and wiped her hands. "But before you lay the table, lay me on the table." The table was bare, and she lay on it and hitched her skirt up so he could slide off her panties. She helped him on and in but in the heat of their passion she suddenly shouted, "No, no, don't! Think of Alice." At that moment her husband and Alice walked into the room.

"What the hell!" exclaimed Mr Barrett-Smythe seeing his daughter's boyfriend on top of his wife. Alice just screamed and ran away.

Yes, that had been five years ago. He had been played for a patsy. The Barrett-Smythe's hadn't wanted him to marry their daughter and had hit upon the plan to discredit him in Alice's eyes. He had left the house that minute and never seen her again, despite repeated attempts.

Now was time for his revenge but unfortunately, he could not play this out like he wanted to. Time was tight. Not his doing. The people he was working with on this wanted him out of the country. He was booked on a flight which he could not miss. Reluctantly, he had to bring this to a close.

"Hope it was worth it, Beverley," he said, as he shot her once in the head.

Sly sighed with regret then made his way to Alice's room. Her door was closed, and he was careful not to make a sound as he turned the handle and slowly pushed it open. He quickly looked at the luminous dial on his watch. He didn't even have time to wake her so she could see it coming. Another head shot then he turned and left the room, retracing his steps to outside the back door. There were two men waiting for him, one also in a white protective suit and one dressed all in black.

"All done?" asked the one in black.

Sly just nodded, at which the man in black tapped his colleague on the shoulder who then entered the house carrying a rather large can of some flammable substance. The sight of that gave Sly a cold shiver down his back and he gave a slight shudder.

The man in black noticed. "You OK?"

"Sure," said Sly. "Just an old memory."

The man nodded and then spoke again. "You and the boss are now even. Go back to the car and Zeke will drive you to the airport. We never want to see or hear from you again."

"Suits me," said Sly and he set off through the garden.

As he was being driven to the airport, Sly pondered on what might have been. That day five years ago when he had first met Alice. When he had thought he had fallen in love and that he would go straight and marry into a wealthy family. Or the couple of days earlier when he had saved the life of a child. Not any child but that of the local crime lord with whom Sly's own boss had been having a meeting. The meeting had been in a restaurant which was closed for business at the time. There had been a drive-by shooting and the restaurant had been strafed. The boy had been playing among the empty tables and as soon as the gunfire started, Sly, instinctively, dove on the boy and covered him until it was all over.

These two days were inextricably linked now. For saving the kid's life, the crime lord owed him a big favour, as he gladly admitted at the time. Feeling good about himself and not aiming to take up the offer, Sly gave his own boss the slip shortly after and met Alice. It was only a week later when her mother played him for a sucker. Now five years later everything was all square. He had called in the favour. Beverley was dead because she had played him. Alice was dead because she had not let him try to explain about her mother's trickery.

It was always good to balance the books.

PART ONE - PUZZLE ME THIS!

Chapter 1

Whoosh! A whirl of colour. A dragon appeared before me, closely followed by a second. Fear not, a brave knight arrived to stop them. Yet alas. two more dragons fell in behind him. One knight, four dragons.

"Fuck!"

I smacked the table in frustration and just managed to refrain from throwing the laptop across the room. That stupid knight had ruined everything. Five dragons in a row was a £5,000 win. I looked at my bank. It was down to £900. My new credit card had taken a beating. I was only allowed to use fifty percent of the balance as money withdrawal, which included gambling transactions, and I had transferred that amount at 6.30 am. It was now 7.25. I had been playing at £10 a go for a maximum jackpot of £5,000. It was time to reduce that now, or the money would run out in about another 10 minutes.

I just was about to do that when the buzzer rang. Who could that be at this time? I knew it was not the downstairs neighbours complaining about my outburst. I lived over a dog grooming parlour, and it didn't open until 9 am. Anyway, it was May Day Bank Holiday, and they were closed. Irritated at the interruption, but also partly relieved at the break from my self-destruction, I pressed the intercom button to see who was there.

"Delivery for Daniel Andrews!"

"Oh okay! I'll be right down."

Not expecting a delivery, I was curious. Still in the t-shirt and shorts I slept in, I went down the stairs to the front and only door, which was at the back of the business premises. There was no peephole, so I had to risk it. A delivery guy stood outside. a large bubble wrapped package leaned against the wall.

"There are two more boxes in the van," he announced, and left to get them.

I just stood there and looked at the bubble wrapped item, but I was barefoot so didn't step out. It looked like a large picture frame. What could it be? I was going to have trouble getting that upstairs. The delivery guy came back with a large cardboard box which he dumped in my arms and went back to the van. I quickly heaved it up the stairs and came back for the next one. That one I just had to leave on the stairs as the delivery guy wanted my signature.

Has anyone ever replicated their true signature on one of those electronic devices? I have the same thought every time I produce an unrecognisable scribble with my finger. Still, the delivery guy seemed satisfied with the resultant resemblance to snail entrails and promptly left.

I took the other box upstairs. Both had been heavy but had been simple compared to hoisting the bubble wrapped parcel up the stairs, after putting something on my feet. Eventually I managed it and propped it up against the wall at the top of the stairs. Curious though I was, the fever was still upon me, and I rushed back to my laptop. It was on auto play and whilst I had been away £7,000 had appeared in the bank.

Drat! I must have had a jackpot and had missed it. But also, yippee! The money was there. Now what to do with it?

The sensible thing would be to pay back onto the credit card what I had taken out and I did try but whilst it was easy to download money into the site account, it was far more difficult to remove it. The site wanted ID sent over and then they would send a cheque or make a bank credit transfer. Either could take 10 to 14 days. This made me think again. Of course it did. That was the whole point. They wanted you to play the money away again instead of going away a winner.

Less than four hours later it was all over. I had only intended spending just a bit of the winnings. I would still be in profit and may win some more. I switched games and started off playing a higher stake for a quick bigger win. Unfortunately, I won a little bit but then not so much. OK. What if I just spend up to the amount I started with, then at least the credit card would be paid back? Then, later after more losses, alright, I had been happy to spend this much to begin with, so let's start again with that.

When the money is all gone two things can happen. One can still be gripped by the gambling bug and start thinking of ways to get your hands on some more money, just to get back to it, like drug addicts need a fix. Alternatively, one can reach the saturation point, when one is totally defeated and deflated, accepting of fate and swearing never to do it again. This time it was the latter for me. I closed the laptop, made a strong coffee, and sat in the recliner, inwardly remonstrating my stupidity. I felt bad now and would swear off the slots, but it wouldn't last long.

Things had to change. My finances were starting to look extremely dodgy. The backstop money was nearly all gone. The thought of the life assurance turned my thoughts to Laura, and I didn't want to go there. We only had five years together, but that had been the only time I had been truly happy. The best day of my life was the day we met. The worst, the day she died. Or rather, was killed. Murdered in her own home, our own home, during the day and for no apparent reason. Nothing had been stolen. There had been no clues to the identity of the killer or his, or her, motive. There was no evidence left behind except the kitchen knife in her chest. Her murder was still unsolved.

Life had been good then. We both had good jobs, lived in a nice house, in a nice neighbourhood – or so we had thought – and wanted for nothing. We had just started thinking about kids. Then on that one fateful day, I came home and found her, lying in a pool of blood in the hallway. The bottom had dropped out of my world at that moment and at times it felt like I had not stopped falling since.

In hindsight, I guess that the lack of a support system had not helped. I had no real social life when we met, and all our friends were really Laura's friends. They tried to help, but when she was gone, they sort of drifted away. I had been in almost a catatonic state. After the funeral I did not move out of the house for weeks – easy to do now with online grocery shopping – not that I ate a lot. I spent whole days lying on the bed, staring at the ceiling. Bouts of tears were frequent, but sleep was not, and when I did manage to drop off it was not to sweet dreams of Laura.

Then things got worse.

Laura had death in service benefit of four times salary. She was an advertising executive and earned far more than me in my lowly insurance job. She had a very creative mind and rapidly rose in the agency. The total came to well over £300,000. The logical thing to do was to pay off the mortgage, which I did. That left just under £50,000. The next logical thing was to bank the rest to make life easy and continue working. That I didn't do. Well, I did bank it, but it didn't stay there.

I lost my job as an insurance broker. They obviously gave me some bereavement time off but had to let me go when I just didn't turn up after a verbal and two written warnings. I just couldn't face the normality of it. Things were not normal now and never would be. No great issue. I was fed up with insurance anyway and with £50,000 and no mortgage, I reckoned I could manage a couple of years without a job. That was nearly five years ago. That money was gone, the house was gone and most of the money from the house was gone.

Just before I could dwell on that fact and get even gloomier, my phone beeped with a text. I picked it up and on reading it felt a million times better. I could feel my face breaking out into a grin. Nate was back. My best and only friend was back in the country. How long for this time? Not to worry though, at least there would be some fun now. Nate could always cheer me up.

We had met not long after Laura's death. Before things had really begun to spiral out of control. It was funny how it happened, although it had not seemed funny at the time. During a friendly five-a-side game, Nate had taken me out with a vicious tackle. He was all apologies afterwards and as I could not even stand on my leg, he insisted on driving me to the hospital. I was pissed off at this new guy I had never seen before the match, but I had no other offers. Outpatients being outpatients it took a while before an x-ray confirmed I had broken two toes. Nate was again all apologies and drove me home after I had been taped up.

It took six weeks for the injury to heal although the bruising, swelling and most of the pain went after the first week. There was a lot of icing and elevating of the foot. I was confined to home which I didn't mind. The football had been an effort to try and get back into living again. Incapacitated, the sense of loss came flooding back and I was just content to sit, brooding, but Nate kept calling round to buck up my spirits. He brought beer and snacks. We played cards and board games or watched the football. In the end this guy from nowhere became my lifeline.

Nate was out of the country a lot and was usually only back for a few days at a time. His text said he would be around this evening for bowling and drinks. I felt a weight lifted from my shoulders and all thoughts of money problems vanished. When Nate was around, he paid for everything. It was Nate that had found me the flat – rent free – after I had had to sell the house. The dog parlour below belonged to a friend of his and all I had to do was keep an eye on the place when it was closed and keep an eye on any dogs staying over, including taking them for an evening walk. That didn't happen very often and had not been a problem so far. I had never had any pets myself, but the dogs were always well behaved and were just keen to be going out.

Afire with new enthusiasm now, I decided to turn my attention to the parcels, but I realised I was hungry. Breakfast first then. Cereal and toast for a special occasion. I even washed up straight away.

Time to open my presents and it wasn't even my birthday. My mind was full of questions. What could they be? Who had sent them? At the time though I didn't think of the most telling point, although it would hit me later.

Chapter 2

The Incident Room was empty and that was how Detective Inspector Tate liked it. At the end of a successful investigation, he always took a few minutes in the ex-nerve centre of the operation and reflected on the good (dogged detective work, logical deduction, out of the box intuition and just plain luck) and the bad (lack of clues, evidence overlooked, lack of attention to detail). What had they done right? What had they done wrong? How did they prevent the wrong things from happening again? All these matters he mulled over whilst clearing away the remnants of the job. Removing pictures, wiping boards, and generally clearing up ready for the next crisis. It was a task that was beneath him, but one that he liked to do and insisted on. It was cathartic.

Tate had not slept in two days. The arrest went down in the very early hours of that morning. Then around mid-morning there had been a brief debriefing – paperwork could wait until the team had got some rest. Every part of his five feet eleven-inch frame was aching. He had not eaten much over those two days either. Just a sandwich here and there, swilled down with lots of coffee. The lack of food had not lessened the start of a paunch, he regretfully noticed. His eyes were bloodshot, his dark hair with flecks of grey unkempt and his suit crumpled. He could not remember where his tie was. He needed sleep, but he also needed to do this to unwind beforehand.

Just as he was finishing there was a knock on the closed door. His colleagues knew and generally respected his post case reflective period. He looked up at the door and saw it was P.C. Lane, a new fresh faced student officer, unwise to the ways of the station yet, or, he mused wryly, the subject of the probationer initiation. Tate motioned him in. As it happened, he was wrong on both counts.

"Sir! A delivery just arrived for you," Lane announced as he opened the door.

"Well, bring it in then, son."

"Right," acknowledged Lane, as he lifted a box from the floor and brought it into the room. Lane was very tall and lanky. As one wit had been heard to comment, he was head and shoulders and another head above everyone else. With his blond hair and size, it came as little surprise that he already had the nickname Crouchie, after Peter Crouch the footballer. It was also extremely amusing for those that had crowned him with that title to learn that his real first name was in fact Peter.

P.C. Peter 'Crouchie' Lane placed the box on the table nearest the whiteboard, next to the box that Tate had recently filled with relics of the past case. "There are two more packages with it. I'll go and fetch them now." He turned to leave the room but then turned back. "There's just one thing I noticed. It is addressed to you but with the wrong rank." With that, he left closing the door behind him.

Tate looked at the label on the box. It was addressed to P.C. Tony Tate. He had not held that low rank for many years. He regarded the box with puzzlement and just a mite of trepidation. It wouldn't be the first time that body parts had been delivered to a station as part of some sick killer's ritual. There was nothing to identify the sender. The box was sturdy and secured with strong tape. Using a paperknife, he slit the tape and opened the box. Peering inside his fear of a lifeless head gazing back at him disappeared. The box was full of white cubes. He pulled one out and saw that on one side there was a letter C on it. He pulled out some more and each one had a black letter on it.

At that moment there was another knock at the door and Lane entered carrying what looked like a large picture frame enveloped in bubble wrap. He put this on the floor leaning against the table and looked with interest at the blocks. "What is it do you think?"

"Your guess is as good as mine, Crouchie," said Tate. "Hold on a minute." Tate nipped out of the room but was back within three minutes. "Here, put these on." He handed a pair of latex gloves over and was now wearing some himself. "Take the wrapping off that and let's see what we've got. Be careful with it, we might need it for evidence."

Suitably gloved, Lane carefully removed the bubble wrap, revealing a large wooden frame. He stood it upright on the floor as Tate looked at it, rubbing his stubble in thought. The frame had slats inside dividing it into columns. Tate counted twenty-seven. The bottom row already had blocks in place and the letters on each made a sentence. *Let's start at the very beginning.* Tate picked up one of the loose blocks and dropped it into the frame where it ran smoothly in the grooves to sit on the bottom. Tate dropped in the other six blocks he had removed from the box. Some in a separate column to sit alongside the first and one in the same column to sit on top of the first.

"It's a puzzle," observed Lane.

"You're not wrong there," Tate agreed. "Let's have some more of those blocks."

Lane dug into the box and handed over blocks to Tate who dropped them any old how into the frame but always with the letter towards the front.

Lane held up a completely black block. "It's a crossword," he exclaimed, excitedly.

"I think you're right, Crouchie." Tate took the black block and it too fitted easily into the frame.

"But there's one thing missing," pointed out Lane.

"Clues?"

"Exactly. How can you solve it without clues?"

"I think that whoever sent this will be providing those also," Tate observed. "Wait! Did you not say there was another item?"

"Yes! Another box like the first one."

"Go and get it. I have a feeling that one might contain a clue."

Lane immediately left and returned a minute later with another box. Tate moved the relic box off the table to make room. "Now, let's see," he said. He opened the box but just saw more wooden blocks. He started unloading all the blocks. "Empty that other box, Crouchie."

They emptied the boxes, making small piles of blocks on the table. Lane dug deep and came up with a brown A4 envelope. Tate grabbed and opened it. "Look!" Then he passed it across to Lane. It was a list of clues. There were twenty of them.

1. Doe a deer, a female deer, but is that really the start?
2. Sow with Oates to make music. (4)
3. Soccer authority to a tee. (3)
4. Will a Merry Man brighten up your day? (7)
5. Bit part but no Othello. (4)
6. Haggard woman. (3)
7. Whisper, wish will leave each. (3)
8. Silence is golden in this place of tomes. (7)
9. Not working and brother gone. (3)
10. Identical but no head. (3)
11. Little Diane ate one after the eight, almost. (6)
12. The Queen is not here. (3)
13. Be with the right crowd. (2) (LB)
14. Mystery Inc but not all at once. (4) (G)
15. Mink theft. (5) (O)
16. Ape drops his tool. (7) (Y)
17. New Zen bird. (4)
18. Keys can be this or somewhat lesser. (5)
19. The selfish note? (2) (O)
20. Halve maker to get a poke. (4)

"What's it all about?" asked Lane.

"Damned if I know. Let me think for a minute" Tate had been looking at the first clue and digging into this memory. "Are you any good at puzzles, Crouchie?"

"I quite like them," replied Lane. "Although not generally cryptic ones and these seem cryptic to me."

"Well, I can tell you for nothing that you can forget the first clue as the answer is already there. I had enough indoctrination in 'The Sound of Music' as a kid."

"OK. What about the rest?"

"Well, as far as I'm concerned at the moment this is not connected to a crime, so I won't be wasting a lot of time on it." Tate noticed a distinct look of disappointment in Lane's expression. "I've been awake for the last fifty-one hours tracking down Dent and now I'm off home for a good twelve hours kip. But you keep it if you want. Work on it in your spare time."

"OK thanks, I will. I can't take it home though. I've got no car and it's a bit bulky to take on the bus."

"I meant work the clues on paper, not take it with you."

Lane was silent, considering this for a moment, turning one of the blocks over in his hand. "I think it will be easier to work on the real thing. Have you noticed? Some of the blocks have dots at the bottom of letters. In different colours. I will need the blocks to try to sort the colours."

"Well, you know we cannot take evidence out of the station, let alone home." Tate paused for a moment, thinking. "On the other hand, we don't know if it is evidence yet. I suppose you could take it, but the moment it becomes clear that this is involved in any investigation, it comes right back."

"Yes, Sir!" agreed a beaming Lane.

"OK. Put it in my office for now and I'll get a patrol car to drop it off at your place later. I'm off home for a bit of shuteye." Tate then changed his mind. "No, take a taxi, I'll reimburse the fare."

Tate left the room. Moments before his mind had been solely on his bed but not now. Whatever was going on it seemed it was connected to his time as a P.C. and there was something from that time that he did not want to surface. That is why he agreed to let Lane take the stuff home. He sincerely hoped his past was not going to come back to haunt him.

Chapter 3

I stood there, metaphorically scratching my head over the packages I had received that morning. What had seemed to be a picture frame, now divested of its wrapping, turned out to be a large wooden frame. The two boxes were filled with lettered wooden blocks. I had counted them. There were seven hundred and two – or seven hundred and twenty nine if you counted the ones already in the frame, because the whole bottom row was filled with blocks already. The frame looked to be an exact square and twenty seven squared equated to seven hundred and twenty nine.

I used to be good at puzzles but not for a long time. Laura and I used to compete at the puzzles in the paper, both against the deadline time and each other. The Daily Express had been our favourite, especially on Sunday. Since her death I had not even tried a Sudoku. It was all too painful. With not working either, my mind had become lazy. I did manage to work out that it was some sort of crossword but only because of some completely black blocks. The list of clues I found at the bottom of one of the boxes made no sense to me as I cast my eye over them. All except one. Mystery Inc related to Scooby Doo. The clue read, *Mystery Inc but not all at once.* That must mean the answer was either Fred, Daphne, Velma, Shaggy or Scooby Doo. There was no way to know though which one it was, except of course there was. Dumbo! The four in brackets must mean the number of letters so obviously it was Fred. No clue as how to fit it into the puzzle though.

I had been at it for a couple of hours and was tired of it. Time for some lunch and then it was time to do some real work. I had to start on my fantasy football team for the forthcoming World Cup. It was quite easy to waste away a couple of hours that way, which is what happened, then it was time for the afternoon TV quizzes. That would take me up to 6 o'clock when Nate was due to arrive.

By that time, I was getting a bit excited. A night out. I didn't really go out on my own and Nate was in the country so seldom that these occasions had to be savoured. It wasn't that Nate paid for everything, although he did usually, but the fact that he was the only person who did not treat me like a loser.

Bang on the dot at 6 pm the buzzer rang. I rushed down the stairs, without using the intercom, and opened the door. Nate was stood there grinning.

"Long time no see, mate," was his greeting.

Anyone seeing us together might think we were brothers. We were both of similar height, around six feet, with dark hair. Nate was lean and wiry though whilst I was carrying a bit more weight, more than I should be. Nate had a moustache while I was clean shaven - well, every other day I was. In between shaves there was stubble but not of the designer variety. I had to wear glasses too. We came together for a man hug.

"Are we going now?" I asked. "Or do you want to come in for a bit?"

"Taxi's waiting so just grab your keys." As Nate was in the country so little he didn't own a car and used to hire one if necessary. If any drinking was involved though he always used a taxi. "Meal first and then bowling."

"Great," I called behind me as I rushed back upstairs to put on shoes and grab my keys.

It was four hours later when we got back, and this time Nate did come in. We were both merry, having been drinking whilst bowling, but not drunk. I made some coffee. No alcohol in the flat because of my addictive personality. I would be an alcoholic in no time. The gambling was bad enough.

"So, Danny, looking forward to the World Cup?" Nate called through to the kitchen from where he sat in the living room.

"Sure!" I shouted back.

I entered the room carrying two steaming mugs. "This young team of Southgate's has got no baggage. No penalty misses. No pressure. They can't do any worse than previous teams. We have done nothing since 1990."

"Too right. I might have some business in Russia so I may get to see a game," grinned Nate.

"Lucky you. I will be glued to the box. Got the wallchart up already. Look!" I pointed at the door to the room which had the wallchart stuck on it. "It's weird. The first time I can recall that the competition starts on a Thursday, but there is only one match. Then three a day after that for the first two weeks."

"Wall to wall football. Good job you're not working."

"I will need to be soon."

"Still playing the old slots then?"

"Yes, and you know it's your fault. If you hadn't taken me to that casino that time I would still be on the wagon."

"Yeah. Sorry about that. Change of subject. What's that?" Nate had just spotted the wooden frame propped against the wall behind the old table I used for my meals, when I was not eating in front of the TV. The blocks were still laid out on it.

"Don't know. It arrived by courier today. Some sort of puzzle but I can't work it out."

"Let's see," said Nate eagerly, bouncing up from the sofa and making the two strides across the room. He picked up a couple of the blocks. One white and one black. Then he looked at the frame. "I assume they slide in, right?"

"They do, I tried one. There is a list of clues on that paper there but there's no way to know where the answers go even if I knew what they were."

Nate picked up the paper and started reading. "Pull the frame out Danny. Let's have a look."

I lugged the frame out and placed it on the floor in front of the table and looked at Nate who was thoughtfully stroking his moustache.

"OK. It looks like you have the first clue done."

"It came like that. Those blocks are glued in."

Nate stood and thought for a few moments. "OK. Now it makes sense then that the next clue is going to be a down clue. You see those little dots on some of the blocks already in. I think that is where a down clue joins up. There is a dot on the first letter, the L see. So, my guess is that the second clue is a word that goes there."

"And?"

"Well, the clue is, *Sow with Oates to get music*. That seems quite easy."

"Not for me it isn't" I pointed out.

"Sure, it is, you just need to think laterally. See how Oates is spelt. Not O A T S as in sowing wild oats but with an E and a capital letter. It's a name. There was a duo called Hall and Oates. You will have heard their music. Never heard "Maneater?"

"Can't place it."

"You'd know it if you heard it. Anyway, I think the answer is Hall which fits. Four letters which is what the number must mean. So, in the first column put H…A…L."

I rummaged through the blocks and slotted those letters in the first column so Hall read downwards.

"Actually, no that's not going to be right," Nate said. "Take them out. The dot on the L is yellow so try and find an H, A and L with yellow dots."

It was harder getting the blocks out than in, but I managed it and hunted round for yellow spotted letters. There were quite a few of them. I eventually found the three needed and dropped them in.

"Now," said Nate, "because this is a crossword a black square will go on top of the H."

I duly dropped one in.

"That's got you started then." Nate took a sip of his coffee. "When I've finished this I've got to go. Off again tomorrow so need a good night's rest. Got to get back to the hotel near the airport. I think we can get a couple more done before I leave though." Nate looked at the paper again. "OK. *Soccer authority to a tee*. Well, it is a T that is dotted next along so I would say it was there. Let's think about this, Danny. What are the soccer authorities?"

I thought for a second. This should be up my street. "UEFA, FIFA and, oh, the FA."

"Right. Now which one of those gives a word ending in a T?"

"Well, only the FA if you want a word that means something. FAT."

"Right again. Drop in and F and A followed by a black block. Then because we have two down words on the L and the T, I think it is safe to drop a black block in the second column. There is no dot on the E so no word coming down."

By the time Nate left, we had gone right along the row and inserted answers to the down clues on the dotted letters of the already completed bottom row. There were ten. In between these words black blocks made up the remainder of the second row. Nate had not given me the answers but made me work them out with a little prodding, so, he said, I could continue on my own in the same way. Not tonight though, I decided, after Nate had gone. As Zebedee used to say, time for bed.

As I waited for sleep, I pondered who had sent it to me. What did it mean? Then I had another thought, a far more disturbing one. There should be no deliveries on a Bank Holiday, so how had I got the package? That meant the delivery guy was not what he seemed. Was he the person that sent the stuff or was he working for someone else?

That kept me awake for a while but eventually I dropped off.

Chapter 4

The first was an accident, although in fact it was not his first, but he did not know that at the time.

It happened in Manchester. She was a prostitute called Annie Betts and he had picked her up near Chorlton Street Bus Station. She was the best of a bad lot. At least her hair and nails were clean, and she didn't have a fag drooping from her lips. She was slim, maybe a bit on the thin side, had short blond hair and was dressed in a sparkly top and short skirt, bottomed off with the obligatory high heels.

Annie liked to be presentable, which gave her a head start on the others, and she could do it when she had an available stash. She had to do it too, when she was running low and had to top up. She was running low now, so she had to give a good performance.

"I gotta place," she smiled as she got into his car.

"Good", said the punter. "Saves on the upholstery."

It was a basement flat, down some stone steps, behind green railings. The peeling paint on the door was an indication of the surroundings but the punter was too eager to notice. He practically pushed her in as she unlocked the door.

"Easy, Tiger." This one would be quick. She could tell. He was younger than her. Might as well have done it in the car, she thought. She would have to change her modus operandi slightly, but it was still worth a shot. It had to be. In a few hours her last fix would be wearing off and she would be climbing the walls.

"What a shithole," observed the punter, eying the surroundings. The place was damp and dirty. One small room with a kitchenette in one corner, comprising a mini-cooker and a small fridge. There was one other door which led to the bathroom. The unmade bed could be glimpsed in an alcove behind a long curtain. The carpet was filthy and the wallpaper peeling.

Annie saw the disgust in his eyes. "You want a fuck don't you? Not to buy the place?" She walked over to the bed and pulled back the curtain. She started to take off her clothes and lay them over a chair by the wall. The punter, his distaste forgotten, began to quickly disrobe, letting his clothes drop to the floor. By the time he was down to his dirty white boxers she was slipping naked between the sheets.

"I could do with a drink first," she said. "Over there, by the sink. Mine's a gin. Have one for yourself."

Keen as he was to start, the punter wandered over to the tray of bottles near the sink. There were no glasses, but he swilled out a couple of dirty mugs in the sink, pouring gin into one and whiskey in the other. Annie smiled. They never touch the gin, good job too. The punter brought the mugs over, handed one to Annie and downed the other in one. Annie took a sip from hers then placed it in a little niche in the wall behind her. Then she got down to work.

Annie put on one of her best performances. A lot of the time she was mostly passive, letting the punter do what he wanted, but this time she wanted him tired out, so she went for it like a sex starved rabbit.

An hour later the punter was asleep as planned. Four of the bottles of booze were drugged. The fifth, the alleged gin, was merely water. No one ever took the gin. He wasn't heavily drugged and soon she would be able to wake him. Just enough time to divest him of his money. Annie had played this trick before when she was low on funds. When she woke him up, she would act all frantic, pretending she had fallen asleep too, and throw his clothes at him, screaming that her pimp was due any moment. What with the drug and being rushed, the punter never checked his wallet, her fee already having been collected in the car before they had arrived.

Annie felt her grip on reality slip. She needed a fix soon. She picked up the punter's trousers from the floor and searched the pockets, finding a wallet in the rear one. Forty-five pounds. She had hoped for more, but it was enough with what she had already. He had eight pounds in coins too, but she didn't take that as he might feel the weight loss of loose change.

Annie climbed back over the punter and took her place in the bed next to the wall. Then began Act Two.

"Wake up! Wake up!" she yelled whilst shaking him.

"What? What is it?" he asked, sleepily.

"Come on! You've got to get out of here. We've been asleep. My pimp is due here any second now. He'll be furious if he knows I slept on the job." She literally pushed him out of the bed. He half fell to the floor then steadied himself and started putting on his clothes.

Annie climbed out of the bed, pulled on a robe, and tying it around her middle, wandered over to the window. "Oh God, he's here!"

The punter looked over at her standing by the window, peering out from behind the net curtain. She seemed close to tears. The punter was not given to many moments of philanthropy, but he suddenly felt sorry for her. Anyway, she had been good. Very proactive. She deserved a bonus. He reached for his wallet and found it empty. The look of horror on her face proved she was not quite the actress she thought she was.

"You bitch!"

Annie started to move towards the kitchen area to get a knife, but the punter was quicker. He caught her across the face with the back of his hand.

He threw it with such force that she spun around, fell, and smashed her head on the old stone fireplace. Her lifeless body crumpled to the floor.

The punter stood stock still in shock for a few seconds. Christ! What had he done? There was perfect silence. Not even the sound of traffic outside penetrated the fog in his mind. Was she dead? She looked dead. She had a limp rag doll look. Still in a daze he bent down and felt for a pulse, trying her wrist and neck. Then he tried to find a heartbeat. Nothing. Definitely dead. The dull lifeless eyes staring up at him said so. More than said it, yelled it from the rooftops.

The punter was less traumatised now but more frantic. What to do? True, it had been an accident, but with his past form would anyone believe him. He had only been arrested for petty offences, but they constituted a criminal record. He *could* contact the police and tell them the whole truth. The evidence would back him up. No. There could still be a manslaughter charge. He was not going to prison.

On reflection he knew he needed to flee and quickly. Her pimp was due. Yet he couldn't leave evidence. His prints were in the system. Now what had he touched. He tried to go through it in his head. The door he had banged shut with his foot as he had lunged for Annie as soon as she got the door open. The bottles and the glasses. He needed something to wipe these. He opened the door that led to what he guessed was the bathroom and found a towel. He wiped the bottles. Washed the glasses and then wiped them. Now what else. Her clothes. Had he touched those? Probably, whilst she was still wearing them. What about the bedclothes and the bed. God knows where his hands had been. And her body. Forensics were so detailed now. They could get a fingerprint from a body. He could wipe the body, but not the bedclothes. They would have to go. He couldn't be seen leaving with them.

He was starting to panic. Then it hit him. There was only one way to do this. To get rid of all the evidence and the body. He had to torch the place. How to ensure a good fire? He had no petrol. The mini cooker was electric. However, it was not necessary for the whole building to burn. Just the bed and the body. He hadn't seen Annie smoke but there was a lighter and a packet of fags on the fireplace. Smoking whilst in bed then falling asleep. The perfect scenario. He lifted Annie's body onto the bed, took off her robe and pulled the sheets up to her armpits, leaving her arms free above the covers. Next, he lit one of her cigarettes, got it going with a few puffs, and then he put it between her lips ensuring a lipstick smear and finally placed it between her fingers. The sheet started to smolder but not quickly enough. He walked over to get the bottle of whiskey, careful to use the towel, and emptied it over the area. The flames caught and he took his leave of the flat after helping himself to his own money. He was sure Annie would have some other money stashed away but he didn't have time to look for it. He had stayed too long already. At the door he took one last look around to see if he had left anything incriminating in case the fire didn't spread to the whole flat. He had briefly considered starting two or three fires but discounted this idea. Fire investigators could identify the seat of a fire and would know if there were more than one which would throw out the smoking in bed scenario. Satisfied, he left, leaving the lights on so the flickering fire would be seen less easily than in a dark room.

Once outside he considered leaving the car. However, it was stolen with false plates. If it was found in the vicinity it might arouse suspicion so he climbed in and drove off, determined to dump it as soon as he could.

Now that the action was over and the adrenalin had stopped pumping, he was aware of how fast and loud his heart was beating. His hands were shaking too. He was sure his driving must be erratic and the last thing he needed was to be pulled up by the police. He turned into a side street that turned out to be empty. Derelict houses on one side and a demolished site on the other. There was no one on the street and he felt sure that none of the houses were lived in. He stopped the car. He wiped the steering wheel, gear lever, seatbelt, mirror and door handles with a couple of paper hankies he had found in the glove box. Then he walked away, leaving the car unlocked and the keys in the ignition. Hopefully, someone would steal it.

Annie's killer walked for a good while until he hit a bus route. He could have hailed one of a couple of taxis for hire that passed him, but he didn't want anyone remembering him. Less chance of that on a bus. Consequently, it took a couple of hours to get back to his hotel room – if you could call it a hotel. On reaching it he collapsed on the bed in a cold sweat.

He had done some bad things in the past, but this was in a different league. All he had wanted was an hour's distraction. If that cheating whore hadn't tried to rob him everything would have been alright. It had been a total accident but by running and covering the death up it would probably be commuted to murder. Could he get away with it? Had he got away with it? He decided that even though he was still persona non grata down South it was time to get out of Manchester.

Next day when he awoke, he didn't immediately remember the night before. Instead, his thoughts were filled with what the Bettinger brothers would do to him if they caught him and how long he would have to stay out of London. He had the same thoughts every day upon waking, ever since he had siphoned off some of their profits from their drug empire. He had been quite close to one of the brothers at one time but that would not save him now.

All at once, the events of the previous night came flooding back and his insides tightened as though they were in a vice. His craving for breakfast vanished, replaced by a nervous tension that almost made him physically sick. With trepidation he got dressed and wandered down to the hall table outside the breakfast room, where he knew the morning papers were put so guests could read them over their cereal and toast.

He had been lucky to get a room, even in a dump like the one he was in. It was Euro 96 and Manchester was crammed. The Group C games were being played at Old Trafford and Anfield. Germany had all their games at Old Trafford, so the place was full of its countrymen.

He took a copy of the local paper and a national one. Walking into the dining room he deliberately sat in the corner farthest away from the few other guests who were late risers. Normally, he would have turned straight to the back pages to read about the forthcoming England v. Scotland game that was to kick off later, but football was the last thing on his mind then. He had hardly started looking through the pages of the local paper when Mrs Gilbert, the landlady, came sailing over.

"Morning Dearie," she greeted with enthusiasm. "You'll be wanting your normal will you? Complete fry up with extra beans and fried bread?"

He was extremely nervous about coming across his deeds in the paper. His mouth was dry and his hands clammy. "What…..eh, oh, Mrs Gilbert. Just toast and coffee this morning please." On seeing her disappointed face, he added, "Upset stomach," by way of explanation.

"Ah. A wee dram or two last night, was it?"

"Something like that," he agreed.

She nodded in understanding. "Ah, well. Toast and coffee it is then, coming right up." Off she went to the kitchen, tut tutting that the demon drink had taken preference over her culinary delights.

Five minutes later he was feeling a lot better. There was nothing in the national and only one small paragraph about a fire in the local one. According to the paper, the cause of the fire was unknown but speculation from neighbours was that the fire had probably started due to the occupant, a known prostitute, smoking in bed. It was stated that there were no suspicious circumstances. He was in the clear and he almost laughed out loud as the tension dissipated as if by magic. His hunger quickly returned, and he considered changing his order but reasoned that this would arouse questions from Mrs Gilbert.

Little did he know it, but something was to happen at 11.17 that would blow his transgression right out of the papers, so he need not have worried at all. It was Saturday 15th June 1996. The Arndale bombing by the IRA. His little fire would be like an extinguished match in comparison. Over 200 people injured and massive property damage and disruption, in one of the host cities for Euro 1996 with the usual crowds swelled by visiting fans. All the emergency services would have their hands full.

Chapter 5

Peter Lane was up late. Later than he should have been bearing in mind he had to be back at the station in less than six hours. He could not help it though. He was fascinated with the puzzle. More so now that he had more idea on how it should be solved.

Peter lived in his grandfather's house, in a basement flat. He had encountered some trouble getting the large frame down the outside stairs which had brought Joe, his grandfather, out of his front door. He was not long seventy but still stood tall, or as tall as he was at 5 feet 8 inches. He had a fine mane of grey hair and glasses that rested halfway down his nose. He was there to lend a hand but once they had manoeuvred it through the tight doorway and set it up against the wall in the sitting room, Peter could not get his grandfather out again. He was too intrigued with the whole thing. It was a good job too because he had made the initial headway. He was a crossword nut, not having much to do all day since his wife had passed away.

As Peter had brought down the boxes of blocks from outside, Joe had been looking at the clues.

"Most of these don't seem too bad, Pete," he said.

"Really Pop? That's good. Can we eat first though, I'm starved."

They had a quick meal of egg and chips in the kitchen of the main house and while Peter was washing up Joe was writing something down on paper. He had brought the clues up with him and had been working some of them out.

"I think I have got the hang of this," said Pop Joe, when they were back in Peter's flat. "Look at this."

Peter looked at the paper on which Joe had drawn a grid representing the frame and had the bottom row as it arrived but now had words coming down into the bottom row. Nine in all.

"What?" exclaimed Peter. "You got them so fast. I must be slow."

"Not really," said Joe. "They are sort of cryptic. Not the type you would see in The Times or any real cryptic puzzle. A bit like an amateur had tried to create one." He took the paper from Peter. "Look here. The first answer is in already. The dots on some of the letters denote where other words intersect. The only one I cannot get is the one that ends in the E of 'the'."

"Hey, that's great Pop," declared Peter. "Now we can start to put them in."

"We could, but I think we should write what we can get down on paper first, just in case we make a mistake."

Plan of action agreed they set down to work on Clue 5 which was the one Joe had not got yet. Othello confused them. Joe was not so hot on Shakespeare. Peter wanted to miss it out and plough on with others, but Joe insisted they try to work it out because it was like putting up a building from the ground up. Each answer supported another. They solved it in the end. Once they worked out that 'bit part' was 'cameo' and take off the 'O' for Othello that gave 'came' which fit.

The next difficult bit was deciding where the first across clue went. That was the first across word that had to be worked out, because some of the down clues had already spelt three words across 'her', 'in' and 'spa'. The first two were in the second row and so would be clues 12 and 13. Joe confirmed that 'her' was the answer to 12 – *The Queen is not here* – take E for Elizabeth from 'here' and you had 'her'. Clue 13 – *Be with the right crowd* – meant the In Crowd according to Joe, but it also had letters in brackets after the number of letters – LB.

"OK," said Joe "I think we have a good fix on the first words to insert down but we need to resolve the colour issue I fear before we can start going across."

"Well, four of them end in a yellow spot so I guess the other letters will be yellow," Peter observed.

Joe was silent for a few seconds and then smiled. "Not only that but we have ourselves a clue." He saw Peter's puzzled look. "Look at the yellow dots and the words that they represent."

"Hall, scarlet, library and dining?" Peter was still in the dark.

"Cluedo!" said Joe.

"Oh yes, you're right!"

Once they had discovered that they took all the blocks with the yellow spots and spelt out the suspects, weapons and rooms with them. Thy found blocks with yellow spots for all the letters but a fair few of these had another colour spot also. One spot on the left of the letter and the other on the right. Joe felt that where there were two spots this meant intersecting words crossed using the same letter.

After this there was a brief stop for tea which Joe was a bit addicted to, needing a cup every hour or so. It gave them some thinking time on where to start with Clue 14. This was where Peter was able to have some real input as Joe had no idea what "Mystery Inc" meant.

"Scooby Doo," explained Peter. "Mystery Inc is the Scooby gang. Fred, Daphne, Velma, Shaggy and Scooby."

"OK," said Joe. "I will bow to your superior knowledge in such matters. So, the clue says, not all at once. That must mean it is just one of those names. Now if you look at Clue 16, what do you think that means?"

"Ape drops his tool," read Peter. "No idea."

"Monkey wrench," said Joe. "American. Which over here means spanner. And what do you see on row three?"

Peter only needed a quick look. "S P A is already there. It's not spa but spanner."

"Precisely. So, on that line before spanner, we have two words to fit in. And from those names you gave only Fred would fit for 14. It would start from 'fat'. Clue 15 means 'stole' as in theft and also mink stole. And Clue 17 is 'kiwi' which is practically already filled in."

"Great," enthused Peter. "This is going great. Spanner will be yellow from the Cluedo er… clues. It has to be "Fred" for Clue 14 and the G in brackets must mean a green spot."

"Right," agreed Joe. "And 'stole' must be orange and 'kiwi' has nothing in brackets so presumably is just black. Or rather no dots at all. Also, we can now put in black squares in all the empty columns for the second row and between the words on the third row." He quickly shaded in the boxes on the diagram they were creating. Then he yawned and looked at his watch. "Is that the time? I'm off to bed. I will leave you to fit the actual blocks in from the diagram."

It was only nine fifteen, but Joe always went to bed early and read for about an hour before he dropped off. Peter got to work slotting the blocks in, so the first three rows were complete and some columns above that from longer down words. He also put black blocks in on top of the down words.

It was not yet ten o'clock and he was keen to continue but by nearly midnight he had got no further except for possible answers to two of the clues. He was still wide awake, but his mind was fuzzy. He decided to leave it for the night and turn in. As he lay there waiting for sleep to come, his thoughts turned to who and what had set up this puzzle. Was it a serial killer taunting Inspector Tate or something else entirely? And why?

Chapter 6

July 1988

In fact, it had all started a long time ago. It began with a boy. A fifteen year old boy called James Perkins who felt utterly betrayed. It had been that way for what seemed a long time. Four years can seem an exceptionally long time to a child.

He had not always felt like that. Life had been full of fun and laughter before he found out. They had been a happy family. His mum, dad and twin brother. Mike had been his best friend in all the world, and they had been inseparable. They had done everything together, always thought alike and never fought. That was gone now. Sometimes he wished it could be like it was before. It could not be though. Never. Ever. Not after what he now knew.

It was just luck that he had found out. Bad luck really. Bad luck and idle curiosity. He had heard somewhere that curiosity killed the cat. In this case, curiosity had made the brat.

It had been late at night, or so he thought. He had awoken feeling thirsty so climbed down from his top bunk and crept to the bathroom to get some water. On the way back to bed he heard voices from downstairs. It was far too late for his parents to be up so who was down there? His parents' bedroom door was shut as always, and he didn't want to wake them. He thought he would investigate first.

He crept down the stairs and saw a light coming from the lounge. The door was ajar, so he went over to peek through the crack by the hinge. To his surprise, it was his parents, but when he thought about it, it would be more surprising if it were someone else, like burglars. Satisfied, he was about to return to bed when he caught the last thing his mother said.

"When should we tell him? Them? Both?"

Now "them" could have been anybody but he felt it was about him and his brother, so he stayed to hear more.

"Do we need to tell them?" asked his father.

"Of course we do!" he heard his mother reply. "They have to be told, and by us. If he hears it from her then what will he think?"

"We refuse her request and leave it there. There is nothing she can do."

"She can just turn up. Here or at school. There was no agreement." There was a rustle of paper. "Here. Read her letter again."

He would have liked to have heard more but he felt a sneeze coming on, so he had to quietly rush back upstairs to the bathroom. He just got the door closed before it came and he stifled it as much as he could. Opening the door again he was going to go back downstairs but he heard his parents' voices.

"We'll talk about this tomorrow." He heard his father say. "We need to get some sleep."

They were coming to bed. He quickly slipped back into the room he shared with his brother and quietly closed the door. He got back into bed as he would learn no more that night. He did not sleep at all though. It *was* about him and his brother, that bit was clear. More about one of them than the other, but which one? Also, who was "she" who might turn up? The first thing he had to do was get hold of that letter. Usually, any quest he had was shared with Mike but this time he was on his own. One of them was more involved than the other in this and he needed to find out who first.

It took him a while to find the letter, over two weeks in fact, searching every chance he got when his parents were out. When he did find it, his world came crashing down.

It was handwritten and it took him a while to decipher it. It was written by a woman who had given up her baby to his parents because one of their twins had died shortly after birth. The woman said that although she had given up the baby willingly at the time, knowing he was going to a good home and would be better cared for, now she wanted to know her child and wanted to meet him.

Shock was the prevailing feeling. So, he had no brother. And these were not his parents. And his real mother had got rid of him at birth. He had no doubt in his mind that it was himself and not his so called brother that was the interloper. He had tried to deny it for so long, but the seed had been there. He had always harboured the hidden feeling that his so called parents showed favouritism to Mike. Now he knew why. It all made sense now. Why they were twins but unalike in looks. At school they had been called the Lopsided Twins or No Peas in a Pod Twins. It had never really bothered him before, but it did now. Why had everyone lied to him?

What the letter did not say, and what he could not know, was that the woman that had given the baby up had been raped. Her baby was a product of a heinous act and she had not wanted any part of him. The arrangement had been a blessing for her at the time. Would this have been better or worse for James to know? At that age would he have understood?

For four years he had lived with the truth, the truth as he knew it. At first he tried to hide it and act normally but as time went on the worm of resentment grew. Now, he hardly associated with his brother and was surly to his parents. His schoolwork had suffered, and he had even been referred to a doctor. The woman, his real mother, never turned up. It was a good job really, he often thought. She was the biggest traitor of all. It was like he was at war with everyone now, or, as he saw it, everyone was against him. Enough was enough. Time to change things. Time to go.

He clicked on the torch and looked at his watch. Two thirty five in the morning. They must all be asleep by now, he thought. He slipped out of bed in T-shirt and shorts and pulled on tracksuit bottoms. He did not share a room any more due to his inability to get on with his faux brother. His bag was already packed, and he placed it at the door. He eased it open and listened hard. No sounds other than snoring from his parents' room. He placed the bag outside on the landing and turned to pick up his trainers. Then without a glance at the toys, books and posters he closed the door on that part of his life. Gone was James Perkins. Killed by treachery.

He crept down the stairs. The front door was locked and bolted. He could not reach the top bolt, so he went through the kitchen to the back door which only had a key to turn. Just as he was about to step out and leave forever he had an idea. A nasty idea. One born out of pent up anger, frustration and resentment. One that he did not even think about, because if he had then he would undoubtedly have had second thoughts.

He picked the pile of newspapers that had not yet been put out by the bin and spread them around the front door, hallway and partly up the stairs. Then on his way out he took a box of matches from the fireplace in the lounge. Once outside he locked the back door and threw the key up the garden. He then circled the house to the front door. He lit and match and popped it through the letter box.

Let the traitors die, he thought. He did not need them anymore. Then the fifteen year old boy walked away down the street.

Chapter 7

The morning after Nate's visit I felt strangely restless and could not settle. Tuesday, and all normal people were back to work after the Bank Holiday. The parlour was open below because I had heard some barking. I felt that I needed to get out, and although I almost never went for a walk just for walking's sake that is what I did. As I came around from my door and past the parlour shop window, I waved at Jackie who was attending to a dog on the grooming table. She waved back.

I didn't know where I was going, and I just ambled along thinking. Mainly about money. I had to start earning some soon. I only knew insurance though and I didn't fancy getting back into that. I had the inkling of an idea, although it was a bit far-fetched to think I could make a living from it. I was not bad at drawing. Not serious artistry like portraits or landscapes but sketches of generic people and things. I had on a few occasions sketched something for Laura to use on a campaign. Maybe I could offer my services to others for illustrating books or something. It would be better than a nine to five office job. On the minus side of course, it meant running my own business, which meant advertising, creating a website, paying taxes etc. It was a nice idea but would need seriously thinking about. I made a conscious decision to really look at my finances when I got home to determine how much time I had.

I noticed that I had somehow wandered into the local park. It was quiet, with just a couple of dog walkers around and an older couple sitting on a bench. Why then did I suddenly feel uneasy? I shivered, despite the heat in what was turning out to be one of the warmest Mays on record. I felt as though someone was watching me and did two complete spins but did not see anyone taking an interest in me.

I told myself to pull it together and headed to Tesco to pick up some lunch. Even inside the store I could not shake the feeling that I was being watched. So much so that I just grabbed and paid for a hot cheese and ham Panini, then headed home. Just in case someone was watching and for something to do to take my mind off it, I ate the Panini on the way back, then at my door I dropped the keys because my fingers were greasy. Once inside I let out a pent up sigh of relief. What was wrong with me?

I was a nervous wreck, but why? I plonked myself on the sofa and tried to work out what was going on. Yesterday I had felt fine. Well, not fine exactly. I wasn't happy, I never was these days and doubted if I would be again, but I had been doing OK. The only odd thing that had happened recently was the arrival of the puzzle. I decided that was what it was. Someone had singled me out to play a practical joke on or even something worse. I had no idea who it was or what it was about, and it had unnerved me.

That being the case then there was only one thing to do and that was to solve the thing. I pulled the frame out from behind the table where I had shoved it again after Nate had left. Now it was a bottom line with ten vertical words and three others spelt across where those vertical words were right next to each other. I lifted the frame onto the table. It was heavy and there was no way I would be able to lift it if all the blocks went in. It was going to have to stay on the table and I would have to eat looking at it.

Nate had ticked off the clues as we had answered them, so including the first one that had already been in the frame we had thirteen done, although technically the last two had completed themselves. Eerily, number 14 was the one I had had a bit of a handle on when I first read the clues. Nate had told me that the next word would be across and as an aficionado of Scooby Doo ever since my childhood I had the answer almost immediately, but then I had to rethink. The clue was different. All the clues from then on were different because they had one or two letters in brackets after them. In fact, on studying the clue paper further, I noticed the letters did not start with Clue 14 but Clue 13. I had missed it because we had not had to work that one out – 'it' had spelt itself. I figured the letters meant a colour, to correspond to the dots on most of the blocks. Clue 14 was G for green presumably. So 'Fred' was in green. There was only one F and one R with green dots but there were three E's and three D's. Then I noticed something else.

The F had the green dot on the left and the R had it on the right. The F only had the green dot but R had a black dot on the left. All the dots on the bottom row which had shown us where to put the down clues, had been on the left. Therefore, dots on the left could mean at that letter words crossed. The colour on the right must be groups. That meant that the R ended a word going down.

Of the E's there was a single green dot but that was on the left so that meant a crossing. Then there was a green and yellow but that also meant a green crossing of a yellow group. That left the only other E which did have a green dot on the right and an orange dot on the left.

The D was more difficult. There were two D's with a green dot on the right. One had a black dot on the left and one had a yellow dot. There seemed to be no clue as to which one to use. However, what this did mean that on the word 'Fred', there were three consecutive words coming down.

Something else hit me and I felt so stupid. I should have seen it earlier. It had been staring me in the face. Four of the down clues I now had in which ended on the bottom row, had been denoted by a yellow dot. The answers we had were Hall, Scarlet, Library and Dining. I had the connection on these now. Cluedo. These were all in yellow but now I had the pattern of crosses I needed to check we had used the right letters.

'Hall' had been the first word down, on the first letter of the already inserted answer. Now the second L, the first block dropped in was only one block away from the A in 'Fat' and that block was black, so no word across and therefore an L with no left hand dot and yellow on the right. Same for the A because that had one block before the start of 'Fred' which would have to be black too, so A also was yellow on the right only. On the H, I was not sure. There were a number of those with yellow on the right, but some had dots on the left. However, unless there was going to be a two letter word across, any word that started across on that H would join over the F in 'Fat' thus stopping that word being 'Fat', therefore I felt safe in using an H with just a right yellow dot too.

The coloured dots were crucial then. They grouped words together – although the significance of that was not yet apparent – and they also denoted where words intersected. Even though I had all the words coming down onto the bottom line already in with Nate's help, we had not considered the colouring. The other three yellow group words were harder to work out and I realised I would have to wait until I had more of the across clues worked out, to see where they crossed. I had no idea on Clue 15, but I quickly had 'Spanner' and 'Kiwi' on that row, so Clues 14, 16 and 17 were solved.

So, the third line across now read 'A', blank, 'Fred', 4 blanks, 'L', 2 blanks, 'A', blank, 'Spanner', blank, Kiwi. The answer to clue 15 was between 'Fred' and 'A' – which was in the word 'came' coming down – a five letter answer with L as the fourth letter. The clue had (O) after it so it was an orange group word.

It took me about fifteen minutes but then I had the word. At first I thought it was 'Steal' but that would not fit because the L was in position and that meant 'Steal' would join right onto 'Fred' with no black block between. I eventually worked out it was 'Stole'. That meant I had the whole of the third line in. Next, there would be several down words ending on the third row. Also, I knew that there was an answer coming down and ending on the S of 'Stole'. There were only two S's with orange dots on the right but they both had dots on the left, one blue and one yellow. Another one I may have to change later.

The next clue was 18 – *Keys can be this or somewhat lesser*. What types of keys were there? Door keys, car keys or any key that opened any type of lock. There were the keys on a typewriter or any keyboard. Wait, there was also a musical keyboard. Musical keys can be major or minor. And minor is lesser. I had it. 'Major'. I already worked out that there was a word coming down on the R of 'Fred'. The left hand dot was black, so I assumed that meant no colour group and I found all four letters of the word free of dots. I dropped them on top of the R plus a black block on top.

There were also words coming down on the E and the D of 'Fred' so these would be the next two clues. I was on a roll. Maybe it was coming back. The puzzle power I used to have when Laura was alive before I had slid into the pit of despair. I was certainly starting to get the hang of it again. Or I thought I was. By the end of the afternoon though, I was not much further because there was a lot of trial and error with the coloured dots, and I had also got stuck on one particular clue. I was annoyed because getting stuck on that one seemed to throw me off and I could not get the one after either. I was about to call it quits when there was a knock at the door anyway.

"Hi Danny!" It was Jackie, who always knocked rather than use the buzzer. "I have a boarder tonight. He's a big one. A Great Dane called Scrappy."

"You are joking," I said. Who would call their Great Dane Scrappy? Everyone knows that Scrappy was the worst thing that happened to Scooby Doo. The fact he was the same type of dog as Scooby and Scrappy was too big a coincidence for this to be random.

"What do you mean?" asked Jackie, a puzzled look on her face. She was only about thirty or so and probably did not understand the reference. It would take too long to explain.

"Nothing Jackie. Just something from my childhood. When does he need his walk?"

"Around 9pm please. He will have been fed. He is very friendly, but he pulls a bit."

"OK. Leave it with me."

So, I had a 9 pm appointment being dragged around the park and picking up great piles of dog poop. Still, I couldn't complain. I was living rent free.

Chapter 8

Tate got up earlier than usual. He had not been able to sleep much because his mind was whirling with thoughts of the past. He stood staring out of the bedroom window for a while. Not seeing the houses opposite, the cars in the driveways or the few lights that were on behind closed curtains. He was back in 1990. The year England had their best World Cup since 1966 but also the year that was blackened in his memory by one specific incident. One small action. One lapse of the copper code.

He tried to snap himself out of it. He turned from the window and saw his wife still sleeping. The alarm was due to go off in thirty minutes. He decided to go and make breakfast, which would be a nice surprise for Beth, who usually ended up making it for him and the kids.

In the kitchen he decided to make a proper breakfast rather than the usual cereal and toast. It would be ready by the time the rest of the family got down, so they would lose no time and be no further behind. The smell of it cooking might even get the kids out of their beds quicker than normal.

As he stood there, frying bacon, sausages and eggs, his mind wandered again back to the time he was trying not to think about.

He was not long out of Hendon and in his first posting, which was in the East End. Not the most salubrious of neighbourhoods but after a few months he started to get some respect from the law abiding locals, if not from the criminal fraternity. There was less danger to him from them than his own colleagues. Or rather just one colleague. Detective Inspector Jackson.

Jackson was a maverick. Good entertainment if you were watching Martin Riggs in 'Lethal Weapon' but not so good if you had to live with it. Jackson was not bent but he did bend the rules to fit. Tate as a P.C. did not get involved with C.I.D. but this time Jackson had approached him to help on a case. They needed a young guy to mingle with people in a nightclub and keep an eye out for anything amiss. Tate was twenty-one at the time. It was obviously at night, after he had done a full day shift, so he had not been at his sharpest. Something went down and he missed it, so although Jackson knew who was responsible, there was no evidence. He was not best pleased. Jackson wanted his man. Everyone knew he was guilty. Everyone knew that Tate had let him off the hook. Jackson left Tate with no doubt that he had to make amends. Jackson told him what to do and reluctantly he did it. He planted evidence and that put an indelible stain on his career before it had even started.

The evidence had been planted on someone low down on the food chain so that they had leverage over someone on the inside. He was hardly more than a kid, maybe seventeen, but once they had him bang to rights, Jackson put the squeeze on. Eventually the pressure paid off and the main target was arrested, convicted and jailed for ten years. He also took everyone else down with him including the kid. That was twenty eight years ago but Tate was sure that the past had come back to bite him. The only thing was that the main target of that operation, a gangster called Bannister, had died in prison during a brawl. If anyone was digging this up for revenge then it had to be one of the others that got caught in the net. The trouble was he did not know who they were. After he had played his little part he was kept out of the loop. He could not even remember the name of the kid. He had blocked it all out like a bad nightmare and now he hoped he was not about to relive it.

He came back to the present as he smelled burning. Now he was in trouble. He like crispy bacon and burnt sausages but the others didn't so he started a new batch for them. He was just laying it out when Beth appeared in the doorway in her dressing gown. She was ten years younger than him, petite, with long dark hair, currently tousled.

"This is new," she said, stifling a yawn. "Is it my birthday?"

"If it is, I have forgotten to get you a present."

"You'll do." She wrapped her arms around him from behind and gave him a hug whilst he was still removing the last of the bacon from the pan. Then she went back out of the door to the bottom of the stairs to shout up at the kids to get a move on.

When she came back into the kitchen, Tate went and closed the kitchen door. His wife looked at him with suspicion that quickly turned to concern.

"What is it, Tony?"

"Nothing really." He tried to smile but it didn't reach his eyes and she saw it. "Just something from my past might crop up. If it does, I want you and the kids to go somewhere for a bit."

"What? Where? Are you in danger? Are we in danger?" There was immediate panic in her voice and her eyes. He did not want her to start panicking.

"Nothing like that yet," he assured her. "Something was delivered to the station that might be connected to a past case. I don't know yet. If it is then someone is messing with me, and I don't know what that means. I just want you to be ready to go if I say so."

"But what about school? They have half a term left and exams."

"It might not come to anything but if it does, I'll sort the school out."

Just then their two children, Katie and Sam, came bursting through the door so the conversation stopped. "Hey, bacon!" shouted Sam, the younger of the two at eleven. He was always bouncing around so sometimes they called him Tigger. Katie, at fifteen, was more of a young lady than a teenager and she just took her seat. Tate looked at them all, his family. Nothing and nobody would harm them whilst he was alive.

Later at the station, Tate had to go and debrief the team on the case they had just wound up, but when free he tried to locate P.C. Lane to see how he had got on. Unfortunately, he was out on patrol, so it had to wait until the end of shift. When he did manage to get hold of him, it had gone 4 pm. He collared him in the locker room and asked him to come up to CID when he had finished getting out of uniform.

"Well, Peter, how did you do with that thing when you got it home last night?" Tate was trying to act casual, although a summons to his office probably negated that strategy anyway.

"Great actually." Peter was beaming. "My grandfather was really into it quickly and we got a few clues solved. Here, I set it down on paper for you." Peter drew a folded paper from his back pocket of his jeans and opened it out before handing it over.

Tate looked it but it did not mean anything to him although he did pick up the Cluedo reference.

"What do you make of it?" Peter asked him.

Tate frowned. "Not a lot I'm afraid. In fact, nothing, except that we have a number of Cluedo references."

"Yes. I noticed that. No secret message in there that you can see?"

"Not so far. Maybe it all must be solved before anything is clear."

"That may be the case, but we only have twenty clues and that is nowhere near enough to fill the whole frame."

"In that case, Peter, we can expect another delivery. We better keep an eye out for that and grab the courier when he comes in. I'll tell the front counter staff."

"Right!"

"You go home now Peter. Do some more if you can. The sooner we can work this out, the sooner I can know if it is just a wind up and bin it."

"Right! Night, Sir!"

When Peter had left, Tate sat at his desk and wondered if this was really about what had happened all those years ago. It made no sense so far. Why the elaborate set up? What was it supposed to achieve? Whatever the case, they had to nab whoever brought in the next delivery.

What about the Cluedo element, he thought. Is there something to read from that? He looked at the sheet of paper. Three rooms – hall, library and dining, one weapon – spanner, and one victim – Scarlet. Miss Scarlet to be precise. Had there been a murder involving someone called Scarlet in one of those rooms, with a blunt object like a spanner? Or did they have to wait for the whole puzzle to be completed to put this together? Or was it all just one big wind up?

He had just two lines of enquiry if he wanted to waste his time on this yet. Firstly, he could dig into the old records of the case against Bannister and get the names of all the others jailed, then check their current whereabouts. If this was connected to the 1990 affair, then the delay of twenty eight years might mean it was someone who got a long prison sentence and maybe got out recently. Secondly, he could have a check done for anything recent involving the name Scarlet. The latter option was a very long shot.

There was still no actual crime that had been identified yet so he still did not have to bring it in house. The problem would be if this all did tie into a real crime. Bring it in and the story may come out. He might have to investigate in his own time. He did not know it at the time, but he was going to have all the time in the world to investigate.

He was just about to pack up his desk and leave for the day when the phone rang. It was an internal call summoning him to Superintendent Grearson's office. It was never usually good news to have that summons, so wondering what else could go wrong, Tate made his way there.

Grearson was a big man with greying hair and moustache. He was only a few months from retirement and was increasingly becoming risk averse so as not to rock the boat. He was not smiling when he offered Tate a seat in front of his desk.

"Good job on the latest case," Grearson began.

"Thank you, Sir. A nice result if I do say so myself. He will be looking at a lot of time."

"We have to hope so," said Grearson, in a way that made Tate worried.

"What makes you say that? We have him bang to rights."

Grearson seemed to visibly prepare himself to give some bad news. "We have had some information."

"What information?" Tate knew something bad was coming.

"Information that mentions possible police corruption in past actions. Your actions in fact."

"What? When?" Tate had a feeling he knew though.

"We have not had the details as yet, but it dates back to when you were a P.C."

"There you are then," declared Tate. "Nonsense! My record over the years speaks for itself."

"It seems so. But if there is any doubt, any doubt whatsoever, it must be investigated. The last thing we want is for all your past convictions to be declared unsafe."

"Who is my accuser?" demanded Tate.

"Anonymous for now," admitted Grearson.

"And you are putting faith in some anonymous tittle tattle then?"

"Better to be safe than sorry," said Grearson. "I think it might be wise if you took a bit of time off. Just until we get this sorted."

"You are joking?" Even though he had an inkling of what was involved, Tate was surprised it was being taken so seriously without any proof. "Would you be doing this if you were not out of here in a few months?"

"No need for that, Inspector!"

"Sorry Sir! It's just that we've nabbed Dent and there is a lot to do."

"All the more reason we don't need the press sniffing around this. Take some time off and put some distance between yourself and the case for now."

"Is that an order?"

"I would rather not make it so," said Grearson.

"Very well! I'll be at home if you need me." Tate turned and left.

On the drive home, Tate realised this was going to be more problematic than he had thought. He was angry, angry at being manipulated like this, but he was also scared, very scared for Beth and the kids. He had to get the family away and to somewhere safe before anything else hit the fan.

Chapter 9

Despite having made a good start on the puzzle, I didn't feel good. I was still uneasy that someone was messing with me, and possibly even spying on me. I had no idea that by the end of that day I was going to feel so much worse and by this time the next day, I would be a nervous wreck.

I got a surprise in the early evening when Nate rang. From what he had been saying the night before I expected him to be out of the country by now, but he was still local and wanted us to go out again that evening. I didn't even have to think about it because I knew it would take my mind off whatever was going on.

No bowling this time. We went for a meal in a pub / restaurant. With it being a Tuesday evening, it was not that crowded, but at a nearby table there were a couple of young women enjoying a meal. I thought I was imagining it, but they kept looking over our way. Nate noticed it too and gave me a wink. I wasn't really interested but I could see Nate was. As there were two of them and two of us, I figured I was lumbered if he decided to go for it.

We decided not to go for a starter but dive right into the main course. When I eat out, unless it is Italian, I usually go for steak and chips. I don't really cook so steak is something I don't eat at home. I always say to people who ask that I just heat things up as per the directions on the tin or packet. Laura had been the cook and a very good one too. Nate decided to follow suit. Well done for me, medium rare for him.

Of course, the drinks came before the meal. Two beers, which at the rate Nate quaffed half the glass in one go, would not last long. We started talking about the World Cup. I was really looking forward to it. I was not working so could watch all the matches. Even though it was in Europe only some of the matches were in the evening. There were also matches in the afternoon with 1pm, 2 pm or 4pm kick-offs. Three matches a day mostly for the first two weeks or so, except the first day. As hosts this was Russia's first game, but unusually it was to be played on a Thursday. Nate sounded like he was well into it too, but he kept looking over at the girls and they kept smiling back and giggling. What was going on? They were extremely attractive girls in their late twenties or early thirties. One with long blonde hair and one with shorter red hair. They both wore short summer dresses showing a lot of leg. We were just two blokes nearer fifty than forty. And in my case not the least bit handsome. I was worried that Nate was going to invite them to our table, but then the food arrived and we tucked in.

I found I was ravenous so there was not much talking until we finished eating.

"Are we going for dessert?" I asked Nate, who as usual was paying.

"If you want some," he replied. "Personally, I think my dessert is over there."

I didn't need to see where he was looking. The girls had finished and had their table cleared of dishes but were tarrying over coffee, or so it seemed to me. Now my fears were confirmed as Nate stood up and went over to talk to them. I could see them nodding and still giggling. I saw Nate point over to me and I think I literally shrank back in my seat. Nate didn't notice and just carried on talking to them. Eventually he came back over but not before he collared a waiter, presumably asking for the bill.

"We're on," he said. "The girls are going to see a film and I said we would be glad to accompany them." He reached for his wallet as the waiter came back with the bill. He quickly paid in cash and told the waiter to keep the change, then he leaned over. "By the way, the redhead is called Tiffany, and she really likes you."

I looked over at Tiffany and she waved back. I wondered what the film was. I hoped it was not scary or romantic. Oh, for a laugh out loud comedy where there would be no need for hand holding or cuddling.

As it turned out it was one of the *Avenger* films. A strange choice for two young women, I thought. I found it difficult to follow because I had not seen any of one the previous ones, although I had seen *Iron Man* and *Thor*.

I didn't really need to worry about the plot though because I was too busy trying to fight off the sub-plot. We were sat Nate, Gloria, Tiffany and me. Tiffany tried to hold my hand as soon as I sat down but then quickly withdrew it. I knew why. My hands had been badly burned when I was younger. There had been some surgery and skin grafts, but you could still see and more importantly feel the damage. She turned and whispered something to her friend that I did not hear. Nate and Gloria were having no such hanging back issues, in fact, at least two people in the seats behind told them to get a room. I tried to concentrate on the film, but Tiffany kept trying, after getting over her initial surprise, and when she put my hand on her leg I finally decided I just had to go with it.

We didn't stay until the end of the film and were soon in a taxi heading to my place. Nate was dropping Tiffany and me off then taking Gloria to his hotel. My hands came up briefly in conversation, but I quickly quashed that subject. By the time we got to my place we had explored each other's body as well as one can do with clothes on, and our tongues were on good terms. I could hardly get the key into the lock fast enough. We rushed up the stairs and I started to drag her into the bedroom, but she held back.

"Where is the bathroom, Baby? I need to freshen up." I pointed the way, and she headed in that direction but at the door to the bathroom she turned. "You be naked when I get back, so I don't have to waste any time."

I didn't need telling twice and by the time I heard the flush, I was laying stark naked on top of the bed. She came through the door, surprisingly still fully dressed, took a quick look at me and uttered "Oh!" Not what I had been expecting or hoping for. "Stand up a minute," she said.

I was a bit confused but did what she asked. She stood there and looked me up and down for a few seconds then she burst out laughing.

"Is that all you've got?" She managed to get out when her giggling was under control. "I'm sorry but it would be too embarrassing." With that she turned and left.

I was floored but even in that moment of downright degradation, I still shouted, "Go home in a Tiff then!"

I lay on the bed stunned, not believing what had just happened. Nate had set me up for this. He had been the instigator. He had pulled the two girls. He had selected Gloria and left me with Tiffany. Had this ever happened to any man before? My thoughts immediately turned to Laura and then I was glad I hadn't done anything. I cried in my pillow for my lost love and might have been there for a while but then I heard a loud howling.

Oh God! I thought. I forgot about the dog. It was twenty past ten and he should have been walked at nine. I got some clothes back on and went downstairs. Opposite my front door was one that was kept locked, but which led to the back of the dog saloon. I opened it with a key that hung on a hook by the door. The front saloon was alarmed but this back area was not. I headed down a set of stairs to the basement where there was a large, caged area for overnight dogs. There were smaller cages for cats along the walls outside the dog area.

Scrappy was waiting for me. He stopped howling when he heard me coming. "OK Scrappy! You can have your walk now." I got a lead off some hanging on the wall. It had to be a longish one because I knew this dog would pull. Jackie had been right, he was friendly. His paws came over my shoulders when he jumped up and almost knocked me over. And with the face licking, I wouldn't need a wash that night. I eventually got the lead on him, and we left the building via my front door.

He pulled like a train and keeping control was a full time job, so it stopped me thinking of what had happened not twenty minutes ago. Scrappy knew the way to the park and pulled along at a rate of knots so we were there in no time. Jackie had given me no instructions to keep him on the lead and when she didn't I was free to let him off in the knowledge that he would not run off. I watched him as he frolicked in the night air. I couldn't let him get too far away or I wouldn't be able to see him or where he pooped. I moved in closer to where he was standing sniffing the air. Then I noticed something.

There were two entrances to the park, one at either end. It was not a very large park and at the opposite gate to where we entered I saw a girl sitting on the bench just inside. There was a lamp near the bench, and I could see that she had short red hair and a short dress. As I looked a car pulled up outside the gates and she walked over to it. A window came down but I could not see inside. A hand came out and handed something over which Tiffany stuffed in her handbag and then walked off. The window went back up and the car drove off.

What the hell was all that about? I wondered. The girl that had just ridiculed me to the point of tears was getting paid. Who by? It hadn't been the front window of the car that had come down but a back window. The car had been a taxi. What was going on?

Damn! I had got distracted and I couldn't see Scrappy now. He had wandered off. I started calling for him but whether he would come to me as a stranger I did not know. I tried louder "Scrappy, do come here!" Suddenly he loomed up behind me. I grabbed his collar and put on the lead. I was assuming he had done his business. I had no chance of finding it in the dark so the pooper scooper I had with me would be unemployed that night.

Before I knew it I was back in my flat. I had got back home, put Scrappy back in the basement and locked up, all on automatic pilot. I was still trying to work out in my head what was going on. It had been a very strange couple of days. First, I get three anonymous packages containing one large puzzle, then I feel I am being watched, then I am totally ridiculed by a woman and then I see that same woman being paid off. How did it all tie up? Did it tie up or was it all coincidence? I made some coffee, lay on the couch and tried to figure it out.

The frame and the blocks came first. Addressed to me, so I was meant to get them. A puzzle from an unknown source that I was meant to decipher. I racked my brain as much as I could but there was nothing there as to who or what was behind this conundrum.

Feeling watched when I went out could just be psychosomatic. I was on edge about being sent the puzzle in the first place and what it could mean. Yet some people had a sixth sense. Did I have it or was I just being paranoid?

This evening's two events had to be linked somehow. Why else would the girl that had played me like a Stradivarius be taking a payoff minutes afterwards and in such a clandestine manner? The girls were already at the restaurant, so they did not follow us. I tried to remember when the restaurant had first been mentioned. I think Nate had told me in the phone call we had. Did that mean my phone was bugged or maybe the flat itself? Why though? Why anything? Why the puzzle? Someone was definitely playing with me, and I was fed up with the game. The question was though, was it just a game or was it a prelude to something more sinister and deadly?

My first instinct was to ring Nate, but he would be at the hotel with Gloria, unless he was being played too. Maybe I should warn him. Then I thought, if that had happened then he would have rung to check in with me. As he hadn't things must be alright at his end, and I would only be disturbing him. I held off but I couldn't think straight. My brain was all fuzzy. I had to get some sleep. Easier said than done. I was tossing and turning for ages before I dropped off. If I had known what was to happen the next day, I would have chosen to sleep forever. Rock bottom? Not yet. There was a bit further to fall.

Chapter 10

Tate was up early the next day; in fact, he had hardly slept during the night at all. All his thoughts were how to get his family to a safe place. He had told Beth that she needed to go and take the kids. She was not happy about it, but he managed to lay it all out for her, as much as he knew, and then she was as adamant as he was about getting the kids away. The only difference was she wanted her husband to go too, and Tate knew he could not do that. He was the centre of attention and he had to stay well away from his family to keep it away from them.

It was all a question of how much his tormenter or tormenters knew? Were they under surveillance for instance? He had tried to keep vigilant but too much curtain twitching would attract attention too. He had not seen anyone suspicious on the street or in a parked car, but you never knew. They could be renting a nearby house or even holding neighbours hostage. Better to assume that they knew the daily rituals and routines of his household. To get away clean they would have to act as though everything was normal.

By the time the kids were at the breakfast table he had a plan. He had made calls – not on his mobile, nor the landline, but on an old 'pay as you go' he kept for contact with informants when he used them - and everything was set. Beth was in on the plan, but the kids were in the dark, they could easily let something slip at school.

The plan was in two parts. The getaway and the destination. Obviously they could not be seen carrying suitcases to the car because that would be a dead giveaway. Fortunately, Beth's job provided the answer to that problem as she worked at a charity shop. They loaded three large cardboard boxes into Beth's car, for all intents and purposes, donations to the charity shop. She drove off to the shop and if anyone followed her they would just see the boxes taken into the shop. The boxes were actually filled with clothes and essential items for a long stay away from home.

Tate drove the kids to school, the only detraction from normal, but the ungodly knew he was off the job because they had initiated it so it should come as no surprise. What, hopefully, they did not know is that Tate had spoken to the headmaster about what he wanted to do. It had taken some persuasion but in the end it was all fixed up.

After dropping off the kids at school, Tate went to the station, ostensibly to clear his desk, but he was also hoping that any tail would be on him and not the others in his family, who would be ensconced in their everyday locations until well into the afternoon – or so anyone would believe. Tate's real reason for going to the station was to see Peter Lane. He now had the time to concentrate on the puzzle because he had no doubt that it was connected to his enforced leave of absence. The clues may be a red herring, but he had nothing better to do. He cornered Peter in the locker room.

"Morning P.C Lane," he said formally because they were others around. "Can I have a word about that thing we were discussing yesterday?"

"Of course, Sir!"

"Come to my office then when you are changed." With that Tate left. He hoped he still had an office. It was only the morning after the evening of his strongly recommended leave of absence, so there should not be a new incumbent yet.

There was no one in his office so he took a seat and waited for Peter, who knocked on the door not five minutes later. Tate got up, ushered him in and closed the door.

"Peter, no time to mess about," he began. "You will learn later that I am on leave. Enforced leave. I am sure it is connected to this puzzle thing. I can take it off your hands now as I have nothing else better to do."

"Oh! OK." Tate noticed he sounded disappointed.

"Having too much fun with it are you?" he asked.

"Well, it is interesting," admitted Peter, "but it's more Pops. My grandfather. He is really into it, and we would not be so far along without his help. It is all set up in my flat which is in the basement of his house."

"Oh OK! Would he mind us working it together then?"

"I don't suppose he would mind at all. In fact, it would be a great thrill for him to be working on a case with the police."

"An unofficial case with a policeman under suspicion," pointed out Tate ruefully. "Look, I've got to go otherwise I might get kicked out. Give me his address and I'll call in later this morning. Give him a quick call though if you can, to warn him."

Peter nodded whilst writing down an address in his notebook and ripping out the page. He gave it to Tate who shook his hand. "Thanks for the help, Peter. I may see you around as you live at the same address." They left the office together but then Peter headed off to start his patrol and Tate went back to his car.

All in all, thought Tate, things were probably for the best. If his home was under surveillance and he could carry out his investigation elsewhere, in a place unconnected with himself, that might work to his advantage. He just had to make sure he was not followed. Not yet though. For the time being he was happy to be followed, whilst his family were making their getaway.

He was relying heavily on two other people. A couple Tate and his wife knew from a holiday they had a few years back. They did not meet up too often, so Tate was hoping they were off the radar. The whole plan relied on them playing their roles to perfection. He looked at his watch as he turned into the road for home. It was 9.30 am and almost time for things to spring into action.

Jack and Brenda Fox were indeed playing their part. Jack had rented a car and driven it to a back street near to the charity shop. Whilst he was doing this Brenda visited the charity shop and after a while came out loaded down with carrier bags which she took to her car. The bags contained everything that had been in the three cardboard boxes. No sooner had Brenda left the shop than Beth exited through the rear door and out through the yard, walking to where Jack was parked up. Then they drove to the school but not the front, a side street off towards the back of the school where a pathway led to a gate at the back of the school grounds. This was opposite another gate which led to the school playing fields. The path bisected the school grounds and playing fields. Beth waited at the gate for her children, who had been surprised at the headmaster pulling them from class and ushering them out of the school buildings towards the playing fields.

"Here they are then, Mrs Tate," he said by way of greeting. "I hope everything works out alright."

"Thank you, Headmaster. I hope so too."

As the headmaster turned to leave, Sam could not contain his curiosity. "What's going on Mum?"

"We're going on a trip. Come on hurry," urged Beth, as they almost ran back down the path to the car.

Sam would not shut up with his questions, but Beth was too worried and tense to answer. So far so good, or so she hoped. Jack drove them to a prearranged rendezvous point where his wife was waiting in their car. She had packed all the clothing and other things into two large suitcases which were transferred to the rental car. After quick hugs all around, Brenda drove off home. Jack got back behind the wheel of the rental. They had a long drive ahead.

Tate was back at home not doing much of anything but thinking hard when he got a text on the secret phone. *The sparrow has left the nest.* He smiled. So far so good, they were on their way. That was a weight off his mind. He would not get the confirmation they had reached their destination for a few hours though. Now was the time to start his own investigation. It was off the books, but he still needed access to records. Time to reach out to one of his contacts.

This time he was not using the secret phone because he was only doing what the ungodly would expect him to do and if they were monitoring his communications they might find it odd if they did not hear him asking questions internally. That would then alert them to the fact he had another form of communication, which he wanted to keep quiet for now.

"Hey Frank!" Tate greeted his long-time colleague from the early days who he had not been in touch with for years. "Long time no speak."

"Whoa, is that Tony Tate?" came the gruff voice from the other end. "Did you ever get that sweet partnership?" There was a roar of laughter after this.

It was an old joke. It had always been said at that time that he needed to have a partner called Lyle.

"No, but I'm sweet enough, Frank. Listen I need a favour."

"What Tony, no walk down memory lane first? Straight down to it?"

"Afraid so. This is a bit of an emergency."

"OK, shoot, I'm still all ears," which referred to Frank Jessop's large, almost elephant like ears that had been the source of much mirth in the old days too.

"Right. First things first, Frank. I'm on leave – if you know what I mean."

"God Tony, what have you done?"

"Nothing but accusations have been made and the top brass are being cautious. Unsubstantiated rumours as far as I am aware." Tate was mentally crossing his fingers as he said this. "I need you to dig up what you can on an early bust I was involved in. Peripherally involved that is. Back in 1990. The Bannister case. A few went down with him. I know Bannister died inside but if you could dig up the whereabouts of the others it would really be a big help."

"So, the accusation goes back that far then?"

"No idea." That was almost the truth because at this time he did not actually know what the accusation was. "All I know is that it goes back to my P.C. days."

"OK Tony. I'll have a nose around. Not going to be easy though. Paper records in archive. It will take me some time."

"Good man, Frank! Quick as you can though. Got to go now but when this is all over maybe we can catch up over a beer."

"Well, yes, but it will be a few and you're buying. The lot."

"Sure Frank. Thanks. Get back when you can."

Despite what he had just said to his friend, Tate knew that was the only blot on his record. The only people that knew about it were Jackson and his team and the guys who got caught. Tate knew Jackson was also dead now and the other three in that team would want this thing to remain buried forever. That left one of the guys jailed for it. Twenty eight years ago.

They would all have been out by now if they had not made any other infractions whilst inside. Tate could not remember how many were incarcerated with Bannister but had a feeling it was about half a dozen. He could not remember any names but the boy they had fitted up had been called Mickey, he now seemed to recall, having racked his brain for hours to remember that fact. Tate never knew what happened to him. He had been bundled back to uniform as soon as he had done his bit and had not even been in on the arrest. Jackson though had warned him to keep his mouth shut.

There was nothing more he could do on that side until Frank came back with some names and locations. Tate did not want to just sit around twiddling his thumbs and waiting for news of his family. It would be a while yet. He decided to have an early lunch then go and see Peter's grandfather. Might as well waste his time on a real time puzzle and keep his mind off things.

Chapter 11

The next day I awoke strangely down and lethargic. It might have been due to the trouble I had in sleeping – I had awoken a few times – but I had a feeling it was a prelude to a deeper depression I couldn't afford to let myself get into. Someone was after me and I had to have my full wits about me. I need not have worried, because something was just about to happen that would shake me to the core and keep me as alert as a cat on a tin roof above a furnace.

It was ten o'clock and much later than I usually woke up. It was stifling hot too. I refused to sleep with any windows open. I dragged myself out of bed and opened all the windows in the flat, all two of them, but after making coffee just lay down again on the sofa. I was trying to collect my thoughts together when the buzzer rang. I sat up like a shot and immediately thought of the last time my buzzer rang unexpectedly two days ago. That had heralded the start of all this queerness.

"Who is it?" I asked into the intercom.

"Delivery for Mr Andrews."

Not again I thought as I trudged down the stairs. I was just undoing the locks when I heard a loud crack, there was a thud in the door, and something went whizzing past my ear. I fell on my rump in surprise and shock. There were three more thuds and then nothing. I stayed exactly where I was. I was too petrified to move. I knew what had just happened because when I turned my head I could see the holes high up in the back wall. Bullet holes. Someone had tried to shoot me.

I don't know how long I lay there on the floor but eventually I realised that the shooter must have gone. I was taking no chances though, so I crawled back up the stairs, keeping low in case someone was taking aim through my first floor windows. I rang 999 and then, as if I wasn't floored enough, the "Which service do you require?" took me back five years to when I was reporting Laura's killing. I was stymied for a few moments, trying to hold back the sudden grief that threatened to engulf me, but I managed to give my details. I then went and sat on the floor behind the sofa where no one could target me and wept. I wept for Laura and maybe out of fear for myself too. This was too much. Far too much now.

Again, my instinct was to call Nate and this time I did not hold back. The number I had was only for emergencies, he had told me once. He was always in meetings, mostly abroad, so it was usually him that contacted me. I think though this counted as an emergency, and I just needed someone to talk to. Until the police arrived that is and maybe after too. The night before

I had held off so as not to disturb him, but things were getting out of control now. Too much for me.

He was one of the few contacts in my phone so was easy to find but I never got to talk to him because the number I rang was not recognised. That was very weird. Had he been attacked too? That wouldn't affect his phone service though. Had he turned it off so he couldn't be tracked? Would that though have resulted in the unrecognised response? This was all I needed. Cut off from my one and only ally. What the hell was going on?

***

"Hey Crouchie! Get a move on, we have a shout!"

Peter ran over to the patrol car and got into the passenger side before the car sped off sirens blaring and lights flashing.

"What is it?" he asked his colleague, Sergeant Buck Wilson, as he dropped the two Cornettos into the cup holders. Bang went their cool down break.

"Shooting on the High Street. No casualties according to reports but Armed Response have been notified," Buck informed him. "Your first one? Firearms offence?"

Peter nodded.

"Pretty straight forward. We wait for the firearms officers to check the area before we go in."

Peter nodded again and settled back for the short ride. Inside he was both excited and nervous.

***

The police arrived after only ten or so minutes, but it was a complete surprise to me when I answered the buzzer. There was a stocky guy outside wearing body armour and a black cap with 'POLICE' on it. He had a sidearm holstered but also had a larger firearm with a strap. He looked at the bullet holes in the door.

"Mr Andrews-White?" I nodded, temporarily having lost my voice seeing live guns for the first time in my life. "I'm Sergeant Hopkins, a firearms officer. Any injuries or fatalities?" I shook my head. "Can I take a quick look inside?" I moved out of the way so he could climb the stairs. I waited where I was and he was back in thirty seconds or so. "OK. Seems all clear. My team will now check the area and the locals will be here soon to chat to you." With that he was gone.

When I answered the buzzer the second time, I was told that Sergeant Wilson and P.C. Lane were outside. There was a *Dad's Army* joke there somewhere, but I was too scared to try and bring it out. When I opened the door, I was facing two uniformed officers. One in his early forties and one in his early twenties.

"Hello Sir," said the older of the two. He was dark blond and sported a fine moustache, a la Thomas Magnum. "Are you Daniel Andrews-White?"

"Err … yes," I stammered, which must have seemed odd, but he had momentarily put me on the back foot. I hadn't realised with the first guy because his weaponry freaked me out, but Andrews-White was our married name. Laura had been the White. I dropped it a couple of years after she died. In my panic I must have given my full name to the emergency operator.

"May we come in, Sir?"

"Yes, of course." I turned and went up the stairs leaving them to follow and close the door. That way they would get a good look at the bullet holes if they had not done so already. What did one do when the police came to visit? Did one offer them refreshments?

"Can I get you a tea or coffee?" Then I realised that was stupid. It was still before noon, but it was incredibly hot. "A cold drink perhaps."

"Actually, something cold would go down well, Sir."

Whilst they took a seat I popped to the fridge and got two small bottles of coke – my last two in fact. I didn't think to bring glasses and they didn't ask. They were sat on the two seater sofa, so I sat in my recliner which was at an angle to them facing the TV.

"Now Sir," It was still Sergeant Wilson talking, "you say you were shot at?"

The P.C. who had not spoken yet was tall, very tall, also blond but a much lighter blond, and clean shaven. He reminded me of Peter Crouch and was sat there, poised not with a notebook and pen but some type of electrical device. I assumed with surprise that he must be going to take down what I said with that. I just hoped it wouldn't be used in evidence against me at some time in the future.

I was a bit incredulous. "What? You saw the holes in the door?"

"We did see the holes in the door," Wilson admitted. "Our ARV is checking the area to see if they can find the culprit. You did speak to the AFO in charge?" I must have looked blank. "The Authorised Firearms Officer?"

"Oh yes! Sergeant Hopkins. He was in and out then off."

The sergeant nodded. "Speed is of the essence in shooting incidents. Now, how about you tell us what happened from the beginning."

"Er … OK." I gathered my thoughts, which was a bit difficult because they were all over the place. I needed a sheepdog to round them up. "It was less than an hour ago." I looked at my watch. It was ten thirty three. "I guess it was about ten past ten. I was lay on the sofa and the buzzer went. The guy at the other end said he had a delivery, so I went down. As I was unlocking the door this loud bang took me by surprise. Something whizzed past my ear. I fell over backwards and there were three other bangs. I knew they were bullets because of the holes in the back wall. I rang for you guys straight away. You were quick in getting here."

"We were in the area," admitted Wilson. "You got all that Crouchie?" Then he realised his mistake. "I mean P.C. Lane."

"Yes Sarge!"

I didn't even smile that my guess at Crouchie had been spot on. I doubted that they were allowed to use nicknames in front of the public. It must be used a lot to make it slip out like that.

"We'll get someone from forensics to take a look and remove the bullets. Do you know of anyone that has a grudge against you?"

"Would want to kill me, you mean, Sergeant?"

"No. I mean someone who might want to scare you? If he had wanted to kill you, he would have fired centre mass straight through the middle of the door. All four holes are high and wide. It was just a scare tactic."

I hadn't even considered that. I did so quickly but could think of no one. I didn't really know a great many people. I was not working so could not have made anyone angry that way. I had no neighbours to speak of as I lived over a shop in the High Street. I didn't have any family. I shook my head.

There was a buzz of a radio. Wilson listened and then said. "They have done a quick sweep of the immediate area. The ARV think the gunman has left. One of the shop owners heard the shots and looked out. He saw a man getting into the passenger side of a car that screeched off."

"Any chance that you will catch him?" I asked, not quite convinced of the scare tactic suggestion, and thinking that he might want to try again.

"There's always a chance, Sir!" said Wilson, in a tone that hinted probably not. "It happened fast, and the guy had a hat on obscuring his hair. We know the car was a blue Golf, but the witness got no index number."

That was that then. No chance without a registration number. On TV they would just get a list of all the blue Golf owners, visit them all and hit the right one on the third go. I doubt it would even get that far here. No one had been killed or injured. It would not be a priority.

"So, Sir? Is there anything else you can tell us? Anything strange happened in the past few days?"

What a question. Everything that had happened in the past few days had been strange. Where to start?

"Now that you mention it, a couple of things have been weird."

"Go on, Sir." P.C. Lane sat up and got even more attentive. I thought he must have writers' cramp by now bearing in mind all the keying he had been doing. I think he was literally taking down every word.

"Well Sergeant, it all started on Bank Holiday Monday when I got a delivery."

"There are not usually deliveries on Bank Holidays. At least not official ones."

"So I realised afterwards. I got this." I pointed to the frame on the table.

Both officers got up and went over to have a better look and that was when Lane gave what can only be described as an involuntary exclamation. Wilson looked at him with curiosity. "Are you alright P.C. Lane?"

"Yes Sergeant."

"This came with these," I said. Pulling out the block boxes from under the table. "And this." I waved the paper with the clues on it at them.

"Do you know who sent this to you or what it means?"

"No idea. The frame was empty except for the bottom row, and you have to solve the clues to put the other words in. As you can see I have not got too far."

"And you have no idea who sent this to you?"

"None at all," I stated emphatically.

"You said there were a couple of things."

I should not have been that forthcoming because now I had to tell them about the Tiffany case – but I got no Bond ending. I tried to make it as little demoralising for me as I could. Told in the light of day it did sound like a set up.

"And where can we get hold of your friend, Nathan?" asked Wilson.

"Well, he has no permanent address as his job takes him out of the country a lot. He was staying at a hotel somewhere near the airport. I can give you his mobile number though, although I tried it a few minutes before you arrived, and it is as though it never existed."

"Strange," agreed Wilson. "Give it us anyway please."

So they took that and asked a few more questions then asked me to read and digitally sign a statement on the device. It was only a brief one and they told me that a more detailed statement may be required by C.I.D. but that would do for now. Whoopee! I wondered what happened if you never turned up to give a statement. I was going to find out because I had decided to take off. Go to ground. Laying out all the happenings of the past few days had made me realise that something mighty peculiar was going on and I wanted no part of it. I was off. But where could I go?

Then before I could think about that very much I remembered what I had done. I didn't think of myself as Andrews-White anymore. That part of my life was over forever. Why had I done that? It only made me think of Laura again. Bringing me down further when I needed to be clear headed. Why had she needed to die?

Chapter 12

She was feeling in a good mood that day. It was nice to have some time off work. A free day to pamper herself. She had seen her husband off to his job and now had the whole day ahead. She cleared the breakfast paraphernalia from the table and washed up. She was still in her dressing gown but there was plenty of time before she had to be in town for her Zumba class and hairdressers appointment before lunch with a friend.

Life was great. Or it was now. She and her husband had just celebrated their 4 year anniversary. They lived in a nice semi-detached house in a new housing estate. Her job was going spectacularly for her age. It had all been so different a decade earlier. She shuddered as she went upstairs to get dressed. She didn't want to think of that time.

She didn't shower because she would do that after her class. She dressed in her exercise gear and packed her favourite blouse and skirt combination neatly in her bag with fresh underwear. She looked at herself in the mirror to check she looked okay but only briefly because she was not vain or into her looks really. The woman that looked back at her was slim, with long red hair, oozing health and happiness. The red hair was going to be a bit shorter by the end of the day.

She drove into town and parked at the top of the multi-storey car park. She always did that. Not only was there always space there but the walk down and back up the stairs was good exercise. Not that she needed the extra workout as she was just off to a class anyway, but it was her standard practice now.

It was a typical June day, so she had to take her umbrella with her, although it was not raining yet. Despite the cloudy sky, she had not a care in the world until the sight of something brought her up short. Or more precisely, the sight of someone. It was only a brief glimpse. and she might have been mistaken but she thought she had spotted someone she knew. Someone she did not want to see. Someone she had thought had gone from her life forever and someone she never wanted to see again. He had left her alone for so long now that she had thought he had given up on the idea.

By the time she got to the hairdressers after 45 minutes exercise and a long shower, she was talking herself out of it. She hadn't really seen him. It was just a trick of her imagination. But why now? When everything was so perfect. Fortunately, her favourite stylist, Petra, was a phenomenal talker and she soon forgot her fears as she heard about holidays and boyfriends and who was doing what with who. So much so that during her lunch with her friend it was not even in the farthest corner of her mind. However, once she was alone again and driving back home, it resurfaced making her wonder all over again if she really had seen him.

Ten years ago, she had been in a right mess. Just turned twenty she was struggling to make ends meet in London where everything was so expensive. Her typists' salary was hardly enough to live on, let alone live it up. She lived in a tiny bedsit and although it was kind of grotty she tried to keep it clean. Living hand to mouth though left no money for savings so any unexpected bill was serious and so proved the case when she got one for council tax arrears which she could not pay. And that was how she fell into prostitution. It was only supposed to be once or twice to get the money to pay the bill but once that was paid it was a case of, OK just a couple of more, then she could buy some new clothes. Or a few more and maybe she could get a car.

Fortunately, she was only just edging over a slippery slope, that could have taken her a long way down, when she met him. He had not been a punter either. They had met in a coffee shop. They had literally bumped into each other, and she dropped her coffee. The lid came off and quite a few customers had to take emergency backward jumping action. He had apologised of course and offered to buy her another cup. This time though it was not to go, and they had sat at a table talking for quite a while.

He was quite a bit older than her. Ten years seems a lot older at that age although now she was married to a man ten years older with no thought of it at all. Also, he was bald, and she had never thought she would go with a bald man, it had never turned her on before. Maybe it was because he had money or maybe the fact that he did not seem to want to just get her into bed. They did end up in bed a few days later and that was when her life changed.

He got her a better job by putting in a word for her. A ground level one to be sure but one with prospects which she hadn't had as a typist. He also got her a much better place to live. They were together for a few months then he changed and that was when she realised she had been duped. It had been one massive, long con and she had fell for it. He needed her to do something, and he had the goods on her. She liked her job, and she loved her flat but one word about what she used to be and it would be all over. The threat of that was what he held over her head. Do what he wanted, or he would ruin her new life.

What could she do? There was nothing that she could do. She had to go along with it. There was no great hardship to it. Just playing a role. A long term role though. The thing was though, he had made her check in from time to time over that first year, then he just disappeared, and she had never seen or heard from him again. Until now. If that is who she had seen.

Anyway, she said to herself, if it was him, I saw him but he didn't see me so everything should be alright. She hoped so. She needed to get her head on straight. She was nearly home now, and she had a visitor coming in about an hour. She had found a way to get some money for her husband. She was keeping it as a surprise for now until she knew if it would work out. A man was coming to talk to her about making a PPI compensation claim.

She got home and went up to the bedroom to collect her husband's tin box. It was where he kept all his important documents going back years. What she was keen to get her hands on were old loan agreements. She found various documents going back to the late 90's. She hoped that this would be enough. She didn't know that much about this well publicised PPI scandal but loads of people were getting on the bandwagon now, so when the email popped into her inbox about the possibility of a claim she had made enquiries - hence today's appointment.

She spread out the documents on the dining room table and went to put the kettle on. Mr Chapman was due in a few minutes. In fact, the kettle was still boiling when the doorbell rang. She opened the door to a tall moustached gentleman with grey hair, dressed in a raincoat and carrying an umbrella and a briefcase.

Soon they were sat down at the table with mugs of tea and a plate of biscuits before them as well as all the papers.

"Now, as I said on the phone, it isn't going to cost you anything just to enquire," said Chapman," however, if a claim payment is forthcoming then we would take fifteen percent for our services."

"Eighty five percent of something is better than a hundred percent of nothing," she replied.

"Precisely, my dear. I wish everyone would see it that way." He picked up some papers and started sifting through them. "So, it looks like we have a couple of old loans here. Are these settled now?"

"Yes. We have no loans now, other than the mortgage of course."

"Ah, well, there could be PPI on the mortgage too. How long have you had it?"

"Oh. We've only been here about eighteen months. It is our second home – an upgrade you know."

"I see. What about the old mortgage?"

"Well, that was with the same bank. We just transferred it over and added a bit on."

"Okay then. Well, if you can give me the details we can always check it out. No harm in looking."

"Fine, I'll just have to go and search out the old mortgage papers. I think I know where they are. If not though, is it alright if I send them across later."

"Sure. But take you time. I'm in no hurry. You are my last appointment today."

She goes upstairs to look for the necessary details. After a few moments, Mr Chapman gets up from the table and starts to wander around looking at things. Presently, he walks into the kitchen and starts opening the drawers. He finds something interesting and places it in his inside jacket pocket. By the time his prospective client comes back downstairs, he is back in the chair by the table.

"Did you find it?" he asked her.

"Afraid not. My husband will know where it is, but I was hoping to keep this money we could get as a surprise. I will try and find out and email it to you. Have you got a card?"

"Sure. Here you are," said Chapman pulling a card from his top pocket. A single card that he had had printed up only the day before.

"Thanks. I will get the details over to you as soon as I find them."

"No rush. We can be starting on what we have already. I just need you to sign this authority for us to be able to approach the lenders on your behalf." He took a form out of his briefcase and showed her where to sign which she did.

"I need take up no more of your time then. Thanks for using our services and I will be in touch soon." He stands up and starts to put on his raincoat again. Buttoning it all the way up.

"Do you think that we will be successful in lodging a claim, Mr Chapman?"

"Most assuredly. I can confidently predict that your husband will be coming into some money in the very near future."

She smiled at this. "That's good. I want to surprise him."

"I am sure he will be surprised at this turn of events," said Chapman.

He started to leave the room and walk towards the front door. She followed him and as he approached it said, "Well, goodbye Mr Chapman. Thanks for your help." She held out her hand.

Chapman had his back to her, his briefcase in his left hand and umbrella under his arm. He whirled round with the knife he had taken from the kitchen and stabbed her in the chest. Her eyes were filled with pain and then just before the end with incomprehension because the man she had thought was Chapman pulled off a wig and moustache to reveal a bald man she knew. She died with a question on her lips. "Why?"

He did not answer her because she was already dead. Chapman – if that was even his name, which it was not – saw that a few spurts of blood had got onto his raincoat. He took it off and folded it inside out and placed it over his arm with the glove he had speedily put on before grabbing the knife in the pocket. Then he let himself out.

"Mrs White in the hall with the dagger," he said. Well, Mrs Andrews-White, but close enough.

Chapter 13

After the police had gone I just sat there numb. What the hell was going on? Three different incidents in three days. They had to be connected, or I was on the worst run of luck ever. I did not know what to do. Was I safe in my own home? The police seemed to think someone was just trying to scare me. Well, bully for them, job accomplished.

It was still before noon and I did what was now a norm when I was angry, fed up or depressed - back to the online slots. This time I was using my debit card as the credit card was used up as far as cash was concerned, although I still had nearly half the limit left for other purchases. It was a bit silly to have a credit card really because every month I had to pay it off from the money left in my current account. That dwindling amount that I would soon have to top up. It currently stood at £19,372.28, which may sound a lot but not at the rate I had been spending.

I transferred £2,000 to my casino account and started playing. Everything gets forgotten at such times except the pursuit of winnings. I had been playing for about an hour with a few wins and some losses, but I was still nearly even. Suddenly, things turned, and I had the sort of luck that you dream about. I was playing at £10 per go again so the winning jackpot would be £5,000. It came in again. Twice in three days. Spookily, the same three days that I had been having horrendous luck with everything else. There was more. I had ten auto-plays left on that game and after three of those one of the features came up and paid me another jackpot. I had almost £12,000 in the bank. I should have stopped then, but I swapped to another game and stepped it up to £20 a go. The feature came up on that game too and whilst it did not pay the jackpot it did pay another £8,000. I was ecstatic but needed a toilet break.

It was on the way back to the laptop that I passed by the puzzle frame and that brought me right back down to earth. I had a voice now screaming in my head. Get out now! You have the money! And for once I listened. The best place for me was away from here, certainly for the time being. I sent over the ID the site required and arranged for a bank transfer. A cheque was no good because I had no intention of waiting in my flat for fourteen days until it arrived. If it arrived in my bank then I could access it from anywhere.

I decided the best thing to do was to get out of the country for a while. I had no idea who had it in for me and was playing mind games, but they could not continue to do so if I was not there to play with. I was not much of a traveller and had not been outside the country for years. I had always wanted to go on a cruise though, so I started searching for likely departures. Of course, trying to book a cruise at short notice was not going to be easy. Some people booked more than a year ahead. As it turned out there was only one option, a seven day north Europe cruise calling at Amsterdam, Hamburg and Le Havre. It left Southampton on the Saturday before the late May Bank Holiday which was more than two weeks away.

I nearly didn't even get on that cruise because my passport would just have about six months left on it when I got back in the country. That was on the borderline, but I was told it would do. There were other things to check like inoculations and obtain a European Health Insurance Card. I also had to arrange travel insurance.

In the end I didn't bother with the first two because these were concerned with health treatment in foreign countries. I doubted very much there was anything in The Netherlands, Germany and France I needed to get jabbed for and I would not need treatment in a foreign hospital as I was not going to get off the boat. There were various trips arranged from each port, but I felt it safer to stay on board, not knowing who was after me and how far their reach extended.

What I had to do though was find somewhere to stay until departure. Somewhere I was off the grid. An idea came to me and it involved some more web work – not the Spiderman kind. Again, I was lucky to find a space although I had to pay for more than my needs. Fortunately, there was enough left on the credit card as I had paid for the cruise out of my bank account, knowing that the transfer from my winnings would be in there before I had to embark.

Now, all I had to do was get there without being seen. If I was being watched, leaving with a load of suitcases would be a dead giveaway. It looked like I would have to leave everything here and buy new stuff on the way. Calling a taxi was out of the question too.

Just as I was realising that there was no point in putting things off and I may as well leave straight away, the buzzer went. Who the hell could that be? Not the police again surely? I was as jumpy as a kangaroo with ants in its pouch. It turned out to be the police of sorts – a tech guy here to take the bullets out of the wall. As the shooter had not even entered the house, he just took the bullets and prints from the outside of the door, in case the shooter had placed his hands on it. He was gone inside twenty minutes. That reminded me though that I may be needed at the police station sometime to sign a more detailed statement. That would ruin all my plans. On the other hand, I didn't want the police pursuing me as well.

I decided to prepare my own statement. Eating a sandwich, I opened my laptop and crafted an account of not just the shooting but everything that had happened since I had fatefully risen from bed on Bank Holiday Monday, just two days ago. That way it was a double safety net. Firstly, I was fulfilling my obligation to give the police a sworn statement for that morning's events, but also, if anything happened to me they would have all the facts to investigate.

It took me about an hour until I was satisfied and then I printed out two copies. One I addressed to Sergeant Wilson at the police station and added a first class stamp. The second I just put in an envelope with the words police written on it which I left on the table. My statement did have a little PS on it that I was scared for my life and was going to ground, and I hoped that would suffice. There was no one else that I needed to tell where I was going other than maybe Jackie downstairs, although I discounted that in the end as she was a known gossip.

At 1.33 pm I locked the flat door behind me, knowing it would be almost a month before I would be back there. I was carrying nothing except my phone, wallet, passport and the stamped envelope to put in the first post-box I passed. And one more thing; a wad of papers. Obviously, I could not lug the frame and blocks with me, but I could not help feeling the puzzle was important in solving my problems. I had the list of clues and multiple copies of the grid I had sketched out as it stood so far – my printer was also a photocopier. I also had photos of the frame and the blocks on my phone. Instead of going down the path onto the street, I went around the back of the shop and through a back gate into an alley. I had never used that exit before and was not sure where the alley came out. It was better than advertising to any watchers that I was off out though.

The alley came out into a residential street, and I just ambled along as if I did not have a care in the world until I came to a main road. There was a bus stop a hundred yards away and one was just arriving. It was going to Croydon which was where I needed to be for the railway station, so I sprinted to catch it. The front seat on the top deck was free so I sat there, knowing that I had been the last person to get on the bus, so no one had followed me. I relaxed as much as I could for the half an hour bus ride.

At East Croydon station I bought a ticket to Manchester. I was going a bit of a circuitous route to my destination, but I had time as I couldn't check in until Friday. To get to Manchester I had to travel into London and get to Euston via tube. My hope was to get in and out of London before the rush hour started. From East Croydon trains went to Victoria or London Bridge and I just got on the first to arrive which happened to be London Bridge. Unfortunately, it called at all the stations in between so it took twenty five minutes. It was now nearing three o'clock, so I had an hour to get across London which was easily doable if the tubes were running without delays. Fortunately, they were, and the Northern Line went straight from London Bridge to Euston, so I was in the station within thirty minutes. By four I was in my seat and whizzing up to Manchester.

I didn't have a reserved seat, but I managed to find one next to a window. During the journey, as the train filled up, I swapped with the lady who sat next to me so that I was in the aisle. I had deliberately delayed getting onto the train so that I was one of the last ones on so I could check for tails, and I wanted to be one of the first off too. It might seem a lot of trouble to take when the chances of being followed were slim, but I was a worrier and felt better taking all the precautions that I could.

I was booked in at a Premier Inn which was five minutes' walk from Piccadilly station. I always stayed in a Premier Inn when I was away from home, which was hardly ever, rather than try a hotel. It was a lesson learned from a client visit when I was an insurance broker. I was account handler accompanying an account executive on a visit to a client, the distance dictating an overnight stay. He picked out a hotel which was more expensive than the Premier Inn although it would have been Travel Inn at that time. The rooms were tiny, the beds single and with lumpy mattresses and the breakfast left a lot to be desired.

There were a few I could have booked in Manchester but the one near the station sufficed because it was within walking distance of Market Street where all the shops were and I had quite a bit of shopping to do, having left home with nothing. I couldn't buy anything then because it was nearly seven o'clock in the evening. I could last one night without luggage although I did get some odd looks when I booked in without any.

At least I could have a meal at the restaurant which I did. I had three courses too, as I realised I had only had the one sandwich all day. Finally sated, I went up to my room and lay on the bed flicking through the TV channels trying to find something to watch. I had been keeping my eyes peeled when out and about but had seen nothing to make me nervous, so I was a bit more relaxed. I watched a film and then went to bed, sleeping in my underwear.

Tomorrow was Phase 2 of Operation: Get Lost.

Chapter 14

```
            M           S           L
        A   P           C           I               D
        J   R           A           B               I
    H   O   M O         R       C   R               N
    A   F R E D   S T O L E   A   S P A N N E R   K I W I
    L   A               E       M   H E R           E   I N
    L E T S S T A R T A T T H E V E R Y B E G I N N I N G
```

Tate knocked on Peter's grandfather's door at about 1.30 pm. He had driven around various blocks for a while trying to see if he had a tail. Not seeing one he decided it was safe to travel to his destination. The door was answered almost immediately by Joe. Tate saw a smallish guy with lots of grey hair, dressed in suit trousers, white shirt and a green cardigan.

Tate held his hand out. "Joe Lane? My name is Tony Tate. Did Peter call you and let you know I was coming?"

Joe took the proffered hand and Tate felt he still had a strong grip. "Yep! He told me. You're the one that got this damnable puzzle sent to you, right?"

"That's correct, Joe. I thought I'd come along and see how it was getting along and try to help if I can."

"Come in then." The frame's downstairs in Peter's flat but there is something I think I ought to show you first. Knocked me a bit sideways when I saw it this morning."

Tate entered the house, closed the door and followed Joe through a long hallway into the kitchen. It was an old house but a fairly modern kitchen with polished worktops and integrated white goods. There were stools by a breakfast bar and Joe indicated that Tate could sit there. He went over to a pile of post on the kitchen table and came back with an envelope, handing it to Tate. It was addressed to himself. Tony Tate, Care of Joseph Lane, at that address.

"How the hell!" growled Tate, shocked and stunned. This was the first time he had been here. No one had overheard his conversations with Peter Lane.

"I wondered that too," said Joe. "Does that mean we are in danger?"

"To be honest Joe, I have no idea." admitted Tate. "Someone is playing with me. They have already got me kicking my heels." He thought for a few moments. "Have you anywhere you can go? I have sent my family away just in case."

"No one is making me run away," Joe declared flatly. "Tea? Coffee?"

Tate nodded. "Coffee please? Need to keep alert."

Joe got up to fill the kettle. Meanwhile Tony opened the envelope. He had already guessed what was inside and so it proved to be. Another list of clues. The next thirty this time.

21. Ben Hurd he was among them once. (6) (LB)
22. Genuflect at the man on the moon at Christmas. (4)
23. Before, he was in charge, did he make chips? (5) (P)
24. A powder within man. (3)
25. Action replay maybe? (5)
26. US shaggy lawyer. (1/1)
27. Not like Methuselah but still tells the tale. (1/1)
28. For ever and a day, a father figure within. (8) (Y)
29. Negative one almost. (2) (LB)
30. Male goat is not soft when it comes to a ball game. (8) (Y)
31. Spelling insect. (3)
32. What has a box but no lid? (5)
33. Pat Pending. He was wacky and nutty. (9) (Y)
34. Doggy business, halved. (3) (G)
35. Porkless pigswill. (4) (LB)
36. It's ragged but take a stab (6) (Y).
37. Band on the run but only an insect leaves. (3) (DB)
38. Proud bird. (7) (Y)
39. Five go in search of their creator. (4)
40. A Tory outhouse. (12) (Y) **(Not yet can you insert)**
41. Wine and dine? Magnum's gone so that just leaves the food. (1/1)
42. There is no logic but there's poetry in it. (5) (P) **(Now you can)**
43. Not knowing? What ecstasy. (5)
44. Even Superman would not see through this. (4) (Y)
45. Mind it or mend it. (3)
46. Where are you clue? (6)
47. I'm having one of these (4).
48. ABBA in danger. (3)
49. Initially a Norwegian composer for example. (1/1)
50. Extra for Thomas and Kenneth. (4) (LB) **(Not yet can you insert)**

He held them up to show Joe, who just nodded and carried on getting two mugs out of the cupboard.

"That might be a good thing, those arriving now," said Joe. "As I was about to tell you. I have solved the first twenty."

They took their drinks downstairs, and Joe showed Tate where they had set up the frame. The first thing Tate did was take a photo of the puzzle as completed so far.

"Great Joe. You've done a brilliant job so far. How have you been finding it?"

"Well, it's strange. Some clues are easy and some tricky. It's like the guy who created this does not know what he is doing. Or what level to pitch it at."

"As long as you get him," said Tate.

"Now Tony, the general rules appear to be as follows," Joe thought an explanation in order so things would flow more quickly. "It seems to be like constructing a building from the ground up. If you like, the words across are floors and the down words columns. The coloured dots on the right appear to be groups of words. We worked this out from the yellow Cluedo clues. The dots on the left appear to denote where a word crosses. For instance, take 'Fat'. The word across is 'Fred' which is denoted as G for green. Therefore, the F has a green dot on the left to show it crosses 'Fat'. Where a clue crosses another word it is the one already in place that takes precedence. So, you see 'Spanner' here. Now that is a Cluedo weapon so is a yellow group but 'She' was in first and that is in the orange group. Therefore, the S in 'Spanner' has yellow on the left and orange on the right. It was in the orange group but a yellow word crosses it. The other letters of Spanner have the yellow on the left because that is their colour group. All clear?"

"As mud," laughed Tate. "Let's just crack on and you can explain as we go through."

"Okay," said Joe. "Clue 21 is referring to the film Ben Hur. I am guessing here that the word is 'slave' or 'slaves' rather because it is six letters. It says *used to be among* them and he was a slave before earning his freedom. Clue 20 was 'prod' and came down at the end of 'Fred'. If this is 'slaves' it will go at the beginning of 'Stole'. The clue has LB after it which I think means light blue for the dots. 'Stole' is orange so the shared S will have to have light blue and orange dots. Now if we just look at the blocks here you can see we have an S here in the right colour. So, we can swop that for the one that is already there. Then we need S, L, A, V and E blocks with light blue on the right coming down.

"Genius," admitted Tate. "I can see it all when you explain it. What about 22?"

There was silence for quite a while whilst Joe worked on it. Finally, he gave a satisfied grunt.

"That one was not easy," admitted Joe. "And that's where I can see this guy – if it is a guy – is not sticking to tried and tested cryptic methods. It is a bit here, there and everywhere. Genuflect can mean kneel. The man on the moon was Neil, Neil Armstrong. Then Christmas is Noel. Get it? No L. Take the L off kneel to get knee."

"Ah, that's tricky. I would never have got that in a million years," Tate said. "Which raises another interesting question. Why would this person send me something I cannot solve? Despite him appearing to know my movements – the last batch of clues coming here – he had no way of knowing at his planning stage that I would have help. That sort of suggests I was never meant to solve it and it was just meant to play with my head.

"Maybe," agreed Joe. "We will never know until you catch him. And the fact that he has sent the second batch of clues here seems to indicate he is not bothered if you do solve it with help."

"True," agreed Tate, draining the last of his coffee. "Now let's look at these other clues."

They sat down at Peter's small dining table and laid out the sheet of clues where they could both read it.

"Now the problem with this puzzle, Tony, is that with the across clues especially it is difficult to know if there is a downwards clue that crosses it or ends on it. There has been a lot of trial and error so far, but I think we are close to what it should be. I think probably now, we need to solve as many of the clues as we can before we try slotting them in. Less need to keep pulling blocks out, which is a lot harder than dropping them in. Anyway, Peter and I have been putting the answers down on a paper version first. Here." Joe pulled over a hand drawn grid on a piece of A4.

"Makes sense," said Tate. "Let's do it. You solve them and I'll write them down."

"Okay but I may need some help from your brain too."

They looked at the next question, Clue 23, and Joe smiled. "That seems easy enough."

"Really!"

"Yes. Another word for 'before' is 'prior'. And a prior can be at a monastery full of friars. Before being a prior was he a friar?"

"Okay. I see that now. That would have taken me a lot longer."

"Now, the next one is already in for us."

"Where?" asked Tate.

"On Row 4 here you can see 'omo' is spelt out and there is a clue here for it. Number 24."

"A powder within man," read Tate. "What does that mean? Never heard of Omo?"

"Omo was a brand of washing powder years ago. It might be still going today for all I know. And 'homo sapiens' is man. Powder within man."

"You are pretty good at this Joe," praised Tate.

"Not much else to do," replied Joe. "This has given me something to get my teeth into."

Joe was silent for a few moments. Reading the next few clues. "I need to think about the next three but look at Clue 28."

Tate read it. *For ever and a day, a father figure within.*

"Aha" shouted Joe with glee. "He's made a mistake! Reverand is within the phrase 'forever and' but spelt with an A. So 'Reverand' is right and wrong at the same time. Right because it is in the puzzle and wrong because of the spelling. Look here. The R of 'Prod' and the V of 'Slaves' must be where this goes. Now did he spell it wrong accidently or on purpose?"

"How do you mean Joe? Why would he do it on purpose?"

"Because if he spelt it correctly then 'Scarlet' would not work going down."

"I'll ask him when I catch him," Tate declared.

"And look!" Joe was excited now. "Clue 36. Proud bird"

"Peacock!" enthused Tate. "Even I can get that one."

"That's what I mean, Tony. Some of them are ridiculously easy and some quite tricky."

They worked away all afternoon and got answers written down for most of the clues. They ended up with the following list.

21. Slaves
22. Knee
23. Prior
24. Omo
25. React
26. D.A.
27. N.T.
28. Reverand
29. No
30. Billiard
31. Bee
32. Voice
33. Professor
34.
35. Will

36. Dagger
37. And
38. Peacock
39. Enid
40. Conservatory
41. PI
42. Rhyme
43. Bliss
44. Lead
45. Gap
46.
47. Ball
48. SOS
49.
50. More

Some of them took a while to work out. Tate was pleased when he got one that Joe couldn't. Clue 31 referred to Professor Pat Pending off the old cartoon show *Wacky Races.* Made before he was born but he remembered watching it as a kid. Once they had the clues listed other than the few they could not get, they then wrote them in the paper grid and when they were happy started dropping blocks into place, where they could. There were still some blanks. They were still at it when they heard a key in the lock and Peter walked in.

"Crikey! Is it that time already?" exclaimed Tate, looking at his watch. It was gone six.

"How are you getting on?" asked Peter enthusiastically.

"Not too bad," replied Joe. "We might get on better now you are here too. Three heads are better than two. I think we need some grub first though."

"Sorry Joe. Can't stay," said Tate. "I have something to do. I shouldn't have stayed this long as it is." He had not heard from his wife, and he had been expecting to hear a couple of hours ago. He checked his phone and saw that there was a text. *The sparrow has landed.* They were safe. In all the concentration he had not heard the message alert. "Actually, maybe I can."

"You might want to," advised Peter. "I saw something today that directly relates to this."

"What?" asked Tate.

"We got a call to this flat on the High Street. Someone had taken some shots through a door and the guy inside thought they were shooting at him. Turns out they were only trying to scare him as they shot high on purpose. However, that is not the only strange thing that has happened to him over the past few days. He got a delivery on Bank Holiday Monday. One large frame and a lot of little wooden blocks."

"You're joking!" gasped Tate.

"No. And what's more. He has more clues than you were sent. I didn't see exactly but he waved a paper at us, and it had writing on both sides. In fact, there may have been more than one sheet but I'm not sure on that last bit."

"Sorry Joe," said Tate. "Have to pass up on the food. Peter, show me to this guy's place. I need to see for myself."

Tate drove fast because he felt that this might be the break he needed but when he got there he knew he might have saved himself the trouble. There was no answer to their knock but seeing the holes in the door, it could be said there was a credible threat to a member of the public, so Tate broke the door in. There was no one inside. On the table was an envelope addressed oddly enough to 'The Police'.

"You read it, Peter," said Tate. "Technically, I am not part of the Force at the moment."

Peter opened it up and quickly read the contents. "It's his statement of the facts we went through this morning, a more detailed one than he signed then. We did tell him C.I.D. might want more details. He left this copy here and posted one to the station."

Peter then pointed at the frame which was still on the table. It was not as far on as they had got. The clues were not there though.

"Damn!" shouted Tate to no one in particular. His one and only lead was gone.

"What do you think?" asked Peter.

Tate stood there contemplating for a moment, gazing at the frame. "I'm not sure. This guy has the same puzzle, and who else would have it other than the person who created it. Yet, this looks like he is trying to solve it too. If he had created it then it would be here completed surely? On the other hand, you said he has more clues than us, so did he create all this?"

"He's gone though. And not taken it with him," said Peter. "Mind you I wouldn't want to lug that thing around with the boxes of blocks too. Maybe he is going to do it on paper like us. Why take the clues if not to continue?"

"Ah, but did he take the clues to continue feeding them to me or to solve them because he has been sent them too?"

Whilst he was there, Tate had a look around the flat. There wasn't much to see but in the kitchen he found something that at least answered one question. Stood against the wall behind the pedal bin was the same type of cardboard box that the frame had been delivered to the station in.

"That settles that, Peter. He was sent it too. I had a feeling. What are the chances that a spasmodic shooting would bring me to the person who is trying to torment me?"

"On the other hand, what are the chances that such a shooting would bring you into contact with a fellow victim of this er… puzzler?"

"Good point! Maybe this was planned all along. Come on we better go."

As they went downstairs to the door, Tate noticed that it looked like the bullets had been dug out of the wall. "Peter, tomorrow, if you can, dig up everything you can on the guy that lived here? What was his name?

"Daniel Andrews-White."

"And try and see what forensics came up with, if they have even looked at it yet."

There was a bit of good news waiting for them when they arrived back at Joe's house. He was still in Peter's flat and stood triumphantly in front of the frame which now had a lot more blocks in.

"I managed to get most of the other words in. Still a few blocks which might have to change because of colour but we are almost up to date with the clues. The answers we were missing were Scooby Doo – that was two answers and I got that from something Peter told me yesterday – and E.G. which are the initials for Edvard Grieg a Norwegian composer. There is only Clue 50 which we think is 'More' to fit in. The other word that could not go in straight away was 'Conservatory' which was possible after 'Rhyme' was in."

"Well done Joe," said Tate. "That being the case then it looks like there is nothing more we can do tonight. I'll be off home."

Before leaving Tate took a photo of the puzzle as it currently stood. He wondered when the next set of clues would arrive. Would he have been expected to solve them so soon, even if he had not really done so himself? If they did arrive soon that means the ungodly were keeping very close tabs on things.

Chapter 15

Phase 2 of Operation: Get Lost was in two parts. Part One was to go shopping and get myself kitted out for the next month, so a visit to Market Street and the Arndale Centre was called for. Whilst I was on my way there, something hit me. I had never been to Manchester before, but it all seemed familiar. Too familiar, it was very déjà vu.

I spent a couple of hours buying clothes, footwear, toiletries, an electric shaver and a couple of suitcases to carry it all in. I had to check out of my room by midday, and I had to get all this stuff back there and packed in the cases properly to look like a normal person on holiday. I didn't have time to check everything fitted and just hoped that the sizes on the tags were correct. I had bought mislabelled stuff before which didn't fit when I later tried it on.

I was so busy buying and lugging it all back, I forgot to keep a wary eye out, but nothing bad happened so I was probably just missing worrying about nothing anyway. However, by the time I was checked out with two newly packed suitcases and wearing fresh clothes, I was on high alert again.

Phase 2 Part Two was another trip. This time to Nottingham. It was a straight journey from Piccadilly which was less than two hours. I had plenty of time, so I bought my ticket but then went for some lunch - I had eaten breakfast early to hit the shops as soon as they opened.

By mid-afternoon, I was once again ensconced in a Premier Inn room but this one in North Nottingham, the closest one to my destination for the next day. I could have gone out and explored Sherwood Forest but there was going to be plenty of time to do that in the next two weeks. Also, I was still wary of too much moving around in the open. I was almost positive that I was well away from prying eyes so why ruin it now. Tomorrow I would be off the grid completely.

The next day I checked into Center Parcs for a two week stay. Friday to Friday to Friday. That then left me a day then to get down to Southampton for the cruise departure. The ideal thing for me was that Center Parcs was self-contained, and you did not need to leave the park at all for the whole period. I had been before, to Elveden, near Thetford, but had chosen Sherwood because I had wanted to get as far away from home as possible.

When I checked in I found I had been upgraded. When I had booked online, there had only been a 6 berth cabin left but now I was in a two floor one bedroomed lodge. One of a row with car park spaces at the front. Bedroom and bathroom upstairs, living area with kitchenette on the ground floor. It more than suited my needs.

After unpacking I went for a walk around the park, weaving in and out of the groups and happy families. I was not here to enjoy myself, just stay off the grid until I could get out of the country. The fact that I would be here longer than I would be on the cruise had not escaped me. Still, I was away from the flat so no one could send me complex puzzles, or bullets.

There were loads of people around because it was checking in day. Intakes were Fridays and Mondays so all the new people were out exploring but as leaving guests could stay on all day, provided they had vacated their accommodation, there were more people on site than there would be on other days. The Village Square was always the busiest because that was the hub of the park. Usually, I hated crowds but strangely I felt safer with all these people in holiday mood than sitting alone looking over my shoulder. Not that I thought anyone could know where I was now. I had taken quite a circuitous route to get there. I would have to take a more direct route when I left for Southampton though, due to the time factor.

Decision time. Was I going to eat out for every meal, or did I stock up the kitchen? The on-site supermarket was always packed on intake days. I decided I could eat out on that first day and decide about stocking up tomorrow. I needed to check how clean the kitchen area was before I knew whether I would be happy cooking meals there. An unclean oven for one would put me right off.

After a while I tired of the throngs and headed a longer way back to the lodge so I could say I had done some exercise. A couple were unpacking their car at the next door lodge, and they gave me friendly nods as I walked down the path to mine. I could see other people unpacking cars further along the row too. I think I had got through check-in quicker because I did not have to queue up by car, which at times could tail back right to the entrance of the park. My taxi had dropped me near the entrance, and I had walked in with my bags.

Inside the lodge I just lounged on the sofa for a bit. I had nothing that I needed to do or any place to go and just for a second it was as though I was totally relaxed, but that didn't last long. The spectre of the past few days was still there, hovering like an ominous dark cloud, and the problem now; I was going to have too much time to think. I was in a holiday camp where people came to enjoy themselves and there were lots to do but for the others but not me. There was only so much one could do there on one's own. Take part in the organised competitions, play a round of crazy golf by oneself or spend an hour taking pot shots on a snooker table. Mainly though it would be wandering around trying to waste time or staying put in the lodge.

I suppose it would be different if I was into swimming because the big indoor swimming complex was one of the main attractions of a Centre Parcs' camp. Swimming was not for me though. I had only managed to get my length certificate at school.

Eating out was always tricky, especially in the evening, because the restaurants could not really cater for a single diner taking up a table for two or four. For this reason, I had to dine early before the crowds. That meant I had to be going out to look for food between 5 pm and 6 pm which was only about an hour away.

I could use that hour to get cracking on the puzzle. I had the clues and I had taken pictures of the frame as it stood and all the coloured blocks before I left. If I had thought about it, I would have hidden the frame and blocks before I left, but they were where I had left them for anyone to see. Not that there should be anyone to see, but as I had left abruptly I supposed that Jackie or even the police might let themselves in to check on things.

I called up the photos on my phone but just one look at them and the futility of it all washed over me and I put the phone down again. I needed to take my mind off it really. At least for a while and let my brain reboot itself. I decided to get out early and visit a booking point to see what tournaments I could put myself down for before I went for a meal.

And so began a very quiet two weeks. Compared to the previous days, one could even have said they were boring.

Time dragged by in my Sherwood hideaway. There was just not enough to keep me busy. I played in four badminton tournaments and two five-a-side tournaments but that was about it on the activity side, other than a lot of walking around. I soon tired of eating out – or rather, I got tired of trying to find a table for one – so I stocked up the kitchen and started making my own meals. Easy to make stuff though. Laura had tried to teach me in the early days but in the end she just did the cooking herself. For me, especially these days, eating was just a fuel stop. You did not have to create a tantalisingly appealing look or smell, just top up the tank. And taking three hours to cook something one could eat in under twenty minutes seemed a bit like my favourite quiz show - pointless.

I did have a lot of spare time for the puzzle. The problem was that I didn't use it. I got out the clues and brought up the photos several times, but I barely tried to get any further really, other than a few possible pencilled scrawls against a few of the clues. I knew that at some point I would have to sit down and give it a good crack, but I was not there yet. I could not get back into that mind-set I had before Tiffany and the shooting. I didn't think I was in danger just then, although I did keep a constant vigil when I was out of the lodge, but my mind *was* all at sea.

I had tried to ring Nate a few times – when I could get a signal – but his number was still unavailable. I didn't know whether to be worried or annoyed about that. Maybe he just used that phone to ring me and then kept it turned off so I could not ring him. If so, I was going to have a few words with him about that next time I saw him.

I was glad when the two weeks was up, and it was time to make my way to Southampton. I feared though that it was just going to be the same on the cruise. There was going to be some fun before then though because the night before I had done some last minute checking and had discovered I had made a booboo. To get on board I had to print off a boarding pass and luggage labels which meant I had to get to a cybercafé or a library or somewhere to print them off.

If that wasn't enough, there was a dress code on board in the evenings. T-shirts and jeans or shorts did not do it so there was more shopping to do. I had to get to Southampton as quickly as possible to give me time to do all this. On the Friday morning, I was up early and out by taxi to Mansfield station, being the nearest. Nottingham itself is about 18 to 20 miles from Sherwood as the arrow flies. Phase 3 of Operation Get Lost was a go.

I had planned my journey out as best as I could on my phone. The first leg was from Mansfield to Nottingham. Then I could have gone back into London, taken the tube to Waterloo and got a direct train to Southampton from there, but I didn't really want to go back into London. Instead, I took a slightly later train to Birmingham New Street and then one from there to Southampton. I paid for first class tickets. Less crowding and more chance of spotting a tail. Not that I was too worried about that now. If everything had run to time it would have taken five and a half hours, as it was it took just over six. It was quite a relaxing journey though.

At Southampton I got a taxi to another Premier Inn – one within walking distance to the docks. Premier Inn were doing well out of me in recent weeks, maybe I should invest in their shares. Fortunately, and I did not plan this, the hotel was across the road from West Quay shopping centre, so I was able to get the rest of the stuff I needed.

In the evenings on board ship, there was a smart casual code and there were even two nights of black tie, although the latter was not compulsory. I was not going to buy anything fancy. I could get away with dark trousers or black jeans and a smart polo shirt. I had seven nights on board so I bought dark chinos and black jeans so I could swap it around, plus four polo shirts. I almost forgot proper shoes and had to go back a second time. I bought an extra holdall too as I didn't think my cases could take any more.

Back in the hotel room, I tried everything on to see if it fitted and then packed it away. I only had the essentials unpacked – change of clothes for the next day, sleeping shorts, shaver and toiletries.

By that time, it was late afternoon and I had to think about getting something to eat. There was a bit of a queue at the restaurant, so I went back over the road to the shopping centre and wandered up to the food court. There were various outlets there to choose from and I ended up having pizza with the usual problem of getting a table for one. It was still quite early though, about 6 pm, so I managed without too much trouble.

After that I just watched TV in the room for a bit, but all the travelling had tired me out. I decided to get an early night before the historic day tomorrow. My first adventure on the high seas. I didn't realise at the time, but I had not thought of the puzzle or the shooting for the past few hours. For once it did not take me that long to fall asleep.

Chapter 16

Tate was getting bored. It had been quiet for a few days now. Nothing much had happened since the last thirty clues had arrived. Not from the ungodly side anyway. Consequently, the puzzle had got no further. This suggested to Tate that maybe the ungodly were not keeping such close tabs on him as he had thought, which was good in a lot of ways. He still could not contact his family though because that was what he had agreed with his wife before they left. Not until this thing was over.

To say that he had nothing to go on was not strictly true. He had tried to analyse the puzzle so far. Well, not just him - the team – Joe, Peter and himself. There was not a lot to be gleaned from it except the Cluedo references, although it was also obvious, to Joe that is, that the other colour groups must mean something too. They tried to put them together but could not get the pattern, other than the Scooby Gang were in a green group – names not yet in the puzzle being Daphne, Velma and Shaggy. There seemed to be six other colour groups. Red, orange, pink, light blue, dark blue and purple. Joe felt that when finished the coloured letters would spell out a message but that was as far as they could get on that side.

The other thing that could probably be assumed was that the person behind this was not that young. This was due to the older references to *Scooby Doo* and *The Wacky Races.* According to Peter, the former was still a favourite of children even today and new stuff was still being made, but the latter was a 60's cartoon which one could probably find on a kids satellite channel but not mainstream. It suggested someone as old as or possibly slightly older than Tate himself.

As he had nothing else to go on, and even now he still did not know if there was a crime involved, Tate thought he might as well waste his time on the Cluedo angle. In the game there were six suspects, six murder weapons and nine rooms. When they had collated all the yellow blocks together and taken into account where there were crossovers of two yellow words, so they shared the same letter – signified by a yellow spot on the left and right of the block – they had the six weapons but seven names and ten rooms. Doctor Black and the cellar were included but these are the victim and his place of discovery in the game. What this signified Tate had no idea.

After about a week, Frank came back to him on the information he had asked for. Whilst grateful for this, Tate needed more assistance now, so he had asked Frank to check into any incidents involving the names of Peacock, White, Scarlet, Green, Mustard and Plum, even though the last two were highly unlikely. Tate suggested looking just recently and not digging into paper files at this time. If this was about murder, and it is usually serial killers that like to play with the police authorities, then it was unlikely this involved cold cases. Frank grudgingly agreed to do it but said it could take some time which Tate had to accept, he had no pull now.

If it was a serial killer, he was going to be hard to track because it looked like there was going to be no common thread. Six different weapons and seven different types of people. These were the sort of killings that without some sort of forensic evidence to tie them together would be treated as separate incidents. No one would be looking for a connection. They might have one now but were looking at it from the wrong end. Or were they? Had the crimes been committed already or was the puzzle an early warning of what was going to happen?

The information that Frank had come back with was interesting. Five people had been arrested with Bannister. Two of these had died inside like Bannister. Two had served their sentence but were back inside for further offences after they got released. They were both now approaching their sixties. The other was the young lad that had been coerced into helping them, Mickey Perkins. He had only been about sixteen or seventeen at the time and ended up in a Young Offender Institution. After his release two years later there was not much further information. A couple of checks found him working at manual jobs and keeping his nose clean. It appeared though that Perkins dropped off the map in 1999.

That's that then, thought Tate. If all this relates to that trouble in 1990, then it must be this Mickey Perkins that was behind it. If he has been off the grid since 1999 though it was going to be bloody near impossible to track him down. Probably living under an assumed name. Why would he do that if he had gone straight? Tate figured putting out an APB would be a waste of time, not that he had the power to do that anyway.

Tate did have another angle to work on - Danny Andrews -White's statement. As he had already sent one to the station in the post which, Peter had been able to confirm, had arrived, Tate had kept the one found at the flat. He was intrigued by the three incidents that were referred to there, which all in all would seem far-fetched but he had first-hand knowledge of the first. The fact that he had willingly offered up the information about the puzzle when the officers had been there for the shooting suggested he had nothing to hide. Therefore, he had also been sent the puzzle which was borne out by the packaging they had found at his flat. This raised two questions in Tate's mind? How was this guy involved in this thing which related to Tate's own actions back in 1990? He did not know him or know of him. And why was he sent a lot more clues than Tate himself?

Then there was the shooting. Obviously a scare tactic but nothing like that had been aimed at Tate. The girl incident, Tate was tempted to leave out as a red herring, except for the fact that enquiries had been made to track down Andrews-White's friend Nathan but no hotel near the airport had him registered as a guest and the mobile number was unobtainable.

Tate was frustrated that Danny Andrews-White had disappeared as he would have liked to question him about all these events to see if he could make any sense or connection out of them. He was another person of interest to Tate, but again one he could not follow up on because he had no authority for a man hunt. It seemed to Tate that Andrews-White was running away from a threat rather than being the cause of Tate's problems, but they must be connected somehow.

It could be that Andrews-White had also wronged the person behind the puzzle, so he was in the same boat as Tate. Maybe this was to a lesser extent, so he had more clues to help him. On the other hand, was it a worse slight so that his end was coming quicker?

When Frank eventually came back to him on his enquiries into any possible crimes involving the Cluedo names, the need to locate Danny Andrews-White became more urgent. It was well after office hours when Frank rang.

"Hi Frank," greeted Tate, he had seen the number come up on the phone. "Any news?"

"Maybe Tony," replied Frank. "I was sceptical myself and there is no perfect match but listen to this. About five years ago a woman was stabbed in her hallway. Guess what her name was?"

"White? If she was married."

"She was. And it was. Or rather Andrews-White. On her marriage she went from White to Andrews-White."

"Good god!" exclaimed Tate. He had not been expecting that. Danny Andrews-White. He had to be the husband. "What was the husband's name?"

"Daniel," confirmed Frank. "He was cleared of any involvement. He was at work at the time and there seemed no motive at all for him to hire someone."

"Was anything stolen?"

"That was the puzzling thing," advised Frank. "The only thing that seemed to be missing was a knife from the kitchen which was believed to be the murder weapon."

"OK. Thanks Frank. Is that the only one?"

"So far Tony. I have only checked Surrey and the Met so far but thought you would want to know ASAP."

"You were right there. Thanks Frank. Let me know if you get anything else."

Tate was a bit shocked. He had so far ruled out Andrews-White as part of the plot against him and more of another victim. The fact that his own wife could be connected to this could not be a coincidence. The thing is, no one would draw attention to themselves if they had gotten away with a crime. Or would they? On the other hand, that could be the reason that Andrews-White was being targeted. Either he did do it, and someone knew about it and was playing with him, or the killer was the one setting the puzzle. If so, what was the connection between Andrews-White and himself?

Obviously the person behind all this was the common denominator. It was someone who had come across both Andrews-White and himself. Someone was mad at both of them and wanted to make them pay. Tate knew it was even more important now to get in touch with Andrews-White so they could put their heads together on this. Always provided of course that this was not a double bluff and the guy had killed his wife. Tate didn't think so though. That was just not logical.

Tate was not sure what to do now. There was still no definite crime linked to the puzzle but there was now a tenuous link to one. Did he take it to Grearson? If so, he would lose track of the investigation. His current stand down status would see to that. Was there enough to put it forward anyway? Tate decided to hold off for a bit.

It was all a waiting game now. Waiting for the Puzzler. Waiting for Andrews-White to pop up again. Waiting for the decision about his past conduct. Tate was an impatient person, and he was not good at waiting but fortunately he did not have to wait that long. A couple of days later Frank came back with some more information.

"I was wrong Tony, last time. Didn't check all the facts."

"How do you mean, Frank?"

"Well, one of the guys that went back inside, did in fact get out again. Found God during his second stint. Went straight and moved to Scotland."

"OK," mused Tate. "That leaves me two to track down. Perkins and this other guy. What's the name?"

"No Tony, you misunderstand. There's more."

"Well go on then man! Don't leave me in suspense."

"Greenhalgh was his name. Dylan Greenhalgh."

Tate picked up on the tense. "Was?"

"That's right, he's dead. Clobbered on the head with some blunt metal object."

"Where did this happen?"

"In a library."

Bingo! That was too much of a coincidence. Yes OK, it was not Reverend Green in the library, but it was near enough. That connected the puzzle to that period in his life. It left Mickey Perkins in the frame as the most likely, although why he would kill off one of his own was a mystery.

"And when?" This could be crucial in working out how long this had been in the planning.

"October 2013," replied Frank.

"OK Frank, Thanks a lot."

Now there were two definite deaths linked with what was going on. Both five years ago nearly, so whatever was going on had been a long time in the planning. Enough to investigate surely. Tate could still not go near it whilst on leave, but he felt it was probably time to report recent events. Not long after putting the phone down on Frank, Tate picked up his keys and made to leave the house. Then he hesitated. Was this Greenhalgh thing connected or was he just looking for a link that was not there? How much of a stretch was it?

He was still in two minds when he opened the front door. He had no chance to react as the man outside fired the stun gun. There was just severe pain and he blacked out.

Chapter 17

Dylan Greenhalgh got up at roughly the same time every morning, around 6.30, and the first thing he did was make a mug of strong coffee which he drank sat at the small oak dining table in the kitchen. It was at these times that he reflected most on his past, his dark past. It was in these early hours of the day he felt depressed and morose. Not the persona that everyone else saw. He kept these reveries and the mood they caused well hidden.

He had been to prison twice and deeply regretted the things that he had done during that time in his life. It was during his second spell in prison that he found God and had tried to make up for everything he had done since. He was fifty five when he got out and that was a lot of years of bad deeds to make up for. He had been involved in drugs, prostitution, blackmail and extortion. He had beaten people up and killed a few. His past actions still gave him nightmares even now.

He had been out eight years now and had been trying to make amends ever since. Not that his atonement was totally without sin, but he viewed it as a lesser evil to propagate good. His old boss died in prison, and he had known where the ill-gotten gains were stashed. Yes, it had been obtained through the pain and suffering of many innocents but to throw it away would have been a greater sin bearing in mind all the good it could do.

In the first instance, he had sent anonymous donations to some of the people he had caused pain and suffering to. The ones he could remember. There were so many that he could not recall them all, which was also a regret he carried with him. He found though that living in the old neighbourhood where he had wrought such terror was too painful, so he had moved far away. He had been in Scotland now for just over six years and things were going well. It was a small village he lived in. He helped the local priest with various jobs. Paid for repairs to the church roof and established a small library. The village did not have one of its own and the mobile library never came anywhere near there. Not so necessary now with half the world reading e-books but some people still liked to read a proper book. The people of the village looked upon him as a generous benefactor although he doubted if they would be so vociferous in their praise if they knew where the money had come from.

His reveries came to an end with his coffee. He placed the mug in the sink and went to get dressed. Time to open the church for the vicar, something he did every day. He and the vicar, the Reverend Angus Mackintosh, had become good friends and he helped him out with various things. Sort of a handyman and caretaker. He didn't get paid or want to be.

It was his way of apologising to God and paying his penance. Having found God in prison, he hadn't tried for the cloth himself because he didn't feel worthy but helping a man of faith suited him to the ground.

The morning was cold and bright. The sky was clear and there was a frost on the ground. Dylan liked this type of weather. Better cold than wet. He made his way to the church which was about half a mile away from his cottage and it took him only about ten minutes brisk walking. Walking up the path to the church door, he noticed a man intently looking at gravestones in the adjoining cemetery. He had red hair with a beard and wore a heavy parka. Giving him no more mind. Dylan unlocked the church doors and went inside.

He was so preoccupied tidying up hymn books and removing dead flowers that he did not notice at first that the red headed man had entered the church. He was sat in the front row of pews, head bent as if in prayer. Just as he did notice him the man looked up.

"Excuse me, Father," he said. "I'm just passing through. Having a motoring trip through the wilds of Scotland. Is there a hotel around here?"

"I'm afraid not. There isn't a hotel for twenty miles. Mrs Beesley in the village though sometimes takes in boarders, you know, bed and breakfast. She runs the post office."

"Thank you, Father. Perhaps you can tell me how to get there."

"Surely I can but I am not the vicar, I just help him out," explained Dylan. "Although the folks around here call us the brother Fathers and do call me that sometimes. Strictly though I am not in the clergy."

"We all do God's work in our own way," offered up the man. "Now the post office you say."

"Yes. Just go down the road into the village proper and you can't miss it. Too early now though. They don't open until nine."

"No rush. I hope though there is somewhere I can get breakfast?"

"Certainly. Betty's café which is only a couple of doors down from the post office. She will be open now."

"Thank you kindly," said the man and went on his way.

Dylan thought no more about the man afterwards, except the stray thought that it was strange to be looking for a hotel in the early morning rather than later in the day. If one were just passing through that is.

The red headed man left the church and as instructed walked down to the village street. He already knew where the café was because his car was parked right outside. He had no intention of getting a room so didn't need the post office, but he thought he may as well have some breakfast. He had hit the road early and been driving since 5 am.

Inside the café was not big but then again it was only a small village. It looked more like a tearoom, with square patterned tablecloths on the eight tables. There was no one in except the grey haired woman with large glasses who was behind the counter.

"Good morning to you," said the man brightly. "I hear I can get a good breakfast here."

"That you can, young man," agreed the woman. "I'm Betty. Go take a seat and I will be over for your order."

The man ordered a full fry up and by some skilful questioning gleaned the location of the library, which was the only building in town he was really interested in. This too would be open at 9 am and closed at 3 pm. The man wanted to get there early when it was empty because he had something he wanted to check out, although this was not a book.

The library turned out to be a large portacabin which was situated to the rear of a cottage. The man knew who the cottage belonged to and that it was that person who had set up the library. It looked a sturdy and weatherproof structure which it would need to be to store books. An unusual library though, thought the man. When he entered it was just gone 9 am. The cabin had bookshelves all along the sides and one or two running down the middle. There was one small reading table with two chairs. Dylan was there rearranging books on shelves.

"Hello again," boomed the red headed man.

Dylan jumped and dropped a book. "My God man, you gave me a start!"

"Sorry. Heard that there was a small library and thought I would take a look."

"Well, here it is. Just a small thing we pulled together."

"I think you are being too humble there," the man pointed out. "I understand that it was all your idea."

"Well, I may have been the driving force," Dylan admitted.

"And where did you get the money for all this."

Dylan faltered for a moment. "Erm … a small inheritance."

"That's a nice way of putting it, Knuckles."

Dylan's face dropped and he went white as a sheet. He never expected someone from the old times to find him here. The use of his old nickname meant this guy must be from that time. His fists balled automatically as he went on the defensive.

"It's alright Dylan, Your secret's safe with me. It's Mickey. You know. Little Mickey. Or Squirt as you used to call me."

"Oh right. Mickey! What brings you up here then?"

"Oh, I just thought I would visit an old friend." The man was smiling. "But then again we were never friends, were we Knuckles? You used to treat me like a piece of shit, especially when the boss wasn't there."

"I wasn't a very nice man in those days Mickey, but I've mended my ways now. I regret what I did and how I treated people then and I've tried to make up for it."

"Sure. Sure. How about we have a chat about the old days. I may have something to interest you."

"No way. I am out of that life for good now."

"No, it's nothing like that. It may prove to be illuminating for you, bearing in mind your current activities. Tell you what. You are busy working now. Why not meet at the café when you finish, and we can chat over a brew."

"Okay," Dylan hesitantly agreed. "I lock up at 3 pm so what about 3.15 at Betty's."

"Done. See you then." With that the man walked out.

Dylan was extremely disturbed by this turn of events and wondered what Mickey wanted. He tried to stay his usual breezy self to those that came in for a chat and a book, but it was difficult. The last customer left at around 2.30 so he did all the tidying and then sat at the table to think. Unexpectedly, just as he was about to close up he got another visitor, Little Mickey, who was not so little anymore.

"Hi Dylan. I was walking and coming past here so thought we could walk around together."

"Fine," said Dylan, a little suspiciously, as he got up from the table.

They were walking to the door when Mickey turned around. "You've missed one," pointing at the floor behind them. It was the oldest trick in the book and Dylan should have been wise to it but for the merest second he looked and that was all the time Mickey needed. He whipped out a bit of metal pipe from a special inner pocket of his parka and hit Dylan hard on back of the head. Dylan went down but he was not out. He put a hand to his head and it came back bloodied.

"What the hell, Mickey!"

"Stay down Knuckles," Mickey suggested in an even tone. "Now, you might think this is payback for all those digs and punches you gave me but no. I don't hold grudges like that. You just happen to fit nicely into my plan."

"What plan?"

"It would take too long to explain. It is a work in progress. Going along nicely though. And by the way, I was being up front before about what I can offer you." Mickey smile again. "An early chance to meet your maker."

The pipe swung again, and this time Dylan was out and not just for the count.

"Father Green in the library with the lead pipe," Mickey announced to himself. Dylan had not been a reverend and the pipe was not lead but one had to get creative sometimes.

Mickey took the keys out of Dylan's dead hand and turned off the light before locking the door. With any luck it would be some hours before they found him. By then the car he had stolen would have been abandoned some place remote and he would be back in England.

As he was driving away he pulled off the red wig and beard leaving his natural bald headed look. Two down, he thought. Four to go. His game of Cluedo was coming along nicely.

PART TWO - ALL AT SEA

Chapter 18

It was massive, that was my first thought. I had just caught a glimpse of the ship as the taxi drove up to the terminal. It was like a building on the water, towering way above the terminal building, like a monster waiting to pounce. Well, it did carry 3,000 passengers, according to the website.

I had never been on a cruise before, so it was all new. No sooner had I paid off the taxi than my case was whisked away by a steward and trundled over to what look liked a laundry chute. I followed the crowd into the terminal carrying my hand luggage to where staff were checking boarding passes before letting passengers up the escalators.

"Sorry," I said to the friendly woman who glanced at my printed e-ticket – in the end I had begged to use a computer at the Premier Inn to print it off. "I'm very early. Premier Inn kick you out at noon." My boarding time was 3 pm and it was only 12.30.

"That's fine," smiled the woman. "We are free flow at the moment, just go on up."

I followed the crowd, up the escalator, and across a large court to more waiting staff checking tickets. There were lots of seats for people waiting but these were less than half full. People were waiting to join the queue to a roped off avenue which led to several counter service points. Before sitting down, I asked one of the staff how long it would be and after looking at my ticket they said I could join the queue straight away.

It took about fifteen minutes to get to the counter where my ticket and passport were checked, credit card verified, and photo taken. Then I was handed a plastic card. That was my cruise card, I was told, and very important to keep safe. It was not just the key to the cabin but also the means to pay for anything on board. It seemed weird but there were no cash payments allowed on the ship. Everything was billed to the cruise card account, and all settled in one go off the credit card at the end of the cruise. There was also a little map of the ship handed over.

Next security. Standard stuff. Anything metal in the tray together with my bag and walking through the detector. About fifty people must have gone through before me without nary a beep but I couldn't help thinking of 'Airplane'. The detector though kept its vow of silence for me too.

It felt weird zigzagging up the gangway towards the even more gigantic ship, now it was seen up close. I passed a guy with security on his jacket and then entered the ship proper where there was another check point and my new cruise card had to be scanned. There was a bit of panic before I remembered that for safe keeping it was in my wallet.

Once through the checkpoint, I was stood in an enormous atrium. There were lots of people milling around and I felt a bit claustrophobic. I walked down a passageway past the lifts to a quiet corner and got out the map. After a while I worked out I was on Deck 6 which was where Reception was located. There were loads of people queuing for advice already. Even though I knew I could not get into the cabin yet, I thought it would be a good idea to find it. Cabin A315 which was on Deck 12.

Lots more people were waiting for the lifts. Fortunately, there were several and I was able to squeeze into the third that came. On Deck 12 I went the wrong way twice until I found the right cabin. The passageway was quite narrow and various bags and cases were being dropped outside doors by the stewards. One of them told me I could not get into my cabin yet, which I already knew. He was a bit curt, but I guessed he was busy and stressed getting everyone's bags to the right door. No matter, having located my cabin I could explore the ship.

According to the map, it seemed the main decks for exploration would be 5 which had shops and a library, 6 which apart from reception had a casino and bar, 7 which also had shops and a Costa, then it was all the way up to 15 which was the Lido Deck.

Decks 5, 6 and 7 did not take long because everything was closed. The shops and casino were only open when the ship was at sea. The Lido deck was crowded because it was there that most people gravitated to. The pools were on that deck and later this was where the Sail Away party would be.

I strolled the deck enjoying the warmth of the sun. I might have looked like everyone else, taking it easy and ambling around the ship prior to departure for a relaxing holiday, I was in fact as serene as a swan. Beneath the surface my insides were thrashing with tension and nervousness like that royal bird's webbed feet beneath the water on which it glides. Despite trying to act nonchalantly, I was keeping an eye out for anything suspicious. Anyone taking too much of an interest. I felt more exposed here than at Center Parcs. I couldn't wait to get into my cabin. There were too many people around.

After a couple of hours, I was able to gain entrance to my berth. It was about what I expected. On the left as you walked in was a mini aisle with a full hanging rail on one side and the bathroom opposite. At the end of this aisle was a cupboard which was open showing shelves and a small safe, also open. Past this aisle was the main room consisting mainly of the double bed and a dresser of sorts with a set of drawers and one cupboard that housed a fridge. There was a large mirror above the dresser and a chair beside it. On top was a kettle and a tray with a couple of glasses and tea / coffee etc.

I dumped my bag on the bed, on the rubber mat there for that purpose, and retrieved my case which had been waiting outside the cabin. Then I locked the door and lay on the bed too. I discovered that it was not a double bed, but two twin beds put together. No sleeping in the middle then because of the crack. I lay back and had my first chance to think in a while.

Was I safe here? I thought so. It was a last minute booking – three weeks is sort of last minute for cruises which some people book a year or more in advance - and I had told no one where I was going. The statement for the police and the note I pushed through the dog parlour letterbox telling Jackie I would not be able to walk the dogs for a while, just said I was going away. No mention of where. The two weeks at Center Parcs had helped because I was sure no one had followed me after keeping a vigil all that time. Then surely no one could have followed me down to Southampton from there and even if they did, they would not be able to get on the ship without a ticket. I figured I was as safe as I could be in the circumstances.

What was it all about? The crossword? The shooting? It must be connected. Never mind the police saying that the shooter had deliberately tried to miss. If it was meant to scare me then it had done the job, and rather well at that. The crossword must be the clue, if you pardon the pun. I had to work it out and see what it revealed. I decided there and then to stay in the room for most of the trip to try and work it out.

Having hit upon a plan of action, I unpacked and put water in the kettle to make a coffee, but just as it was boiling, the call for all to muster sounded throughout the ship. I had forgotten about the safety drill. It was mandatory and there was a rollcall as such, with the cruise cards being scanned, so they would know if I did not attend. The orange life jacket was on the shelf over the hanging rack. I grabbed it and left the cabin, ensuring to put the cruise card back in my wallet. Would not do to get locked out of the cabin.

The muster station for my deck was in one of the restaurants. There was no room to sit by the time I got there so I just stood in the corner. I did feel out of place among the couples and families. We were all shown how to put on and secure the life jacket, then had to try it for ourselves. Members of the crew went around making adjustments where necessary. Then when all had it right we were allowed to go. I hurried back to the cabin as fast as I was able bearing in mind the throng of people leaving at the same time.

Going down the corridor back to the cabin I spotted the steward and asked if I could get food sent to the cabin and was told I could. That was good. No having to eat in the dining rooms with all the other passengers.

It was almost five o'clock which was the stated departure time. I thought I would feel easier once we were underway. If no one had followed me aboard then once at sea I was safe – for a week at least. Having never been on a cruise ship before, part of me felt the need to get out on deck to experience the sail away. After all, staying in the cabin all the time might arouse suspicion in these days of extreme terrorist alert. People came on cruises to enjoy themselves. I might just take a chance. I could then see if anyone was taking an unusual interest in me.

And so, when the ships tannoy announced that we were leaving port, I left the cabin and made my way back up to the Lido deck. However, once I got there I changed my mind. The place was heaving and there was loud music blaring away. I went back down to Deck 7, where one could go outside and walk around the ship. There were less people here. Some sat on chairs taking in the late afternoon sun and others stood at the rail watching the dockside recede. I decided to do a whole circuit. I did this leisurely, looking out over the sides like everyone else but also checking no one was taking an interest in me.

It was better on the port side (left) than starboard (right) as it appeared all the smokers were on the starboard side. That must be a thing, I thought. Standing at the front or back were best, although it was very breezy at the front. I stood for a while getting thoroughly buffeted just watching the passing landmasses. Once we got to what one nearby passenger advised was the Isle of Wight, I had had enough and set off back to the cabin. Time to order something to eat.

Dining for the passengers was split into two sittings. One at 6.00 pm and the other at 8.00 pm. If you booked a certain ticket you could choose your sitting, but I had made a last minute booking, so I had had no choice in the matter. A note, which had been left in a little slot outside the cabin, told me I was on second sitting. As I was eating in the cabin, that was of no consequence.

There was a TV in the room, but it was obviously not live. There were a few films one could watch but one had to pay to watch the better ones and I had seen a lot of them anyway. Instead, I tried what I knew I should be working on non-stop. I got a little further with the puzzle but not massively so. There was a lot of trial and error. I was having to pencil in words on the paper grid and there was a lot of rubbing out. I had given myself a target of Clue 50 – which was not even a third of the way through – but I didn't even make that. I wasn't confident on all my latest answers anyway. I did manage to get most of them to fit in the grid. The colour scheme had gone out of the window though. I was just trying for the clue answers.

After a couple of hours, I got fed up and packed it away. I ended up watching some film I had seen before, but never finished it because my eyes were tired. In the end I was in bed probably earlier than I had ever been in my life when on holiday.

Chapter 19

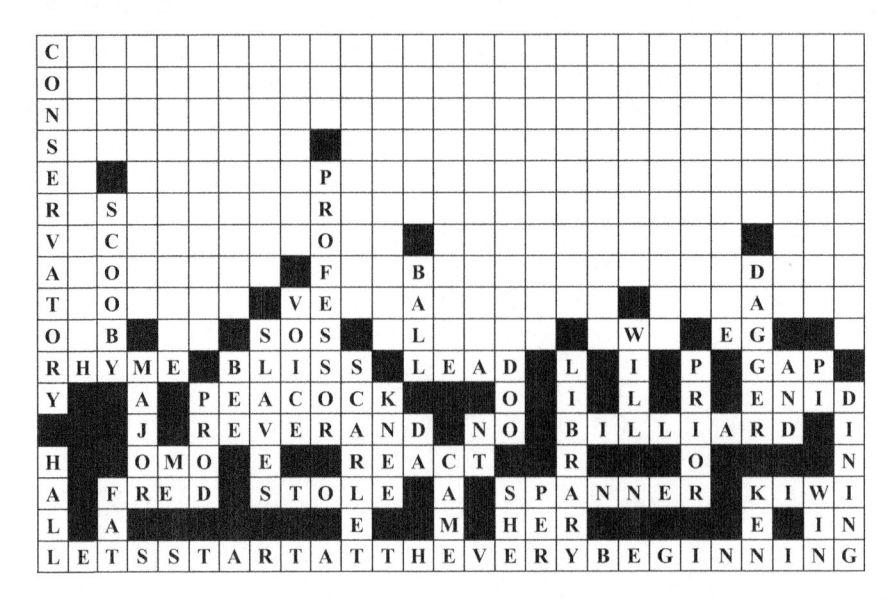

C																			
O																			
N																			
S																			
E						P													
R	S					R													
V	C					O													
A	O					F		B							D				
T	O				V	E		A							A				
O	B			S	O	S		L				W		E	G				
R	H	Y	M	E		B	L	I	S	S		L	E	A	D		L		I	P		G	A	P		
Y		A		P	E	A	C	O	C	K		O		I		L		R		E	N	I	D
		J		R	E	V	E	R	A	N	D		N	O		B	I	L	L	I	A	R	D		I
H		O	M	O		E		R	E	A	C	T		R				O					N
A		F	R	E	D		S	T	O	L	E		A		S	P	A	N	N	E	R		K	I	W	I
L		A							E				M		H	E	R					E		I	N
L	E	T	S	S	T	A	R	T	A	T	T	H	E	V	E	R	Y	B	E	G	I	N	N	I	N	G

    The next day was a sea day as we did not arrive in Amsterdam until early the following day. I was already going stir crazy in the cabin and therefore decided it was probably safe to get out for a bit. I had only been on the ship about twenty four hours. I had been sticking to the cabin most of the time, except when the steward was cleaning it. I breakfasted there and had a lunchtime sandwich too.

    Maybe it was better to have a proper break now I was here. I had seen no one suspicious on my few bouts outside the cabin and we were now at sea. I should be safe.

    Having noticed in the ship's daily newsletter that there was a shuffleboard competition, I wandered up to the Lido deck for the 2 pm start. Deck 15 was popular due to the hot weather, and I had to pick my way through sunbathers and swimmers dripping from the pool. My eyes were still constantly searching for possible danger, but everyone though was just intent on enjoying themselves as far as I could see.

    It took me a while to find the shuffleboard court, as I was still having trouble with forward and aft, but eventually I got there with about ten minutes to spare.

    There was a young couple already playing. They were both of slim build. He was about five feet nine or so and she was about three or four inches shorter. His hair was short and – as his wife described it later – dark ginger and fuzzy. He sported Clark Kentish glasses. She had long, dark hair, although only wisps could be seen poking out from under the hood of her coat – it was quite breezy in this part of the ship, which I thought was pink at first but on closer inspection was white with pink flowers.

Never having played shuffleboard before, I watched them for a while to learn the rules. When they introduced themselves, Rich and Jenny said it was their first time too. They had picked it up quickly enough though, especially Jenny who had won four times in a row. On my first try I did not even reach the scoring grid and the second hit minus ten. My last one sailed past the end of the grid as I tried to exert more force. There was obviously a knack to it.

Just as we were finishing that game, which Rich won easily, one of the ship's hosts arrived to take charge of the tournament. Unfortunately, only the three of us had turned up. After waiting ten minutes the host, an attractive twenty something girl called Issy, called off the tournament, advising there had to be a minimum of six. She said we were free to keep on playing though.

Rich and Jenny had already been playing for some time before I had arrived, so they were much more proficient in the game. Jenny beat me and then Rich. Rich beat me and then lost to Jenny again. So did I, although I did manage to win the final game against Rich.

"There is supposed to be a quoits tournament at three," I told them, looking at the newsletter I had brought with me. "I haven't played that before either."

"Neither have we," said Rich. "Shall we give it a go?" he asked Jenny.

"Why not," she replied, "although we had better get something to eat first."

"We haven't had lunch yet," Rich said to me. "You're welcome to join us."

"I don't want to intrude."

"Nonsense. We would be pleased to have your company."

We went to the all-day buffet restaurant which was on that same deck. Rich and Jenny went to select their food. As I had already eaten, I quickly grabbed a desert and went to find a table. I waved when I spotted them. They came over carrying their trays. Rich had a soup and a couple of rolls while Jenny had mainly salad. While we ate, we chatted about general topics.

They were from some unpronounceable town in Wales, but I could not have placed them as Welsh from their accents. Jenny ran her own flower shop and Rich was a dog trainer, looking not a bit like Barbara Woodhouse. Walkies! It was Jenny's first cruise, but Rich had been on one with the lads a few years before – the same ship we were on in fact.

They were easy to talk to and I found myself telling them all about myself and Laura. I was quite open but did not mention the shooting. I did tell them about the puzzle though which they were interested in. They were keen quizzers and played in a weekly pub quiz team. Before we finished and went to find the quoits court, I said I might call on their assistance if I got stuck. Who was I kidding? I was already stuck and had been since the beginning. True, I had made some headway but each time it was hard going and there was no way to tell if what I had done was correct. Three heads would be better than my one. Any one head would be better than my one.

After lunch we ambled across to the quoits court which just happened to be almost directly opposite the shuffleboard court on the other side of the ship. This too got cancelled because of lack of participants. None of us had played before but as we were trying to work it out, a guy came over who had been on a lounger, beyond the plastic dividing screens of the playing area. He agreed to show us how to play. He partnered Jenny which left me and Rich. He didn't stay long but we had a couple of games, Jenny once again the star by being the only one of us to get her quoit perfectly over the centre spot. After the guy left, we all went our different ways. Rich and Jenny were going for a stroll around the ship. I was headed back to the cabin. We agreed to keep a look out for one another in the bar later so we could be on the same quiz team.

Funny how one's plans can change. I had anticipated another evening holed up in the cabin. That was why I was back there now. I figured if I was going to ask for my new friends' help on the puzzle, I needed to have it in the best possible position. Time to really get my thinking cap on. I had the clues, the drawn grid – plus copies in case I made a mistake – and the photos of the coloured blocks. Having abandoned the colour scheme, I was still able to use this for one aspect. Any clues with Y in brackets after them were all related to Cluedo which helped, and I had also discovered that the green clues were all members of the Scooby Gang. It had been impossible to glean anything from the other colours which was why I was concentrating on the words. When I got back home, whenever that was, I could sort out the colours.

I had resolved another aspect to the puzzle. The clues that stated 'Not yet can you insert' related to answers that could not be placed because it attached to another word which was a later clue. There were so many nuances to this puzzle, it was so irritating.

I made a little progress because I found answers for the next five clues, including 49 where I cheated and used my phone to look something up. I just managed to get Clue 54 (Velma) in when I felt unaccountably tired. I lay back on the bed for a bit to rest my eyes and before I knew it I was being jerked awake by a knock at the door. I looked at my watch which said 6.30. At the door was the steward with my evening meal. Beef Stroganoff with rice and lemon meringue to follow.

By 7pm I was all finished and the tray with the dirty plates was outside my door. It was time to get ready for the quiz. According to the timetable there were loads of quizzes on throughout the day. The main one in the evening was at 8 pm. I had to get showered and changed because of the dress code after 6 pm. Smart casual except on Captain's dinner evenings when many dressed up to the nines. The first of these was on was Tuesday evening – they were usually on sea days, and we would be in Amsterdam the next day. I wasn't going to partake. I had never worn a dinner jacket in my life and wasn't going to start now. That night I just had on dark chinos and a polo shirt. I didn't get dressed up often.

Chapter 20

The quiz was in the main bar on Deck 6. Just behind reception. I walked down the six flights of stairs for some exercise. I crossed paths with a couple of people but not many. The stairway came out at the back of the bar, which shared space with the casino. On the left as I went in there were fruit machines all along the wall and a couple of dealer tables – one for roulette and another for cards. The actual bar was in the centre of the room and surrounded by tables and chairs. On the top wall there was a small stage. Two of the ship's hosts were there preparing for the quiz.

Still twenty minutes to go before the quiz but the place was already crowded. I managed to get a table for four then kept an eye open for Rich and Jenny. I had to deter a few people and hoped they would be there soon. Whilst I was waiting I overheard a couple of guys talking on the next table about the Champions League Final the night before - Liverpool playing Real Madrid – which I had forgotten was on. Sounded like there had been some trouble in the bar and one couple had been thrown out.

After about another five minutes Rich and Jenny arrived and I waved them over.

"Hi. Glad you made it," I said. "I had to fight off a few people who wanted your seats."

"Thanks," said Rich as he pulled out a chair for Jenny then sat in the other himself.

Their smart casual was a lot smarter than mine. Rich had on a proper shirt and Jenny was in a dress.

"How does this work?" asked Rich. "Been to one before?"

"No, this is my first one too. I guess we'll find out. Are you two good at quizzes?"

"We are in a pub quiz team," replied Jenny. "Every Tuesday."

"Oh, that's good. I'll rely on you then. Do you win often?"

"Now and again," said Rich. "What do you want to drink, Jen?"

"Just water I think for now," she replied.

I must have looked surprised. "Jenny doesn't drink," Rich informed me. "And I don't partake much either. Only on special occasions."

I was a Marmite drinker. Unlike most people who love it or hate it – Marmite that is – I can take it or leave it, so too with alcohol. In deference to my new friends, I opted for a diet soda.

"Ladies and gentlemen," called the male host from the stage. "We will be ready to start the quiz in five minutes. If each team can come up to the front and take an answer sheet and pencil we can soon get started. I stood up and went. I took 3 sheets and 3 pencils just in case.

"Who's got the neatest handwriting," I asked as I got back to the table.

"Jenny has excellent penmanship," said Rich.

I gave an answer sheet and pencil to Jenny. "We can use these for scribbling on," I suggested putting the rest on the table.

I was not a regular quizzer myself although I did watch a lot of TV quizzes and I was hoping I had sucked up a lot of knowledge by osmosis, or rather as my favourite was *Pointless*, by Osmanosis. It was a general knowledge quiz with twenty questions and we didn't do too badly. We didn't win but we were in the top five. Jenny seemed to be an expert on the bible – regular Sunday school she told me – and Rich's specialist subject was technology based subjects, especially computer games but also sport. I was poor at sport other than football and even on that I did not have the encyclopaedic knowledge that some football fans seem to have. TV used to be my best subject and still is but with the bulk of programming now geared to soaps, documentaries, and factual stuff – and I include cooking in that – I am not as good as I used to be. Cop shows of the 70's and 80's would be my best area. Nothing from that came up but I was able to hold my own.

The quiz only lasted half an hour. Rich and Jenny were going to one of the shows at 9 pm which was in the small theatre they had on board. There were shows on every day, from magic shows to comedy and all the singing and dancing you wanted in between. We were sat idly talking until they had to go when Rich nudged me.

"I think you've got an admirer," he winked and nodded back over his shoulder.

"What do you mean?" I asked worriedly, my paranoia jumping back in with both feet.

"That girl three tables behind you, the one in sunglasses even though there is no sun in here. She keeps looking at you."

"How do you know that? She is more probably looking at you. Or maybe Jenny even."

"No," put in Jenny. "We saw her watching you before. At lunch whilst you were sitting at the table waiting for us. We didn't think much of it at the time."

"Why don't you go over to talk to her," urged Rich.

"Nah! It won't be that kind of interest, if any at all. I can't even get lucky on a dating website."

"Ah! Funny you should mention that," said Rich smiling. "That's how I met Jen."

They looked at each other with a knowing glance.

"No shame in that," I agreed. "It seems most logical these days. Doesn't seem to work for me though."

The girl must have seen us looking because she got up and left quite hurriedly. Now she was out of her seat I could see she was quite short, with black hair in a short ponytail.

The fact that she had been watching me was worrying and didn't say much for my observational skills. I had been on the lookout for anything suspicious since I got on the ship and hadn't spotted her. Was she involved with whatever was going on?

I tried to take my mind off it. "Hey, do you two want to help on the puzzle I was telling you about?"

"Sure," enthused Rich. "It sounded interesting when you mentioned it before." I looked at Jenny and she nodded.

"OK. I don't think there is enough time now. You need to get off to your show. What time does it finish?"

"I think it's about an hour," said Jenny.

"So that's a finish at ten then. I guess it's too late after that to start puzzling?"

"A bit," agreed Rich. "And tomorrow we are in Amsterdam."

"Oh yes. I'd forgotten about that," I said, with a hint of disappointment which I hoped was well hidden. "I'm not on any tours as I booked too late." Not strictly true as there were a couple I could have got on, but I had never intended to leave the ship until it got back to Southampton. "Which tours are you on?"

"We are on the Anne Frank tour," replied Jenny.

"Then after that, we are just going to do our own thing," added Rich. "So, we will be out pretty much all day."

"OK then. Tomorrow evening then if that's OK with you two?"

With that sorted they left to go to the show, and I was on my own. I felt strangely at a loose end. It hadn't bothered me before, sitting in the cabin by myself, but now I had interacted with the cruise and the people on it for the first time, I was loathe to go back to the cabin. Also, surprisingly, I think I had caught the quizzing bug. We hadn't done too badly in the first one and I had certainly contributed more than my fair share of answers. There was another quiz at 10 pm and I decided to go in for that too.

I had about an hour to kill, and I was in a dangerous place for me. The slot machines were calling to me with their siren song, so I had to get out of there. I wandered around the ship for a bit. Popping in one or two of the shops which were now open. I found a coffee shop that was not too crowded. Probably not the best time to be drinking coffee but my excuse was that I wanted to be wide awake for the next quiz. At 9.45 I got up to find my way to the quiz venue. This was in a different place. Not in the bar but in another room, near to the theatre as it happened. I found my way there and poked my head inside but then retreated. The room was almost full, with teams sat at square tables. I felt like an intruder and left. |

As I was nearing my cabin, I bumped into someone hurrying the other way along the narrow corridor. "Sorry," I apologised automatically, although it was she who had bumped into me. Then I saw who it was. The girl who had been watching me.

"Hey!" I called out, but she had gone running down the stairs.

Now I was troubled again. What had she been doing there? Had she been in my room? I don't see how she could have done without my card. Only the steward would have access other than me. I hurried down the corridor, but the door was tightly closed and opened with a click and green light when I inserted my card. Nothing looked disturbed but my mind was. It took ages for me to fall asleep.

Chapter 21

When I woke up the next day after a restless night we were in Amsterdam. Or at least I assumed we were as my cabin had no porthole. I had to go out for breakfast because I had forgotten to leave my order for the steward. I could either try one of the restaurants for a proper full breakfast or I could have a DIY one in the buffet on Deck 15. I decided to go up.

It was going to be another hot day. As I came out of the doors from the lift area I saw the cloudless blue sky. It was only 8.15 am so it was fairly cool then with a nice breeze blowing. We were in port but looking out all I could see was industrial type buildings – definitely no windmills. I could see people on the dockside. Some walking away from the ship but not many because the tours had not started yet. Most left at 9 am.

The buffet was more crowded than I thought it would be. I don't know why I expected it to be empty. I did find an empty table to eat my cereal and toast. One had to get coffee from the urns at the end of the room. There was a queue, so I decided to skip it. Orange juice would do, I was probably over caffeinated anyway.

I was halfway through my food when I noticed someone watching me. It was that same girl from the night before. She was a few of tables away but there were not many people in between us. As I chewed slowly, I wondered what to do about it. Go back to my cabin and worry about it or go and face the problem head on? After all what could she do here, there were too many witnesses, and if she was involved maybe I could get some answers?

When I had finished eating, I headed for her table like a heat seeking missile. She quickly looked away, but I was on a mission. I dragged out a chair.

"Mind if I join you?"

"Who are you then?" she demanded in mock outrage. She had her hair in a ponytail again but no sunglasses this time so I could see green eyes. She had on a pink t-shirt which is all I could see from my position.

"I could ask you the same question?" I pointed out, trying to maintain eye contact, not being very good with conflict normally. "You have been following me around the ship?"

"Who says so?" she asked, defiantly.

"You were seen by friends of mine, and I saw you last night. Are you involved?"

"With what?"

Now she had me. If she was not involved then I didn't want to say any more about it. I prevaricated. "You would know if you were involved? Why are you following me?"

"I'm not. I was here first. You could be following me." Truth be told, I couldn't swear that she had not been at her table when I sat down.

"OK then. Why were you watching me last night? And earlier in the day? You were seen and not by me?"

"Why do you keep going around like a cat on hot bricks, always looking here there and everywhere, checking for something?"

So, she had been watching me, probably right from the beginning, because I had been most watchful when I had first got on the ship and my vigilance had gotten progressively less diligent as time had gone on. Not that I was any good at spotting anything suspicious anyway because I hadn't spotted her. If she was involved though would she have mentioned that at all?

"I am just naturally cautious," I said.

"And I'm Meghan Markel," she replied immediately.

"Really! Nice to meet you Miss Markel, or is it Mrs Windsor? I watched you in *Suits* from the first episode. I must say you look a bit different off screen."

This verbal sparring was getting me nowhere and she must have been of the same opinion. She was silent for a moment, taking a sip from her coffee cup. Then she smiled. "Look, cards on the table. I'm a reporter. I'm not on here on a case, just finished one. I just have an instinctive curiosity and when I spotted you looking as nervous as a sack of kittens, let's say it was piqued."

OK, I thought, that seemed reasonable and why would she tell me she was a reporter if she wasn't. Most people try to avoid them, so it was not wise to advertise. "Okay then," I conceded, "that seems to explain it."

"Well then? Are you going to tell me why you are acting like public enemy number one trying to evade capture?"

"There's no story for you here!" I told her emphatically. "There is just someone I need to avoid. That's all."

She looked me straight in the eyes, coolly appraising me. "Okay then."

I couldn't believe she was just letting it go but I wasn't about to argue. "Fine. Thanks. Have a good day."

With that I left and made my way back to the cabin. On the way I just glanced over the side and saw the docks was now full of people making their way to coaches in a nearby car park. I could see tour guides pointing the way to different coaches and checking lists.

Back in the cabin, I sat on the bed to do some thinking. I had nothing particular to do. I couldn't say I was a good judge of people, but I believed her to be a reporter. It made sense. No doubt I had been acting peculiarly to someone taking a particular interest. If she was a reporter she must have investigative instincts, and maybe good sources of information. Could this be a blessing in disguise? If I promised her the story – and if she wanted it of course – maybe we could partner up to investigate the mysterious events that had started on Bank Holiday Monday. The earlier Bank Holiday that is, because I realised that it was also Bank Holiday Monday that day too.

It was 9.30 am. I had planned to participate in the various quizzes during the day but now I had something else to do. I had decided to sound out the reporter, so I wanted to get my facts straight. It was time to write down what had happened. I had done it once, in my statement to the police, I just had to recreate it now. I bought a writing pad from one of the shops and headed back to the cabin to begin.

It had all started with the parcels. Delivered on a Bank Holiday Monday, so the delivery man was bogus and may have been the person behind the whole thing. Unfortunately, I couldn't remember or describe him. I had not taken much notice having been completely surprised at the delivery in the first place. Why this had been sent and who had sent it was an unknown.

The next thing that happened was the Tiffany affair. But was that even connected at all or just a massive coincidence? Meeting the girls at the restaurant could only have been by chance. It was not pre-booked or certainly not for more than a few hours. Nate could have booked it beforehand, I never asked. Then they came on strong though. Not surprising for Nate but it was for me. Perhaps Tiffany was just going along because she was her friend's wing woman but then when it finally came to the crux she could not fake it anymore. On the other hand, it had been a massively humiliating experience, and could someone hate me that much to fabricate such a scenario? Who though? I tried to recall that night in more detail.

Nate was engaging with the girls almost from the off and it was Nate that was practically pushing me into Tiffany's arms. Now I came to think of it, two nights out with Nate on the trot was strange in itself. Not since the early days when my leg was broken had we spent more than one night out. He was always on business jetting here, there, and everywhere.

Tiffany's actions were odd too. She was all over me in the cinema and the cab, then when we got back to my place it was like a switch had been thrown. The fact that I saw her paid off must mean that she had been paid to do a job. What job? Work me up and then drop me like a stone? Also, if she was getting paid did that mean she was a working girl? If I was a deliberate target then someone had known beforehand where we were going to eat. I hadn't known. Nate had picked the place. Nate! Had he set me up? Why would he?

Nate had left in a taxi with Gloria. If Tiffany was a prostitute there was a good chance Gloria was too. How much time had elapsed between the taxi dropping us off and Tiffany's dramatic put down? No more than ten minutes probably. Then ten or fifteen minutes later Scrappy and I were in the park. Tiffany was waiting for someone. Waiting for a payoff. The person paying her off came by taxi and the last time I saw Nate he was in a taxi. That was a bit of a stretch. Purely circumstantial, as they say in cop shows. On the other hand, there was no smoke without fire.

I was stunned. It couldn't be. There was no reason for it. Or no reason that I could see. My first reaction was to ring Nate immediately and talk it through, but I was not in the place to do that and anyway he had been out of contact since the shooting. Had the police been able to contact him even? The fact that he was uncontactable wasn't damning in itself, but he had told me to use that number in emergencies and therefore it should not have been unobtainable. I should have been able to leave a message. I had a nasty niggling feeling and I didn't like it.

I sat there and thought back to when I had first met Nate and what had happened ever since. What did I know about him after nearly five years? Well, if it had not been for that tackle then we would not have been friends. He had been a great help to me after that. Keeping me company and helping out with stuff. Paying for nearly everything. I could not have managed without him.

Then it hit me. Before I met him I was sort of on an even keel. I was grieving of course but I was more or less together. It was after meeting Nate that I started gambling again. He had taken me to a casino and when I told him I shouldn't go on the slots because I had a problem, he had laughed. "Don't worry," he had said. "Play with my money." And I had done that night and won. I was only going out with Nate though and on my own I stayed in. So, I gravitated to online gambling and that had been the start of the great slide into the pit. He had put me on that path and even though he had at times paid off some of my debt, I had wasted a whole load of money.

Another thing I realised was that I didn't really know him. I had never been to his house – he said he did not own one because of all his travelling. He stayed in hotels or sometimes rented a house if he was in one place for a few weeks. I had never met any of his other friends or family. He didn't even talk about them.

Had this been a set up all along? A long con? A very long con? But to what end? It sort of made sense but it also made no sense at all. Had I been the biggest mug of all time? It was difficult to swallow especially on top of what had happened with Tiffany – although it now appeared that could be all connected.

If Nate had gone that far, was he the one that had sent the frame? Come to think of it, he had been very keen to get me started on it that first night. Helped me solve the first clues. Was he able to help because he knew the answers?

That brought me to the third and final event, the shooting. That had to be connected. Something else to scare me and make me feel small. Was that Nate too? It would make sense then that I had been unable to contact him since.

I looked at the notes I had made and realised there were not too many notes and too much doodling. I must have been dwelling too heavily on events and not concentrating. I rewrote my notes on a clean sheet. It was an account of everything that had happened up to that point. Was it enough for a story? I didn't really care if it was enough for me to get help working it all out.

Chapter 22

I think I had become addicted to quizzes. Not a real surprise considering the amount I watched on TV. On the ship there were about six a day one could take part in. I planned to do them all but was also on the lookout for the reporter too, which was of more importance. I had taken part in The Battle of the Sexes Quiz - exactly what it sounded like, men versus ladies, had lunch, got beaten in the table tennis tournament and had an ice cream, before I spotted her. I had even been back to the cabin.

It had occurred to me that whilst I had a copy of the grid which I could give to Rich and Jenny, I had no copy of the clues so I would have to write them out. I decided to write them all out as this could then be a second check on what I had done so far. Other than the clues that were already in the grid, I didn't give any answers. I had some scribbled in against some of the clues on my copy, but I wanted to see if my new friends came up with the same thoughts.

After this I was on my way to the 4 pm quiz. I was not so keen to stay cooped up in the cabin now. I was starting to get into the cruise life and started believing that I should be enjoying this as a holiday rather than just an escape from whoever was trying to get me. I was feeling more confident and less worried. Nothing had happened to me for nearly three weeks now. I still had to be cautious, but I was sure as I could be that there was no one on the ship after me, provided my feelings about the reporter were on the money.

I never got to the quiz because who should I see at the lifts but my shadow reporter.

"Hey! I'd like a word with you," I called out to her. "Sorry, I don't know your name."

"Vicky," she said, warily. "What do you want? I thought we were sorted now."

"You wanted to know what I was being so furtive about didn't you? Well. I'm going to tell you. If you think there's a story in it then I want your help."

"Er...okay. Where do you want to talk?"

"Your place or mine?" I had always wanted to say that.

"I'd prefer a public place," she replied. I hadn't lost it, but only because I had never had it in the first place.

"Fair enough, but it needs to be quiet. We cannot be overheard."

We wandered about the ship for a bit looking for somewhere public but quiet. In the end we sat right in the corner of one of the coffee places. There were some other customers but not as bad as it would be on a sea day.

Once we were happy we had the best position available and had drinks in front of us, Vicky got down to business. "OK, spill the beans." So, I did. I told her about everything except for the humiliating part. On that I just said that Tiffany had come in then had a sudden change of mind and left. I did, of course, tell her about the subsequent payoff, plus the next day's shooting.

When I finished there was silence for a while. "Well?" I asked. "Is there a story there?"

"I honestly don't know," she replied deep in thought. "There is something there. Someone appears to be messing with you, but it could all be a big prank. I am freelance so whilst I am free to follow whatever story I like, I need to be certain it is going to be worthwhile, otherwise I don't eat."

"Maybe the puzzle will convince you." I pulled out my phone and opened my photos. I didn't have many, so the ones I wanted were quite easy to find. I passed the phone over to her. "There, that is the frame. You can see how the blocks fit in. Scroll on one and you can see some of the blocks. Someone has gone to an awful lot of trouble with this. Surely too much for it to be a practical joke? There must be something deeper although I've no idea what."

Vicky studied the photos for a while, flicking back and forth between the frame and the blocks. "Looks custom made," she conceded. "If you look at the isolated incidents though they could all be practical jokes. You have been sent a nearly unsolvable puzzle. Then you get teased and then fobbed off by a girl. These could have easily been set ups. Even the shooting. A bit extreme but again it could be a lark."

"So, you don't want the story then?" I was disappointed, having banked on her doing some legwork on this.

"I didn't say that. I'll just need to look into it a bit first. Check a couple of things out." I nodded, taking what I could get. "We can't do anything until we get off the ship anyway. Meantime could you write it all down, so that I can read through it again when the cruise is finished."

"I already have something down," I informed her. "Already done and waiting in my cabin."

"Fine. Let me have that and then we can just enjoy the cruise. I don't think anyone is following you, I would have noticed."

"OK. I will get the notes to you!

"No rush. We are not back in Southampton until Saturday. Plenty of time." She looked at her watch. "Now I have a spa date, so I have to go." She got up from her seat and started to leave then she paused and came back. "Full disclosure. I am on here on a job, keeping an eye on a certain person and his er… companion."

"Oh… you're one of them. A gossip reporter?" I don't know why I was surprised. She didn't look like a grizzled investigative reporter with her petite frame and pretty face.

"I do what I can to live," she declared feistily. "I have been looking for an investigative gig, so nothing has changed. Okay?"

I had no choice really and someone was better than no one. "Okay!"

This time she did leave, and I was left feeling a little disappointed. She was unlikely to have the relevant contacts to investigate the situation I was in. Still, it would be nice to have at least one person on my side.

It was too late now for the quiz, so I went back to the cabin to change for dinner. I had forgotten to book something in my room again, so it was back up to the buffet. I dined leisurely. There was nothing on until a James Bond quiz at 8 pm. I was hoping that Rich and Jenny would be there so I could hand over the puzzle clues to get some fresh minds on it.

As it turned out I didn't see my new friends that evening. They didn't turn up for the quiz and whilst it was a bit frustrating for me, it was nothing to worry about. They could have been late getting back in from Amsterdam, as they were doing their own thing. Or could be watching another of the theatre shows. I ended up being in a team of one, but I didn't mind that because on Bond I could really hold my own. I scored 18.5 out of 20 and lost to a table that got 19. My half point lost was on a question about the three items that made up Scaramanga's golden gun. I forgot about the cufflinks. The other point lost was on the title on one of the newer films. I was almost perfect on the Connery and Moore films but had difficulty in putting the Brosnan and Craig films into order. Still second place for a team of one was pretty good if I did say so myself – which I did.

After the quiz I just mooched around the ship. I had to get out of the bar because the slot machines were still calling to me. It was a balmy evening, so I ambled around the whole ship but gave that up when I got to the smokers' side and moved inside instead. I kept an eye out for Rich and Jenny or even Vicky but saw no one I knew. In the end I was back up in the cabin early. I had not achieved as much as I had wanted that day but felt I had made some headway by gaining a possible ally.

Chapter 23

Vicky had been busy since she left Danny. Her spa visit only lasted an hour and after that she was keen to get started on what she felt was going to be a good story and one that might even get her the crime slot she was craving. Currently. she was only managing to sell salacious stories on celebrities and politicians, but she did not want to be with the gutter press for longer than she had to be. There was the question of eating though, so she had her current assignment to complete too.

She was following a recent ex-footballer who was fooling around with someone who was not his wife. She had only managed by chance to discover he was coming on this cruise and had booked on the same trip at the last minute. She was not bankrolled by a paper, so it was her own money and she had taken the cheapest cabin available. Having said that, even though it was a single berth, the price was nearly what she would have had to pay for a double berth. The room was small but sufficient. It was a single bed - a mattress on a wooden frame which was secured to the wall, rather like the bottom half of a bunk bed. The mattress was quite thin. There was closet space and a mirrored dressing table / desk and a shower cubicle. The room backed onto the casino. All the rooms in the one corridor were single occupancy.

She went back to her room after the spa to change for dinner but more importantly to get her camera. She had spent a good portion of the past two days taking photos of the ship, the sea and anything else she could be expected to take photos of whilst getting the real object of attention in shot. She had plenty of shots of the ex-pro with his companion but no money shot. She just needed one real kiss and it was wrapped up.

First though she had something to do on her new assignment – if that was what it proved to be. She went down to the ship's library which was on Deck 5. It was possible to pay to use the internet here which she did. She entered her email account and sent an email to a contact she had in crime reporting, hoping that he could do her a favour. Once done she checked her other emails but there was nothing of interest and she left after only using ten minutes of her thirty minute session.

Her target and his companion always had the 8 pm slot for dinner and Vicky had made sure she was on the second sitting too. Not that anything ever happened at a table with four other people, but it allowed her to eat whilst not losing sight of him.

He was a family man with rather a large family of four kids, living in a nice house, with his interior designer wife. No one would recognise him now. He had grown his hair and a beard virtually obscuring his facial features. If Vicky had not known who he was she would not have recognised him. That was why he felt safe coming on this trip she supposed. He had been the Mr Clean of football. Hardly ever booked, never sent off and no scandals whilst he was playing. That was why this would be a dynamite story because he was so regarded as an upstanding citizen. Not that Vicky felt good about doing it, but when a meal ticket like this came along one should not turn it away.

Vicky had to multitask at her table; eat, surreptitiously keep an eye on the prize and try to follow the conversation at her own table just in case someone brought her into the conversation. There were two couples and an older guy. With a set sitting you were put on the same table for the whole trip which meant your dinner companions were always the same. No doubt designed to breed companionship and maybe friendship on board. Vicky usually only participated if she was asked a direct question but had to try and follow the conversation just in case this happened.

It was also tricky planning the courses. If her target did not have a dessert then neither could she but to time each course with his was a bit impossible. Still, she knew where they lived. As it happened this evening, she was having to dawdle over coffee to make it last. The two couples had already left the table and there were some awkward silences between the older guy and Vicky.

Suddenly, Mr Ex-Pro and his paramour were on their feet and leaving. Vicky held it a few seconds until they were out of the doors then rapidly looked at her watch, drained the last of her coffee and excused herself. She had her digital camera in her evening bag so could just follow them and see if she could get lucky.

The restaurant was on Deck 6 - a deck on which one could walk around the ship outside which is what her target did. Vicky sauntered after them, seemingly in no hurry. Outside she walked over to the side and leant on the rail, ostensibly to watch the sun setting. Taking out her camera she took a few shots, then ambled along in the wake of her subject. Mr Ex-Pro and his lady did not notice as they only seemed to have eyes for each other, and Vicky was just about to get very lucky indeed. As they reached the prow of the ship, the couple stopped and looked out to sea, then just moved out of sight around the corner. Vicky came around the slight curve and came upon the couple in deep lip lock. She walked unconcernedly past, hoping they would not stop, then just before rounding the curve out of sight, she took a couple of quick snaps. The couple were none the wiser, but she nearly bumped into another passenger as she turned to walk away. She apologised and moved on.

Back in the cabin she was smiling to herself as she wrote up the story. Job almost done. She knew which paper was most likely to buy it. If she could get it out before she left the ship then there might be a nasty surprise for Mr Ex-Pro when he set foot in Southampton again. She felt sorry for Mrs Ex-Pro but no doubt she would do well in any divorce proceeding.

She wondered if it was too soon to expect a reply from her contact on her possible other story and figured it was, it took time to get information out of police sources. The library closed at 10 pm but it would be better to try again in the morning. The night was still young, so she grabbed hold of the ship's newsletter to see what shows were on that evening.

There was a loud knock on the door. Without thinking she opened it and there stood Mr Ex-Pro. A glowering, angry, Mr Ex-Pro – all six feet two of him. He pushed her into the room and followed with the door shutting automatically behind him. "Where is it?" he growled.

"Where's what? And what right have you to come barging into my private cabin?" Vicky demanded.

"You were seen taking that photo. Where's the …" but he didn't need to finish the sentence as the object of his attention was lying in full view on the bed. He snatched it up. "This is going over the side," he snarled. "And I better not see you around again."

"No! No!" yelled Vicky, trying to grab hold of the camera but it was quite tiny, and Mr Ex-Pro was a big unit and his fist nearly closed around it. "Get off!" he said, pushing her again and she fell on the bed.

By the time Vicky was on her feet again he was gone but from the smile on her face you would think that she was not too bothered. True, the cost of a new camera was an expense she didn't need, but the photos had already been uploaded to her laptop. It had been open on the dresser where she had been writing the article, but he had not taken any notice. She decided to quickly polish off the article and get her email off to her target market, which is what she did. The email was in drafts where she could send it tomorrow when she logged on to the internet in the library.

It was still early but she decided to call it a night and slept like a baby. In the morning, feeling refreshed, she went for a run around the deck before many other passengers were up and about. Then she showered, changed and went for breakfast. For once she didn't have to be in the same place as Mr Ex-Pro. In fact, as he had suggested, she felt it better to stay completely out of his way for the rest of the trip.

As soon as the library opened at 9 am she was there, paying for a session and logging into her account. First, she sent off the email out of her drafts, with a virtual sigh of relief, and then she glanced through her new emails. It was probably still expecting too much to have anything back from her crime contact, but he owed her a favour and he usually acted on things fast. In this case he had and there was a reply from him.

Vicky read the reply and felt the thrill of the beginning of a chase flow down her spine. This might be the one. The story that landed her into the big time. She had to be careful because her contact was the crime writer and he wanted to know what she had got. She would have to let him down gently just in case she needed him again. Time for that later though. For now, her mind was abuzz with what the email had said.

Firstly, it seemed like Danny had been telling the truth. There had been a shooting in Surrey which had been earmarked as a scare tactic. The interesting point was that the bullets were from a Luger. An old German gun, used by the Gestapo in World War II. The police were at a loss as to what that meant, or so they said, relayed her contact.

Secondly, and far more interesting was that her contact had learned that a police inspector, from the same area as the shooting, had disappeared. No one had seen him for nearly a week. The last people to see him before his disappearance were a young police constable and his grandfather. The same P.C. that had got called to the shooting.

It got better. The missing inspector had been on leave – rumour was this was enforced – but the P.C. admitted that he had last been seen at his grandfather's house and that he was there because they had been doing some investigating on the side. Well, not really investigating, puzzle solving. One big puzzle that had allegedly come in the post.

That was all he had been able to get. No names of those involved or any specific details. There was one other bit of news though. Danny had mentioned a name to her – Nathan Black – and she had asked her contact to get anything he could on that name. He had nothing to tell which was strange. He had not had time to conduct an extensive search but there was nothing on social media for a guy with the name and around the age Danny had given her. That was odd these days, especially given he was supposed to be a gadabout wheeler and dealer.

It was time to find her new best friend and delve a bit more into this story. Get his reaction to the news that his friend was a ghost and that a police inspector also had been sent an anonymous puzzle but was now missing.

Chapter 24

Tuesday. Day four of the cruise and I was back to eating breakfast in the cabin. I was late too. I had difficulty sleeping and must have dropped off about dawn. I had ordered breakfast for 8 am but it was after 8.30 when I opened my door to bring in the tray. The toast was cold and the coffee lukewarm. Not the best start to the day.

I was getting dressed after a shower when there came a loud banging on the door. "Just a minute!" I yelled trying to make myself respectable, or as respectable as I ever looked. I went to the door in bare feet but otherwise clothed and looked through the peephole. It was Miss Gossip Column Reporter, so I opened the door.

"Hi! Not interrupting anything am I?" she breezed in.

"Er… no, but what's the emergency?" I asked, closing the door.

"Just got a bit of information and wanted your reaction. Bed or chair?" She was asking where she could sit.

"Take your pick." She sat on the chair, so I sat at the end of the bed. "So, what's the big news?"

"Well, I don't know if you would call it big news but certainly interesting," she informed me. She seemed to be excited about it anyway for her eyes were shining. "I have this friend who is a crime reporter, and he has his contacts. I asked him to check on the shooting and he came back with a few things."

"What things?"

"Okay. Well, first, the shots through your door were made with a Luger?"

"Okay. I'm not sure what significance that has?"

"Me neither," she admitted, "but that was just the opener. Do you remember the police that interviewed you? Their names?"

"Er… I think so." I scrolled back through my memory to that day I had been unsuccessfully trying to forget for nearly a month. "Sergeant Wilson and … Lane, the constable was Lane."

"Great!" Suddenly, there was a notebook and pen in her hand, and she was writing a note. I had a feeling I had just been played. She saw me glaring at her and held her arms up. "Sorry, just my guy couldn't get the names."

"Go on then."

"Well, P.C. Lane – if that is the constable – was in touch with a Detective Inspector who has since gone missing. He wasn't on your case as he was on leave at the time but … drum roll please." I didn't oblige her.

"That same D.I. had been sent a puzzle in the post and Lane and his grandfather were helping him solve it."

I was temporarily lost for words. Another puzzle? Was there a serial puzzler running loose? Was this connected to my puzzle? It had to be, didn't it? It would be too much of a coincidence otherwise. "So, this police inspector has gone missing?"

"Yes! He was supposed to go in for a hearing or something, but no one can find him. The last people to see him were Lane and his grandfather."

"Did he solve the puzzle?" Maybe that was it. Solve the puzzle and then the Puzzler made you disappear.

"I honestly don't know." Why was she grinning like the Cheshire Cat?

"You seem to be enjoying this," I observed dryly.

"Well, no, not enjoying exactly, just pumped. I have been trying to get into serious journalism for a while now and it looks like I've got a story here that no one else has."

"Except the crime reporter you've just been talking to," I reminded her.

"Yes, but he doesn't know anything. Or he doesn't have what I have. Ties with a person in the middle of the story."

"Well, I hope you know what you are doing. Whilst we are trying to solve this riddle we don't want the Puzzler to know what we are up to, so I hope you contact doesn't write something himself."

That kept her quiet for a moment. She was thinking hard. "All he has from me is the name of your friend."

"Nathan?"

She nodded. "The thing is, I asked him to check up on him and it appears he is a ghost."

"What do you mean, a ghost?"

"He has no online presence which today is unheard of. No social media presence at all. I mean my contact has not done a deep dive, birth records etc. but it is strange."

"I guess there are people who are not on Facebook or Twitter." It didn't tie in with Nathan's man about town persona. It did though underline my own fears.

"Possibly but not likely," she stated.

"What do we do now then?" It would be good to have a plan.

"Well, firstly, I am with you all the way. I am going to stick to you like glue."

I couldn't help it and glanced at the bed in an obvious way.

"Not that stuck. No offence but you're not my type."

"That's what they all say," said with my most deprecating smile.

She wanted to put the record straight though. "I prefer someone nearer my own age. And someone with X chromosomes only." It took me a moment to work that one out.

"Oh!" I said and left it at that.

"Other than that," she continued, "I need to talk to the grandfather. Much better than the P.C. who will be under orders not to talk to the press. Then we need to do an exhaustive background check on Nathan Black. Of course, I cannot really do anything now until we finish the cruise because I don't want to involve any other people if I can help it. This is my baby, and I don't want to share."

She got up to leave. "You off now? I thought you wanted to stick to me like glue?"

"Yeah but you cannot go anywhere on here can you? I won't put the leash on until Southampton."

With that she was gone, and I was left alone with a maelstrom of thoughts. The most gobsmacking was the fact that there were two puzzles. At least. If two why not more? Two puzzles but surely only one Puzzler. That person was still a mystery, but there must be a connection with the D.I. if he had the puzzle too. So, was I connected to the D.I. or to the Puzzler? Even if he was missing it would be a good idea when I got back home to check in with the station. I wanted to know if it was the same puzzle or a different one. If it was the same then that one might be further on than mine.

The fact the D.I. had disappeared was disconcerting. Had he been kidnapped or was his body going to turn up somewhere? On the other hand, if I was going to be killed then the bullets would have not been shot high. Maybe he had been taken because he was getting too close to the Puzzler. After all, as a policeman his detective skills would be much better than mine.

If he had been getting too close was it safe to continue to try and solve the puzzle? Was I putting other people in danger by getting them involved, especially innocent people like Rich and Jenny? Vicky was slightly different as she was going into it eyes wide open, and with a gung-ho attitude too.

Then, of course, what about Nathan? I had been already thinking about his possible involvement and now it seemed there was certainly something to think about. Having already acknowledged to myself that I didn't really know him, did it surprise me that he had no media footprint? Did he not exist then? My previous musings had highlighted to me that my current financial circumstances could have been down to him. Was he playing a very long con, manipulating me for some unknown purpose of his own? No media footprint. His phone number unobtainable. I bet the police were unable to contact him either, for they only had the same number.

I was still not definitely sure that he was connected to the puzzle, but things were damning for him as regards the Tiffany incident. He had made the restaurant booking. He had been the one egging the girls on. He had even pointed me in the direction of Tiffany. Not forgetting the payoff in the park from the back of a taxi, the same type of vehicle he had last been seen in. OK that last one was a stretch of sorts, but it all tied in.

He had been interested in the puzzle and had got me started but I couldn't see how that tied in nor how it was connected to the D.I. that had gone missing. What were the chances that the same person had a grudge against me and a police detective that was known to the constable who came to investigate my shooting? That seemed to suggest a localised area but then something hit me between the eyes. It was Nathan who had got me the flat and I had moved a fair distance from where I used to live. He had moved me into the same area as his other target. Maybe Nathan was the Puzzler after all.

This was still all conjecture of course. I had no proof of anything. There were two indisputable facts. There were at least two puzzles that meant two people at least who were targets. And now one of them had disappeared. Even that though could not definitely be connected as it was likely the D.I. had made many enemies over the years.

My mind was going around in circles, and I decided to leave it until there were some substantial facts to go on. At least my idea to get a reporter involved had paid off to a certain extent and it was possible with her contacts that she could find out more. Whatever happened I was not too bothered about her reporting on the story because I was not in the wrong.

Suddenly, however, a certain chill travelled down my back. Yes, she could dig into Nathan as much as she wanted to. I would be glad to learn anything she could discover. What I didn't want though was for her to be digging into my past because that would not stand up to too much scrutiny either.

Chapter 25

I woke up screaming or so they told me, ripping out a few of the wires to which I was attached. I didn't know where I was. I was hyperventilating and sweaty. About half a dozen people were milling around me, lying me back down and reattaching the wires. After the initial shock of waking, I was aware of pain in my hands and my back. I lifted my arms and saw that my hands were heavily bandaged. Lots of questions were coursing through my head and I had to get some out.

"Where am I? What happened?" It was more of a croak than human speech, but I think they got the gist of it.

"Get the Doctor!" I heard a voice say.

I closed my eyes for a moment because the light was hurting them for some reason. When I opened them again the throng of people had gone leaving just one. She was a nurse, I could tell that, so therefore I must be in hospital which tied in with someone calling for a doctor. That was all I did know though. What had happened to me and how I had ended up there was a complete mystery.

"What happened Nurse?" I asked again, still croaky but more audible.

"Best wait until the Doctor gets here," she replied, going round the bed and tucking in the sheets which I had obviously dislodged.

At that moment a white coated woman arrived. She was about fifty, average height and of Oriental heritage. "Hello, I'm Doctor Tan. Glad to see you are awake. You had us very worried for a while there."

"Why is that?" I asked, eager for information now.

"Well, you've been in a coma for three days, since they brought you in from the fire," she informed me, picking up the chart from the end of the bed and reading it. "Three days, three and a half hours in fact."

"I was in a fire?" I looked at my hands and she saw where my gaze was. "Badly burned I'm afraid but you will be able to use them again. A few skin grafts. There will be some scarring."

"My back hurts too." I told her.

"Yes, your back was badly burned and your hair was singed too."

Fortunately, there was no mirror for me to see that. I was silent for a few moments trying to collect my thoughts. "Does anyone know what happened?"

"Not much. There was a fire in a warehouse and while the fire brigade were trying to put it out, you came staggering out ablaze. They got to you fast and doused the flames. You were unconscious when the ambulance arrived and have been so until just now."

I tried to think back but my mind was a blank. A complete blank as was demonstrated when the doctor asked the next question.

"You had no I.D. or anything on you when you came in," she said. "We don't even know your first name. Can you tell me please?"

I just looked at her suddenly dumbstruck. There was nothing there. "I don't know," I managed to get out eventually.

"What can you tell us?" asked Doctor Tan. "Do you know the year for instance?"

I thought about it for a few seconds and realised I didn't. I shook my head.

"Could be temporary amnesia. Nothing to worry about at this stage. Let's leave it a while and things might start coming back." She cast her eye at the various monitors. "Your vitals look good. We'll keep you wired up for a couple of days to keep an eye on things. How do you feel?"

My head was swimming with the fact that I didn't know who I was, so much so that I had to concentrate fully just to work out how I felt physically. "Mentally knocked for six," I replied. "Physically, my hands and back are hurting, I have a headache and my throat is as dry as a bone."

"We can give you some morphine for the pain and as for thirst we can deal with that straight away. Nurse, please!"

The nurse filled a glass of water from a jug, both of which were on a bedside table, and held it to my lips because it would have been too hard to hold bandaged as I was. I quaffed the lot in two seconds and handed the glass back for a refill. I took my time with the second glass. As I sipped the doctor was writing things down on the chart.

"Well," she said, "I will and come back and see you later. Nurse Simons will see to your pain relief and then can no doubt find you a sandwich if you're hungry. Mid-morning, a bit early for lunch. I will pop back to check on you later." Just as she was going out the door she turned back. "By the way, it is 1997."

The nurse did some tampering with the drip in my arm and after a while my various pains started to ease but I also felt sleepy which I tried to fight. I needed to stay awake and work out what had happened and most importantly who I was. Unfortunately, the morphine had other ideas.

When I awoke again the room was empty but there was a sandwich and a packet of crisps together with a fresh jug of water. I had no way of knowing how much time had passed since I had emerged from my three day coma. I obviously had no watch on with my hands bandaged and there was no clock in the room that I could see. It was still daylight, I could see through the window, so possibly not too long. Not long enough to get my memory back though. Everything was still a total blank.

I was freaking out now and wanted to scream the place down. Nothing was coming at all. No images, no indistinct stirrings. I tried to think back to when I was a kid. Parents? School? Toys even? Nothing would come. It must have been the trauma of the fire. How long did temporary amnesia last? A few hours? Days? Months? What were the chances of permanent amnesia? That was a much scarier thought.

I had nothing better to do and I was a little hungry, so I started on the sandwich, which was tricky to say the least and the crisps were out of the question. The sandwich did give me a little hope at least. There was lettuce on it and after just one mouthful I realised that I didn't like lettuce. I couldn't pick it off, so I put the half I had bitten back on the plate. Fact Number One – I didn't like lettuce.

That was as good as it got in those early days. Hospital food is not renowned for being of the culinary arts, but it did highlight what I did or did not like. There seemed to be quite a lot I didn't like. Most fruit and vegetables for one thing. I wasn't keen on mashed potatoes but liked roast potatoes and chips. I was obviously not a vegetarian so did eat meat but seemed to have a gristle aversion, in as much if I found a piece then that put me off the whole sausage.

I became free of all the monitoring equipment after a couple of days and was able to take my first steps out of bed. I got a look at myself in the mirror. The bearded face looking back at me seemed strange. This was no five day growth of stubble but a full beard. It didn't seem to be me, and it didn't go with my extremely cropped hair do which had been necessary to make it less fire damaged. The beard would have to go.

The beard did go a couple of days later, but nothing came back in return. I was a special case apparently. There appeared to be no head trauma. Therefore, it was probably psychological trauma that was giving me a sort of dissociative amnesia which usually did not involve totally losing one's sense of self, although it was not unheard of, the doctor told me. A common treatment of subjecting the patient to stimuli – persons and places that should be known to them – was not available to me because no one came forward to claim me. I was not reported missing to the police, and nobody came enquiring for accident victims at the hospital.

There was no way of checking my identity either because of the injury to my hands I had no fingerprints, they had burned off. Not that this would make a lot of difference unless I had a criminal record which I sincerely hoped I didn't. The police did take a DNA swab which I thought was odd at the time, that method of crime detection not having filtered through to the TV I watched. They told me a DNA Database had been started in 1995 but would only bring up a result if I had been trouble with the police since then. Nothing came of that, so I obviously hadn't broken the law recently – or been caught anyway. It was strange though that no one was missing me. I must have been a complete loner, which was a particularly sad thought.

The police had wanted to talk to me about the fire, but I was unable to tell them anything obviously. I got the feeling they thought I might be faking. It was arson and I had been the only person around at the time. They kept coming back but nothing did for me. They were as forceful as the doctors would let them be, but they were flogging a dead horse. They threw names at me but none of them rang a bell. They told me the address of the warehouse, who owned it and what it was used for, but it meant nothing.

They were obviously looking at me as the arsonist. The only person to benefit would be the building and business owner – who was the same person – but they were unable to tie him to me. A good thing from my point of view. The last thing I needed to learn was that I was an unsavoury character that burnt down buildings for money.

Then they changed tack. If I was not the arsonist and I didn't work in the warehouse, confirmation of which they already had from the owner, then maybe I was an intended victim. Someone had wanted to get rid of me. That was something else I didn't want to learn either but that was the one that bothered me. If someone had been trying to kill me and found out that I was still alive, then I was still fair game. When they suggested doing an appeal to find someone who knew who I was I declined. My view was that if I was missed then someone would have at least been searching for me. I would rather be a live nobody than a dead somebody.

After a week in hospital, other than the complete memory blank, I was as fit as a fiddle so there was no need to keep me. The problem was I had nowhere to go. No money, clothes or accommodation. One of the nurses took pity on me and offered me a room rent free whilst I sorted myself out. Gwen was a senior nurse and rather matronly although not yet a matron. It was a purely platonic relationship. She was in her late forties, and I was … well, I didn't know how old I was. Early to mid-twenties was the consensus in the hospital.

After collecting some second hand clothes from thrift shops using a small loan of money from Gwen, I started to do odd jobs to earn something towards paying her rent. As the weeks went by though and my memory did not return something more permanent had to be arranged. I needed a proper job and to get that I needed a proper identity, so Daniel Andrews was born … or in fact created. They had started calling my Danny in hospital, they had to call me something, rather than just calling me that man, so that became Dan the Man then Danny.

I applied for any jobs I could and eventually got one at a firm of insurance brokers. It was hard because I was competing with guys of a similar age who had worked there since school so had far more experience, or university degree students. Needing to get a life started though, I worked hard and achieved the relevant qualifications. That took four years and before that I had moved out of Gwen's house and into a flat of my own. I was working in London, but my small studio flat was in Balham. Even though it was only a studio flat I could only just afford the rent.

By the time I met Laura about seven years later, I had moved up in the company and was on quite a nice salary, living in a much better flat in Surrey Quays. She was the only person who knew of my lack of a past, other than Nathan who I had confided in at one time.

This was the secret then that may come out if Vicky started digging. Not that I had anything to hide, or did I? I had no way of knowing the type of person I was before or if I had done bad things. After those first few weeks with no one coming forward, I had decided I was better off not knowing. Someone who had been on the earth twenty odd years that did not have one person to miss them cannot have been such a nice person. My memories have never returned, not even in the form of dreams, as far as I knew, and that is how I wanted things to stay. Who knows what might come out of the woodwork if Vicky really started digging. I might be in a mess already but always better the devil you know.

Chapter 26

```
C . . . . . . . . . . . . . . . . . . . . . . . . . .
O . . . . . . . . . . . . . . . . . . . . . . . . . .
N . . . . . . . . . . . . . . . . . . . . . . . . . .
S . . . . ■ . . . . . . . . . . . . . . . . . . . . .
E . ■ . . P . . . . . . . . . . . . . . . . . . . . .
R . S . . R . . . . . . . . . . . . . . . . . . . . .
V . C . M . O . . . . . . . . . . . . . . . . . . . .
A . O . O ■ F . B . . . . . . . . . A D . . . . . . .
T . O V E R ■ V E L M A . . . . . . T A . . . . . . .
O ■ B . E . S O S ■ . L . . . . W . E G . . . . . . .
R H Y M E . B L I S S . L E A D . L . I . P . G A P .
Y . . A . P E A C O C K . . O . I . L . R . E N I D .
. . . J . R E V E R A N D . N O . B I L L I A R D . I
H . . O M O . E . R E A C T . R . . . O . . . . . . N
A . F R E D . S T O L E . A . S P A N N E R . K I W I
L . A . . . . . E . . M . H E R . . . . . E . I N . .
L E T S S T A R T A T T H E V E R Y B E G I N N I N G
```

About half an hour after Vicky had gone I was leaving my cabin when who did I see? None other than Rich and Jenny exiting a cabin two doors down and across from my own. "Hey!" I called and they turned towards me. "Fancy you being so close. I could have thrown a sock and hit your door; you are that close."

"Strange thing to say," observed Rich, "but if you like."

"I mean a balled sock obviously," I explained. "Like being a stone's throw away."

"We had no idea you were in this corridor," said Jenny.

"Probably a good job for you," I responded quickly. "Is now a good time to show you the puzzle?"

"We're just off for a late breakfast," Rich told me. "We had a bit of a lie-in. We don't get much chance at home. You're welcome to join us."

"No, it's okay, I've had some in the cabin. We can do it later."

"We can be back here by eleven," offered Jenny.

"In your cabin?"

"Why not," said Rich. "We can sit on the balcony." They were on the opposite side of the corridor to me which meant they had an outside cabin and a sea view.

"Fine. See you then. And bon appetite."

I had been going up to Deck 15 again because there was supposed to be another shuffleboard competition, but I wouldn't get back in time, so I stayed in my room getting things together. At precisely eleven o'clock I took a pair of balled socks out of the dresser drawer and threw it at their door. The angle was too acute though and it bounced off the door jamb. Then I had to go and sheepishly pick it up under the gaze of a couple of passing passengers. In fact, Rich and Jenny were not inside because by the time I had returned the socks to the drawer and grabbed the required sheets of paper and a pen, they were walking down the corridor. I saw them and stayed in my doorway until they had passed – the passageways were not very wide. I held up the papers as they did.

"Hiya!" sang out Jenny.

"Have a good breakfast?" I asked.

"Great," answered Rich, "but I suppose it was more of a brunch."

"Delicious," enthused Jenny, beaming.

"You seem pretty happy," I said to her.

"We're getting a puppy!"

Rich was opening their cabin door. "We have been thinking about it for a while," he said over his shoulder.

"What breed?" I asked, as we went inside.

"Border collie or a cockapoo," he replied.

"Border collie!" said Jenny emphatically.

"Border collie," Rich grinned. "Jenny's family always have border collies."

"My parents have one called Timber," Jenny added.

"Got a name for him yet?"

"Cluedo!" Jenny told me.

"As well as quizzes we play a lot of board games," explained Rich. "Cluedo is Jenny's favourite."

A bit of a strange name for a dog I thought but certainly unique. "Better than Rummikub. But if you get a cat will you call it Mousetrap?" Like most of my jokes this just got a groan. "Wait a minute though, what a coincidence?"

"What do you mean?" asked Rich.

"There is a Cluedo theme running through the puzzle. You will see when you see it."

Their cabin seemed a bit bigger than mine but that might have just been because of the light streaming in through the balcony doors through which I could see the sea rolling by.

"It's hot out," said Rich, "but we should be cool on the balcony."

I looked out and saw that there was a small table and two chairs. "You and Jenny take those outside," I suggested. "I will take this one from the dresser and sit just inside the doorway. We don't want the papers blowing away."

That was agreed so we all got into our seats. I got out my phone. "Now this is what the frame actually looks like," I said, bringing up the picture. "You can see how far I have got but, of course, that might not all be totally correct." I brought up other pictures. "I've got photos of all the blocks too."

Rich and Jenny took turns with the phone, having a good look at the photos. Then they handed it back.

"Someone has gone to a lot of trouble with this," observed Rich.

"Yes I know," I agreed. "I have racked my brains to work out who but with no luck." I was debating whether to tell them the whole story, now that it was out in the world with a reporter, but I didn't want them in any danger. I handed over the sheets of paper containing the whole list of clues and the frame I had filled in so far. "This is where I have got up to. There is no guarantee that what I have in is correct, but it seems to fit."

They edged their chairs around to each so they could both look at it at the same time.

"Looks impressive," said Rich. "Where should we start?"

"Have you seen the Cluedo theme?"

"I saw it," smiled Jenny. She counted. "Thirteen words so far."

"Me too," joined in Rich.

"If you look at the real frame in the photo, you might just see the yellow dots. All the Cluedo clues have yellow ones."

They both had a quick look and nodded thoughtfully in unison.

"Well, I guess we should go through the clues and see if any answers jump out at you. Fitting into the grid takes longer. There is a colour issue too. The words seem to be in different colour groups, but the dots also show where words intersect either across or down. It is quite a complicated set up. I decided to abandon the colour scheme for now as I couldn't show it in the drawn frame you have there."

"There are no numbers in this diagram," observed Jenny, "so what number are we up to?"

"Yes, the numbers do not make a lot of sense as regards a normal puzzle because one, for instance, is the clue right along the bottom of the frame. It is like a construction from ground up. That's why I didn't write the numbers in – and it would have been a bit cramped. Assuming everything I have done so far is correct, we are up to fifty five, but fifty two is not in yet either."

The next set of clues was on page two which started at number forty seven. We all looked at the rest of the clues which covered almost two and a half sheets of paper, Rich and Jenny looked at the copy I had written out for them and me at the original. I had been careful when copying them down to have the same number of questions per sheet as the original, so we were always … er … on the same page.

47. I am having one. (Y) (4)
48. ABBA in danger. (3)
49. Initially a Norwegian composer for example. (1/1)
50. Extra for Thomas or Kenneth. (4) **(Not yet can you insert)**
51. Yours lies in your own hands. (4) (LB)
52. The road may not be winding but it certainly is this. (4) (P) **(Not yet can you insert)**
53. When the fat lady sings. (4) **(Insert 50 now you may)**
54. The nerd in the gang. (G) (5)
55. Liam kept losing his family. (5) **(Insert 52 now you may)**
56. Frog croaks with silent partner but prospers in the mix. (LB) (6)
57. Salty salesman below. (Y) (6) **(Not yet can you insert)**
58. A mackerel but not clear. (DB) (4) **(Not yet can you insert)**
59. Escape a vacuum (LB) (4)
60. Agent of the Mysterons loses rank (Y) (5) **(Insert 57 and 58 now you may)**
61. Initially, Magic Roundabout Spinoff (Y) (3)
62. Off the cuff but not liberal. (2)
63. You are a long time this. (4)
64. Who is in the house? (Y) (6)
65. Circumstance may make you this. (6)
66. Some French fighters were all for this. (LB) (3)
67. In the end it is for nothing. (LB) (3)
68. Your country needs you, he said, but not the queen. (Y) (7)
69. An English queen loses her head to give a direction. (1/1/1)
70. Part nut, in the army (Y) (7)
71. Twee but no alien (R) (2)
72. Never ending tear. (4)
73. Divert stream to expert. (R) (6)
74. Oliver found in an instrument. (4)
75. D'you make her in there? Writer with no surname. (G) (6)
76. Gamble on old Ireland. (4)
77. Batman gets back one of these from Bolivian capital (3)
78. Which shop follows in line? (P) (4)
79. Already in once but we can begin again. (R) (5)
80. Wolf or freedom, which one to yell. (3)
81. You can hang soap with this (Y) (4)
82. In the soup with no back end. (2)
83. Reputation is all here, even abbreviated. (1/1)
84. For each, never yesterday. (5)
85. It's local and bright (DB) (6)
86. Get your sick note for school lesson. (1/1)
87. Can you cut it? You need a spoon. (Y) (7)

88. *Noun to adjective roared the lions. (5)*
89. *Solve it with a monkey tree. (R) (6)*
90. *Bend it but not with Beckham (DB) (4)* ***(Not yet can you insert)***
91. *Iron out Rough to be electrically charged. (3)* ***(Not yet can you insert)***
92. *Abba did one about this and this and this. (2)*
93. *Hi to this girl at the holiday camp (5)* ***(Not yet can you insert)***
94. *Handicap's woman (3)* ***(Not yet can you insert)***
95. *This maker followers the meat man and bread man (Y) (11)* ***(insert 90/91/93/94 you may)***
96. *Insect compilation that shot to the top (Y) (8)*
97. *I and Tara went on ahead. (5)*
98. *US letter guys, government but not postal. (1/3)*
99. *Stella goes back after losing a note. (R) (4)*
100. *Sounds like you need a drink but place it instead. (O) (5)*
101. *A Known Injury initially sounds like renal trauma. (1/1/1)*
102. *German man posts silent letter by mistake. (3)*
103. *Serve it cold although you may be hot to give it (P) (7)*
104. *A Scottish insect travelled back in this (P) (4)*
105. *Plunder but German ready to fall. (4)*
106. *Shame on you for not completing task. (3)*
107. *Serious accident but ending to come out. (6)*
108. *New French cheese shows who sent it. (O) (4)*
109. *Initially, One More Ends means urban utterance. (1/1/1)*
110. *Is it afoot? (R) (4)*
111. *A pet goes wild due to tangled flare. (5)*
112. *A horror flick for Del Boy's baby. (4)*
113. *One hundredth of a dollar for acid, it's an emergency. (8)*
114. *Hot but not when on cake (Y) (6)*
115. *At the treble musically (4)*
116. *Do this to Bill but not Ben (DB) (4)*
117. *Whittle with sword to get this up (DB) (4)*
118. *Oh, what has little Faith lost? (2)*
119. *Threat without bible study leaves the thing. (4)*
120. *Soon the end will be. (DB) (4)*
121. *Was Mr Wallach in the bible? (3)*
122. *Trouble here but remove blemish to become expert. (O) (3)*
123. *If you fail make a rugby touchdown again. (DB) (3)*
124. *Your mission is to remove the atom to leave her alone. (Y) (4)* ***(Not yet can you insert)***
125. *Evil clown tagged so now he's this. (2)*
126. *Flap about at Christmas to get an F. (4)*
127. *That history included something. (Pu) (4)* ***(Insert 124 now you may)***
128. *Where has W gone to? (R) (4)* ***(Not yet can you insert)***
129. *Town, drink or bread? Or is it a facial thing? (3)*
130. *I need this to tango (P) (3)*

131. Not evening wear but suits as a place to loiter. (6) *(Not yet can you insert)*
132. This word sounds like a letter, over to who? (DB) (3) *(Not yet can you insert)*
133. Bad hair day for this member of the gang (G) (6)
134. The lowest form then you and you out. (DB) (2)
135. Dip them in but cut off half (Pu) (2)
136. School pudding, take off the head and time has passed. (P) (3) *(Not yet can you insert)*
137. Double this means average. (O) (2) *(Not yet can you insert)*
138. Go for this colour (Y) (5) *(Insert 128 now you may)*
139. It will be all this on the snowy night (Y) (5) *(Not yet can you insert)*
140. Custard flies (P) (5) *(Not yet can you insert)*
141. Sherlock did this in a sort of red. (Y) (5) *(Not yet can you insert)*
142. Definite thing (Pu) (3) *(Not yet can you insert)*
143. Be he North or South he was the main man. (4) *(Not yet can you insert)*
144. Cut head off Don to be right there. (2) *(Not yet can you insert)*
145. Vie but lose con to leave the task (DB) (4) *(Not yet can you insert)*
146. A plate you cannot eat off. That's the title of this clue. (4) *(Not yet can you insert)*
147. Digit fruit for a guy in the corner (Y) (4) *(Not yet can you insert)*
148. Map book does not fit to a tee, shame. (4)
149. Witches transport but let the buzzer tick down. (5) *(Not yet can you insert)*
150. Be possessive with top of a puzzle (R) (2) *(Not yet can you insert)*
151. A mischievous little car of yesteryear. (3) *(Not yet can you insert)*
152. Second half of Saturday morning kids show definitely existed (O) (3)
153. They are in the stream but exile these lands. (Pu) (2) *(Not yet can you insert)*
154. I see no African country but I did have it. (O) (3)
155. Jumping stick is po-faced so just leave (Pu) (2) *(Not yet can you insert)*
156. Same as 153. (2) *(Not yet can you insert)*
157. Instinctual desire to be known. (2) *(Not yet can you insert)*
158. More than one slaying at the same time. (7/3/5/4/3/5) *(Insert others now you may)*

"Let's just see if we can pencil any answers in against the clues," I suggested. "I've been doing this a while now, so I sort pf have a handle on this guy's mind set. Not all the time though."

"Okay," agreed Rich and Jenny nodded. "Looks like we need to solve fifty five to get to fifty two, *Liam kept losing his family*."

"Now, is it a real Liam or an anagram like mail or Lima," I said. "What Liams do you know?"

"Liam Gallagher," from Jenny.

"So, losing his family? Does that mean a falling out with Noel?" That was Rich.

"Don't know much on Oasis," I admitted but something had just occurred to me. "However, what about Liam Neeson?"

"Taken!" said Rich.

"Exactly. It makes sense. He lost his family three times. Write that one in. It is going to be an across clue after Velma but there are two spaces at the moment. We do have T and A in the second space but the other one is five columns long so it could go there too."

"Next," grinned Rich, as Jenny wrote this down next to the clue.

I cast my eye down the next few clues, but nothing jumped out of me until I got to number sixty. "Got sixty. The Mysterons were the enemy in *Captain Scarlet* and their agent on earth was Captain Black. If you lose the rank that would be 'black'.

"Fifty nine," said Jenny. "A vacuum is a void and to avoid is to escape. Four letters so it could be void."

"Good thinking, Jenny. Jot that one down too."

Nothing came to us for fifty six, seven and eight, but I had a bead on sixty one. "Use of the word 'initially' usually means use the initial letters of the following words. This is a three letter answer and that would be M R S or Mrs, which ties in with the Cluedo theme."

"Are we assuming that all the rooms, weapons and suspects are going to be answers?" asked Jenny.

"A fair assumption on what we know so far," I replied.

"Okay then first we can go down the list and pick out all the yellow clues left and work those out. There is a limited pool so we should be able to do that fairly easily."

"Sounds like a plan," agreed Rich.

Jenny being the expert was quick to calculate. "There are nine rooms, six suspects and six weapons so twenty one in total. So far we have six rooms, four suspects and three weapons, but you can see that some of these are split up. Where they are two words they must be separate clues. In total then more than twenty one. Let's just write down what is missing."

"Okay said Rich. Suspects we have Professor, Peacock, Reverend and Scarlet so we are missing Plum, Mrs, Green and Miss, plus White – assuming Mrs will not crop up twice - and Colonel Mustard."

"Right," agreed Jenny, writing them down on the back of the clue sheet. "Then on the rooms we have Room missing and if that does not crop up multiple times it might come up as Rooms. Also, kitchen, lounge and study."

I hadn't played Cluedo in years but didn't want to be left out. There were only six weapons. "Weapons. Let's see. We have spanner, dagger and lead so obviously missing piping. Then rope, revolver and er ... candlestick."

"Great," said Rich. "How many is that Jen?"

"Fifteen to find," she replied.

Off we went on a Cluedo hunt.

"Got one!" yelled Jenny. Rich and I looked at her. "Number 70. Part nut. In the army. Part of a nut is the kernel. In the army colonel. So, half of Colonel Mustard." She wrote it down.

"Got another," cried Rich. "Number 80. You can hang soap with this. Soap on a rope so Rope." This was written down too.

We were at it for a couple of hours, and we did get a fair number written down but surprisingly did not find all the Cluedo ones. Even though we had the yellow answers some of the clues were so obscure that we couldn't make them fit. We did in passing work out some of the other easy ones though. By the time we were ready to think about lunch we had the following possible answers:

55. Taken / 58. Make / 59. Void / 60. Black / 61. Mrs / 62. Ad / 63. Dead / 68. Kitchen / 69. N.N.E. / 70. Colonel / 71. We / 73. Master / 74. Reed / 78. Next / 80. Cry / 81. Rope / 83. P.R. / 87. Mustard / 88. Proud / 89. Puzzle / 91. Ion / 92. On / 93. Heidi / 95. Candlestick / 97. Tiara / 99. Let's / 112. Omen / 113. Accident / 115. Clef / 116. Kill / 118. Ye / 119. That / 121. Eli / 125. It / 131. Lounge / 132. You / 133. Shaggy / 138. Green / 139. White / 147. Plum / 155. Go

We had enough to be going on with, or rather I did, as I would be me trying to fit them into the frame. Rich and Jenny were going to give it a go themselves on their copy. I felt that I had taken up too much of their time already that day so when they invited me to lunch I gently declined. I crossed the corridor back to my cabin and debated with myself. Carry on whilst I was in the groove or go and get something to eat. My rumbling stomach won the argument.

Chapter 27

						C					K								D				C
(Grid shown above)

It was a close call on whether I got something to eat. This was the first time I had made any great headway in one session on this dratted puzzle and part of me wanted to keep at it. I needed a small break though and a trip up to the buffet for a quick bite did just that. I was back in the cabin in less than forty five minutes.

I had a list of clue answers now and I needed to try and fit them into the frame, or paper grid as it happened. They were not all consecutive answers but if I could get some in it might help me solve the blanks. There were forty one answers written down, although there was no guarantee that they were all correct.

I beavered away for some time and made some progress. Of the forty one answers I was able to fit in twelve and whilst doing this I came up with the answers for another seven. The frame now contained answers up to Clue 75 except for 56 and 57 which I could not get. The latter was particularly annoying because it was a yellow clue so should be a Cluedo term.

I was excited now that I was making real headway. I had almost half of the puzzle filled completed and I had more answers to fill in. I was a bit annoyed therefore when there was a knock at the door. I had a good mind to just shout out for whoever it was to go away but thought better of it. When I opened the door I found it was the erstwhile reporter again.

"Do you ever leave your cabin?" she asked, breezing in.

"I must do otherwise you would not have been able to follow me, would you?" I countered. "What brings you back?"

She sat on the bed without invitation. "Well, I have been doing a bit more investigating. Preparatory work you could call it."

"Okay. Have you found out something else?"

"No! But I have a theory."

"Shoot!" which I immediately regretted saying, the shooting incident still too recent a memory.

"Well, you have been sent this puzzle. And so has the police. Or at least a similar one. Now, in most circumstances where the police are goaded by a criminal it is usually a serial killer."

"Really? That truly happens?" I thought it a film and TV thing to make plots more intense.

"Certainly. In America they had the Zodiac Killer among others and even Jack the Ripper sent letters to the police."

"So, what are you saying? That I am being stalked by a serial killer?"

"I don't know. I am just hypothesising."

"Goading the police, I can sort of understand, but why would I be included."

"Maybe you're the next victim?"

"Charming. Any other good news?"

"No. That's it for now. Just thought I would let you know my thoughts." Then she was on her feet and heading to the door. Just before she went through it she had a word of warning, "Watch your back!"

Great! I had been feeling a bit more relaxed over the past couple of days but now I could feel myself going into paranoid mode again. Thanks a lot Vicky!

I tried to think about it logically and it made no sense. Why would a serial killer go to such lengths to torment his victims? Also. If it was a serial killer why had this modus operandi not been in the papers? That was another thing. Was he or she not more likely to send clues to the papers so they got published rather than to the police where they would be a closely guarded secret?

On the other hand, only one other person that we knew of had received the same puzzle and he had disappeared. No body had been found but that did not mean anything. Maybe Vicky was onto something after all. But then, how did this all tie in with Nathan who, I was now almost convinced, could be mixed up in this somewhere?

Whatever was the answer I could do nothing about it on the boat. I still figured I was safe here. No one had followed me or knew where I was.

The time to worry was when I had to go home. My concentration had been disturbed though so I could not get back into the puzzle. With more than a little annoyance at this I left the cabin to go for a wander round.

I was wandering around the ship, but I wasn't watching where I was going and only avoided a couple of head on collisions at the last second. Even though I was trying not to think about it, my mind would not let it go. From almost the beginning I had believed that someone had been messing about with me and then later I had been convinced that from some reason Nathan had been setting me up for something. But a serial killer? That was far more complicated and more dangerous for me. The logical part of my brain still said that this was not a likely scenario, but logic never overrides panic.

After a second round of apologies, I just sat down on an empty seat, to avoid any more near misses whilst my mind was elsewhere. I didn't stay there long though because it was the smoking side of the ship. It was almost 4 pm so I decided to go down to the bar and see what sort of quiz was on.

As it happened. Rich and Jenny were there sat at a small table near the front, opposite the small stage the hosts used. They were chatting so didn't see me approaching. "Hi guys!" I greeted them. "OK if I pull up a chair?" They were at a small round table with two chairs, but it was possible to get four around it, often done during the quizzes.

"Sure," said Rich, so I pulled a chair over from an empty table. The afternoon quizzes were not as crowded as the evening ones. With the hot weather passengers tried to get as much sun as possible before coming inside.

"We are glad to bump into you," said Jenny.

"We have made some further progress," added Rich, grinning.

"Great! What did you find?" I was getting excited that the possibility of having the puzzle solved before I got off the boat was becoming more and more feasible.

"The notes are in the cabin," said Rich. "We can let you have them later. We think we have all the yellow clues now." That meant all the Cluedo answers.

"Yes," agreed Jenny, "and we realised that we made a mistake earlier. There was one person who we forgot about, because it is someone that never really takes a part in the game." I must have looked puzzled because she continued, "Doctor Black, the victim. His body is found in the cellar which is the whole scenario for the game itself."

"That makes sense," I said. "We had Black already and I got Doctor later when I was trying to get the answers we had into the frame. But cellar? Is that another of the answers?"

"Yes!" exclaimed Jenny. "What clue number was it Rich?"

"Can't recall offhand but it was the salty salesman one?"

"Oh, that one! Clue 57. That one has been bugging me," I declared. "How did you get it?"

"Well, it was the last one we got actually," Rich informed me. "We had done all the other yellow clues and realised we had Doctor Black, so we assumed it was cellar and then worked it backwards. Salty salesman. A salesman is a seller."

"And then you have a salt cellar," Jenny contributed. "Then below means down below. Cellar!"

"Great! That one was giving me some problems. Are you having fun helping me crack it? Do you want to do some more later?"

"Can't tonight," advised Rich. "Captain's Dinner. We are getting dressed up, then off to a show. What I will do though is stick what we have in your door slot when we go to get changed and you can work on that for now."

"There is mistake though," Jenny pointed out. "We think it might be deliberate."

"How do you mean?" I was intrigued. The Puzzler had made a mistake.

"Reverend is spelt with an E at the end and not an A. It is A in the puzzle, but we think it is deliberate because of two things. Firstly, the word Reverand with an A is in the actual clue question. Secondly, because without the A you cannot get in Scarlet which is the word that comes down through it."

"Okay. I will have a look at that. Seems odd though that he would go to all these lengths to get something so complicated and then make a silly mistake." Silly mistake that I had not noticed.

"That is why we think it is deliberate," said Rich.

We got not further because the host declared we were about to start and to get pencils and answer sheets from the front. I did the honours. It was just a general knowledge quiz this time and not themed. We didn't do too badly and got sixteen out of the twenty. We only came third though. It was about half past four by then.

"Got to go and get ready in a minute," declared Rich, looking at Jenny who nodded. "We'll put the notes in your slot before we go to dinner. We did get a couple more than just the Cluedo ones by the way. There was one I was pleased I got."

"Which was?" I prompted.

"What was it now?" He thought for a second. "A Scottish insect goes back in this." Pause for effect. "Scottish insect. McFly. So, the answer is time."

"Rich is very much into any sort of time travel," Jenny said.

"Bet you're a big *Back to the Future* fan then?"

They both grinned at that. "Rich had never seen that film until he met me," explained Jenny.

"Really!" That was surprising. It was the time travel epitome.

"No," confirmed Rich. "It was Jenny who introduced me to it."

"I love it myself," I told them. "Some of the best films were made in the 80's. *Back to the Future, Raiders of the Lost Ark, Beverley Hills Cop, Police Academy.*" The last one got a groan from both.

"On that note, we'll be off," said Rich.

He and Jenny got up and went to get dressed up for dinner. This was one of the two nights when most passengers would be in black tie and evening dresses. The thing one had to remember on such nights was that if you were not taking part in such finery then you were not allowed in certain parts of the ship. In the atrium, which was the central part of the ship where reception was on Deck 6 and the decks below, and at any of the main restaurants. Not that worried me too much. I was having dinner in the cabin and could do a bit more work on the puzzle. I did find out though by asking one of the hosts, that it was permitted to join the quiz at 8 pm in the bar without being in fancy dress, subject to the usual evening dress code of course. I might try that if I got too cabin crazy.

It was just gone 5 pm and my dinner would not arrive for about two hours so that gave me a good bit of time to work on the puzzle. True to their word, there was a sheet in my cabin slot from Rich and Jenny. It was not the clue sheet because obviously they had kept that for further puzzling, so it was just a page of lined paper with their guesses written down.

57. Cellar
64. Doctor
85. Colour
86. P.E.
96. Revolver
102. Err
104. Time
114. Piping
124. Miss
129. Rye?
136. Ago

140. Birds
141. Study
149. Rooms
158. Killing Two Birds With One Stone

    Okay, I thought, we now have all the yellow clues. All the Cluedo references. And a few more to the list I already had. A lot of the Cluedo ones were already in and I could not insert some of the others yet because they were further on than I had managed to get. However, 'cellar' had been the one I was missing before and that one could go in straight away.

    The next couple of hours passed swiftly as I was engrossed in what I was doing. I took a couple of chances, jumping ahead if I thought I could fit something in. Such as inserting 'Candlestick' which was Clue 95 and meaning I had to insert nineteen words in between that and Clue 75 'Daphne' which is where I had left off. I managed to fit in nine.

    Times flies when you were having fun they say. I didn't think I was having fun, but I was achieving something, and time had flown. There was a tap at the door. I looked at my watch, 7.04, so that would mean my meal was outside. I got up and realised for the first time that I could feel the rolling of the ship a bit. We were still in warm weather or were last time I had been able to see out, but the swell must have picked up. The movement was not pronounced but it did feel a bit weird. No matter. I opened the door and retrieved the tray. Today's culinary delight was chicken and sautéed potatoes followed by jelly and cream. Yes jelly. I couldn't resist when I saw it as an option on the menu. Lime. Not the best but enough to take me back to being a kid.

    Wait! Was that a memory? I tried hard to bring it back, but it was not there. I was confused and annoyed. That was the first time anything had triggered something in the subconscious. I had given up all hope of getting my memory back after all this time. I focused hard but there was nothing there. What was that then? Just someone recalling they used to like jelly as a kid. Just a feeling not a recallable memory.

    For all that I was still disturbed by what was an infinitesimal shift in my mind. The mood was broken again, so after eating I got changed into normal evening attire and went down to the bar for the quiz.

Chapter 28

That evening's quiz should have been right up my street – it was on TV themes. I was in the bar only about ten minutes before the start, but I was able to get a small table to myself at the front. I guessed a lot of people were hobnobbing with the captain. However, a steady stream of people entered until the start time, and they were all making me very self-conscious. I felt like a sparrow in a waddle of penguins. All the men were dressed in their Bond tuxedos and the women in mostly full length evening dresses. A couple of them came to sit at my table.

"Hi," greeted Jenny, as she sat in the chair Rich pulled out for her. Rich was dressed as most of the other guys and Jenny wore a green dress.

"Hi guys," I responded in surprise. "I thought you could not get here tonight."

"Well, we finished dinner, and the show isn't until 9 so we thought why not," said Rich sitting down himself.

"Glad you're here." As they sat down I got up, but only to go over and collect an answer sheet and pencil. "TV themes," I informed them as I sat back down. "Any good for you?"

"Depends what it is," said Rich.

A passing waitress asked if they wanted drinks. Rich looked at Jenny and somehow knew the answer. "No thanks," he told her.

I had noticed that before. They had a sort of silent telepathy at times. You could tell how much they loved each other by the little touches and glances. Something I felt I would never have again myself.

I was expecting to do well at TV themes, but I got a nasty surprise because half of them I didn't know. Jenny and Rich were doing better because they got things like *The Apprentice* which I would not have got in a million years. I only watch escapism on TV i.e. stories by writers, acted out by actors. I only got the older ones and there were not that many. No 'The Professionals' or 'Dempsey and Makepeace'. The kicker though was one tune right near the end. I knew it. I knew I knew it, and knew it well, but it would not come to me. I didn't get it until we had handed the papers to a neighbouring table to check, getting theirs in return. There was a massive irony here. The tune was the 80's quiz show *Telly Addicts* with Noel Edmunds. I watched it every week and I gave rather a large groan of annoyance when it was confirmed a bit later.

The fact is though, and I put it down to this, I wasn't feeling well. Whatever it was, it had crept up on me gradually, but I felt quite queasy by the time the quiz ended. We were not in the top five this time. Something must have been showing in my face too because as they got up to leave

Jenny looked at me with some concern. "Are you alright Danny? You seem a bit pale."

"To tell you the truth I feel a bit queer. It came on me quite suddenly."

"Might be seasickness," observed Rich. "Jen gets it quite badly sometimes."

"Why would it happen now though? I have been on the ship for four days."

"Who can say? It can happen at any time I think. Maybe there is more movement in the ship."

I remembered thinking that before. "Funny you should say that. In my cabin earlier I was feeling that a bit."

"Could be that then."

"I think I'd better go and lie down." I got up too, staggered and almost lost my balance. I felt an idiot. People were staring at me from other tables. "I'm alright!"

"You sure?" asked Rich.

"Yes fine. I'll just go back to the cabin. Enjoy the show." With reluctance they turned to go but I remembered I had something to tell them. "Oh! I've got a bit further with our project. I don't think I will be doing any more on it tonight. I will leave the grid in your slot. You can copy it down on yours and then let me have it back."

"Okay," said Rich.

"Hope you feel better soon," added Jenny.

I made my way slowly back to the cabin. I had been using the stairs mostly to get anywhere in the ship. For exercise and also so as not to be in a confined space with a possible killer – short though the odds were on that. This time though I went straight for the call button. The lift was empty, and I didn't see anyone on the trip back to the cabin.

I tried to evaluate my symptoms to see if I needed to call for the ship's doctor. In the main I just felt sick and a bit sweaty. I had no headache and although for that one moment downstairs I had been lightheaded that was gone. I just felt that I should go to bed and see how I was in the morning. I just took off my outer clothing and got straight into bed which may have been a mistake. I hardly noticed it before but now I could feel the rocking of the ship constantly, as though every wave we hit vibrated through the cabin. It made me feel worse, but I didn't want to move either.

I couldn't get to sleep and after about an hour I did move, rather rapidly, and just got to the bathroom before I was violently sick. Weirdly after that I felt slightly better. I still had trouble sleeping but the movement was not causing me as much grief. When I eventually dropped off I had this rather vivid nightmare. Well, I say vivid but that is probably not quite accurate. None of my dreams tend to be that. If I can remember anything at all when I wake up it is just vague images of people or things that were said. There was no logical start or beginning and places or events just mixed up in my brain. One moment I could be outside and the next moment I could be inside but standing by a car talking to someone. Nothing ever made sense.

This time was different. I was there but I was also watching me too. There were two of me. I was following myself around for a while and saw myself doing rather nasty things. I threw a bike through a shop window and stole some jewellery. I then pushed a man into the street who got hit by a car. In the dream I was in shock seeing myself do such things. I kept thinking to myself, what are you doing? You are going to prison.

Suddenly we were being chased by the police. I could see my other self running with the policeman behind him, but I was also running myself because I was out of breath. The other me ran into a building and suddenly that building was on fire. The policeman had disappeared, so it was up to me to try and get into save him, or was it me? The door was locked, and I could not break it down. As I banged on the door suddenly my hands were on fire and I screamed.

I woke up sweating and thrashing about in bed. Then I realised where I was. I was actually shaking, and it took a few minutes for me to calm down and persuade myself that it was only a dream. I tried to think about it, what it meant, but I must have dropped off to sleep again because when I awoke again it was daytime. Not that I could tell because no light filtered into my room, and I still needed to put the lights on. My watch though said 8.24 am and I could hear conversation and people walking by outside in the corridor.

The queasiness had gone but I felt listless and weak. I didn't realise how weak until I got up to go to the bathroom. It took me a while to get there, and I had to hold onto various surfaces to aid me. My legs and arms felt so heavy. The bathroom stunk of sick, probably because it was still in the toilet which I hadn't flushed. I did the necessary then washed my hands and threw some cold water on my face. It didn't do much good. All I wanted to do was get back in bed, so I did.

We were supposed to be in Brussels that day and I guessed we had already docked as I knew some of the trips were due to leave at 9 am. Not that it concerned me. I was not booked on anything and could stay in the cabin all day if I needed to. I must have dozed off because I awoke to a banging on the door. I looked at my watch, it was gone 10 am now.

"Mr Andrews! Are you alright, Sir?" came a voice through the door.

I managed to get there and open it a peep. It was one of the stewards.

"Ah! Are you alright, Sir? Your breakfast tray was still there so I was a bit worried."

"Yes. I'm fine." A little white lie. "Just a bit under the weather."

"Do you need the doctor?" he asked with concern.

"No, I'm okay," I assured him. "The worst of it was last night. Just a bit weak and tired."

"Do you want me to get you some more breakfast? This is all cold now."

Just the thought of food made me feel queasy again but what I did need was strong coffee. "No food but I could do with some coffee." I could make some in the cabin from the sachets, but it was not as good as that from the kitchen I had found.

"Right away, Sir."

He went on his way. I couldn't tell you what his nationality was but like all the staff on the ship he was not originally from the UK. I had wondered about that. It was strange to me. Only the hosts were British, and we seemed to have the full collection there – Scots, Welsh and Irish. The officers of the ship I had never spoken to but certainly all the lower ranks were foreign.

I was back in bed but had not fallen asleep again when there was a tap on the door. Just so he knew I was still alive I made my way to the door to take the coffee in. There was a pot of coffee and one cup and saucer plus sugar and a milk jug. I quickly made myself a cup. Not quite black but just a drop of milk and two sugars to try and kick-start my brain. I sat in bed sipping it slowly.

As I sat there, I remembered the dream and wondered what all that was about. There had been two of me. It was like I had been split in two. There was the normal me watching and then a really vile version of me doing nasty things but then getting burned to death in a fire. What did it all signify? Did it signify anything? It was odd though that this had occurred the same night as I had had that déjà vu feeling with the jelly. Maybe my subconscious was trying to break through the amnesia after all. I was not sure I wanted it to succeed.

What would happen if I suddenly got my memories back? Would I be a different person? Had a been a bad person? Would I revert to being a bad person? All in all, I figured it was better to stay as I was, even though I was in a bit of trouble right now. In fact, was the trouble related to my past? Maybe that was it? Maybe this puzzle had something to do with the past and because I had no memory I could not work out the significance. Wait though! If it was something to do with my past then it had caught up with me because that would mean the person behind the puzzle knew more than I did.

Or was it like Vicky had said, just a serial killer getting his kicks? But then why me and the police? The only reason could be if I was in fact an intended victim. A serial bad guy with no memory but whose past is back to haunt him or the next victim of a sadistic serial killer. What a prospect. It was too much to think about. I poured myself another cup of coffee and thought about what I didn't want to think about.

It all came back to the puzzle, solve that and hopefully it would give me some answers. Or would it? Was I meant to solve it? Were the police meant to solve it? No! The detective who had been sent it had disappeared. If I hadn't scarpered maybe I would have disappeared too.

The serial killer angle did have some traction though. The puzzle was heavy with Cluedo clues. Six suspects and six weapons. What if the suspects were victims? Could that mean that there were six dead people already. That was a bit hard to swallow. Yes, I could conceivably believe a serial killer could have taken six victims and wants to goad the police but why involve me? Did I know the six people? The Cluedo character names could only be like pseudonyms then. There could be no real Colonel Mustard. It might be possible to find a Green, White and Peacock. Scarlet possibly – it was used more as a first name these days – i.e. Miss Scarlet as in *Gone with the Wind* but again Professor Plum would be difficult.

Suddenly I was stricken with the most horrendous feeling. The thought process of naming the Cluedo characters had them running around my head until I got to Mrs White. As I had said, the killer could not have got victims with exactly those names, but he would get as close as he could. I knew someone close to one of those names. Mrs Andrews-White. My god! Was I dealing with Laura's killer?

The coffee cup fell from my hand onto the bed and rolled onto the floor, but I did not notice. Anger was building up inside me and the listlessness and weakness disappeared as trees before a lava flow from a volcanic eruption. I had to solve that damn puzzle! I was going to find out who was doing this to me, and if it was the person who had killed my Laura then they were going to die.

Chapter 29

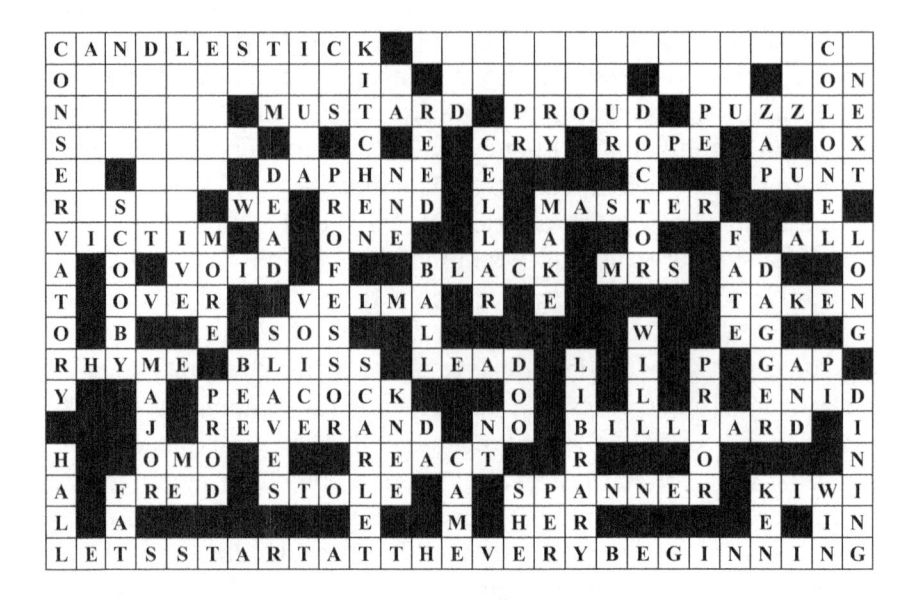

C	A	N	D	L	E	S	T	I	C	K															C	
O										I															O	N
N					M	U	S	T	A	R	D		P	R	O	U	D		P	U	Z	Z	L	E
S							C		E		C	R	Y		R	O	P	E		A		O	X
E				D	A	P	H	N	E		E				C					P	U	N	T
R		S		W	E		R	E	N	D		L		M	A	S	T	E	R			E	
V	I	C	T	I	M		A		O	N	E		L		A			O		F		A	L	L
A		O		V	O	I	D		F			B	L	A	C	K		M	R	S		A	D		O
T		O	V	E	R			V	E	L	M	A		R		E				T	A	K	E	N
O		B		E		S	O	S		L				W		E	G						G
R	H	Y	M	E		B	L	I	S	S		L	E	A	D		L		I		P		G	A	P
Y		A		P	E	A	C	O	C	K			O		I		L		R		E	N	I	D
		J		R	E	V	E	R	A	N	D		N	O		B	I	L	L	I	A	R	D		I
H				O	M	O		E		R	E	A	C	T		R				O					N
A		F	R	E	D		S	T	O	L	E		A		S	P	A	N	N	E	R		K	I	W	I
L		A								E			M		H	E	R					E		I	N
L	E	T	S	S	T	A	R	T	A	T	T	H	E	V	E	R	Y	B	E	G	I	N	N	I	N	G

Hope you are feeling better. If not you could try one of Jenny's seasickness pills (enclosed). We are off into Brussels on a chocolate making tour. No doubt see you later. Rich and Jenny.

That was the note they left in my slot with my grid back. I was glad that they had returned it. My blood was boiling, and I was itching to get back to it. I didn't want to leave the cabin, so I ordered a sandwich to be delivered to the room via the steward. Yep, I was hungry now.

Now where had I got up to? There was a bit of a gap on the left hand side of the puzzle. I had been working on Row 14 because at the beginning of that row I had worked out was Clue 79 and going down from that was Clue 56 for which I already had the last three letters – IVE. Going back to the colour scheme and using my phone for this, I found that 79 was 'start' and 56 'thrive'. That got me going and I ploughed on, managing to get all clues in up to 'mustard' Clue 87 on Row 15. Appropriate as it happened as my sandwich arrived with a knock at the door at that precise moment. What I didn't want was mustard on the sandwich, but there was little chance of that as it was cheese and pickle. I wolfed it down without realising it, I was so engrossed now in what I was doing.

I managed another five words, so now I was up to 'candlestick' and well over halfway. The grid was twenty seven squares by twenty seven so Row 14 was halfway.

I was still angry and visibly shaking. Who would kill Laura and then taunt me with it? That suggested someone I knew otherwise what would they get out of it? That brought me back to Nathan and the chagrin I felt about being hoodwinked for so long. Nothing was definite though, just a lot of conjecture. I had decided on one thing. No more running. When the trip was over I was going back to the flat. Let him come, it could be she but somehow I felt it was a man at work here. A totally diabolical person, whoever it was, but let them come for me. I was going to be ready and waiting, wanting a confrontation now.

This new train of thought made me feel I was actually safer than in Vicky's theory. Here, I was not the actual next victim, I had already been made a victim and was being played with. If I had a personal connection with the killer, so much so that he got a kick out of making me his plaything, then did that mean that the policeman was too? Or was he just the figure of law and order that the killer was also stringing along? If he had not been missing, maybe we could have joined forces. But he was missing, and no body had turned up so he could still be alive. If so, was he being held captive? Was I supposed to be a captive too? Had I spoiled the plans by running away?

Lots of questions but no way to get the answers … yet. One thing I did decide though was to put everyone in the picture. There were three people caught up in this now. Two just in the outermost strands of the web and one trying to work her way into the centre. I felt a council of war was called for. Rich and Jenny needed to be put into the picture. I didn't feel they were in any danger. All they had been doing was helping me with the clues. The P.C. that had been helping the missing inspector had not been harmed.

I put the tray with the plate and the earlier coffee things outside the door. I wanted to get right back to the puzzle, but I noticed I was starting with a bit of a headache. I decided to take a walk around the deck to clear my head. We were in port, so Deck 15 was not as crowded as usual. It was a fine, hot day, as all the days had been so far. There were some people sunbathing on the loungers around the outdoor pool. The shuffleboard and quoits courts were both empty. I found I was still hungry – maybe this was the fresh air after the stuffiness of the cabin. On that deck around the corner from the pool was the ice cream kiosk I had tried before but right next door was a pizza kiosk. They were making pizzas all day and you could just take a slice or two from those displayed. I did and got an ice cream too.

I sat at one of the tables to eat. As usual as soon as I sat down a waitress came around to ask if I wanted a drink. I declined this time. I was just finishing up when I noticed that on one of the loungers by the pool was

Vicky. She looked hot in her white bikini and I wondered how many times she had been hit on by guys who she would have turned down. Did I want to disturb her? I didn't want a long question and answer session but then I did need to know if she had anything more for me. I made my way over.

As I came out into the sun from the shade I had to cover my eyes to see her. She had sunglasses on so I couldn't tell if she was awake or not.

"Hello Vicky!"

"Hi," she replied without moving.

"I just saw you here and wondered if you had found out anything more?"

"No, nothing else to report. I am just enjoying what is left of the cruise."

"Fair enough," I said. "What size is your cabin?"

She sat up at that question, and took off her glasses to look at me. "What sort of question is that? You know I am not into you?"

"No… it's nothing like that," I laughed. "It's just, I've decided to call a meeting and I wondered if your cabin was bigger than mine."

"No way. It is smaller than yours. I am in a single cabin. There is a corridor of these that run along aside the casino. Just room for a bed and a chair. How many in this meeting?"

"Four. You, me, Rich and Jenny."

"Who are Rich and Jenny?" Vicky had picked up her bag that had been by the side of the lounger and was scrabbling inside it, presumably for her notebook.

"Don't bother. They are just new friends who have been helping me solve the clues. You will meet them later."

"Okay. What's the meeting about?"

"So everyone is in the picture. They don't know the background to this, and I think they need to, just in case. Also, there is now possibly something personal going on."

"What?" she asked, her reporter instincts kicking in.

"I will let you all know later."

I took her cabin number so I could drop a note off about time and venue once I had agreed this with Rich and Jenny, then it was back to my own cabin to carry on with my work on the puzzle. I wondered what time Rich and Jenny would be back. Usually, the excursions were back well before evening meal. The first sitting started at 6 pm. It was just gone 3 pm now. I guessed I could try their cabin in a couple of hours.

In fact, I never did get any further on the puzzle that afternoon because when back in my cabin I dozed off, probably due to the bad night I had the night before. I had been out for a couple of hours, and it had gone

5.30 when I awoke. I tried Rich and Jenny's cabin but there was no reply. I then went back to mine to shower and get into evening attire. I had not booked any dinner in the cabin, so I had to go out to eat. I still had not been into the restaurant where I had been allocated a table. I would then be sat at a table with up to seven strangers. I wasn't in the mood for that, so it was back up to the buffet. It did occur to me that other than my cabin, and the bar where the quizzes were, I spent all my other time on that deck. Maybe I would book a cabin on that deck next time, save all the stairs. Little did I know that it was good to be getting all that exercise now as soon I would not be having the chance.

Chapter 30

[Crossword grid]

    The council of war did not take place until the next day. Thursday. The last sea day. We were due to have a day in Guernsey on the Friday and then would be back in Southampton on Saturday morning. Initially Rich and Jenny were surprised at my request for a private meeting, but they had agreed and as they had the biggest cabin, that is where the four of us met. It was around ten thirty and we had all breakfasted but not together. The time had been agreed the night before when I had caught up with Jenny and Rich at the evening quiz. I had then left a note in Vicky's slot outside her door.

    Jenny and Rich sat on the bed while Vicky and I sat on the chairs from the balcony which we had moved so we were all inside the room. After I had made the introductions, I went first because Rich and Jenny did not know the whole picture. I went through the whole thing from the delivery of the puzzle, the Tiffany case, the shooting, my suspicions of Nathan and how I had run away and hid out before joining the cruise. Then Vicky told them what she had found out about the missing policeman. I had left one bit out though because even Vicky was not in on that yet.

    It was difficult to tell from their expressions what they were thinking when we had finished. They could have been of the mind that they were dealing with a mad man, and who would have blamed them.

"So, you were sent the puzzle by an anonymous person who you think is playing games with you and may be a person you have known for five years, except that you don't know him very well at all? You have been shot at and a police inspector, who has also received a puzzle in the post has gone missing? And you are on this boat hiding from whoever is after you?" Rich summed it up rather succinctly.

"That's about the size of it," I acknowledged. "Obviously I didn't really know how far reaching this had gotten until Vicky told me what she had found out. I thought it was just someone after me. The shooting, I was told by the police, was someone trying to scare me and not harm me, so I was sure I wasn't putting you two in any danger. With what I know now though, I think you need to know the truth."

Rich and Jenny looked at each other and a silent message seemed to be passing from one to the other. Vicky was looking at me in a puzzled fashion. Maybe she had noticed I had said "need" rather than "needed", meaning there was more to disclose.

"There is something we saw yesterday when we were getting back onto the ship," Rich announced. "We thought it odd at the time but didn't think to mention it."

"What?" I was intrigued and not a little apprehensive.

"When we were walking through the terminal there was a man who was shouting at the officials," Jenny told us.

"Some Custom types seemed to be escorting him out of the terminal against his wishes," added Rich. "We asked one of the ship's crew in passing. He had tried to sneak on board with other passengers, but he had no cruise card. Apparently he was there as a surprise for a passenger."

That could have meant anything and need not relate to my troubles but a paranoid mind latches onto anything, so obviously I thought he was after me.

"They've found me!" I wasn't exactly paralysed with fear, but I felt that a visit to the toilet would be necessary in the very near future.

Nothing was said for a few seconds, then Vicky piped up. "There's nothing to worry about. He didn't get on the ship even if he was after you."

"No, but that means there will now be someone waiting at Southampton. Maybe even Guernsey."

"Well, if they try to get on in Guernsey, they will have no better luck than here," she pointed out sensibly. "And at Southampton we will just have to make some plans won't we?"

"And is it likely that guy was here for you?" asked Jenny. "There are three thousand passengers aboard the ship."

It was possible I had to admit. Even probable. It did not detract from the fact though, that stranger things had happened to me in the past month. Better to be safe than sorry although there was nothing to be done right then. At least if that guy had been after me, it meant that there was currently no one on board in the ranks of the ungodly. Time to get back to the matter in hand.

"Okay, we'll forget about that guy for the moment," I said. "I have one more thing to reveal. A realisation I came to yesterday and one if it is true makes this very personal for me." I looked around and saw that I had their undivided attention, but I couldn't begin. I was instantly struggling with two overriding emotions – grief and anger. I was desperately trying not to let any tears flow, but I could feel them coming. Two emotions, both negative, but one got you nothing except maybe sympathy, the other got you going. I angrily wiped my eyes and glanced again at the surrounding faces, which now showed surprise rather than expectation.

I tried to get back to the logic of my thoughts. "If Vicky is correct and this is a serial killer we are dealing with, then the Cluedo aspect could sort of make sense. Instead of six suspects we may have six victims." No one contradicted me so I went on. "Now, it is very unlikely that the killer would have been able to find people with exact matching names to the Cluedo characters." I got some nods on this. "Colonel Mustard would be a definite no and Scarlet is more of a first name these days. Therefore, he may have gone for as near as possible. If I am right, and in some ways I hope that I'm not, I could be connected to one of the victims."

Jenny gasped and Vicky's mouth dropped open. Rich inched closer to Jenny and put his arm around her, a thoughtful look on his face.

"Five years ago, a woman was knifed in the hallway of her house. She was called Laura Andrews-White." There was a blank look on the faces, and I remembered that they did not know my surname which had never come up. "I am Danny Andrews but when I was married my surname was Andrews-White. Laura was my wife."

This last statement was met with absolute silence. No one knew what to say. I decided to excuse myself for two reasons. One, I was still holding back the tears. Two, to give the others the chance to talk it over.

"Is it Ok if I use your bathroom?" I managed to croak.

"Sure," said Rich, and I quickly headed for the door off the bedroom, locking it behind me.

I sat on the turned down toilet seat for a while, tears rolling down my face. I thought I had gotten over the real heart wrenching grief of Laura's death but maybe not. Or maybe it was just the digging it all up again with the probability it was tied up with something else. By the time I had composed myself and washed my face, it must have been fifteen minutes later. I made a lot of noise unbolting the door, so they knew I was coming back into the room.

As I took my seat again Jenny said, "We can't imagine what you have been through, but we are happy to help if we can."

"Anything we can do," added Rich.

"Thanks," I mumbled. "I don't want to get you two into any trouble though."

"Hey! What about me?" asked Vicky.

"Oh! Well, you wormed your way into this for a story so you're on your own." I tried to smile but my heart wasn't in it.

"I don't think we have anything to worry about," Rich informed me. "No one knows us or that you have confided in us. We're just helping you out on a puzzle problem."

"Right!" It was time for the anger to kick back in and the adrenaline flowing. "And I have made a bit more headway. Have a look." I took out a folded bit of paper from my pocket and spread it out. "I still have not been able to fit in all the answers to the clues we have solved but we are over halfway now."

I showed it to Vicky who was new to this and had only seen the photos of the frame and blocks on my phone. She took a photo of it with her phone. Then I passed it over to Rich and Jenny who had been instrumental in the progress so far.

"It's all fitting together rather nicely," observed Rich.

"So where are we up to in the numbers?" asked Jenny.

I looked at the clue sheet, glad to get my mind back on solving the puzzle rather than lamenting on past tragic events. "Candlestick was Clue 95. That suggests that 96 is the next clue across and you two have solved that one. It was on the list you did when you managed to get all the yellow clues. Revolver. And we can easily see where that fits in."

There were four heads on it now. Vicky brought new eyes and came up with a few answers that had stumped us. We made some progress but still by the time we called lunch we only had six answers in the grid and a couple of extra clues solved.

We all went our separate ways. Rich and Jenny went off to go up to Deck 15, to have a walk around and get something to eat at the buffet. I felt like I wanted something from there myself, but I felt they needed a break from my company. Vicky was off like a shot because she said she had something to check out. I popped into my cabin for a bit and then something hit me like a brick wall. The adrenalin boost from the anger, which had aided my recovery from feeling ill, seemed suddenly to evaporate and I began to feel queasy again. I quickly lay on the bed and hoped it was going to pass. It didn't pass quickly, and it was getting on towards evening before I felt any better, having this time taken Jenny's pill. We never got back to the puzzle that day.

Chapter 31

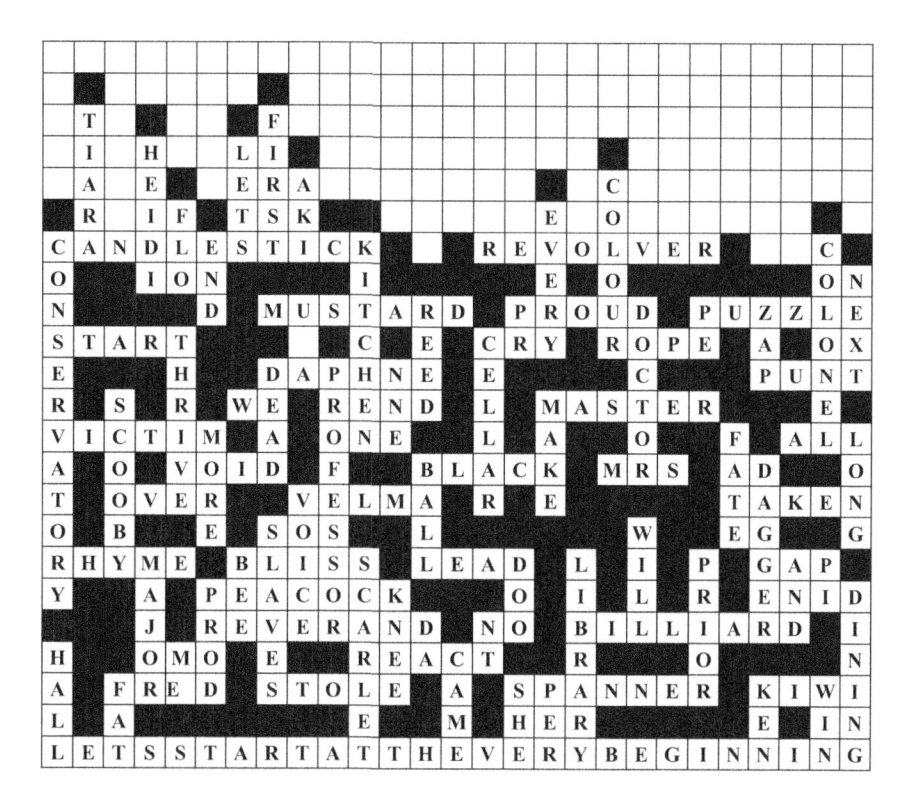

[Crossword puzzle grid]

It was late when I got up the next day, gone nine o'clock. Ever since that first recognition of the rocking ship when I first started feeling ill, I could not stop feeling it when I was in my cabin. Far from rocking me to sleep it kept me awake for long periods. The queasiness had gone though, for the time being.

It was Friday, the last day of the cruise because we docked in Southampton the next morning. Today, we were in Guernsey and, not that it mattered to me, this was different than the other ports. There was no docking and the ship had to moor offshore and passengers had to get to land via the ships' tenders. I hadn't booked anything so had no need to go ashore. Jenny and Rich had, and Vicky was going to take a trip ashore too.

We had discussed this briefly the night before. After I had spent the whole afternoon in the cabin under the weather, I had made a bit of recovery by evening. I had a bite to eat and we all met up for a quiz. I had decided that as it was the last day and it being a port day, only I would be wasting time on the puzzle. No one argued with me, so I think it was unanimous. I did get a little bit of assist though because Vicky had been using the library computer again and she had looked up the two words that had stumped us. The answer to Clue 101 A.K.I. stood for acute kidney injury and Clue 105 was Reif – meaning plunder or booty, but also meaning ripe in German.

I guessed the others were ashore already as the tenders started about 8 am. I didn't feel like breakfast, but I did feel like I needed a strong coffee, so I headed down to the coffee place on Deck 5. There were more people around that I expected. I didn't get it at first. I took my coffee to a single table where I could see out of the window. I wasn't especially surprised to see the sea and assumed the land to be on the other side of the ship. I then noticed that we were moving which did surprise me, but that then explained more people being around.

I remembered what I had heard a couple of passengers saying – not that I was eavesdropping at the time. Apparently, if the weather conditions were not totally mild then the tenders did not get sent out. If the swell was too high no one got into Guernsey. That must have been the case that day because just then on the tannoy the captain apologised for not being able to stay in Guernsey and that we were having an extra sea day before home.

I wondered what the others were up to then. I wasn't going to chase them down. Let them enjoy their last day as they saw fit. I had taken up too much of Rich and Jenny's time already. I wondered what I could do today. I hadn't had a look at the programme in my room but it was probably changed now anyway due to it being a sea day. More activities would have to be slotted in.

I didn't feel like wandering around the ship just then so after I had finished my coffee I went back to the cabin. I decided I would just have one more go at the puzzle and try to tidy up what we had started the day before, then after lunch I would just try and enjoy the rest of that last day. When next would I have time to rest, relax and enjoy myself after that? Life could get pretty hectic once I got home. Or maybe not? I had a sneaking feeling I had blown things up out of all proportion whilst on board that ship, far away from reality. Or was that just because I was now running scared? The anger of the day before seemed to have absconded. Courage overboard!

Back in the cabin, I got out the sheets of paper and tried to collect my thoughts on yesterday. Now where had we got to? I remembered the last thing was Vicky coming up with two answers. What were they? I had written them down surely. I looked at the clue sheets and sure enough there they were - 103 'revenge' and 107 'emerge'.

I managed to fit in eleven more words, a couple of which we didn't have written down but I managed to solve, when there was a knock on the door, which startled me because I had not realised how engrossed I was in what I was doing. When I opened it all my three new friends were there.

"Fancy a game of shuffleboard," asked Rich. "There is a competition on in just over an hour. Just time to get something to eat." Jenny and Vicky seemed keen, so I agreed. The puzzle could wait because now I could see the light at the end of the tunnel. It was not so vital I got it finished before I got off the boat because I now knew it was doable.

We got something to eat at the buffet and then headed towards shuffleboard. It was still a bright blue sky, but it was a lot breezier than earlier in the week. This time there were enough entrants for the competition. Obviously enough, it was a pairs game, so Rich and Jenny were together and Vicky and I. There were eight of us in total. Best of three ends then the winners met in the final. Vicky had not played before and with my lack of expertise too, we were out quickly. Rich and Jenny got to the final on the back of Jenny's uncanny knack at the game. They lost out though after a hard fought battle to a couple who were die hard cruisers and had probably played hundreds of times.

As it happened, just on the other side of the ship, there was a quoits competition just as the shuffleboard finished so we entered that too, with a similar result. Vicky and myself out first round and Rich and Jenny losing in the final.

Both games together only lasted about a couple of hours, so it was about three o'clock when we finished. There was a quiz in the bar at four, so we grabbed a table and despite the breeze all had ice cream from the kiosk.

That final day went the quickest of the lot for me because I was with other people and not spending it on my own. After the quiz, where we came second, everyone went to get dressed for dinner. We couldn't eat together because of allocated seating in the dining rooms. I had not once taken my allocated seat and the last night was not the time to get acquainted with new people, so it was back up to the buffet for me.

That evening Rich and Jenny were off to see a final show and Vicky said she had things to do but we all agreed to meet up at 10 pm to do the final round of the Continuous Quiz. We could be one team of four unless anyone wanted to join us. After eating I was at a loss at what to do. As usual there was an 8 pm quiz but I didn't feel like doing that on my own. There was though a show on about the life of Glenn Miller, I liked a bit of his music and had seen *The Glenn Miller Story* with James Stewart. I decided that was the thing I was 'In the Mood' for and went off to see it. It wasn't bad as it happened. One of the ship's hosts narrated his story and a band was on stage to play many of the hits. It was a good a way as any of spending an hour and a bit.

As arranged we all met up in the room where the Continuous Quiz was held. I was first, then Vicky with Rich and Jenny arriving just before the start. It appeared that most of the teams had been playing all week so were well ensconced and that meant we were just a team of four. The other three in their late twenties or early thirties, they looked to me for the age questions which made me feel very old. We didn't do too badly and managed to come second out of eight.

"Not bad," said Rich, as everyone packed up and handed their pencils and spare paper back to the host.

"No," I agreed. "It would have been nice to win just once but second is not bad."

"Well, that's it then," said Jenny. "Home tomorrow."

"Yes. I am not looking forward to it in one way," I replied to that. "On here I was safe and now I have to go back to whatever game someone is playing. On the other hand, I keep getting so mad when I think of Laura being killed that I want him to come and get me, so I can get some justice."

"Be careful," advised Rich. He gave me a piece of paper. "Our contact details. Keep in touch and let us know you are safe."

"Thanks guys!" I was touched that two people I had met briefly on a ship liked me enough to want to stay in touch.

"He won't be alone," pointed out Vicky. "I'm going to be sticking to my exclusive."

We all then said our goodbyes as there was no guarantee we would see each other the next day. There were two ways of disembarking the ship. If you wanted your luggage taken off the ship and left in the baggage hall then one had to congregate in various disembarkation points on the ship the next day when groups of passengers were let off the ship in some sort of coordinated order. Otherwise, if you were prepared to carry off your own luggage, you could make your own way off from about 7 am. I was going to do that, but Rich and Jenny were in no hurry, they had their car in the long term car park. Vicky was getting off with the first batch too, but she had to go home first before starting her watchdog assignment. She lived over in Essex so it would take her some time before she got over to where I lived. It could possibly be the following day, Sunday.

As I lay in bed that last night after packing as much as I could away into my luggage, still feeling the rolling of the ship, I wondered what I was letting myself in for. There was a fiendish puzzler, possible murderer and kidnapper, against little old me and a gossip column reporter. I was scared and angry with alternate thoughts and I was hoping that it was the latter which would prevail if I came face to face with my foe – whether it be Nathan or someone else.

The puzzle was afoot, as Sherlock liked to say, or certainly something like that.

PART THREE - CAPTIVE AUDIENCE

Chapter 32

Tate woke up groggy. He was confused. Why couldn't he move his arms or legs? He tried to open his eyes, but it was like they were gummed together. Eventually he was able to force them open, but his vision was blurred and he could not take in the surroundings straight away. He realised that he had been drugged and then he remembered the guy with the stun gun, which brought him to alertness with a jerk.

It was then he discovered his predicament. He was upright but appeared to be attached to a post. He looked down at his feet and saw that they were clamped, then glanced over at each arm to see the same. His arms were spread out attached to a cross beam. Crucified. Why?

He tried to clear his vision then looked around. He didn't recognise the room, but it was laid out like someone's lounge. There was a sofa, armchairs, a coffee table and a massive TV on the wall. He could see no windows, although he could not twist to see behind himself. There were lights on though, so he guessed there were no windows. From his fixed position he could see two doors, both closed.

He tested his restraints and found them immovable. His wrists and ankles were cuffed to the post. Strangely, there was another post by the side of him, a few feet away. He could see that it was a black painted sturdy metal affair. There was like a small platform or ledge, two feet off the ground with a cross beam and two ankle cuffs. Then a much longer cross beam with two cuffs for the arms. It did not take a genius to work out that there was another prisoner expected and Tate reckoned he knew who it would be. Daniel Andrews-White.

He had no idea what time or even what day it was. There was no clock in the room that he could see. He had been taken on Friday. Was it still the same day or had he been out of it for a while? The lack of windows and therefore daylight meant he couldn't even guess at the time of day. Then as the grogginess began to recede and he became aware of his senses and his body, he had an answer. He had the most powerful urge to urinate. He was still in the same clothes he was taken in and was not wet or smelling so he had been out a few hours at the most. He could still sleep eight hours without having to get up to pee, so it was most likely still Friday. Of course, that did not help him with the immediate problem, and he was damned if he was going to wet himself for the amusement of his captor.

Suddenly, Tate heard a click and a sort of swooshing sound. Then he knew someone else was in the room because he heard a voice before he could see anybody.

"Glad you could join us," said the voice and then the owner moved into view. Tate was sure he had not seen the guy before. It couldn't be the guy who stunned him because this guy was bald. Tall, thin and as bald as a coot. "Hope you don't mind hanging out here?" The guy smiled at this own joke.

"Forgive me if I don't clap at your comedic genius, I seem to be a bit tied up?" growled Tate. "What the hell is this all about?"

The man came right up to where Tate hung and as this was off the ground he had to look up slightly. "Do you know who I am?" he asked.

"I can guess," replied Tate. "One Mickey Perkins. Low level gangster wannabe."

"Partly right, Tony. You don't mind if we use first names? Yes, I was Mickey Perkins. So, if you know that, you know why you are here, right?"

"Probably some ill-judged revenge for some slight you still feel from the past."

"A slight you say," Tate's captor smiled, then his voice changed. "You fitted me up! You fitted me up so I would have no choice but to help you take Bannister! You made me a grass and in fear for my life! Not only that but I still went to prison."

"Not prison. Young Offender Institution I would guess," Tate said. "You would have known about it if you went to prison."

"Be that as it may, Tony, it was like a prison to me at that age."

"Look man, get over it! It was over twenty years ago. Nearer thirty. I was a young P.C., and I was forced to do what I did by the D.I. in charge. It was not my choice. They just wanted any young copper to mix in with the crowd. That was my bad luck. I had to do what he said, or it was my career. It should not be me you are mad at."

"All you say may be true," the man conceded, "but Jackson is dead, and you are the only one left on the force that was involved. Someone must pay."

"It looks like someone else is going to pay." Tate turned his gaze to the other post.

"Ah yes! You will be having a companion soon but that is a different matter entirely. He has so much more to suffer for than you. He put me in that position in the first place."

"Danny Andrews-White?"

"You know? Well, there was always a chance that would happen, but it matters not."

"So, what is all this nonsense with the puzzle then?"

"Ah, you will see detective." The man came closer, and Tate could see sweat glistening on his head. "You may die in this room. On the other hand, you may survive. That puzzle is the only way you might."

"Are you a killer? Or just a headcase? What is all this Cluedo crap?"

"I have killed no one that did not deserve it. I am not a bad man. I am a wronged man. A wronged man seeking justice. I could explain it all now but then I would have to do it a second time when my new guest arrives. In fact, to be perfectly honest, this is all a bit too early. You were destined to be here in the end, but I wanted to play with you both a bit more first. Danny disappearing like that made me change my plans. I had to pick you up before you disappeared too."

"Ha. So, your other plaything has outwitted you then? That's something."

"Not for long. I have eyes everywhere. He may have pulled a fast one, but he will be found and as soon as he is, he will be brought here too."

"Well, this is all fine and dandy," said Tate, "but I trust you will not be leaving me up here until you find him. I'm about to pee my pants."

"Er … no, Tony. Apologies, I should have realised. Let me explain the rules here." The man moved back into the room. "This is my panic room. A panic room with a difference because it cannot be opened from the inside. As you can see it is comfortably fitted out as a living area. There is a bedroom and bathroom behind those doors. You are free to do what you like. When I leave here, the cuffs will be electronically released and you will be free to move around. Now, listen carefully. When I want to come in here I will announce it and you will then come back to this position and place yourself in the cuffs which will electronically close. I will not enter until you are secure. I want no surprises. I don't like surprises. Got all that?"

"It's clear," said Tate. "What makes you think though I am going to be so stupid as to let myself be chained up again after being free? I don't care if you come in here again or not."

"You say that, but that is not playing the game. Besides, you will need food from time to time. I can only bring in supplies when you are secure. Think it over. I am sure you will come to your senses." The man turned to leave.

"Hey!" Tate called out and the man turned back. "You said that you used to be Mickey Perkins. Who are you now then?"

"Doctor Black. Doctor Nathan Black. Not a medical doctor though, so don't go injuring yourself. Now I must go. We will talk later."

Black walked out of sight and Tate heard a click then nothing. Five minutes later the cuffs holding his arms and legs clicked open and he nearly fell off the post. He gingerly stepped down and sank on the sofa. What the hell had he gotten himself into?

Tate couldn't afford to lie on the sofa too long because he really had to relieve himself. He managed to stand but his journey to the bathroom was far from smooth. There were two visible doors in the room. The first one he tried was the bedroom, with if you could believe it or not, metal bunkbeds, not unlike ones would find in a prison. The bedding looked new and clean though. It was the other door that led to the bathroom which in turn led to extreme relief for Tate, but of course it was only temporary because then his mind was free to take stock of his situation.

He was starting to get feeling back in his legs, so he began to check the place out. The bathroom was small but had all it needed; toilet, sink, bath / shower. The bedroom was a surprise. Apart from the bunks there were two wardrobes – the type with lower drawers. One of these were empty but the other one was full of his own clothes. Trousers and shirts on hangers with socks and underwear in the draws. Surprising on the one hand, why would his captor bother? On the other hand, not surprising how they had got there. After stunning him and then drugging him, his captor would have plenty of time to go through the house and collect stuff.

There was no separate kitchen but in one corner of the main room there was sort of kitchenette area with some units and a microwave and kettle. There was a fridge / freezer, and the latter contained numerous frozen meals for one. The fridge had long life milk, butter spread, bottled water, soft drinks, and there were some boxes of cereal in one of the cupboards along with coffee, tea bags and sugar. There was crockery and cutlery in the units but only of the paper and plastic variety. The reason for that was obvious. No metal knives or forks to use as a weapon and no ceramic or glass to break to use for similar purposes.

All this said one thing to Tate. This was meant to be a long term stay. He couldn't get his head around that. This had obviously been planned well in advance. This place had been kitted out to accommodate two people for a considerable period. This was not then going to be a quick kill for revenge then. Of course, that sort of tied in with the crossword puzzle, which was very complicated and could have been a long drawn out affair.

Talking of the elephant in the room, it was obvious that the crossword was not finished with. On the back wall, behind the post he had been secured to, was a much larger replica of the frame he had received in the post. There was a pile of blocks to the side, also much larger – each bigger than a Rubik's cube, and in the frame the first row was complete as it had been in the one he received. Tate had to assume from this that he, or they when his companion in abduction arrived, still had to complete it. No wonder then the long term supplies. It could take ages now he did not have his support team. He was under no illusion that it had been Joe who had put most of the clues together. He was not sure he could even remember what they had achieved so far.

Tate noticed that his watch had been taken and there was no clock in the room. He went to turn on the giant TV but there was no remote that he could see and there were no visible buttons on the screen itself. Tate sank back on the sofa feeling slightly defeated. It seemed there was no communication with the outside world. The panic room had no visible external door. He had looked when checking the room, but wherever the exit was the seam was invisible. He was at the will and mercy of Mickey Perkins or Doctor Black or whatever he wanted to call himself.

Tate suddenly felt very tired. He still had no idea what the day or time was, but he still felt it was late Friday or very early Saturday. A drugged sleep was not very restful so it made sense he would be getting tired now. He also had a headache, no doubt an aftereffect of the drugging. He wondered whether that had been considered by his captor. He got up and went back into the bathroom. He had noticed a bathroom cabinet on the wall but had not opened it. He looked inside. There were two new toothbrushes in their packets, a new boxed tube of toothpaste and what he was looking for, a packet of paracetamol. The cabinet also contained deodorant and indigestion tablets plus some plasters and bandages. No razors though.

Tate opened the box of paracetamol and looked carefully at the foil strip of pills. They looked pristine with no tiny holes so he figured they should be safe. He took two and swallowed them with a couple of handfuls of water from the sink tap. Then putting everything back he went back to the sofa.

Dare he sleep? He had no doubt that the whole place was wired for sound and probably there was video too. He would be being watched. Could he let his guard down? Tate was a light sleeper so he reckoned he would awake if he heard anything. He didn't fancy the bunk bed, so he lay on the sofa. At first he tried to think things over and try to come up with a plan but that was fruitless, he had so little to go on. Instead, he soon drifted off to a troubled sleep full of dark mysterious foe and gigantic letters that were chasing him.

Chapter 33

Tate woke up screaming. His last dream had been about his wife and kids being tortured. He was sweating and his heart was pounding. Immediately he realised something he had obviously been too groggy to remember before. His phone. Not his normal phone but the secret one. If Perkins had that then he could trace where his family was. Tate frantically checked his trouser pockets, and it came as no surprise to discover both phones were gone. So were his keys and his wallet.

Were his family OK? They had gotten to safety he knew because they had sent the text, but had they been discovered by this guy that seemed to have extraordinary sources of information? He needed to find out. He also needed to play it cool. If he brought attention to them, if currently they were of no interest to Black, that could be just as worse.

Tate got up from the sofa. He did not know how long he had slept but he guessed it was not that long. His throat was parched so he went over to fridge and helped himself to a bottle of water. After a long swig he realised that he was also hungry. It must be at least twenty four hours since he had eaten last. He didn't feel up to a microwave meal, so he had some cereal from a paper bowl with a plastic spoon.

Whilst he was eating his mind was busy. He had no idea how long he was going to be held there. The chances of escape were minimal. There were no guards he could overcome, and the place had been made practically self-sufficient. He could last in here until the food ran out. He could not work on the door because he could not find it, although if this was a proper panic room it would be extremely secure and indestructible. The only chance he would have would be when Andrews-White was brought in, if he was ever caught, and until then he was just a rat in a trap.

Tate glanced at the puzzle frame on the wall. Perkins obviously wanted the puzzle to be finished. It was part of the game. The question was should he go along with it or not? He had nothing but time on his hands and he may as well waste his time on that than anything else. At least it would keep him occupied. On the other hand, did he really want to be doing what Perkins wanted him to do? Yet, he had said that solving the puzzle was the only way out of the room, and if that were true then no time should be wasted on solving it. Tate doubted whether he could do it alone. He was even dubious he could get up to the stage they had been in before he was taken. He had a photo on his phone but that may as well have been on the moon.

Tate finished the cereal and then realised that there was no kitchen sink. Still with everything paper there was no washing up to be done. There was a plastic swivel top bin, so he just dropped the used bowl and spoon in there. He then realised he was starting to whiff a little so decided to have a shower. He noticed something that had not registered before. The bathroom light came on automatically when the door was opened whilst the bedroom had a switch. The lights in the main room though did not and were always on. It made sense. The bedroom would need to be dark to allow sleep but everywhere else illuminated.

Tate showered and changed his clothes. There was even a laundry basket in the bathroom for his discarded apparel. This guy was something else. Tate felt like a doll in a doll's house, everything kitted out like a normal environment but moved around by an unseen hand.

Whilst he was dressing, Tate found something else which might help him. In a drawer that contained his underwear and socks he found a new boxed electric shaver. Tate always had a wet shave but as he had observed earlier, there was no razor in the bathroom because that would have meant blades which could be used as a weapon. Tate had already noticed his stubble in the bathroom mirror, and it looked to be about a day's growth, which tied up with this being Saturday. The longest he ever went without shaving was three days. He could work out the time lapse from how often he needed to shave. On that basis he used the shaver to get rid of his current stubble. He now had a way of telling time, to a rough degree anyway.

Back in the main room, he went over to look at the puzzle. He was still loathe to bow down to his captor and do what was expected but if in the long run this was going to help him escape he had to give it a go. He tried to remember what Joe had said. The puzzle was built from the ground up like putting up a building. Across clues were floors and down clues columns or pillars. The dots represented where a word crossed or a colour group. All the yellow dots related to Cluedo. That was it. He couldn't recall anything else.

He was just about to start when a loud voice made him jump out of his skin. "Boo!" Tate spun around and saw Perkins on the giant TV screen.

"Morning Tony. I hoped you slept well. Is there anything you need?"

Tate decided to use this opportunity to try and find out about his family.

"Yes. I need to call the wife, to let her know I'm alright, she'll be going frantic."

"Nice try, Tony," chuckled Perkins. "I know that you had your family whisked away to some safe location. Rest assured, I have no quarrel with them, and they are safe. They are in no danger from me."

Tate was immediately relieved, but this was short lived because he was by nature suspicious, a good trait in his profession. "Why should I believe you?"

"I promise you that they are and will remain safe. I have no interest in them."

"Not even to force me to do what you want?"

"My dear Tony. You don't have to do anything if you don't want to. Of course, you will die if you don't but that's down to you."

Tate decided to let the matter rest. It made sense. This was no kidnapping for ransom, and he was already a prisoner under sentence of death. On the face of it there seemed no reason to get his family involved so he would have to just hope that this was the case.

"In fact," continued Perkins when Tate did not respond straight away, "no one else you know is in danger. Not P.C. Peter Lane, nor his grandfather Joe, even though they have been giving you quite a bit of assistance, something I did not anticipate, and another reason I had to bring you in early."

"You seem to know everything, Perkins," Tate stated.

"Not Perkins! He is dead. Doctor Black!"

Tate realised he had touched a nerve and felt that he might be able to use that later, but he let it go for now.

"OK. So now what, Doctor Black?"

The big bald face on the screen smiled. "That's better. A little respect."

"What's this all in aid of? Pure revenge?" Tate wanted to get him talking to see if he would give anything away.

"In simple language, yes," agreed Perkins / Black. "I got to a stage where I looked at my life and saw what a pile of poo it was. I then decided who had been responsible for my life being like that. There were two main culprits, and you were the second."

"Daniel Andrews-White being the first?"

"Precisely! As I said before he perpetrated the far greater wrong and in fact, if I hadn't been going after him, I might have let you off."

"Very civil of you I'm sure," said Tate, "but we are not the only two are we? You have killed others. That puzzle of yours certainly intimates that you have."

"Let's just say, Tony, that I have not harmed any innocent victims. Anyone who has come to harm were not a loss to society."

Tate had walked over to stand in front of the screen as soon as Perkins had started talking. Now he went and sat on the sofa which was directly opposite. He was pausing for effect.

"Like Dylan Greenhalgh? A la Reverend Green in the library with the lead piping?"

"Congratulations Tony! Go to the top of the class! But shed no tears for Dylan. He may have turned to God but that could not atone for all the evil he had already done. Let me tell you something about Knuckles, Tony." The view on the screen zoomed out so Tate could see Perkins sat in an armchair, with something in a glass on a small table behind him. And at the corner the glimpse of a window. There was daylight shining through it, so well into the day then. "Now, we could talk like this, or I could come down to do it face to face. You realise, of course, if I do that you will need to be in the cuffs."

"No bother," said Tate. "This is near enough."

"Okay fair enough. Well, there we were in 1990. I had no home, for reasons I cannot divulge yet, and I was sixteen going on seventeen, as they used to sing in one famous musical. Yes, I was hanging around the Bannister gang, but I was only an errand boy, delivering messages mostly, I never did anything serious. Then you set me up and put me into the clutches of Jackson. What could I do? I had to do what he wanted? He got the glory and I got shafted."

"Just a few months in a Young Offenders Institution," said Tate. "It could have been worse."

"Anyway, I am jumping ahead. I was going to tell you about Knuckles. I never met Bannister or even his number two. Knuckles was as near as I got, and he was bad enough. I saw him kill and torture people, bribe others and many other things to keep them in line. To me he was just a sadistic taskmaster but for others he was the devil incarnate. Quite spooky in fact that his stint inside turned him to worship the complete opposite. No amount of prayer and good deeds could atone for all those he victimised. I meted out justice on their behalf. He was no innocent victim."

"What about Laura Andrews-White then?" asked Tate accusingly.

"You have been busy, Tony. Good show." Perkins took a sip of his drink. It was brown liquid so could have scotch or brandy. "I cannot tell you about that yet. What I can say is this. When I got out of detention, I decided to go straight and that was tough. One menial job after another. Crappy digs. I was living the low life, but my brief incarceration had taught me I could not go inside again, especially not to the big house. I toed the line, but I was miserable. You know what saved me, Tony?"

"I don't know. You won the lottery," replied Tate with sarcasm.

"That's right, Tony. I did. I won a rollover. Twenty four million."

"Blimey!" exclaimed Tate. "I was joking."

"You know what that did, Tony? Yes, it changed my life and took me out of the gutter, but after a while I started to think of revenge. I could not afford it before but now I could. That is what got us to this point. If I hadn't had that win, none of us would be here today."

"You're mad!" Tate observed. "You had all that money. Would never have to work again. You could have just enjoyed life. Instead, you go on a killing spree which will see you in prison for life. Why?"

"Because the scales must be balanced Tony. And not to worry, I'm not going to prison." Suddenly Tate could hear a phone ringing in the background. "Sorry Tony, got to go." Perkins cut the connection and the screen went blank.

And so began days of isolation for Tate. This period started bizarrely because on that Saturday evening the TV screen suddenly came to life and the Champions League Final was showing. Tate was an Arsenal fan but for something better to do he watched it. In normal circumstances he would be rejoicing that Liverpool lost and that they could be without Salah at the start of the next season, but these were not normal circumstances, so he took no joy from it. Even Bale's spectacular goal had no effect. As soon as the match was over the screen went blank again.

The one thing Tate did do then was have another shave although he did not need it. He had the time now from the match so he could count the days down in threes by virtue of when he needed to shave again.

Perkins only made one appearance in the next week and that one was brief. Tate got the impression of underlying anger in his demeanour and although nothing was said about it, the absence of his prospective fellow captive suggested things were not going well tracking him down. Good for him, thought Tate. Tate only saw him on screen but in fact Perkins had ventured in the room and Tate learnt a valuable lesson.

Perkins told him to get into the cuffed position so he could enter the room, but Tate refused. He was happy with a stalemate but soon realised there was no such thing. A hissing sound told of escaping gas and before long he was unconscious. When he came to, he was back on the post. After an out an hour the cuffs clicked open, but he now knew it was pointless to resist this humiliation in future.

Tate did have his angry outbursts too during this period. All he had to do was eat and sleep so despite his misgivings he did keep having stints with the puzzle. He made mistakes and the more he made the angrier he became. Several blocks did take some flying lessons.

He had had two shaves since the end of the cup final, so he figured it was Friday when Perkins came on the screen again all smiles. "Not long now Tony and your roommate will be here."

"Oh, you eventually found him did you?" goaded Tate.

"I know where he will be tomorrow morning and will have eyes on him from then on." Perkins informed him. "The little devil went on a cruise to get away but the ship docks at Southampton tomorrow. Not long now." He was almost purring.

Tate did not know whether to be hopeful or not. Two heads were better than one, but with both captives, Perkins was free to forge ahead with whatever he had planned. Up to now he had been in a holding pattern. The clock was now ticking, and Tate did not know how long there was to go.

Chapter 34

As it happened, Vicky and I did travel back together, or part of the way. She caught the same train as me. I was getting off at Croydon and she was staying on until London, then onward from there to Chelmsford. She would have driven to Southampton but her only means of transport was her motorbike which made carrying luggage a bit difficult. Her intention though was to get home pack some fresh clothes and bike it back to my place in Surrey. The fact that she would have to sleep on the lumpy sofa did not deter her. She had her story and was sticking to it like glue.

We had departed the boat early, about 7.30 am. I had not seen anything of Rich and Jenny but then I had not expected to. I did not know if I would ever see them again. I had their contact information but did not want them in any danger.

It was slightly over two hours to East Croydon. The train was not packed at that time, but we did have trouble getting all our luggage next to us. It would not fit in the overhead racks. We talked quietly at first about the situation, but we had already gone over everything and what was left was guesswork. I had not slept well again, and train travel made me sleepy anyway.

"Can I borrow your phone," Vicky asked me, just as I was nodding off.

"Why?" I asked.

"Just want to check something."

I handed it over and felt my eyelids closing again and this time I let them. I must have been more tired than I thought because rather than dozing I must have dropped off. I woke up with a start, Vicky shaking my shoulder.

"You better wake up," she advised. "Next stop is yours."

I hurriedly gathered myself and my things together. "So, what time will you be around?" I asked her.

"I reckon I get home, check on a few things, pack a bag and be back at your place within a few hours." It was about 10.30. "Say five or six."

"Okay. See you then."

By the time I caught a train to my local station and took a cab to the flat, it was getting on for an hour later. I stood outside my door for a good five minutes in trepidation. The bullet holes before me were a good reminder of what had happened last time I was there. It was hard to believe that was now nearly a month ago. Eventually I turned they key in the lock and went up. I left my cases below. If I was going to get jumped better to be unencumbered.

The place looked the same. The air was a bit stuffy, and the place was like a sauna because the windows had been closed all that time. It didn't look like Jackie had been keeping an eye on the place. I went and opened all the windows to let some fresh air in and went down to collect the cases. I made no move to unpack or get a load of washing on. The puzzle frame was on the table staring at me, but I ignored it. I just dropped onto the sofa. What next?

I wasn't sat ruminating on the sofa for very long because I was aware of a funny smell. I opened the fridge and there was a whiff coming from some milk that was fast on the way to becoming yoghurt and some green cheese. The tub of butter spread was out of date too. I dumped it all in a black bag and took it down to put in the outside bin. Having accomplished that task, my empty fridge now meant I had to get some supplies in. I should have cleaned it out first to get rid of any lingering smell but that was too much work.

I decided to put a load of washing on whilst I was out – two birds with one stone so to speak. It was funny how that phrase kept coming up. I reckoned I had three loads of washing if I crammed it in. Some items would have to go to the dry cleaners.

Before leaving I also checked the cupboards and the freezer. I had been away a month and didn't know what I had in. I had some tins – mainly soup and tuna – and there were mini pizzas and oven chips in the freezer. Not a great variety so I might as well do a proper shop – it was Saturday after all, my usual shopping day. The only trouble was it was the middle of the day, and I usually went early before any crowds. It couldn't be helped this time.

As I walked down the stairs, carrying my bags for life, and passed the internal door to the shop, I again caught a whiff of something. I thought it was just lingering from when I had brought the bin bag down and never gave it another thought. I had just realised something else instead. England had a friendly later that day against Nigeria, the penultimate one before the World Cup started. I wanted to get everything done including all the washing before the 5.15 pm kick-off. Then I realised that Vicky could be turning up around then. Hoped she liked football.

The store was busy but not as busy as it would be an hour or two later. I was back within the hour with enough stuff to last a fortnight, but then I had a guest staying. In fact, I don't know what she liked to eat so I may have to go out again – but after the football.

It was as I came in that the smell hit me again. It seemed more powerful this time, but it could have been because I had been out in the fresh air. It was far worse down here at the bottom of the stairs and I suddenly figured it must be coming from the shop. I hadn't noticed when I had first arrived home, being fearful of what might await me, but I did notice as I passed on the way to the shops. The dog parlour was closed, shut up tight, and Saturday was usually the busiest day of the week. That was strange.

I lugged the bags upstairs and stored everything away, then I got the key for the shop door. I left my outer door open to let the smell out as much as possible. I entered the shop, and the smell was stronger and most unpleasant to say the least. I couldn't check the front of the shop, or the alarm would go off. That only left the small kitchen area which was clear and the basement. As I headed downstairs, I knew I was going the right way as the smell got stronger. The door at the bottom was closed and as I opened it I wretched as the vile stench overwhelmed me. I didn't want to go in, but I had to. I covered my mouth and nose with one hand and switched on the light.

It had been a dry heave before but now I dispelled the contents of my stomach. Jackie's large body was hanging from the ceiling in the dog cage. I didn't go any nearer to check. She was obviously dead. I just turned and ran back up the stairs and out into the fresh air. I gulped it down greedily to get rid of the putrid air I felt I was suffocating on. When I was sufficiently recovered, I went back in to call the police. As I came to the top of the stairs I got another shock because who was there waiting for me, sitting on the sofa. Nathan.

"Hello Mate. Where have you been? I have been worried about you."

I was at a loss for words. All my musings on recent events had resulted in thinking Nathan was the cause. Now he was here in the flat. What did I do? Assume I was correct and run? Or bluff it out and pretend that everything was normal? Or as normal as it could be with a dead body downstairs.

"Sorry Nathan, I must call the police. The landlady is dead downstairs."

I looked around for my phone. I was sure I had left it on the coffee table when I got back from shopping. "Have you seen my phone?"

Nathan looked this way and that. "Er … no. Haven't seen it. Dead body you say?"

"Yes! She is strung up down there in the basement. We need to get the police!" I was laying it on a little bit. "Can I use your phone?"

"Sorry Danny, left it in the car."

"What car? You never have a car. You use a cab?"

"Usually yes, but with what has been happening, I rented one. Look, sit down and tell me what's been happening."

I almost did but something held me back. "No! I've got to get the police. I'll just go outside to see if I can borrow a phone. Or we can get yours from the car."

I was still near the top of the stairs and was about to turn to go down when Nathan stood up. "I don't think we need to get the police involved, do we?" He took something out of his jacket pocket and pointed it at me. I couldn't make it out. It didn't seem like any gun I had seen.

"So, it is you behind all this then!" I hissed.

"I guess the game is up," he smiled.

I wasn't waiting around, and I turned to run down the stairs. I heard a sound behind me but whatever it was had missed me and I was down the stairs. I heard Nathan vent an expletive, but I was gone. Outside I ran out into the street. There was an ambulance parked in front of the dog parlour with two men dressed as paramedics leaning on it smoking. When they saw me their fags went flying and they moved out to block my path, so I just turned and ran the other way. "After him!" I heard Nathan roar.

It was Saturday and the High Street was busy, so my flight was full of dodging and weaving. I didn't look behind me for fear of what I might see. What I did hear though was the siren on the ambulance start up, so at least one of the men was now driving. The noise and presumably flashing lights would clear his path. I was running out of puff already. I turned down a side street where there were less people but that was when it happened. Something you hardly ever see during a chase on TV where people just get out of the way with annoyed utterances. Not this guy. I don't suppose I could blame him. He sees someone running away from a paramedic with a wailing ambulance in the background and wants to be a hero. I was running past this guy when he tripped me. I went sprawling in a heap.

"There you are," he declared proudly to the chasing paramedic. "Caught him for you."

"Thank you very much, Sir," said my pursuer, also out of breath. "He is a bit confused. Off his meds. We must get him to hospital."

He was on me before I recovered and almost immediately the ambulance arrived. The other paramedic got out and I was forcibly helped into the back of the vehicle. "Help me!" I implored to the small crowd that had gathered. "I am being kidnapped!"

"Don't worry, ladies and gentlemen," said another voice. "He is delusional. Once he is back on his full medication he will be fine." I turned. I didn't recognise the voice, but it was Nathan. The voice was a lot deeper than his usual speech. It gave his words gravitas, and I could see the crowd believed him.

I was lifted into the back of the ambulance. The two paramedics crowded in after me and Nathan climbed in too and shut the door. I was cornered. My three opponents were one behind each other. "Here!" said Nathan, passing something to the front guy. He pointed it at me, and I heard the noise again before I was thrashing about in pain before blackness engulfed me.

I cannot have been out for long because when I opened my eyes we were still stationary. I couldn't move though because I was strapped down. I felt a prick in my arm and then everything went black again.

Chapter 35

My head was splitting but when I tried to bring my hands up to massage my throbbing temples they would not move. They were stuck. I had to open my eyes to see what was wrong. Everything was fuzzy at first and then things began to swim slowly into view.

"You must be Danny," said the guy, stood there looking up at me. Tall, dark hair, in jeans and t-shirt.

"Where am I?" My voice was croaky. I tried to move my arms again but in vain. I looked across left then right and saw I was clamped to a post. I looked down and saw the same with my feet. "What the hell?"

"Take it easy! I woke up secured in that position too. He will probably let you out shortly. He did with me."

My mind was filled with cotton wool and questions that I could not frame at that precise moment. Where the hell was I? The last thing I remembered was … oh, being in the ambulance. Nathan must have brought me here. He was behind everything after all. But who was this other guy? A fellow prisoner from the things he had said. It was all too much for my head. At least I could get one question out. "Who are you?"

"Tony Tate," he replied. "D.I. Tony Tate." Police. The missing detective inspector, which I supposed made sense. "I know who you are. You must be Daniel Andrews-White."

"No! Danny Andrews!"

"Okay, Danny. Take it easy. You're going to feel wobbly for a while, especially when you get out of that thing."

"Er…when will that be? Can you let me out?"

"Afraid not. It is centrally controlled. I was let out quite soon after coming round. No reason why you won't be too. I am sure he is monitoring us all the time?"

"He who? Nathan?"

"I don't know who he is, but he is in total control at the moment. He did tell me he was using the name Nathan Black but that's not his real name."

At that moment a voice came booming out of a speaker somewhere. "Tony! I am going to come in. Get back in your restraints please."

"You are joking! Why would I do a stupid thing like that?"

"Because whenever I come into the room you both need to be restrained, you know that after last time. I am not taking the chance on you jumping me and escaping. You can either do it willingly or we can do it forcibly again. And I might not let you out again this time."

I didn't recognise the voice. I thought it would be Nathan's, but it didn't appear to be. I watched Tony as he debated what to do. In the end he went over to another post. Climbed up and turned himself around putting his arms and legs in the open clamps. They snapped shut immediately. "That's a good boy," said the voice.

A few minutes later and someone came into the room, but I was not aware of this until he was in front of me. He was carrying a suitcase – it looked like mine, an old one. The luggage I had used on the cruise had been new as had been all the clothes. I was even more confused now because it was Nathan. "Hi Mate," he said smiling.

"Hey!" interjected Tony. "Where's the other guy?"

I got an immediate shock. Nathan pulled off his hair which was a wig and stood there as bald as a coot. "Voila!"

"What the hell is going on?" I demanded.

"One moment." He held up his hand and turned to carry the case up to a door and went inside briefly then he was back before me. "It's quite simple Danny. Nathan was a part I was playing. One I have been playing for five years. All geared to this moment." His voice was different now and more like the voice on the speaker. It was more cultured and posher.

"Why?"

"Quite simple too, or would have been, but you have spoilt it a bit. I thought at first that your lost memories were just an act but having known you for a while now I know it's not. At first I thought that would take some of the fun away, but then I realised it makes it even better."

"What fun? What are you going to do with us?"

"Ah, us? Yes, Tony is here for a different reason to you. You are the most important person out of the two of you. Tony set me up, but he wouldn't have been able to do so but for you."

"But what did I ever do to you in the five years we have known each other?"

"Ah, but that's the whole point, Danny boy," said the guy called Nathan, who I did not in fact know at all. "We have known each other for a lot longer than that. We are brothers."

I didn't know what to say. I was dumbstruck. I had a brother. Then why was he acting like this? What had happened in the past that I had no knowledge of? He could probably see me struggling.

"Yes, brothers. We were very close when we were younger. We were twins or supposed to be. Then suddenly when you were about eleven you changed. You became all surly and moody. You pulled away from everyone. And finally, at fifteen you ran away. You ran away but you left a leaving present." I could not believe what he was telling me. I had to believe him though because there were tears in his eyes. "You set fire to the house. You killed Mum and Dad! I only survived because a fireman pulled me out of my bedroom window. That is why you are here!"

"No! Noooooooo! You're making it all up!"

"Unfortunately for you, I am not. Your name is not Danny. It is James. James Perkins. I am your brother Mike, or that is how we were brought up."

The name meant nothing to me. It brought nothing flashing back. I shook my head. Nathan turned and pointed a remote he had in his hand at the large TV on the wall. A picture came up of two smiling children. About six or seven years old.

"Do you remember what you looked like when you were a kid?" He asked. "This is us at our seventh birthday party. Look how happy we are. Why did you have to go and spoil everything?"

"Why ask me? I don't know. I don't know you. I thought I did, Nathan, but I obviously don't."

"I often wondered what made you go off the rails. It wasn't until years after, when our parent's solicitor passed me some papers that it all made sense. Somehow you found out we were not twins. One of us was adopted – although apparently not through official channels. The birth mother came calling about the time that you changed. It was all in a letter written by dad in case anything happened to them. They didn't know why you changed. They didn't know you knew, but somehow I think you found out." He just looked at me for a bit then went on. "The thing is, I think you were so upset because you thought you were the adopted one. You felt wronged somehow, not really belonging there. But you got it wrong. I was the adopted one. You were their real son and you killed them."

He wiped a tear away with his hand. "Anyway, that is enough to be going on with. You both now know how you have wronged me. You both know why you are here. I will give you time to let you think on that." He turned and left. I didn't hear a door close, but I was too within myself to care. Was it all true? Had I killed my own parents? What little strength I had suddenly left me, and I sagged letting the restraints hold me up.

"I wouldn't do that if I was you," Tony called over to me from his post, but it was too late. The clamps opened as if by magic and I fell face first onto the carpet. Tony who had been released too had been expecting it. He rushed over to help me up. My big nose had made the most contact and it was bleeding. He led me to one of the visible doors and showed me into the bathroom. I closed the door, sat on the toilet and held a large wad of toilet roll to my nose. This was all automatic because I was still deep in shock at learning who I really was. The type of person I really was. If someone had told me it was going to get a thousand times worse, I would not have believed them. I could not have imagined how it could possibly be worse. It was probably a good job I didn't know.

After a while, there was a quiet knock on the door. "You alright in there?" I didn't want to reply. I just wanted to sit there but there was a little part of me that needed to know everything I could. I needed to know what Tony knew. I got up and opened the door, still holding the toilet paper to my nose. When Tony saw me he asked me the same question. "Are you alright?" I just nodded even though I was nothing of the kind.

"Go and sit down," he said. "Do you want a drink? There is no alcohol in the place. Tea, coffee or soft drinks."

I could do with a very strong coffee and said so. Five minutes later a steaming cup was in front of me. A paper cup which in normal circumstances I would have thought odd, but these were far from normal circumstances.

"What's it all about, Tony?"

"Beats me, Danny," he replied. "This is the guy who sent us the puzzles. I know you got one too. He has been playing a game with us because he obviously thinks we both wronged him in the past. If what he said before is true then he holds a bigger grudge against you than me."

"Can it be true though?" I wanted reassurance. "Could I have killed someone and not remember it?"

"It does happen, although this does seem to be an unusual case I would think, if you have no memories at all of your childhood."

"Not just childhood. I have no memories before walking out of a warehouse fire in 1997."

"Oh! So, you have had amnesia for over 20 years. I guess it's not coming back then."

"No. I am resigned to that now but then I have no way of knowing of what he told me is the truth or not. I don't want to believe it. I am not that type of person."

"Well, I've got to be honest here, Danny. I don't think it matters a jot now. This guy's got an agenda and what you believe is going to make no difference. I think he has a screw loose myself but make no mistake he is smart. He created that puzzle, and he has been ahead of me all the time. You foxed him by going on that cruise, but you are still here now."

"What are we here for though?"

"He obviously wants his revenge."

"Is he going to kill us?"

"Probably. He said as much earlier. He also said though that our only chance of getting out was to complete the puzzle. I don't know if you noticed the life-size version on the wall back there."

I hadn't but I looked now and saw an even bigger version than the one in my flat. This frame seemed to be attached to the wall. Tony had obviously started on it but had not got very far. The same bottom line was there from *The Sound of Music,* so I guessed it was the same puzzle and that we had both been sent the exact same one too. For the first time I felt an element of being in control.

"I think I can help with that."

Tony suddenly put his finger to his lips. He sat down on the sofa next to me and leaned over to whisper in my ear. "Be careful what you say. I think this place is wired for sound and there will be cameras too. Assume we are under constant surveillance."

I whispered back. "I have made quite a bit more progress than what you have over there."

"Well, we did too," Tony informed me, "but I cannot remember how it all fits together."

"Don't worry. I have my workings with me," I said, glad to have one over on Nathan or Mike or whoever he was. That was one thing I had done on the ship when I was packing. My most important piece of luggage was the sheets of paper with the puzzle grid and clue answers, and I did not want them getting lost or stolen. I had folded them up until they fit in my trainer, and they had been there ever since. They might not smell very nice by then, but they were in a small plastic bag so should be fine to read.

There was no way we could work on the puzzle in the dark and anyway, Tony told me that the lights in the main room were controlled from outside and were never off. The only room where we could be in the dark is the bedroom and that would defeat the object.

I sipped at the coffee. I didn't normally drink it black, but I had asked for it strong and that was what it was. I was still a bit groggy and my mind fuzzy from whatever they had drugged me with. I was hoping it would clear the cobwebs.

"What time is it?" I asked Tony, looking at my wrist and realising my watch had gone.

"Not exactly sure," he replied, "but I would say it is early Saturday evening? What time were you taken?"

"It was going on for one when I got back from shopping and found the body?"

"A body? Another one?" Tate was all policeman for a few seconds.

"Long story. I guess Nathan killed her, but I don't know why. Anyway, he was in the flat and there was a brief chase before they caught me. Say one fifteen."

As it happened at that precise moment guessing the time became irrelevant because the TV screen came to life. It was the England match, and it was just about to kick off. That meant it was 5.15 pm.

"This happened last week too," Tony informed me. "Champions League Final. We may as well watch it."

We sat on the sofa and watched the match, surreal though it was. Then after we watched England beat Nigeria 2 – 1, Tony showed me the food situation and we had something to eat. After this I was feeling very tired and had a headache. Tony told me it had been the same for him and he had felt better after some sleep, so I turned in. Tony already had the bottom bunk, so I slept in the top one, my prized possessions now out of my footwear and under the pillow. Tomorrow was going to be one big puzzle day. Or that was the plan. Things don't always have a way of working out how they should.

Chapter 36

Waking up in a strange bed and much closer to the ceiling than normal I panicked and nearly fell out of the top bunk. Then I remembered where I was. The panic did not lessen any. I lay for a while staring up at that ceiling trying to work out how things had got to where they were. Was it all true? If it was then I really was a bad person and I supposed I deserved what was coming. But I couldn't reconcile a person that would kill their parents with who I felt myself to be. I was being pulled in two. For years I had hoped that my memory would come back but now a large part of me was glad it hadn't. On the other hand, a small part of me wished it would so I could learn the truth of things for myself. Inside I was freaking out and there was nothing I could do to calm down.

I could not hear breathing from below so assumed Tony was up already. What was there to get up for though? I was trapped in a windowless room with someone I didn't know but who was in a similar boat. We were helpless and at the whim of a madman it seemed. I could not believe I had been hoodwinked by Nathan for so long. Gullible or what? The thought of that made me angry then. So angry that I did get up and jumped down to the floor.

The suitcase *had* been mine. Tony had briefly told me before I turned in, how his clothes had already been in one of the wardrobes when he woke up here. Looked like I had to do my own unpacking. As I had left the flat all that time ago with no luggage everything I had used for the past month had been new. The suitcase was packed with all my old clothes taken from the flat. The stuff I had brought back, other than that I put in the washer, was still packed but that had not been brought. It was used and soiled clothing, so some thought had been applied here.

I had not been wearing jeans for quite a few weeks because of the hot weather. The room was not boiling hot but at a nice room temperature. I pulled on jeans and t-shirt; I still had underwear and socks on from yesterday and couldn't be bothered changing. I grabbed the important prize from under my pillow and put it back in my trainer before I laced it up. Then I left the bedroom. Tony was stood in the kitchen area eating from a paper bowl.

"Morning Danny," he greeted. "Breakfast?"

I shook my head. I was not hungry, except for knowledge. "I could do with a coffee though."

"The kettle's boiled," he said. "How are you feeling?"

I hadn't really taken stock because I had been too busy with thoughts of being a parent killer. When I thought about it, I was feeling better health wise if not mentally. "I'm okay now I think."

I joined him in the kitchen area and made my coffee. Strong with a drop of milk this time. Tony wanted tea so I made him a cup. As I stirred in his sugar I asked him, "What do you do all day?"

"Think mainly," he said, finishing what had been cereal and dropping the bowl and plastic spoon into the bin. "That and the puzzle."

"That damned puzzle!" I retorted heatedly. "I wish I had never seen it."

"You say that like you had a choice," pointed out Tony. "You didn't and therefore you could not go back and change it."

That was true. It seemed all predestined somehow. "I guess we crack on with it then?"

Tony motioned me to put down the coffee and follow him. He went into the bathroom and turned on the taps for the shower and sink. "I don't know if this will do any good," he said in a low voice, "but I'm not going to make it easy for him. Now what were you saying yesterday about being able to speed things up?"

I stooped down, untied my lace, and slipped off my left trainer. I pulled out the small plastic bag with the folder papers inside and handed it to him. He opened them out and gave a little whistle. "Wow! You have made progress." He was looking at the grid which was about two thirds completed.

I used the same low tones. "I had some help. I think the answers are right, or most of them, but the colouring is out as I didn't have time to check that."

"No problem. We have time now. You never know we could get this finished today."

"And will that get us out?"

"To be honest I doubt it," Tony warned me, "but it is the only thing we can do and in case it is the way out, we may as well."

There was no way we could keep it a secret that we were using a crib sheet, so we didn't aim to try. We were going to take our time and put in the correct colours now. If this was our way out, we were guessing that it would need to be completed perfectly as to Nathan's design. The best plans of mice and trapped men though. We never even got over to the frame before the TV screen burst into life again.

"Morning campers!" boomed faux Nathan's voice from the screen. The screen contained the upper half of his body. "Morning Tony! Morning James!"

"My name is Danny!" I shouted at the screen.

He shrugged his shoulders. "Fair enough. I don't go by Mike anymore. In fact, you stopped using James even earlier. You took the name Sly."

"Sly?" I was confused. "What are you talking about?"

Nathan was beaming. "You know this is more fun than I thought. Informing you of your own life and seeing the disbelief on your face. Are you sure you want to know?"

Forewarned is forearmed and we needed all the knowledge we could get. I looked at Tony who just shrugged. "We'll have any truth that you have," I told him.

"Okay," he agreed. "The God's honest truth. Take a seat."

We both went over and sat on the sofa so we could see the screen. I had a momentary flash of panic. What else was I going to learn that I didn't really want to know? The problem is I wouldn't know whether it was the truth or just an attempt to wind me up.

"Are we all sitting comfortably? Then I'll begin." Nathan was obviously enjoying himself. And why wouldn't he be? He was in charge, toying with us at his own fancy. "I don't know every specific detail you understand but I know enough."

"Get on with it!" I snapped.

"Well, as I said yesterday, when you were fifteen you left home – and left it burning. You got in with a gang and immediately changed your name to Sly. This was in 1988. I don't know how you got in with them or what you did for them, but you got yourself quite high up in the hierarchy. So much so that you accompanied the boss man to the US in 1992 for a business deal. There things could have changed. You met this girl and fell for her. You were going to quit the gang, stay in the US and go straight, except that her parents had other ideas. Without going into details, they turned the girl against you, and she never wanted to see you again."

It was like I was listening to fictional story about someone else. None of this made any sense to me or rang even the faintest bell. I looked at Tony and he just shrugged.

"I gather things carried on as usual after that back in the UK until 1996 when you seem to have overstepped your authority and took something that did not belong to you. You then had a rival gang after you. You disappeared and no one knew where you were, but I found out, I was actually not that far behind you. You went to Manchester. It was June 1996 during the European Championships. You left Manchester the same day as the Arndale bomb." He paused for effect. I obviously didn't remember the events but had read about them since. He must have read something in my face. "Oh, don't worry, you weren't involved in that. A prostitute was killed though in a fire. You were her last customer. You do have a thing for fire don't you, James?"

What was he saying? That I killed a prostitute and set a fire to get away with it? What sort of guy did I used to be? The trouble was we were not dealing with provable facts here. Did I take his word for it? Was I a killer or just a plaything?

Nathan continued. "You had outstayed your welcome in Manchester but still could not be seen back down South, so you hopped a plane to the US. And guess what you did there? You reeked your vengeance on the girl who had snubbed you and her mother who played you. You left them both dead."

God, what more can he heap on me?

"I only learned about that later. I lost you when you left Manchester, and it wasn't until I employed some investigators that I found out about this. You made your escape back to the UK, but I think you had some help over there. That bit is hazy. Then shortly after you got back, the other gang that had been chasing you finally caught up. They left you to die in that warehouse – yet another fire – and then the rest you know. Or rather, you think you do?"

What did he mean by that? I was soon about to find out. Nathan disappeared from the screen and then there was some kind of home movie playing. A blue home movie because there was a guy and woman on screen going at it hammer and tongue. I didn't know what this was to mean to me. I didn't know these people, at least I didn't think so, but then the couple separated, and the guy got up and went off screen. The view then zoomed in to the woman who was knelt on the bed. The zoom got in close until her top half almost filled the screen.

"Noooooooo!" I bellowed. I did know the woman. Different colour hair but the face I would have recognised even if the birthmark above her left breast did not give it away.

"That's right brother. Meet Laura. Except her name isn't Laura or wasn't at that time. This is Angie. One of my favourite companions for a few years."

I was absolutely gobsmacked. I felt as though I had been hit in the face with a bag of wet cement. If I was not already sitting down I would have fallen but as it was I just sank into the sofa. All my strength and wits left me as I looked at the image on the screen. I knew there were tears running down my face, but I didn't care.

The screen changed and Nathan was back. "Oh yes, brother. This has been a long game. I cleaned her up, got her a job and made sure you met up. It all went according to plan. Well, up to a point." He sounded a bit angry with that last remark. "She was supposed to lead you on, even get married to you if necessary but always report back to me. She did for a while but then she stupidly fell in love and called the whole thing off. I guess she thought she had a life for the first time. Once she cleaned her act up she was pretty savvy and took to her job like a duck to water. Well, you know how well she did at work. And she got a loving husband too. I let it go for a while because I had planning to do. In the end though she had to pay."

The anger erupted inside me. I jumped up and ran over to the screen putting my face close. "You killed her!"

"Yes. I killed a lousy rotten cheating prostitute who had stolen from so many of her clients and bribed them before I turned her onto my path. No sorrow there, brother, for she had used you too. To get a life she wanted to lift her out of the gutter and ensure she never went back."

"I will kill you!"

"Honestly James, I don't think you will get the chance." Nathan sat there and peered at his screen. "Can you get back James, I can't see Tony."

I looked over at Tony who had not moved. He had a bemused look on his face. All of this was obviously news to him and why shouldn't it be. All we had was Nathan's word for it. Except his confession that he had killed Laura, which I had thought about before and now knew to be true.

"Now you both know why you are here. You, James, killed our parents and left me in foster care which I hated so this in turn made me run away and start off down a criminal path although I didn't travel down it as much as you did. You, Tony, set me up so I ended up in custody. Now you are both in my trap. There is only one way for you to escape and that is to solve the puzzle. Good luck."

With that the screen went blank. It had sounded a bit final. Was that it now? We were left to finish the puzzle or stay in that room until we died? Suddenly, the screen was back on again. "Oh, by the way," said Nathan, "I have returned your phones. I see you have photos on them which might help you. There is no signal down there so you might as well have them." Then he was gone again. Tony got up and started looking around. He eventually found the phones on top of the uppermost blocks that were in the frame. I didn't know it because I was observing nothing right then, but he was disappointed that his burner phone was not there, only his usual phone.

I was not that bothered about mine. I was literally in a black hole. Nothing I thought I had known was true. Everything had been blown out of the water. I wasn't a nice guy but a cold blooded killer and the woman I had loved was just a mirage. I think Tony was talking but I didn't hear him. I heard nothing. I could take nothing in. I don't know how long I just sat there but it was a long time. I was dead inside so what did it matter now if I was going to be dead on the outside too. He had taken everything away from me just like, allegedly, I had from him when we were kids.

Chapter 37

It was well into the afternoon when I stirred but even then it was only because I had to if I didn't want to wet myself. I rose and like an automaton made my way to the bathroom, closing the door behind me. Trousers down, I sat on the throne and after relieving myself just stayed there. Suddenly the tears came but they were silent as I had no wish for Tony to be banging on the door. Everything in my life was a lie. The life I had been living for the last five years was not great, but I had had the good years with Laura to look back on. Now those were taken away from me, and I had nothing. I don't think I had ever been so low or in such despair. I just wanted it all to end.

The one thing about me though was that I was often down but never out. When I threw the newspaper across the room in anger having made a silly mistake on a Sudoku puzzle, I always later picked it up again to finish it. I never liked to be beaten. That was why I was in so much trouble with gambling. I did not like to lose and always went back to try and recover my losses. Not a good thing in that scenario but it was all part of the same thing. Never give in. It took a while to kick in this time but eventually the anger was back. This time it was all directed at Nathan, or whoever he really was. Brother or tormenter. He had bested me so far, by a long way, but I was not going to let him win. I pulled up my trousers as well as my socks, washed my hands and face and went back into the room. Tony was eating a sandwich.

"Let's get the puzzle done," I said.

Without knowing where the cameras were situated it was pointless to try to hide what we were doing. What we could do was compare the photos on my phone with those on Tony's phone and as far as these had progressed at the time they matched. The paper grid was a lot further on, but we took the time to get the colouring correct and after about ninety minutes we had the frame on the wall filled in according to the paper but with all the colouring resolved as far as possible. We were on row 20.

"OK, that's where I was up to," I declared when the last block was in. I picked up another sheet of paper to show Tony. "These are answers we have to some of the remaining clues." I quickly totted them up. "Twenty."

"And where are we with the clue numbers then?" asked Tony.

"Well, Row 19 is complete across and those are, let's see," I ran my finger down the last full page of clues. "Numbers 110 to 113. We have not got 108 or 109 yet. They will be down clues that end on Row 18. If you look where 'omen' sits above 'emerge' we have O M and M E coming down which means these must be the ends of words coming down. Therefore, 108 and 109 go there. This also means we can black block the rest of that Row as Number 110 is 'game' which we already have in across."

"I'll put the black blocks in then," offered Tony. "To be honest, I didn't do a lot of the solving. It was mainly one of the P.C.s and his grandfather, especially his grandfather."

"Same for me really," I owned up. "I had a lot of help aboard the cruise, which is how I got so far along."

"It's just down to us though now," said Tony. "That could mean disaster."

"We are not beaten yet. And I need to do this" I blurted out a bit forcefully, needing to get out and get my hands on the guy who had been playing with me like a mouse.

"Where do we go from here then," asked Tony. "What's the next clue?"

"Okay, well, 'accident' is 113 and 'nigh' on the next line up is 120, so that leaves six words coming down that end on Row 19. If you look at this list we have answers for 114, 115, 116, 118 and 119. Five of the six. Looking at the left here we have N G in the first column and E F in the sixth column. That must be where 'piping' and 'clef' go. Also, we know where 'kill' goes because there is only one L on Row 19, in 'feral'.

We started to put these blocks in. I explained about trying to keep the colours in mind. The colour denoted by the brackets was the group colour which was the right side. As the blocks reduced in number it got easier but there was still a lot of trial and error.

Of the other three words that ended on Row 19 there were only 6 letters they could come down on – the A, second C, D, E, N and T of 'accident'. I was sort of used now to the way The Puzzler's mind worked by now. Or should I say Nathan's mind as we knew now. Clue 117 was *whittle with sword to get this up*. This suggested whittling away at the word *sword* to get a shorter word. The answer was four letters, so the easiest solution was obviously 'word'. When one considered the expression *word up*, then it made sense. This then would come down on the D of 'accident'. Then we knew where 'ye' and 'that', which were already solved, went.

I quickly explained all this to Tony, and we then had the three down words that ended on 'accident'. We now had the word 'try' above accident. This seemed to fit Clue 123 to me - *if you fail make a rugby touchdown again*. Tony agreed. We didn't have 122 yet and this was somewhere on Row 20, between 'eli' and 'try'. We did have 124 and 125 but 124 was one of those answers we could not put in yet because as had happened once before, it must connect only to a clue that was not in yet. According to the list that would be Clue 127. I did notice though that Clue 125 was already in. The answer was 'it' and that was created by the down words 'piping' and 'tiara'.

"We are not doing too badly at this," observed Tony.

"It took a long while to get started but once you are in the mind set it can get easier," I said. "Also, once you know how the puzzle is structured that helps too." Something had just occurred to me. "Now see here. We have one across word to fill in on Row 20 between 'eli' and 'try'. We already know that 108 and 109 come down onto 'omen' and 'emerge' so that means there is an across word joining them. It is a three letter answer so we know we can black block after the first L of 'kill' and after the E of 'revenge'."

Tony read out Clue 122 aloud. "Trouble here but remove blemish to become expert."

"So, I think we need another word for trouble that we need to shorten," I suggested.

Tony got it first time. "How about problem?"

I thought about it for a bit. "That works. Take out the blemish or in this case just B L E M and you are left with 'pro' which is an expert. Good job." We put this in and then 108 said R O M and 109 O M E. Now 109 was three letters so that had to be the answer although it made no sense to me. I did now see what 108 was though.

"Fromage is French for cheese. The clue says new so no age which leaves 'from' and that is who sent it."

"Okay," said Tony, a little doubtfully.

"So now we have everything in up to 125 except for 124 which as you can see cannot be inserted until we have solved 127." I stood back and looked at the whole puzzle for a while. It was nearly complete. We only had seven rows to complete and thirty three answers to insert – or thirty four if you counted 124 'miss'. Of those other thirty three I had answers scribbled down for thirteen. We needed to get 126 and 127 then insert 124 because after that there were a series of clues where the answers could not be inserted until later – *not yet can you insert*. That looked very confusing. "Tony, let us both just concentrate on 126 and 127 for a few minutes."

We both stood and read the clues, looked and thought. Something was bugging me for a while. Something I had forgotten about. It was literally staring me in the face. Face with a capital F. On Row 21 we had 'it' being 125 then three black squares, L in 'clef', black, F from 'first', blank, I from 'kill', blank, blank, F from 'from'. The two F's were the last ones available and both 'first' and 'from' were in the orange group. Both F's had orange dots but one also had a black dot on the right meaning it joined an across word. This had to be 126 which was four letters. I could not think of a four letter word starting I and ending F which suggested it was the first F which was in the across word. It would then be the first letter with I as its third letter.

"Tony, I believe 126 goes here," I told him, switching the two F's around because the one with the black spot had been in the wrong place. "So, four letters starting with F."

Tony looked at the clue again. "Er… in exam terms an F is a fail. That fit's but I don't know what the Christmas angle is."

"Well, let's not worry about that. We can put 'fail' in and see where it gets us."

This we did with the obligatory black block at the end. Then I had a bit of a brainwave. Clue 124 we knew was a down word, but we also knew that it had to end on Row 20 because Clue 125 'it' started Row 21. There was only one vacant square which was the last one in that row. When we put 'miss' down there that had to mean it joined with Clue 127 because the sheet stated 124 could not be inserted until 127 was solved. This mean 127 was a four letter word blank, H, blank, S which turned out to be 'this' which in the way of some cryptic clues was hidden in the question this time – *that history included something*. We put this in and a series of black blocks in for the rest of that row.

After this we were stuck. There were only five out of the next fifteen that could be inserted, and we had no idea where these would go. We had been at it for some hours, so we decided to call it quits for the time being. It was well gone 5 pm and I had not eaten all day. We microwaved a few meals – I had two – and sat on the sofa eating. My mind would not stop though.

"What do you think is going to happen if we solve this thing?" I asked Tony.

He swallowed his mouthful. "No idea. That lunatic said it was the only way we could get out, but he didn't expand on that. He is probably playing us again, but we cannot afford to overlook that chance."

"I was wondering what it all means though," I explained.

"Well, we know that there is a heavy reference to Cluedo," said Tony. "The victim in the board game is Doctor Black and there are six suspects. He is Black, so he has spun it around and that makes the six suspects into six victims. I know of two. There was a guy called Greenhalgh that was clobbered over the head in a library in Scotland. He had found religion. That would loosely give us Reverend Green in the library with the lead piping. Then … er …"

"Yes, I know. Mrs Andrews-White in the hall with the dagger." It sounded funny to say it out loud. I didn't know how I felt about Laura now.

"That leaves another four victims, or potential victims," Tony observed.

I remembered Jackie strung up in her basement. "There has been another killing," I told him. "But I cannot see how it ties in." I gave him the details.

"Well, she was strung up with a rope but that is the only connection I can see. What was her surname?"

I thought about it. "Do you know what? I never knew it."

"Did you not sign a lease or anything?"

"No. In fact, Nathan, found the place for me."

We both looked at each other because based on what we knew now this sounded like another piece of meticulous planning.

"If I had to guess," said Tony, "I would say he put you there so she could keep an eye on you. Either he planned to kill her all along or when you skipped out he felt she failed in her duties."

It sounded plausible. "If the former then she could be one of the six victims. Not if the latter though."

We thought about that for a bit, finishing off our food, before I had another thought. "Do you think we could be the last two victims?"

Tony thought about this for a while. Meanwhile he stood up and took the empty plates over to the bin. "It's possible. I don't see how we can be pigeonholed into Professor Plum and Colonel Mustard though."

I had to admit he was right about that. I changed tack. "Where do you think we are?"

"On location I have no idea," he replied, sitting back down. "I have no data to go on. I was unconscious on the way here and so were you, so we saw nothing. However, he called this his panic room. Most people install a panic room in their residence. Possibly place of work too but I am guessing the former as he would need to keep things secret." He then lowered his voice and leaned over to my ear. "When he told us we had our phones back he said there was no signal down here. That suggests we are in a basement area."

Suddenly the TV screen burst to life and our tormentor was there in front of us. It occurred to me in that instant that this was because we had been conversing in a tone that he could not hear, and he wanted to disrupt this.

"Good evening gentleman," he greeted. "I couldn't help overhearing your conversation and thought I could confirm something for you."

Tony and I exchanged glances. We now had confirmation we were under constant surveillance.

"You were right," said Nathan. "Jackie worked for me. I picked her up out the gutter and set her up in her dog shop. All she had to do for me was to keep an eye on you, James, and report to me. She let you slip away and didn't even tell me, I had to find out for myself. However, she was due to die anyway, it just came earlier than expected. Everything is having to be brought forward, it really is too irritating."

I couldn't help myself. "Yes, but Jackie does not tie in with your Cluedo murders."

"One has to have some poetic licence in these things," countered Nathan. "Jackie's occupation involved preening and pampering pooches. She was quite proud and boastful herself, bragging how she looked after pets that won exclusive pet shows, including Crufts. She thought a lot of herself."

"Proud as a peacock?" I recalled the clue in the puzzle.

"Precisely," said Nathan. "Mrs Peacock in the cellar with the rope."

"Okay then," acknowledged Tony, "but that still leaves three more."

"Let me tell you about them," offered Nathan. "Are you sitting comfortably?"

Chapter 38

This one was going to be a nice little earner. Plumbing out the whole of a basement flat. The bathroom and kitchen area. The guy was stinking rich if what little he had seen of the rest of the house on his way down was any guide. Certainly, he had not quibbled at the quote he had been given and had asked for a start as soon as possible.

Drew Fairgrove had been a plumber for years and he had a reputation, which is why he almost exclusively dealt with high end clients that could afford his over the top quotes. He did a good job, with no call backs necessary for poor workmanship, and he was very tidy, doing a proper clean up after a job. He came highly recommended.

He had been on the job for about a week and was nearly finished. There had been some tiling work involved too but that was no problem. It went hand in hand with fitting bathroom suites and he had experience in that side of things too. He would be finished with the job that day he reckoned.

It was getting on for lunchtime when the customer came down from the main part of the house. "Drew, I need to go out for about an hour. You will be alright here? There should be no callers or anything."

"Sure. No problem."

"Fine then," said the guy. "I will see you later."

When he was gone, Fairgrove rubbed his hands together. How was that for a piece of luck? He gave it about fifteen minutes then carefully wandered upstairs. He crept around the ground floor then looked out of the window. The Ferrari was gone and only his van remained parked in the long gravel driveway of the house which was in its own grounds.

He quickly began wandering from room to room taking a mental inventory of what each one contained and whether it was worth anything. The last room on the ground floor was the kitchen and he could not believe his eyes. In the back door was a set of keys. He took these out and quickly headed back to the basement. In his toolbox he had a tin of wax in which he made an impression of the back door key and what he thought were the front door keys and a little square one which might be to a safe. Then he wiped the wax off the keys with a roll of kitchen paper he kept for that purpose and returned the keys to the door.

He then had a quick look at the upstairs rooms and then was back down in the basement working before the hour was up. After a short while his mobile rung. It was the customer. He had been ringing the bell, but the sound did not reach this bathroom in the basement. He apologised but had locked himself out by leaving his keys in the house and could Fairgrove open the door which he did.

Getting on for five o'clock Fairgrove had finished and tidied up, leaving everything spick and span. Then he went to find the customer to get paid. He took payment in whichever way it came, cheque, credit card, bank transfer or on the odd occasion cash. This time it was a cheque, which was safely in his pocket, and he was about to take his leave.

"You have a nice place," he said to the customer. "You must have some nice pieces." He indicated the couple of vases standing in alcoves in the hallway.

"Would you like the tour?" offered the customer.

"No thanks, I'd better be off. Surprised though that you don't have an alarm system."

"Ah, I will have soon. Not been here long. That is on a long list of things to do."

"Better sooner than later. You can't be too careful." Fairgrove was now outside the door.

"True," agreed the customer. "Anyway, thank you for the excellent work. If I need any more doing I have your card. Drive safely. Goodbye."

Fairgrove got into his van and drove away. The electric gates at the entrance to the property were open so he drove straight through. They closed behind him, but Fairgrove did not notice. He was thinking hard about his next job which was in the pipeline now but did not involve any plumbing.

If all his clients could have got together and compared notes they would all have been able to come to the same conclusion. They had all had work done by Perfection Plumbing – proprietor Drew Fairgrove – and they had all been the victims of burglary to their homes. Fortunately, they could not compare notes, nor would they know they had to. The burglaries were always at least a year after the job so not a standout event in the run up to the thefts. That is what had kept him off the radar so long. Not that it really mattered because for every theft he had a rock solid alibi – courtesy of his doppelganger who took his place whenever he was out on a non-plumbing job.

However, now he had to throw the rulebook out of the window. This one was going to be much easier if he did it now rather than later. A house where there was no security installed yet and to which he could have duplicate keys by the next day. It was too good a chance to pass up. He cleared his appointments for a week and sat in watch upon the house. After the third day of seeing his former customer leave the house at 10 am and not come back until lunch, he knew he had his window.

On the fourth day, after waiting ten minutes just in case of a quick return, Fairgrove climbed over the electric gates. He had no fear of dogs and there was no alarm system as already determined. He had his duplicate key for the back door – and hopefully the safe – so the only issue was the electric gates. It would be so much easier if he could find the opening mechanism and drive his vehicle up to the door. It was not his normal van of course because that had his business name on the sides. Sometimes it does not pay to advertise.

Once in the house he decided to try upstairs first as he had not had as much of a thorough look up there on his previous reconnoitre. There were a lot of rooms but only one bedroom appeared to be in use, which made sense if there was only one occupant. There were a couple of nice watches in a drawer but not much else. He did find a safe though, at the bottom of a wardrobe. It was an old safe with no combination and just a key. Trembling a bit with anticipation he took out the odd key he had duplicated and to his immense satisfaction it fit perfectly. Inside the safe there was a lot of cash and some other documents. He was only interested in the money and from one of the many pockets in the jacket he was wearing, he pulled out a strong black plastic bag. Into this went the money and the watches. It was then back downstairs to see what else he could take but also to try and find the gate controls.

He got a complete shock when he descended the stairs because waiting at the bottom was the customer. Far from being surprised, the customer was grinning and holding a silenced gun.

"I didn't know we would be seeing each other so soon, Drew," he said.

"There's no need to shoot," Fairgrove said nervously, dropping the bag and putting his arms up.

"Oh, don't worry. I'm not going to shoot you. We are going back down to see the work you did for me." His former customer signalled with the gun. "Go on you know the way."

Fairgrove made his way down to the basement flat that he had worked in. He walked into the main room which was just how he had left it. Empty other than the kitchen area he had worked upon. Then it hit him. The floor was all covered with plastic sheeting. He whirled round to find the customer at the doorway.

"Please don't shoot," he pleaded.

"I told you. I am not going to shoot you. I am going to lock you in so that you can contemplate your sins and see what it is going to be like in prison."

"Why are you doing this? Was this all a set up?" Fairgrove had been thinking this ever since he had been discovered.

"Of course. I needed a professional plumber for my plan, but I needed a naughty one and you have been a naughty boy, haven't you Drew. Or maybe you prefer your real name, Derek." There was shock in Fairgrove's eyes now because not many people knew his real name. "You would have got away with your burglary sideline until you killed someone."

Fairgrove knew what he meant. "It was an accident. Honest. She fell down the stairs. I never touched her." He was referring to the events of over a year ago when a woman had come back home unexpectedly and ran into him at the top of the stairs. The shock had been so great she fainted and fell down the stairs breaking her neck. "Who was she to you?"

"Oh, she meant nothing to me, but that took you out of the burglar class to a killer. Just right for my plan. Now I must call the police so goodbye for now."

Fairgrove had never taken it in before, but the room had no actual door. Just the doorway he had entered many times during his work there. He now saw that a panel slid down from the roof and fit seamlessly into the wall space.

Fairgrove only had time to worry about this incarceration for a few minutes because then he heard a hissing sound and gas began to enter the room from ceiling vents. There was no point rushing to the bathroom because there was no door on there yet or the other room off the main room. Instead, he ran to the section of the wall where the doorway was and started banging on the wall, screaming to be let out. No one came to help him, of course, and soon his attempts grew more and more feeble and eventually stopped. He collapsed onto the plastic covered floor unconscious.

No sooner was he out cold than the doorway opened, and the customer came through wearing breathing apparatus, followed by another man similarly attired. They carried Fairgrove out and up into the back of his van which was now parked outside. The plastic sheeting had not been down to catch blood but for decorating purposes. The customer chuckled at what this had made Fairgrove think.

Fairgrove was driven back to his own house, where in fact his doppelganger was waiting. He was not part of the plan, so they let him go. Once they had Fairgrove in his house and specifically in the kitchen, the other man left. The ex-customer brought in a toolbox from the van. He was now dressed in a hooded forensics suit and gloves. After looking through the tools he brought out a wrench and whacked the still comatose Fairgrove on the head. The power with which he was struck cracked the skull like an eggshell, but he hit him twice more for good measure. Then he put the wrench back in the toolbox, which he left on the kitchen table.

"Professional Plumber in the kitchen with a wrench," said the ex-customer as he took his leave.

***

"Not only is that stretching things a bit far," I snorted, "Professional plumber for Professor Plum, but that is not even connected to the rest."

Nathan was unperturbed. "Poetic licence again. Anyway, as I told Tony before, I am not a bad man, just one who wants a little justice. I have hurt no one who did not deserve it."

"What about Laura?" I snapped.

"You didn't know the real her," he said. "Before I cleaned her up she was a prostitute, drug addict and blackmailer. She was due some retribution."

What? Drugs and blackmail too. Was I such a fool to get taken in?

Nathan was enjoying himself, unloading such titbits. "Anyway, on with Colonel Mustard," he began to say, but then he quickly looked away. "What the hell!"

The screen went blank, so we never found out what happened to Colonel Mustard or for that matter Miss Scarlet. Not then anyway.

Chapter 39

Whatever had disturbed Nathan it was something that he had not planned for, that much was obvious. We couldn't do much about it or turn it to our advantage. That left us with two things we could do, mull over what he had told us or carry on puzzling. We were at a bit of a dead end though with the latter, so we just talked over the situation again, trying to guess what Nathan's end game was. We were no nearer the answer after three hours and thinking we were going to need all the rest we could get, we retired early. Signified by his light snoring, Tony was out like a light immediately. I envied people who could sleep as soon as their head touched the pillow. I didn't think I would get any sleep because there were so many things whirling through my head. Me as another person, a killer. Laura as a common prostitute who had played me from the start. The puzzle too, which had been going around in my head for a lot longer than the other two intrusive thoughts.

I must have dropped off because I woke up some time later with an idea fresh in my mind. I quietly got down from the top bunk and went into the main room, closing the door behind me so the light would not disturb Tony. I didn't care if Nathan was watching his monitors.

I wanted to update the grid on my paper copy. We had got to a place now where a lot of the clue answers could not be inserted until the last clue answer which was 158. I had the answer to that one. 'Killing two birds with one stone.' As the puzzle had been built from ground up like a building, this last answer was then the roof. In effect then we had to put the roof on and then build downwards until we met where we were already. That obviously could not be done with the actual frame on the wall, but I could do that on paper. Or that had been my idea, but I was stumped by one simple problem. I had nothing to write with.

There were no pens, pencils or anything like that in the room as far as I could see. Nathan probably thought they could be used as weapons, although I guess you could cause an injury with a plastic fork if you knew how to. I had the idea at first of breaking all the prongs but one off a fork then using a bottle of ketchup I had spied in the cupboard as ink. It turned out to be too thick. I was wracking my brains for something else to write with when I realised that I didn't have to. I could use the blocks but lay them on the floor face up.

I knew how to start. That last clue had no colour against it so most of the blocks would have no colour on them. Some would be the start of words going down, but most would be plain. If I gathered all the letters in 'killing two birds with one stone' using as many plain letters as I could, then those that I could not find a plain letter for would indicate where a downwards word would be. It was not foolproof because I could use a plain letter where there should be a coloured dot, but it was something.

I got off to a good start because there was only one K left and it was plain. There were several I's left but only one was plain. I needed four so that meant three of them would be down words. I had no idea which coloured dots to use yet though, so I just stuck any in. And so, I went along spelling out the twenty seven letter phrase. There were only two plain N's and I needed three, so one of them started a word, but there were no plain G's so that was another word. There were three plain T's and I needed three so could be right or wrong. There were no plain W's. In the end I had a definite 10 words going down because they were dotted letters. I knew that there were two starting with W, one with G and one with B. The phrase had two W's, one G and one B so I had the position of these words. On the I's, O's and S's there would be a choice.

I could start with the B because it was the only one left and it had a pink spot. I ran through the clues from the bottom up and the first one that had (P) beside it was 140. I had the answer to that already 'birds'. It seemed odd that the same word would go down and across, but I had nothing better. There was only one 'I' with a pink dot and this also had a purple dot which meant a word running directly under the top line. There were two R's with pink dots but one also had a yellow dot, however, there was only one D with a pink dot and that also had a yellow dot so a yellow word across. As it was unlikely, although not impossible the way this puzzle went, to have two yellow words going across above each other, I used the R with just the single pink dot. There was also only one S with a pink dot and this also had an orange dot.

Now to the two W's. There were three of these left but two had a black dot on the left side meaning an intersection of words and a yellow dot on the right on one and orange on the other. The general rule so far had been the first dot was the colour group – right side – and the crossover was the left side. As we were building up 'killing two birds with one stone' was the crossover word or phrase so the black would be on the left. Therefore, we had two words going down off the W's, one yellow and one orange. Going back up the list of clues the first yellow one was 147 but I had 'plum' for that. Then 141 which was 'study' and finally 139 for which I had 'white'. Which W to use though. In the end it was made easier because of already having 'birds' in. That word had a D which needed a yellow word across. I was fine with all the yellow words because we had all the Cluedo answers. I saw that if I put 'white' down using the W of 'two' then the T of 'white' and the D of 'birds' meant I could put 'study' across. This worked out because there was a T with a yellow dot on each side. There was also only one H with a yellow dot and the three I's but with only single yellow dots. There was an E with a yellow dot alone but also one with a red dot. I took a chance on the former.

As regards 'study' I could find an S and U with a single yellow dot, so I used those for now. As for Y though the only on with a yellow dot also had a dark blue dot on the left, indicating a dark blue down word. This would be a three letter word starting with Y. Looking at the clues the first clue going backwards that fitted was 132 and I had the answer to that 'you'. Placing that word down would create 'so' going across from the S in 'birds' so the O I needed would have to be dark blue and orange, which I found, and the U would just be dark blue.

Turning now to the other W for 'with' in the top row, this was going to start an orange down word but from checking the paper I could see that it would only be a three letter word as this would then join the black square over 'revenge'. The clues that had (O) after them were 154, 152 and 137 but the latter was only a two letter answer, the other two were three. However, the two letter clue was easy now that I had the S and O under 'study'. The clue was *double this means average*. I used the expression myself quite often – so,so. The answer then was 'so' and was already in, so it just needed a black block at the end.

The word starting with a W was one of the other two clues. I had no idea the answer to 154 but 152 did seem to fit. *Second half of a Saturday morning kids show definitely existed.* I only knew two Saturday morning kids shows but now I knew Nathan was the architect and his age was similar to mine, it seemed safe to assume it was one of these. I doubted very much it referred to 'The Multi-Coloured Swap Shop' so that left 'Tiswas' and the second half of that 'was' which definitely did exist. The only orange A left was double orange suggesting a crossover word and the only orange S had the dot on the left which means that 'was' was intersecting with a non-coloured word.

It was difficult to tell because I had a disconnected frame with blocks on the floor, but I think I now had two bits of it connecting from top to bottom. Now I had 'you' Clue 132 ending on row 22 which suggested that Clue 131 was also a down word ending on the same row. I had the answer to that clue which was another Cluedo one. That being the case 'lounge' could join either of the L's in 'killing' but which one. I couldn't put that in yet. I had to look elsewhere.

I had put in 137 as 'so' and the answer for 138 I had as 'green', part of the Cluedo set. There was an R – the one in 'revenge' three spaces away and I could not fit in 'green' anywhere else on that row. Now staying in that area, when placing 'was' I had used an A with double orange spots which meant it was used in a word across. There was more than a fifty fifty chance then that there was a downwards word on the S in 'birds'. I had an answer that started with S and had a G as the fifth letter – shaggy. This left me with a place for 'rye' which Rich and Jenny had come up with but as a probable not a definite. It now looked more probable. The colours all worked except for the two E's in 'green'. There were three E's with yellow dots but two were single and one had a right red dot. Now 'green' was Clue 138 and after this it said that 128 could be inserted so this means it must cross 'green'. Therefore, I used the E with a yellow dot and red dot plus one with a sole yellow one. The former had to go second because that was the one that allowed a crossing word to go below that row and as 128 was before 138 that word began on a lower row.

With 'shaggy' and 'was' coming down next to each other there were two words directly below the top line going across one had H A and the other one A S. The H A word was orange and the other one no colour. The only orange clue left in the latter end of the clues was the one I could not get before – *I see no African country but I did have it*. Now this was only 3 letters, and I could not make one with a letter before the H other than 'cha' but then that immediately gave me the African country of Chad. Obviously 4 letters but *see no* could mean no C thus leaving 'had'. This then left me with I D coming down from the 'I' in 'with'. On looking that could tie up with Clue 157 – *instinctual desire to be known* – which was a two letter answer. What's more, there were only two D's left and one had an orange dot. That meant that the A S word ended in those two letters if I put a black block under the D in 'id'.

Things were going well. It was funny, I was tired and my mind fuzzy, but I was coming up with the answers. That was the way sometimes. I recalled that back in the days when I was doing puzzles regularly, I could do one at night in bed before going to sleep that had bugged me during the day. There was sometimes a clarity in the fuzziness. Thinking of this though was a mistake because that made me think of Laura, which then made me think of what I had been to her. That brought a bit of an end to my breakthrough.

Then another thought hit me. I had just remembered 'Tiswas' a show that I had watched before my amnesia. Were things coming back? Would I turn back into the monster Nathan had been telling us about? This in turn led to scarier thoughts. What if we did get out of this? Tony was in the police, and he had heard Nathan's story. He would have to do his duty and I would get arrested for murder.

All these thoughts came to me at once and I had to retire to the sofa where I lay in deep gloomy reverie. How long that was for I don't know but I was abruptly brought back to the real world when Tony came out of the bedroom and into the bathroom. Five minutes later in he was in the kitchen making coffee.

"You're up early. Got something special on?" he smiled at his own joke.

"I've been up for hours. I got an idea to start working on the puzzle from the top down." I said it before I realised that Nathan probably heard that. I stood up and motioned Tony over to behind the sofa where blocks were spread out on the floor.

"Not bad," he nodded. He went back to the kettle. "I take it you want coffee?"

"Yes please! Strong and lots of sugar this time." When it came it was one of those cups of coffee you could stand a teaspoon up in. It was just what I needed.

No sooner had I sat down with mine and Tony was looking to his breakfast than the TV screen burst to life. It was you know who and he didn't look happy. No bonhomie today.

"I have to bring someone in," he said. "Get in the restraints."

"Might as well do it," warned Tony, "otherwise he'll just gas us again."

We got back up against the posts and put our feet and wrists in the clamps that automatically shut on them. No sooner had that happened than we heard the door swoosh and almost immediately Nathan came in carrying someone. I could not make out who it was as he dropped the prone form on the sofa. "Temporary guest," he said and left.

The restraints were soon released, and we both went over to see who it was. Tony's face looked blank as he stared at the woman spark out on the sofa. Not me though, because I knew her. It was Vicky.

Chapter 40

I had to make an immediate decision. Did I let on I knew her or not? However she came to be here, I was sure that her reporter instincts that made them keep stories close to their chests would have meant she would not have let slip our association. Tony needed to know but not our watching Big Brother.

"I wonder where she comes in?" mused Tony.

"Let's not disturb her," I said in a whisper. I then indicated we move away. I went into the bathroom and turned on the taps and the shower. Tony obviously knew I had something to say that was not for the ears of our host, so he just waited for me. "I know her," I began. "She's a reporter I met on the boat. Her name is Vicky."

"What's she doing here?" asked Tony in the same hushed tones.

"I guess she followed. She was supposed to meet me at my flat, a bit later than the time I was snatched. It is not a good idea for Nathan to know this. Follow my lead when she wakes up. I just hope she cottons on."

We went back into the main room, having turned the water off again. Vicky was still out of it. She lay there dressed in jeans and a white t-shirt. Her breathing was regular, so I didn't think there was anything to worry about. I wondered how Nathan had got hold of her. Had he caught her snooping around? I remembered his "what the hell" of earlier and felt that must have been it. Had he interrogated her though? If so what had she said? Again, I didn't think she had said anything about me otherwise Nathan would have said something instead of just dumping her on the sofa. Still, if she had been the cause of Nathan's outburst, which had been early evening yesterday, then he had been questioning her for some time. There were no marks on her that I could see – so no rough stuff.

Tony had got back to making his breakfast and I finished my coffee which was a bit cooler now. By the time Tony had finished eating, Vicky was starting to come round. What I mean by that is she moaned, turned over and was sick all over the floor. I had been standing nearby and rushed over to the kitchen area to get something to clean it up. I whispered to Tony in passing. "You do the honours. Best she doesn't see me until she is more compos mentis if we want her to play along." He nodded and went over.

"Hey, are you okay?" he asked Vicky, who was trying to sit up.

"Er … no. I feel as sick as a dog," she replied. "Where am I and who are you?"

"Well, I'm Tony and you are like me a captive in an underground panic room which in actuality is really an escape-proof room." Talk about telling it straight.

"Oh... I remember now. He caught me." She put her hand to her head, massaging her temple. "God, have I got a headache."

"It will pass," said Tony. "What's your name?" Tony was with the programme.

"Er... Vicky"

"Well, take it easy Vicky. Looks like you were drugged like us." Oops! She picked up on it as well and started looking around. She spotted me and just as her mouth opened I jumped in.

"Nice to meet you Vicky. I'm Danny. Another prisoner."

Fortunately, slightly incapacitated as she was, she still got it. "Hi."

I took her over a cup of water and then tried to mop up the sick as best I could with kitchen towels. I flushed them down the toilet, but the stink was going to hang around though. Vicky was watching me all the time, looking for her cues I guess. After she finished the water, she asked the obvious question that Nathan would have expected. "What the hell is going on?"

We took it in turns to outline the situation which obviously included stuff she already knew. We told her that we were being monitored so not to say anything out loud she did not want our captor to hear. We said that aloud to tick him off. Then when she was up to date we naturally asked her how she had got caught up in this mess. That is when Vicky came up with an idea that had eluded us. She didn't have her phone, I guessed Nathan was checking it out, so she asked for mine. She opened a text and started typing, her thumbs flying over the keys, then showed us what she had written.

We can communicate this way!

I took the phone and took twice as long to write two words. *Great idea.*

So, with a series of texts that were deleted once read, Vicky informed us of how she happened to be there with us. It took a while but surprisingly none of us had anything in the calendar for that day.

***

Vicky had managed to do what she had to do at her place rather quicker than she had anticipated. Having dumped all her holiday clothes at the laundrette for a service wash, other than items that had to be dry cleaned, she had packed a smaller bag with some stuff, had a shower, changed clothes and was back on the road in an hour. Not forgetting to ring her source to get an update on the story. She rode her motorbike fast and arrived at Danny's place just in time to park behind an ambulance although as she did it suddenly took off sirens blazing. She was puzzled to see the door wide open when she approached Danny's flat and having entered the smell hit her from the shop, that door still being open too. Upstairs she noticed Danny's open cases and the washing machine on but no Danny. She went back down and into the shop and found Jackie's body. She called the police about that but left before they got there.

She didn't know where Danny was, but she could find out. When she had borrowed his phone on the train she had added an app to his phone, now she could track him on hers. Stopping a couple of miles away from Danny's flat, she had a look. She could see he was moving and moving fast. She got on her bike and gunned it. By the time she got to where he had briefly stopped she was in a field where the ambulance stood, all doors wide open. According to her phone, he was now travelling even faster. Too fast for a car. A plane or a helicopter. She guessed the latter because of the state of the field, which was not long enough for a take-off by plane. She took off again travelling in the same direction, or as far as she could on the roads. Every so often she would stop to check she was still going the right way.

After a couple of hours Danny, or his phone, stopped moving. It was out in the wilds of Devon or Cornwall but near the coast. It would take her a while to get there. She had stopped at the first service station she came to which happened to be Cobham Services on M25 for petrol. Then it was M4, M5 and A30. The journey took well over four hours, so it was nearly 7.00 pm by the time she arrived at Portreath on the Cornish coast. This was the nearest place to where Danny's phone had stopped. Portreath only counted as a village, there had been a town a few miles back, Redruth, but she wanted to be as near as possible. She was lucky in getting a room at a B & B in view of the busy start of the summer trade.

Using her reporter skills, she managed to wangle out of the rotund landlady that there was a rich gentleman living a couple of miles away in a self-built property on the coast road that, yes, did use a helicopter from time to time. Not much was known about him. He kept himself to himself, but people were not too keen on his mad driving of his sports car, nor the helicopter arriving sometimes in the middle of the night. So not that popular with the locals.

After quickly having something to eat, she then went out to reconnoitre the property. She had trouble finding it at first but eventually located it and saw that it was well secured in its own grounds. According to what she could tell Danny's phone was on the inside. She was at a crossroads, a mental dilemma. She wanted the story, the exclusive story and therefore her instinct was to investigate. On the other hand, she had a friend in there at the hands of a possible madman and / or serial killer. What to do?

It was unlikely she could get the police to raid the place without proof. It was her word against the local rich guy. She had not seen Danny get taken from his place nor seen him transported here. The police might take a dim view of tracking non-family members via a locator app. She had to get inside to check, or at least get to a window. The property was walled all the way around. It was a high wall with no overhanging trees. She had no ladder and precariously standing on her bike did not give her the height. She would have to wait for a delivery. It was something she had done before. The postman was out because it was Saturday and no post the next day. Unless the guy was having a Saturday night pizza delivered the chances were not too good of anything happening until at least Monday. She knew she could not wait that long. She went back to the B & B to make some calls and find a ladder.

As it turned out there was nothing open in Portreath that might sell a ladder. She would have to wait until Sunday opening hours and go to the nearby town. A rope ladder or grappling hook and rope would be best for her, but she imagined that it would be easier to buy a normal ladder. She thought transporting it would be a problem but in the end not so much. She got a taxi, and he knew a place on an industrial estate. She was able to buy a telescopic aluminium ladder that when closed fitted in the boot of a car. It was easier to carry too although heavier than it looked. With a bit of work, she managed to lash it to her bike although she hoped she didn't happen on any police on the short drive.

Then her luck turned for the worse. She had not spotted it when lashing the ladder, but noticed she had a flat tyre as she was about to set off. It was about lunchtime and it being Sunday, the earliest she could get someone out to look at it was mid-afternoon. She had to cool her heels for a few hours, and it was then she noticed that Danny's phone was no longer showing up. In the end it was past 6 pm when she arrived at the property walls. She had no idea of the security, but it made sense to approach from the side because the front and back would have the main rooms presumably.

Her ladder was just over three metres when fully extended, so it was easily long enough. The problem was heaving it up after her to place it down the other side, but she managed to do it. There was absolutely no cover between the wall and the house so she just kept as low as she could and headed straight for it. There were few windows on the side of the very extensive house, but she could see cameras positioned at each corner. She guessed she had been seen coming over the grounds, and maybe the wall, but she now kept close to the wall and edged around the property looking in the windows. It was at one window that she saw Nathan – although she didn't know who he was – watching a TV monitor closely. He was talking but she could not hear anything. Vicky saw enough of the monitor to see Danny, but her reflection must have given her away because Nathan whirled round and spotted her at the window. She fled in a flash. Got to the ladder and reached the top. She looked back and saw Nathan running down the drive towards the gates that were opening. He was going to beat her. Instead of trying to haul up the ladder to get down the other side, she pulled out her phone and hit redial. "Contact the police!" she said and then hung up. She placed her phone on top of the wall where it could not be seen from below. Not a moment too soon.

"Get down here!" Nathan had a gun pointed in her direction.

Without protest Vicky pulled up the ladder and then placed it down the other side to come down. She reached the bottom and raised her hands. "And who are you then?" demanded Nathan,

"Just a friendly neighbourhood reporter," answered Vicky.

"Really! Now why would you be interested in me? We'll talk inside. Move it!"

She had been tied up and questioned but not tortured. Her story was she was a journalist on holiday and had got curious hearing about the reclusive neighbour who came and went by helicopter so had decided to investigate. Nathan had his suspicions, but his ego made him think this was a logical event. He could not let her leave though, so he had injected her with something and that was all Vicky knew until she woke up in the room.

***

I was a bit excited and almost grabbed the phone. After erasing her last message, I wrote, *so the police are on their way?* but she wrote back, *maybe but my contact was not there, I had to leave a message. Don't know when he will get it.* As suddenly as they had risen my hopes were dashed. Still at least we had a chance now, a blind dog's chance it was true, but a chance.

Chapter 41

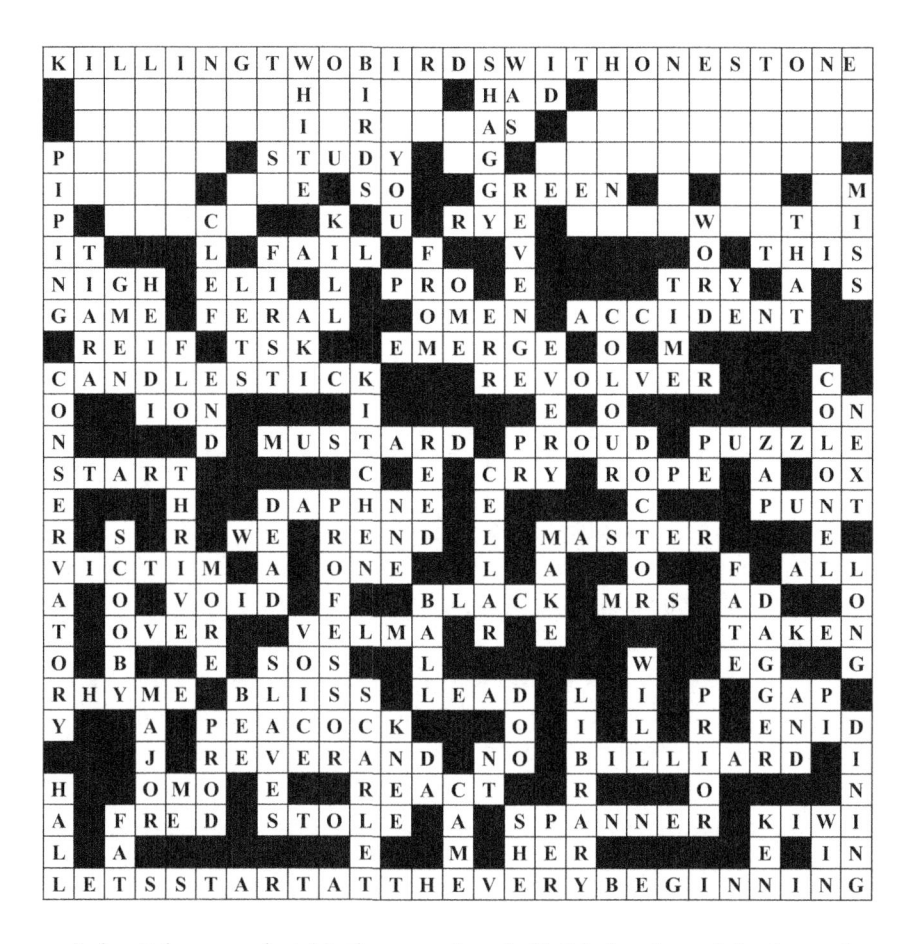

[crossword puzzle grid]

    I don't know what Nathan made of all this back and forth on the phone, but he did not make an appearance either in person or on the screen. Maybe he was not watching us constantly after all. One thing for sure though is that we could not keep this up forever. My battery was getting very low, and we had no charger. We had to keep Tony's battery life in case we managed to get out of the room and could call for help.

    "So how long have you been here?" Vicky asked us, playing along with the stranger's role.

    "I've only been here a couple of days," I said, "but Tony has been here for over a week I guess." Tony nodded at that.

    "What do we do? Just sit here?" Vicky wanted to know.

    "There's not much we can do, Vicky," Tony informed her. "This is a completely sealed room. No visible door and no windows. We do have a task to be getting on with. Allegedly, it is our only way out, but I have my doubts about that." He indicated the puzzle frame on the wall.

Vicky obviously knew what it was from our sessions on the boat. "Impressive but what is it?"

"It's a sort of crossword puzzle," he replied. "Danny and I were getting clues sent to us before we even got captured. We have to complete it but what happens then I have no idea."

"Well, you boys go ahead," said Vicky. "I still feel a bit yucky. I'll just watch."

Tony's breakfast over he could join in. I explained what I had done and why there were blocks all over the floor.

"Looks like you've broken the back of it," approved Tony. There can only be a few words to slot in now."

"Well, if I have ticked them off correctly, we have twenty left and we have answers to five of those." I consulted the list. "Lounge, Ago, Plum, Rooms and Go. I know 'lounge' goes here under one of these L's in 'killing'. Which one though will be a guess."

"We're building this two ways now," observed Tony. "Upwards on the wall and downwards on the floor. This could get complicated if we cannot view both together."

"Well, we could put the middle section in, as we can link up to the top with 'white', 'birds' and 'shaggy' but that will leave us with gaps on the floor which won't help us. We probably need to finish it all now before we slot it all in."

The last full row complete was Row 21. There was currently only one word going across on Row 22 which was 'rye'. The next clue was 130, *I need this to tango*. I was unsure why we had not got this before, surely it was a well-known phrase. I directed Tony's attention to that clue. "Two," he said without hesitation which is what I had been thinking. There was a W on Row 22 being the start of 'word' going down. Now 131 was 'lounge' and we knew that this was a down clue from 'killing' in the top line.

"Ah! Something else to help," I declared. 'Lounge goes there or there," I pointed at the L's. Now that is six letters, and it ends on Row 22. Now look at this. Other than 'shaggy' which we have in, there are no other six letter clues left. That means there are no other words on Row 22 that join up with the top line. Other than under the two L's we can put black squares in the rest of Row 22."

Tony started picking up black blocks but then I realised I had made a mistake. "No! Hold it. I forgot something. Clue 128 could not be inserted until …" I traced my finger down the list "…138 had been inserted. That is 'green' which is in but that means 128 crosses 'green'. It can only be off the E or the N. *Where has W gone to?* Four letters."

"Here," piped up Vicky from the other side of the sofa.

I looked and it would fit if we took out a black square that had been put in Row 21 in error. Now we could put black squares in all the other columns other than the two L's. "Let's put 'lounge' in and see what we can build off it.'

Tony spotted something which immediately helped. "There is only one U left and it has two yellow dots."

"Another yellow word crossing it," I exclaimed somewhat too excitedly. There were only two yellow Cluedo words left – 'rooms' and 'plum'. Obviously only the latter fitted and because of that it also told us that 'lounge' sat under the second L. Under the first the P of 'plum' would be sitting on top of P for 'piping which already had a black square there. Using the colouring we were able to work out a few things. There were three O's with a single yellow dot on the right which tied up because we would need two for 'rooms'. There was only one each of N and E with yellow dots. There were two L's with yellow – one right and one left, which I didn't quite get yet but it didn't matter. The biggest help was the G which had a left pink spot so a pink word going across. This could only be 135 or 136 because 137 was 'so' and we had that in.

"Shout out some school puddings," I said aloud.

"Jam roly poly," was Tony's first attempt.

"Semolina," said Vicky. "And tapioca. Yuk!"

"Sago," put in Tony.

"That's it. Take off the head – S – and you are left with 'ago' which ties in with 136." We were flying now. We could get it finished that day I thought. There was a single pink dot A and O. And inserting 'plum' across used up the other yellow dotted L and one of two M's with yellow dots. There were three P's with yellow dots but one of these on the left.

I thought I had the answer to that now. "Listen, I think I have something. When we have been building this up the colour group is on right and a left dot meant a word crossing. Now we are building down. So, if a blank word came down from the top line – so it was in first technically – and a yellow word crossed it, then there would just be a single yellow spot on the left. So just to check is there a three letter word starting I and ending P?"

The answer had come to me before I had even finished asking the question. There was only one letter that could go in as far as I could see which was M. Now did 'imp' tie up with any of the three letter clues? Imps were mischievous as in Clue 151. Then again something from my past came back. The name of a car – Hillman Imp. No time to worry about it then but at the back of my mind these snippets of knowledge were starting to worry me.

There was a plain M to insert. Now we had one corner filled in too. Staying in that corner 'plum' was Clue 147 and 148 was *map book does not fit to a tee, shame*. I was in the groove now and based on the way some of the other clues had gone I had this. A map book is an atlas, take off the T and you get 'alas' which means pity or shame. Now we were on Row 25 here and after 'plum' we had a black square then blank, blank, I from 'white', blank, R from 'birds'. It didn't fit there but it did fit with the A and S made from 'shaggy' and 'was'. It went there and the four prior blanks were now black squares. We were so close.

Our mounting excitement got Vicky up from the sofa and she came around to help too. It took us another three hours with a lot of trial and error but eventually we thought we had it. We stood looking at the floor then at the frame and trying to check it all dovetailed correctly.

"There is only one way to find out," said Tony.

We carefully inserted all the blocks into the frame leaving the 'killing two birds with one stone' until last. As the last E was dropped in there was whooshing sound and a small square section of wall was gone leaving a small alcove containing a screen and keyboard.

There was the sound of raucous laughter which made us all jump. Turning round we saw Nathan on the TV screens. "You didn't think it was going to be as easy as all that did you?" He was beaming. "Still, I didn't expect you to get this far. Especially as I was expecting you to be doing this by yourselves alone and struggling. You both sort of cheated by getting help. No matter, it is not finished yet and you still have to work out the final bit."

"I might have known that you wouldn't keep your word," snapped Tony.

"Now let's stay civil," Nathan admonished. "As you have completed the whole puzzle I guess it's only fair I clue you in on Colonel Mustard. Not that there is a Colonel Mustard you understand. That person would have been so hard to find. No, I found a Colonel Colman – think about it and you'll get it. He wasn't a real colonel only in his war games. He was a bit of kiddy fiddler though, so he deserved to get included in this production."

"So, we have had the dagger, rope, spanner and lead piping – I glanced at Tony who nodded, having filled me in on Greenhalgh – so was it revolver or candlestick?"

"Well, he liked his war games, so a firearm was the most suitable," Nathan said. "I had a few rooms left to choose but in the end it was in the conservatory of his big fancy house. Not a person that will be greatly missed."

"What do you think you're like?" asked Tony angrily. "You seem to think that you are putting down bad people so that is okay. What about the people in this room?"

"Well, Tony, you know as well as I that you and Danny are both criminals too. The only possible innocent person in there is the reporter – hi Vicky – and she may have to be collateral damage."

Vicky got a wild look on her face then and started looking from one of us to the other then back at the screen. She didn't know the whole story we had been fed whilst we had been there. Fact or fiction? Who could tell anymore? I needed to get her mind off thinking of us as a sudden enemy – if that is indeed what she was thinking.

"You haven't told us about Miss Scarlet," I demanded defiantly.

"Oh, don't you know brother. You did that one."

I must have looked confused, I certainly felt it. Nathan decided to explain it to the ensemble.

"The prostitute in Manchester 1996. No, I could not possibly know how you killed her. It was not the fire which was just to cover it all up. Prostitute, scarlet woman. I felt that you deserved that one." Then he smiled. "Well, in fact you may be getting the others too. I left some of your DNA at a couple of the scenes."

"How the hell?" I spluttered.

"How many times have I been to your place, Danny? This has been long term planning, not a flash in the pan."

I was stunned. Every time he granted us an audience he came at me with even more venom. He looked pleased with the reaction.

"Anyway, time to me to go for a while. I have one other person to cross off my list. I should be back well before you solve the second part. Toodle pip!"

The screen went black, and we were all stood there at what moments before was a scene of triumph but now was littered with suspicious looks. It was Tony that broke the spell.

"Don't let that freak get into our heads," he said. "We've got to finish this. If he's going away somewhere we could not have a better chance of getting out."

"Honestly Vicky, I don't know what he is talking about," I told her. "He has told us some fancy story, but we don't know if anything of it is true. Right, Tony?"

"True. And other than taking that guy down for what he has done, I don't think anything will be coming of it if it is true." That was welcome news to my ears.

"Let's have some lunch and get back down to it," suggested Tony.

"I'm not particularly hungry," said Vicky. "I still feel a bit queasy but you two go ahead." She went and sat back on the sofa, no doubt thinking over what had been said and wondering what she had gotten herself into.

Whilst tucking into our microwave meals, I was mulling the situation over in my mind. "It has to be the colours," I suddenly announced to the room.

"Sorry," Tony mumbled, his mouth full of food,

"The colours. Why is there a group of coloured words? Yes, we know all the yellow were Cluedo words. And for that matter the green ones were the Scooby Gang. What about the other colours though. Do they spell out a message?"

It was an interesting thought so that is what we looked at next. Apart from yellow and green there were red, orange, pink, light blue, dark blue and purple. We listed out all the words for each colour and ended up with the following lists.

Red: we, master, start, puzzle, let's, game, here, name, my.
Orange: she, stole, me, first, from, accident, pro, so, was, had.
Pink: came, prior, rhyme, time, long, next, revenge, two, ago
Light Blue: in, slaves, no, will, more, thrive, void, one, all, kill
Dark Blue: and, make, end, colour, nigh, try, word, you, test, it
Purple: this, the, go, is, to

If each colour was supposed to be a message then purple was a bust, but it was quite easy when you thought about it. As the reporter Vicky came up with it first. "Presumably the purple words are those that occur more than once." It seemed as good an idea as any and fitted with the type of words of that colour.

We had the words grouped and now we had to work out what to do with them. On a whim I pressed the button on the bottom of the screen, and it came to life. There were a set of blank spaces – like hangman with a slash between words presumably. There were four lines consisting of twelve words.

"Well, that is not enough for all the words we have here," I announced. "That being the case I am guessing we have to play one colour at a time. Which one first though?"

We were out of one puzzle and straight into another.

Chapter 42

It was the ultimate frustration. We had thought we were so close and now we were back at the beginning of another brainteaser. Not that we had been expecting the completion of the puzzle to have led to our release, despite what Nathan had told Tony previously. We had already been at it for hours before lunch, so we decided to call an hour's break to give the little grey cells a rest. As Nathan had left the building we could talk naturally, or maybe he had not left the building but was just saying that, so we did talk naturally. I was too riled to care. and my phone was going to be useless now anyway.

I brought Vicky up to date on what had happened to me and then Tony told us both what had happened to him. It was obvious how Nathan had sat as the big fat controlling spider spinning a sticky web to catch us all, even though Vicky was an unintended victim. I think it came over in this chat how worried I was about the type of person he was painting me as. The type of person I might turn back into if I got my memory back. Tony told me not to worry about it as it served no purpose, especially not now. Vicky was half sympathetic but also half curious reporter on an exclusive story.

Eventually the conversation drifted back to the puzzle and what we now had to do, so we decided to get down to it. It was obvious we had to type the words onto the screen using the keypad, but in what order? I looked at the screen and spotted that the first line consisted of two six letter words. From the groups of words we had, only the red and the light blue groups had two six letter words. That meant we had to put in master and puzzle or slaves and thrive.

"Puzzle Master sounds like a name," said Vicky. "The Puzzle Master."

That was feasible particularly as the red group included 'name' as one of its words. I typed it in, and the letters appeared on screen. Next line was two letters, two letters and four letters. Assuming the four letters was name as opposed to game or let's, we could get 'is my name' by using one of the purple words. This made sense because there were twelve words on screen but only nine red words in the group so that meant three purple words. As a short sentence it also made sense. That left us with; start, game, here, lets, we. The next line down was four letters, two and two. That meant 'we' was in there and presumably one of the purple words. After mucking about with it for a few minutes we all felt that the best line out of what we had was 'here we go'. We put that in which left us, start, game lets which with a line looking for four letters, five letters, three letters and four letters. The second word was obviously 'start' and 'lets' seemed the better fit before this, so the last line typed in was 'lets start the game'. There was a beep, and a second screen came up with blanks on four lines as before.

"One down," said Tony.

"An eight letter word to start," Vicky noticed.

There was only one - 'accident' - which meant this was the orange group. This verse, if that is what it could be called, went letter wise like this; first line - eight, five, second line – three, three, three, third line – five, four, two, last line – two, three, two, two. There was only one four letter word in the orange group which was 'from' so we knew that was in the third line. There were two five letter words being 'stole' and 'first'. Line three had a five letter word before 'from' and 'stole from' worked better than 'first from' and that lead us to 'me'. First line then 'accident first' and third line 'stole from me'. That left us with only three and two letter words; 'had', 'pro', 'she', 'so', 'was' and therefore we also needed two purple words. It was the last line that had the two letter words and 'so' was there. This also meant the two purple words had to be two letters so that meant 'go' 'is' or 'to'. That being the case, line two which had three letter words only and the strong suggestion that this started 'she had' or 'she was' which meant the last word had to be 'pro' otherwise there was no sense to the line. It also tied up with prostitute which Nathan had mentioned more than once. That left 'had' in the last line as well as 'so'. The latter did not make a lot of sense being used in the third or fourth position, so the line had to start 'so had' and then of the three two letter purple words 'to go' made the most sense.

Vicky typed it in. 'Accident first, she was pro, stole from me, so had to go' and there was another ping, and a fresh screen came up.

"Two down. Three to go," growled Tony.

I thought this was going too easy. There must be something more to come because Nathan had been so fastidiously clever so far – or thought he had – that this was too fast. "Do you think this is going too well?" I asked the others.

"Why would you say that?" asked Vicky. "It has not been straightforward and needed working out."

"Yes, but it can be worked out logically. Everything else so far has included guesswork which means mistakes and going back to the beginning. This is just falling into place."

"It does seem a bit simple compared to what has gone on before," agreed Tony. "What can we do though but plough on and just be on alert for any tricks."

The first line of the next screen started off with a seven letter word. There was only one and that was in the pink group – 'revenge'. Then it got tricky because there were two four letter words next but there were four of these in the pink group and there were six in the verse in total so that meant two were purple. There was only one purple four letter word so 'this' had to be in the verse twice. Maybe I had been a bit too premature in thinking it was easy.

There were other things to go on though. There were two three letter words in this verse which gave us something to go on. These were 'two' and 'ago'. Line three was just two words, a four and a three. There were also two five letter words in the last line. These would be 'prior' and 'rhyme'. There was also a two letter word and there were no pink ones, so we were back to 'go', 'is;', it' and 'to'.

"Wait a minute!" shrilled Vicky in excitement. "Look at the two previous … verses, I guess we can call them. Name and game. Pro and go. The second and last line rhyme. In this case we have a four letter word and five letter word that have to rhyme. There is only one option – 'time' and coincidentally 'rhyme'."

It didn't take long to see that she was correct. That immediately meant we had the last words to line two and four. Also, as the two five letter words were on the last line, this meant 'prior' was the first word on that line. The use of 'prior' was usually followed by 'to' so that could be one of the purple words. Then to make sense the four letter word would have to be 'this' also a purple word. We had the last line then 'prior to this rhyme'.

Now looking at line three we had possible combinations of 'came two', 'next two', 'long two', 'came ago', next ago', 'long ago'. Taken with the last line we all felt that 'long ago' fitted best' – 'long ago, prior to this rhyme'. This now meant that 'two' started the second line and that left us with three four letter words, two in the first line and one between 'two' and 'time'. There were only two pink four letter words left – 'came' and 'next' so we also needed 'this' from purple. Now 'next' could go on line two and made sense but that meant the top line would say 'revenge came this' or 'revenge this came'. Using 'this' in the second line worked better and this gave us a whole verse of 'revenge came next, two this time, long ago, prior to this rhyme'. Vicky keyed it in, and we got the bleep and the next screen.

The next screen was trickier. This went; Line one: three, six, two, four, Line two: four, two, four, Line three: two, three, four, and Line four: six, two, three, four. Due to the two six letters words, we knew it was the light blue group as the dark blue had only one. There were eleven light blue clue answers and fourteen words in the verse so that meant we needed three purple. One of these was a three letter meaning 'the' but two of these were two letters which left us the choice again of 'go', 'is', 'it' and 'to'.

We had the rhyming aid which this time was two four letter words so had to be 'will' and 'kill' but we obviously did not know which way around yet.

"Not much to help here," observed Tony. 'We know the two rhyming words but not the order and the same with the two six letter words'.

"Let's think about this logically," I said. "The last line starts with one of the six letter words and ends either 'kill' or 'will'. There is then a two letter and three letter. Write down the combinations and see what we have."

Leaving out the two letter word for now we had as follows:

Thrive __ all kill   Slaves __ all kill
Thrive __ all will   Slaves __ all will
Thrive __ one kill   Slaves __ one kill
Thrive __ one will   Slaves __ one will
Thrive __ the kill   Slaves __ the kill
Thrive __ the will   Slaves __ the will

The ones that made any sense when inserting a two letter word were; 'thrive it all will', 'thrive no one will', 'thrive in the kill', 'thrive in the will', 'slaves no one kill', 'slaves in the kill', 'slaves to the kill' and 'slaves in the will'.

"Too many," declared Tony.

I thought about it for a moment. "Yes, but if we look at the start of line one this would have to be either 'all slaves', 'all thrive' or 'the slaves' as the others do not make sense.'

"Looking at line two also," Vicky said, joining in, "you can only have 'more blank will', 'more, blank, kill', 'fate, blank, kill', 'fate, blank, will', 'void, blank, kill' or 'void, blank, will'. Using the two letter words, the one that reads best and ties in with our mad friend is 'more to kill'.

We messed around with it for a long while before we got something we were mostly happy with – 'all slaves to fate, more to kill, in the void, thrive no one will'. I wasn't keen on line three but if the others were correct that was all that was left. Anyway, Vicky typed it in and it worked, and we were down to what was hopefully the last screen.

Dark blue group. There were nine words but thirteen in the verse, so we needed four purple words – a four 'this', a three 'the' and two of the usual twos. However, we did pick up on something quite quickly. Two of the dark blue words were 'end' and 'nigh' and as we knew we had to use 'the' also the phrase 'the end is nigh' came easily to mind and it fitted in the last line.

The first line was four, three and six. There was only one six letter word which was colour. Now we had used 'the' there was only 'and' and 'try' as three letters. Along with 'this', the four letters remaining were 'make', 'test' and 'word'. We all agreed that 'and' was the three letter word. All the four letter words could be used but in view of the whole puzzle 'word and colour' went best. We had been puzzling over word clues and their colour groups for many weeks – or at least Tony and I had, Vicky for much less time.

With the first and last lines fairly certain, we mucked around with the other two and eventually came up with 'word and colour, make this try, you test it, the end is nigh'. Vicky typed it in and then we got a shock. The computer said no! It also said we had two attempts left.

"What happens then?" asked Vicky.

"We don't get out," replied Tony the realist. "If we were ever going to be allowed to get out anyway. I bet after all this the guy is just playing us for the mugs we have been so far."

"Damn, we were so close!" I was frustrated to be stymied at the last. Yes, Tony was right, even if we finished Nathan's game we would probably not get out, but I just wanted the stupid puzzle over. It had taken over my life. I tried to calm myself down. "Okay. Let's not lose it but try and see where we went wrong."

"I am guessing it is in the middle two lines," said Vicky.

"Agreed," I acceded. "I think we were all fairly sure that lines ones and four were correct." I looked at Tony who nodded. "That being the case, as 'this make try' and 'make test try' do not make sense then 'this test try, you make it' is probably the best bet."

"Are we sure?" asked Vicky, fingers poised over the keys.

"Er…no but no need to panic unless this one doesn't work."

"One thing," interjected Tony. "What if it is wrong and there is a time limit on the last try? If this one is wrong we could be here ages trying to figure it out."

"Not a lot we can do about that Tony. Nil desperandum."

"Go ahead then Vicky," agreed Tony.

Vicky keyed in the verse and this time there was a beep and the screen changed to a message.

Congratulations guys! I never thought you would make it. Thanks, it's been a gas!

"Run!" yelled Tony.

Chapter 43

He startled both Vicky and I, but we saw him hurrying to the bathroom, so we followed. "In there," he shouted, pointing to the bedroom as he opened the bathroom door. "Block up the door frame with whatever you can."

I could hear a hissing sound now and guessed what was happening. I shoved Vicky into the bedroom and slammed the door shut. I then raided the wardrobes for clothing to stuff in the space between the door and frame. Vicky was staring at me as though I was mad. "Gas!" She understood then and started helping me. We had jeans along the bottom edge acting like a draught excluder and then anything else we could find that we could wedge in elsewhere.

"You two okay?" Came Tony's shout whilst we were finishing.

"I think so," I called back.

"He gassed me before. There are jets in the ceiling or something. It was only knock-out gas before but if this is game over it might be something more permanent. Have you got the whole door blocked up?"

"As best we can with clothing," I replied. "I guess some is going to get in eventually. How long does it last?"

"No way to know. I guess he gave me only just enough to put me out for a few minutes last time. It might be jetting out permanently for all we know. I would stay far away from the door as possible."

I moved back. Vicky was already sat on the bottom bunk. I shouted louder. "What do you think then, Tony? Knockout gas or something more lethal?"

"That guy's a psychopath. I don't think he had finished playing with us. When he said he was going, it sort of felt like he intended to come back. If that was the case then it is less likely to be lethal. We cannot take the chance though."

We were at it for a while bouncing thoughts backwards and forwards. Vicky was quiet though. She told me later that she was writing her story out in her head. After a while, Tony and I gave it up as we needed to conserve oxygen. I don't know how long I lay on the top bunk, but I must have dropped off. When I awoke I had a headache. It was getting a bit stuffy. I leaned down and saw that Vicky was dozing too. I had no idea how long we could survive, especially if the gas fumes were seeping in slowly. We had to do something. I had a weird thought which may have been due to the start of oxygen deprivation.

"Tony! Are you awake?" I yelled.

"Just about!" came back the reply.

"I've been thinking. If everything Nathan told us was true, then when he told you the only chance of escape was to complete the puzzle maybe that was the truth too."

"How do you mean? We have less chance of getting out now, stuck in here, than we did before."

"Think about it though. All the games he has put us through. The completing of the puzzle released the gas which was either supposed to make us unconscious or kill us. What if, knowing the gas would get us, there is now a way out, but we are incapacitated so cannot use it. That would be just his sort of game."

"I suppose it might be," agreed Tony grudgingly, "but we cannot take the risk."

"We may have to. We don't know if Vicky's message has got through to the police yet. Then how long would it take to mobilise a raid on this place bearing in mind we are in Cornwall and Vicky's contact is in Essex, and you being the missing cop are from Surrey?"

"If the message got through and was taken seriously, forces would be brought to bear," said Tony. "However, you are right in that we don't know how long that will be because we don't know when and if the message got through."

"One of us needs to check out the main room."

"Let me," chimed in Vicky who had woken from her slumber. "I can hold my breath for two minutes."

"No!" Tony yelled. "That compromises two people once the door is open. It had best be me." He was silent for a few moments then yelled again. "No time like the present. I'm going for it."

We heard the bathroom door open cautiously but nothing else until about a minute later there was a loud banging on the door. "Cover your faces and get out here! You were right. The devil has the door open. Not sure how long it will be though. Come on!"

Vicky and I moved as if our lives depended on it, which they did. Holding shirts to our faces we freed the door and peeped out. Tony was in the middle of the room gesturing, a wet towel held over the bottom half of his face. We ran to where he pointed and there was a doorway in the wall which we all rushed through, and we didn't stop until we had climbed some stairs and closed the door at the top behind us. We then dropped our hands and all of us gasped in lungfuls of air. We had been holding our breath without realising it.

We found the lounge and just dropped onto sofas and armchairs in relief. None of us spoke for a while. I guessed it was the most relief for

Tony who had been down there a lot longer than me. He was the policeman though, so he recovered quicker than Vicky and me.

"We need to call this in?" said Tony, standing up. He pulled his phone out of his pocket, obviously having had the composure to recover his from the room, mine was still there. Now we got the benefit of having saved his battery.

While he arranged for the forces of law and order to arrive, Vicky and I went to the kitchen. Whether it was the release of excessive tension we had all been feeling when locked up I don't know but we all agreed we were hungry. The food in the kitchen seemed to support the thought that Nathan was coming back. There was milk, butter, cheese and other stuff in the fridge and bread in a container bin. Vicky made up a load of sandwiches and I found plates to put them on. Then I made some coffee too.

Tony had some news for us when we got back to the lounge. "We only just beat the cavalry," he said. "I spoke to my boss, and they had got the message. Some colleagues are en route to liaise with the local force. They must have been ready or nearly so to raid this place. I told them to call that off now, no need to waste manpower, but I told them to try and track down Nathan, or whatever his name is. My colleagues will be here shortly and the local forensic team. They will take this place apart no doubt."

Something was bothering me, I didn't know how to bring it up, but I had to. "Er … Tony. We are all going to have to give a statement aren't we?"

"It might be more than a mere statement because of what we're involved in. I would imagine that there will be several interviews for all of us."

That was what I was worried about. "Er … what do we say when they ask if we know why Nathan went to all this trouble?"

He knew what I was talking about. If it all came out then I was looking at a possible three murder charges, five if you counted my parents. If it was all true and we still had no proof of that. Tony had a frown on his face and was obviously thinking hard. Vicky had a curious look on her face. I had to remember she was still a reporter at heart and wanted a story.

"We tell them what we know and not anything which is hearsay," explained Tony after a while. "We know he thought he had a grudge against both of us. Mine goes back to when I was a P.C. and he got nabbed with the Bannister gang. You, he thought you were his long lost brother that left home and made life bad for him. That could be true or a pack of lies as you have no memories to back it up. We can also say that we did hear him admit to at least four murders."

"There's something else." Tony and Vicky just looked, waiting for me to continue. "Didn't you notice? The verses in the rhyme? The second verse said something like 'accident first' and the next 'revenge came next'. That ties up with the story he gave us about what I am supposed to have done. He set this all up so I would be the fall guy."

"Don't worry about it," said Tony. "It will all work out."

It was well into Monday evening when the cavalry turned up and Tony was busy showing them all where to go. Vicky and I just sat in the lounge with everyone and everything buzzing around us, awaiting transportation to the local station where we would give our statements. Vicky was alert and wanted to be mooching around picking up bits for her story, but she was not allowed to wander around and had to stay put. For myself, I was bushed, and I started to doze off and would probably have done so but for the noise and running about that suddenly happened. We didn't find out until later, but a forensic tech had been working in the panic room - the controls had eventually been found and the door had been jammed open to prevent anyone getting trapped inside - when gas started gushing out again from the ceiling jets. He was caught by surprise and this time it was of the lethal variety and he died almost instantaneously. Someone caught on and released the doors, leaving him inside but it was obvious he was already dead from the grotesque fatal expression and severe drooling. Tony's view was that Nathan had some surveillance on the property and when he saw it had been breached had a failsafe to make sure his prisoners did not escape. Having triggered that it was obvious that he was not now going to return. Setting a trap with officers lying in wait, which had been the original plan, was scrapped.

As Tony had foreseen, over the next few days we were all interviewed individually, some would say interrogated. There were a few county forces interested in closing cold cases, so information was being shared over a wide spectrum. In the end though our stories must have all lined up with available proof and facts because before the week was out we were all back to our normal lives.

There was no news on Nathan. Having admitted to being a multimillionaire and able to change his name and appearance at will, Tony was not holding out much hope of catching him. That left us all with a cloud hanging over us because he could always come back and start all over again. Forewarned is forearmed though, Tony advised us, so he would not catch us all off guard again.

A thorough search of the house in Cornwall had revealed a lot of surveillance footage, mostly of me, but some on Tony too, and a few other people who were now dead. That on myself dated back to way before I had met Nathan, even Laura, which sort of gave some veracity to his claims. I did not know now how to feel about my dead wife. Her loss had left me with my life spiralling out of control and Nathan had taken that and spun me faster. It did not feel like loss anymore, just the end of a chapter. Maybe Nathan had done me a favour. Maybe I could now move on and get my life back into order. Get a job even.

That was for later though. After the summer. After the World Cup. The Thursday after the captive weekend saw England's last pre-World Cup friendly against Costa Rica which they won 2 – 0 and which saw Marcus Rashford score, pushing himself forward for selection for the more important matches to come. It was just eleven days until England's first match in Russia against Tunisia. As I sat there watching though I could not help thinking of the last match I watched, in that underground panic room where I, and others, had been at the mercy of a madman.

I could not help wondering what had happened to him. Where was he now and what plans was he hatching? In one way he had been a brilliant master planner and strategist. He had had me fooled for a long time but then that was not difficult. There had been a lot of meticulous work in his plan but on the other hand he had an over inflated opinion of himself. He had made the error in the puzzle, spelling reverend incorrectly, and according to Tony he had made several other slip ups. Having said that, he was still out there. Not caught and unlikely to be so from what I had heard.

I shivered at thinking this. Was he out there now, watching me? I knew I couldn't afford to go around looking over my shoulder all the time. I had to move forward. As Franco declared in *The Gumball Rally* as he pulled off the driving mirror and threw it away, "What is behind me is not important."

Chapter 44

Amelia McQueen was smiling to herself as she poured out the wine in her expansive and immaculate kitchen. She did not regard herself as one of these cougars you hear about so much these days, but if a younger man wanted to pay her attention she didn't mind at all. At sixty one she looked good for her age, at least ten years younger, fifteen on a good day, and this was a good day. Her long blond hair had never been dyed but there was no grey to be seen and there was hardly a wrinkle on her face. She had always been slim and the evening gown she wore showed her off to perfection. Time had been good to her if nothing else.

It was only right that she had some good days now because she had experienced a lot of bad days in her past. Meeting her husband had been one. Oh yes, he had been charming and dashing at first, so different from any other person she had met, but she had been so young and easily swept off her feet. If she had only known then how controlling he would be or what nefarious activities he was involved in. Yes, she had served her time, as though it had been a prison sentence, but being in the line he was in, an untimely end was always a possibility and thankfully for her, that is what happened.

He had been careful in his dealings though and although he was taken out by the competition, there was nothing incriminating found after his death to warrant confiscation of his ill-gotten gains, so Amelia was allowed to continue in the life to which she had become accustomed. She had the big house, cars, clothes and more money than she could spend in the bank. For nearly eleven years now she had been living the good life, but she also tried to make recompense for her husband's misdeeds too by her contributions to various charities.

It had been a charity event that night where she had met Felix. They had been seated together at the same table for dinner, at quite exorbitant ticket prices, and although there had been a plethora of younger women there, she had captured his full attention for the whole of the evening. He hadn't danced with another woman all night and when he had escorted her to her chauffeur driven car and she had thanked him for the good time he had responded by betting she could show him a better time. How could she have not invited him home after that?

She carried the glasses into the lounge, bringing the bottle with her under her arm. Felix was sat on one of the sofas. Tuxedo jacket off and bow tie loosened. She guessed he must be mid-forties, in good shape though, short dark hair and a nice moustache.

"Here we are then," she said, handing him a glass and putting the bottle on a coaster on the expensive coffee table.

"It's a very lovely place you have here," admired Felix.

"You can have the full tour later," purred Amelia. "Ending in the bedroom."

"Can't wait," smiled Felix. "It's too early for bed yet though. Tell me some more about yourself."

Amelia sat down beside him on the sofa, slightly facing him with her legs crossed. "There is hardly any more to tell, we talked so much over dinner."

"Well, for a start, you didn't tell me that you were this well off."

"Why? Are you only interested in me for my money?" She was not worried if he was because she came across that all the time. She had received seven marriage proposals since her husband had died.

"Not at all. I have made my own money," Felix advised. "How else could I have afforded to get a place at your gala dinner? Such prices."

"Yes, it is all in a good cause though and everyone that was there could afford it," Amelia pointed out.

"Of course," Felix agreed. "How did you make your money? Business?"

Amelia smiled. "No. My husband ran a business, and I inherited his wealth when he died."

"Oh, I'm sorry. Was it sudden?"

"It was. Hit and run." She didn't say that it was a hired hit.

"Oh my god! So sorry."

"No need. It was eleven years ago and water under the bridge now. How did you make your money Felix?"

Felix gave a little smile. "Well, to tell you the truth, I won it. On the lottery. Well, that is to say, I won the start of it that way, over twenty years ago and have made it grow since with investments."

"Really! I wouldn't have thought that. I would have figured you for a self-made millionaire, starting a company from the ground up."

"No. I got lucky," admitted Felix. "Nice wine. So do you have any children?"

"Alas no," Amelia answered with a catch in her voice. "My husband and I could never have children. He knew and accepted that. We did talk of adopting but it never happened." Her face had dropped a little and Felix could tell she was sad about that aspect of her life. And so she should be.

"Surely not!" Amelia looked at him in surprise. His voice had suddenly changed into a hard tone. "Why, do you not remember you had a child in about seventy three I would guess? You gave him away!"

Felix stood up as he said this, placed his glass on the table, and pulled off his hair and moustache. "Why did you do that, Mother?"

Amelia dropped her glass, and the spilled wine stained the expensive carpet. She clutched a cushion in front of her as though it would afford protection against the irate man before her.

"Who are you?" she asked, with a bit of a stammer in her voice.

"I just told you Mother," snarled Nathan. "I was that baby you gave away to the Perkins. Why did you do that? Why did you abandon me?"

As she suddenly accepted the truth there were tears in her eyes. "You don't understand," she wailed. "I was just sixteen. I couldn't look after a baby, I was still a child myself, and that couple had lost one of their twins. It was the best for both of us."

"If you couldn't look after a baby you should not have got pregnant should you?" Nathan was not to be appeased.

"I was raped!"

That took the wind out of his sails a bit. That was the one thing he could not have known. The records he had been able to find, which were sketchy at best, never mentioned that.

"That's why I could not have any more kids."

"I didn't know that," admitted Nathan. "Then why did you try and make contact when I was eleven."

"I had been married a while by then. I was out of love with my husband, having found out what type of man he was, but we had money so knowing I could never have another baby I wanted to meet the one I did have." Amelia now had tears running down her cheeks.

"And why didn't we ever meet then?"

"The Perkins didn't want it. They didn't write back straight away but when they did they said you were having a bad time of it. You and your brother were suddenly at loggerheads and they didn't want any more trauma in your life. I had to accept it."

Nathan froze. He remembered how James had changed from a loving brother into a stranger. They had been about the right age at the time. Nathan himself had not known about the attempted contact until much later. When he had found out he guessed that James had thought he was the cuckoo in the nest, but his actions had stopped his real mother getting in touch. Maybe things would have been different. James definitely had to pay now.

"You could have tried again. After the fire. Did you not know that Mum and Dad died when I was fifteen?"

"No, I'm sorry. I didn't keep track of you, deliberately. It would have been too painful."

"I wish you had, Mother," said Nathan almost wistfully. "My life could have turned out different. I wouldn't have had so much blood on my hands."

"Blood on your hands? What do you mean?"

So stood there, before the biological mother he had never known, Mike Perkins told her the whole story. His unwritten biography and when he was finished he could see by the horror on her face that there would be no loving reconciliation. That was fine by him because he had not engineered his way there to make one.

Amelia started to get up. "No, Mother! Stay where you are," warned Nathan.

"So, I'm part of your game then?"

"Of course. You were to be Miss Scarlet. Scarlet woman." Despite what he had told his captives, this had always been the plan. "Now that doesn't quite work. However, I have adapted before so I can again." He looked around the room and to his surprise found something better than what he had been looking for, which had been any type of heavy object. "Wow! You even have a candlestick!"

He backed up to the marble fireplace, keeping his eyes on her all the time. He felt behind him for the silver candlestick which had candles in it. He pulled them out and let them drop to the floor. He started to walk menacingly over to the sofa on which Amelia was again cowered with the cushion in front of her.

"Think of what you are doing?" Amelia pleaded. "Killing your own mother. From what you told me those others you have killed were bad people and deserved to die."

"Even my brother and the policeman?"

"I thought you said they survived. But anyway, yes. They wronged my boy." She made one last attempt. "Look we have found each other now. We can make up for lost time. We both have money. There is a lot we could enjoy with each other."

"Nice try, Mother, but it is too late for me now." Nathan now actually had tears in his own eyes. "And therefore, it is too late for you."

"It's not too late, Michael. You have done some bad things. My husband did some bad things. I never told on him, and I would never tell on you. We could just have a normal but good life now. Everything in the past forgotten."

"You know, I wish I could, Mother. In some ways. I must disappear though after this. Make a brand new life for myself."

"We can both do that. I have no ties. I don't have to stay here. We could go anywhere in the world."

Nathan momentarily stopped advancing. Her use of his real name had struck a chord. No one had called him Michael in years. Only Mum had done that. He had always been Mike to Dad and everyone else. A little doubt began to creep into his mind. Maybe he could stop and then they could have a normal, if somewhat delayed, mother and son relationship. For the first time in many years, he had an angel on one shoulder as well as the devil on the other. Amelia could see the indecision in his eyes, and she thought she had gotten through. She smiled and then the devil dug his fork into his shoulder. No! He was not finished. He had to go back and finish off the others. He had to finish what he had started.

Nathan started to move again. "I am sorry Mother. If it is any consolation, this is the only time I have had any feeling of remorse about what I must do." He was in front of her now, having pushed the coffee table aside knocking the wine bottle over so that it rolled onto the carpet, adding its contents to the previous stain.

Even as he towered above her, candlestick raised aloft, he hesitated. She did not. The gun shot came out of nowhere. As Nathan fell to the ground, surprise written all over his face, he saw the smoking gun Amelia had in her hand as she pulled it out of the cushion cover.

Epilogue

One Year Later

Even though I had not been at the best time in my life, I had enjoyed my first cruise so one year later I was back on board. It was a similar itinerary although this time I had taken part in some of the excursions at the ports of call – Hamburg, Amsterdam again and Le Havre where there was a day trip into Paris. The latter was a little disappointing. We only got to see the Eiffel Tower from a distance and most of the time off the coach was spent at Notre Dame. A guided tour inside and then three hours to ourselves afterwards. Unlike the previous trip, I had made no connections this time and spent the time wandering alone up and down, by the Seine so I didn't get lost. I had lunch in a café but my "Parlez vous Anglais si vous plait?" did not go down very well. I did though have a caricature sketch done by a pavement artist.

On board ship, I had partaken again in all the quizzes that were held and shuffleboard, table tennis and quoits competitions. It was a bit lonely though after last time, doing everything by myself.

A lot had happened in that last year but even so the spectre of Michael Perkins – as Tony referred to him now, or Nathan Black as I still thought of him, loomed overhead. No sight or sound of him had been heard since he flew from our place of capture in his helicopter. That was never found either. The fact that he was still out there and could pop up at any moment was still disconcerting to me but as the time went on this was on my mind less.

Tony was reinstated and quite a celebrity having now help resolve several cold cases, even though they were not officially closed because the offender was still at large. His family had arrived home unscathed, and the previous allegations of misconduct died a death. We kept in touch and had the occasional game of snooker. He had kept his puzzle and had it displayed all completed in a spare room upstairs. I suppose it could be regarded as a trophy. Mine had been seized as evidence and when asked if I had wanted it back I politely declined.

Vicky had not been able to force herself onto the crime beat much to her chagrin, but she was going to get the word out in another way. She was writing a book of the whole affair, under strict instructions on what not to put in the book from me – my alleged past former life. Again, we kept in touch but had only seen each other once over the last year.

As for myself there had been a lot of change. The whole thing had been a severe wake up call for me. That and the fact that Laura, that paragon of virtue I had been pining for, had not been that at all. She had still been my wife and I still loved her, but I was not in the heartbroken depths of despair I had been before. The gambling had stopped, and I had a new job – back in insurance unfortunately but beggars cannot be choosers.

Obviously, I had had to leave the flat. Not only were the memories too much to live with but I would always have known that Nathan had manipulated me into living there under the eyes of his watchdog. I was renting a new flat for now until I could save a deposit to buy a place of my own.

Not that the past year had been easy. I had had my share of nightmares and other times when I could not sleep at all. That was in the days and weeks following our release. Rich and Jenny had helped enormously. They had invited me down to their place for a while where I had stayed in their spare room and met Cluedo the bouncing Border collie puppy. Very friendly and always wanting to play tug with his toys. It was easier to forget things down there.

The World Cup had taken my mind off it as well. It seemed as if the whole country had gone mad for Gareth Southgate's team, but my feeling had been that a 6-1 pummelling of Panama did not constitute a trophy winning side. People were getting too excited, and the sale of waistcoats went through the roof. In the end it was another semi-final defeat, although for a while after Kieran Trippier's early free-kick goal against Croatia even I had hope. Still, it was the best effort since 1990.

The day after the Paris trip was a sea day before docking at Southampton the following day and I spent it in quizzing mostly. There was to have been a football tournament right at the top of the ship –Deck 18 where there was a caged tennis court area. The net could come down and there were five-a-side nets. Cricket was also played there too. No host turned up, so it ended up with two dads, their kids and me. It was fun but I don't think they liked it when I scored the winning goal.

Unlike the first time, I was dining in the restaurant at my allocated table and not in my cabin. Other than polite dinner conversation I had not really connected with any of my dinner companions. There were seven of us at the table of eight. Three couples and me. After dinner it was time for the eight o'clock quiz. At every one I had to offer myself to any team that needed an extra player. Sometimes I was taken and others I was on my own. I had not won once in the whole trip and the same was true this time too. I went to watch a show after this and it was not until I went on deck after this finished, to get a breath of fresh air and take a last stroll around the deck, that things took a turn for the worse.

I was at the stern looking out over the dark sea when I felt someone approach from behind.

"Nice view."

I whirled round. I wouldn't have recognised the guy there with dark hair and a bushy beard, but I knew the voice. He was leaning on a thick, heavy cane.

"Nathan!"

"At your service. Nice to see you again, Brother." He was smiling. The smile of a crocodile that has seen his lunch. There was no one else around and at the stern we were out of sight of others who might be standing at the rails at either side of the ship.

"Did you miss me?"

I tried to stay calm. "Not really. You never miss what you never had,"

"Oh. So, you still don't think we are brothers then?" He asked. "Well, brought up as brothers because I was technically adopted."

"No, I don't. And I was hoping we had seen the last of you."

"No chance, Bro." He laughed. "I am sorry that it took so long though. Let me tell you what happened?"

I needed time to think so I let him go on.

"I was feeling really pleased with myself at the time. I flew to a local private airfield where I kept my car. I knew I had the two of you squirreled away and I just had to tie off the last loose end. True, things had not gone according to plan, but even if I do say so myself, I had adapted well, and things were still running quite smoothly. The only fly in the ointment had been the reporter but she was not likely to cause any trouble to me where she was."

He was gazing intently at my face all the time. Trying to read my intentions. As I had not formed any yet, my face must have been inscrutable.

"Anyway, I was almost at my destination when my security alert told me that something was wrong. It was possible that you were about to be saved so I opted for the contingency plan."

"Yes. The poisonous gas. That killed a forensics guy which is another life you must answer for."

"Not in this lifetime I think," was his drawled response. "Anyway, my hopes of eking my pleasure out with you and your new cop friend was gone but I still had the coup de grace. Do you know what that was?"

"I have no idea how a sick mind like yours works," I replied, still furiously looking for a way out.

"My mother. My real mother, who gave me up. I tracked her down. She has a nice life. True, she gave me quite a sob story, but it made no difference to what I had to do. She was really begging for her life at the end, but I underestimated her." Here he laughed again. "You won't believe this. She shot me! Yes. She had a pistol in a cushion, and she shot me."

"Yet you are here."

"Yes. I went down with the impact, but it was the top of my thigh. She went to get help or call the police or something. I managed to get out of there but as you can see not unscathed." He waved the stick at me. "It took me quite a while to get back on my feet. Literally. By the time I had she had beefed up her security so much I needed more time to plan."

"So, you decided to come back and finish me off?"

"Precisely. I knew that this would be quite quick with no major obstacles in my way. I got a hacker to get into your computer and when you booked this trip I made one also. It has been fun, watching you all through the week, thinking you were safe."

His stance changed. He was evenly balanced now on both feet, but I could see the pain in his face. "Now that you are all up to date it is time to say goodbye. This won't hurt … much."

He came at me, and I backed up to the rail. All I could see was his snarling form in front of me but before he could bring the cane down his face contorted and he started jerking. Then he fell to the deck, and I saw the wires attached to his back.

"Payback's a bitch," said Tony, holding a stun gun.

Nathan was on the ground still twitching but he tried to grab my leg. I jumped back, slipped, and cracked my head on the rail. Everything went black.

When I awoke I was in sickbay. My head was throbbing, and I couldn't see straight at first. Tony was there, as was the ship's doctor.

"Are you alright?" asked Tony.

I was confused. "What are you doing here?"

"We have been keeping tabs on you," Tony advised me. "Well, not on you really but on anyone trying to follow you or obtain information on you. Our cyber guys were keeping a close eye on things and noticed someone tracking your movements. We saw they booked this trip after you did and guessed it might be you know who."

"You have been here all trip?" I was astonished. Two people watching me for nearly a week, and I hadn't noticed.

"Keeping an eye on our friend. When he made his move tonight I was ready. I let him talk for a bit to record his admission to you, then before he could throw your overboard I took great pleasure in zapping him like he did to me. Don't worry. He's locked up until we dock."

That was a relief but there was something more of a bother to me at that moment. Something must have been written on my face. "What's up?" Tony's face was full of concern.

"Oh nothing. I've just got a banging headache."

"I'll get off and let you rest then," said Tony. "See you later no doubt."

When Tony had gone the doctor gave me a couple of tablets and left too. I lay back on the bed to think. The headache was not as bad as all that – I had had worse. There was something else. After the bang on the head, there was a brief flash of memory, or I thought it was. Two children happily playing together. Me and my brother. It was transient. There one second and gone the next. Try as I might I could not get it back.

We had talked about this. Tony and myself. What if my memories came back? What type of person would I be? Tony was a pragmatist. What will be will be. If it happened we could deal with it then. Live life going forward. That was what he was doing with his family after the ordeal. There was no point in dwelling in the past. I totally agreed with his sentiment which is why I now had a job and was saving for a house. One flash of memory meant nothing. I would just go on as what was now normal. Nothing to worry about.

Of course, there was. Not the possibility of the returning memory because that was all conjecture. Nathan's capture was not. It had occurred and he was in custody. He would get a trial and at that trial everything could be out in the open. We had not previously discussed that because his capture had not looked likely. I could let this weigh me down, but I had more resolve now. Let the cards fall where they may.

Que sera, sera.

THE END

Also by David A. Wardle

Rewind
A forty year old from 2003 wakes up in his eight year old body back in 1971. Is he dreaming or dead? Either way this is a second chance to get things right. Not as easy as it sounds. An eight year old boy has no say or influence, especially back then. Jason has to battle his parents and find an ally before he can turn around his previous life. Even then it is far from plain sailing.

'This is a great story about a 40 year old man sent back in time to when he was just eight years old. It takes you to an era before mobile phones, social media and all the other mod cons we are now so used to. There are lots of twists and turns which keep you guessing as to where the plot is heading. Jason is a wonderful protagonist, who draws on his adult experiences whenever he is dealing with the 'grown ups'. His has wit and humour that made me smile and yet at times there is a great sense of sadness and regret of the man inside.

This is a really good story and I thoroughly enjoyed reading it.'

Pratt, Pratt, Wally and Pratt Investigate
A newly formed insurance investigation firm has its first case. What seems a simple case of embezzlement to Thomas T. Robel (Tommy Trouble) soon turns into a web of intrigue involving robbery, kidnap and clown murder. Finding himself in prison for a crime he didn't commit can Tommy escape and extricate himself from trouble?

Doctor, Oh No!
S.P.I.D.E.R. Sindy Cobweb (W7) takes on her most ludicrous assignment to date. She must find and rescue the kidnapped scientist, Professor I.C. Nutting, and his new eyesight formula from the clutches of the combined forces of S.M.A.S.H. and S.E.P.T.I.C. who are secreted in their Egyptian lair. A short James Bond spoof.

'This was a quick fun read that brought me back in time to the heyday of the James Bond era. I really enjoyed it!'

Once Upon a Week
Seven new fairy stories, each one based on a proverb. A week's bedtime stories for children with a life lesson thrown in.

'I enjoyed reading this book Once Upon a Week. It consists of 7 different fairy tales (one for each day of the week) featuring different mythological creatures, motifs, and themes. It is middle grade fiction, but adults can read it as well. It is for anyone who is looking for a book that takes them back to the simpler times of the past. It is for the person who is nostalgic about old-school fairy tales and wants to devour more. I give this book 4-stars for its interesting premise, characters, and themes, as well as the life lessons at the end of each of the 7 stories, which undoubtedly are the golden nuggets of this book.'

The Whole in One
Prior to the publication of The Puzzle, I wanted to catalogue my writing journey so far. This is all my previous published work in one volume, in chronological order including background to each one. This includes my very first novel 'Trance' which I wrote at age eighteen so is a simple affair and which has been long out of print as a standalone book. Truly a multi-genre volume.

Printed in Great Britain
by Amazon